Mintie Das
Storm Sisters
The Sinking World

About the author

Mintie Das was born in India, raised in America and lives in Finland. She's been traveling the world since childhood and always finds inspiration from the discovery of the unknown. She has sixteen years of corporate public relations and marketing experience. For the last ten years, Mintie used her background to organize international criminal justice symposiums around the world.

BASTEI ENTERTAINMENT

Digital original edition
Published by Bastei Entertainment, 2016

Bastei Entertainment is an imprint of Bastei Lübbe AG
Project management: Rebecca Schaarschmidt
E-book production: Urban SatzKonzept, Düsseldorf

ISBN 978-3-7325-1701-5
978 1962 560171

www.luebbe.de
www.bastei-entertainment.com

MINTIE DAS

STORM SISTERS

THE SINKING WORLD

BASTEI ENTERTAINMENT ■■■■■▶

To all the girl pirates —
past, present,
and future.

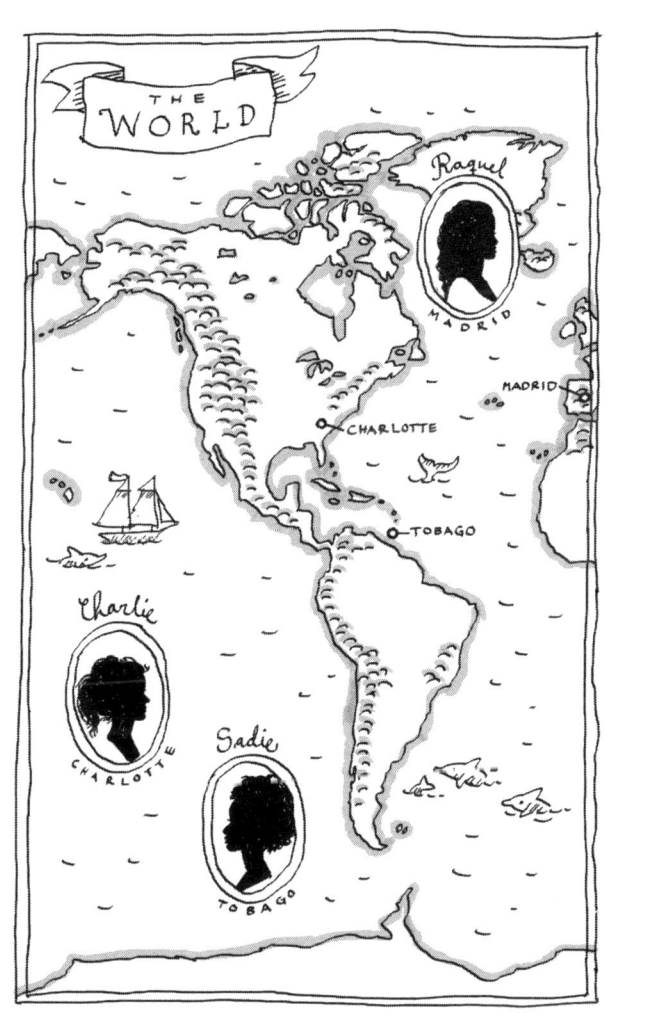

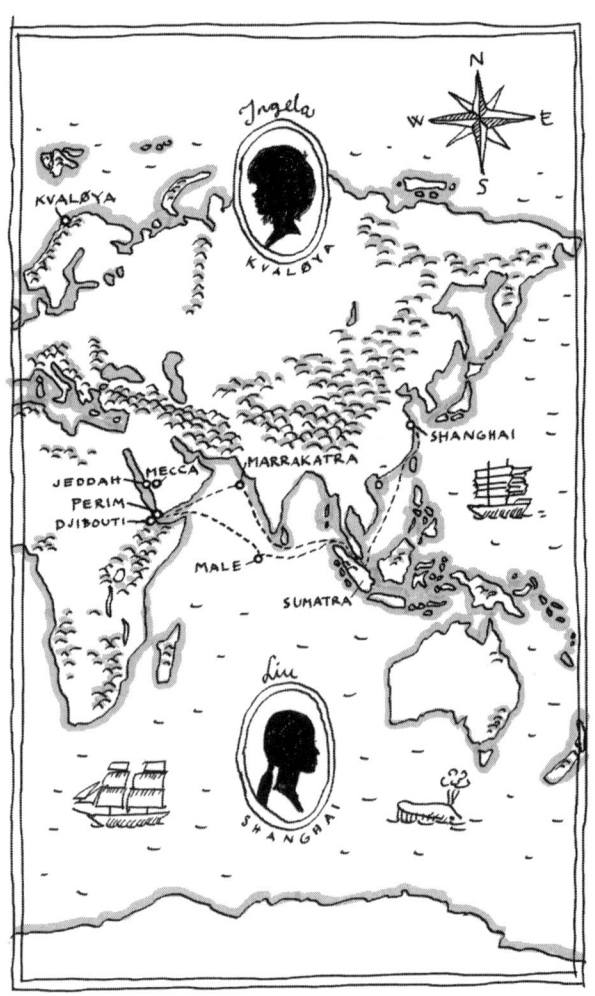

On the sea, we are free. Free to be ourselves, free to go where we choose, free to speak our minds.

We are not judged lesser either by our sex or our skin. Here we are equal.

And so it is on the sea that we choose to live.
Live like our ancestors did.

The history books will erase us. Convince you that girls are not smart, are not brave, and are not powerful. We share our story to show you that we are. Most importantly, we share our story to show you that you are, too.

Chapter
ONE

SHIP'S LOG (i.e. SLOG)

Dear Diary, (Oops! Need to remember this isn't a diary or Charlie will have a fit!)

Dear Ship,

We're about a day away from Shanghai so that Liu can visit her father. She doesn't really want to see him, but she has to ask—or beg—him to let us continue using his ship. Liu's already so nervous that she hasn't kept any food down since yesterday (though I have to admit that we're all kind of queasy after a full week of Sadie's cooking).

I hope I find some cucumber at the market in Shanghai. I'll use some of it to make a yummy salad for Liu (poor darling really needs to eat), and some for my eyes. The dark circles make me look like a raccoon. But the nightmares won't stop. Sometimes, I even have them during the day. It's the same thing over and over again. The man with no face plunging his sword into Papa ...

Oops again! Better just stick to ship business. So, here's all the boring stuff:

Date: July (or is it August already?)
Position: 38° 53.6N 08° 48.6E (I'll ask Liu.)
Av Speed: 5.2 knots
Wind: E, 10-18 knots (Ingela said it was easy climbing the masts today)
Weather: Partly cloudy—my curls are going crazy in this humidity.

Kisses, Ship! (Sorry we can't name you, but Liu says not to get too attached in case her father makes us give you back.)

Raquel ♡

They rowed in silence. The waning moon offered little light. But they were always comfortable on the water. Even on a dark, deep moat leading to a forbidden city.

As per the detailed instructions in the letter that Charlie was holding, they reached the eastern gate of the three-mile wall that surrounded the Old City of Shanghai. Though the brick wall was wide and tall, standing close to 33 feet, the eastern gate was a small, cramped archway, barely big enough to fit the rowboat.

"Swing the back to the left and then I'll paddle through," Charlie whispered to Raquel.

The rickety boat dinged the right side of the bricks but still managed to squeeze through the tight pass. Upon entering through the gate, the two girls crouched down. Any foreigner found trespassing into the Old City was immediately imprisoned. Though the letter guaranteed there would be no guards on this side of the wall, Raquel made a quick sign of the cross when she realized this was actually true.

Charlie pointed to an enormous rockery further down. "I think we need to go there."

They stopped paddling and let the boat gently glide to the shore. As Charlie's cavalier boot sank into the carpet-soft grass, her heart rose into her throat. When she'd received the anonymous letter this morning detailing this mysterious mission, she'd barely had time to process it. But now, as they tip-toed their way onto the bamboo bridge, the danger was starting to hit her.

Not to mention, she had dragged Raquel into it as well. Normally, she'd have taken calm, cool-headed Liu, but with Liu at her dad's, she'd had to settle for Raquel. Raquel was adept at languages, and she did seem to have a sixth sense with people, which was why her nickname was *Embajador*. Plus she was becoming pretty damn good at *panchi*, the Storm's ancient art of dagger fighting.

Panchi, which all the Storm started training in from childhood, was a powerful martial art involving knife-based combat. This was why Raquel had concealed multiple daggers, throwing knives, and even a dirk, her prized Scottish dagger, throughout her body. Each weapon weighed no more than one to two pounds, with single-edged and double-edged blades all measuring between twelve to eighteen inches long, which made them perfect for hiding and absolutely deadly in spots too cramped to wield a sword. All of which, Raquel felt, might come in very handy tonight.

Charlie jumped across the koi pond. Instinctively, she fingered the single pearl hanging on the flimsy silver chain around her neck. As a rule, she hated jewelry. Except this simple necklace her pop had given her on the day Charlie's mother had walked out on them. Ten years later, Charlie had been wearing the necklace on the day she lost her pop, and hadn't taken it off for a single moment in the eleven months since. Though she would never admit it out loud for fear of sounding like superstitious Raquel, she'd even come to believe the necklace brought a bit of good luck. Charlie tucked the chain inside her shirt. She had a feeling that tonight they were going to need as many good luck charms as possible.

"I think you'd better get this." Raquel stepped aside as they reached the huge rockery. Her high-heeled boots were never going to allow her to make it to the top.

Charlie eyed Raquel's footwear. "I told you not to wear those stupid things!" she hissed.

Raquel stomped her foot on the grass. "Faking like a boy isn't as easy for me as it apparently is for you, Charles! I need accessories!"

When they were dressed as their alter egos, the Pirettes, a group of dangerous girl pirates, they happily paraded out in the open unchaperoned, stirring up as much attention as they could. After all, they'd invented the Pirettes alias just so they could get away with things most girls didn't dare do in plain sight. However, when they were trying to stay on the down-low, the best disguise was as males. Because no matter where in the world they found themselves, females were always prey, targets, or toys. Men could literally get away with murder and never receive so much as a sideways glance.

Charlie's long limbs and lack of hips naturally lent themselves to dressing up like a boy. She could wear her usual flat-heeled pirate boots and dirt-stained britches to easily convince anyone she was just an ordinary fellow.

But for Raquel, who at age fifteen was now officially an inch shorter than eleven-year-old Ingela, her petite stature and developing hourglass figure were a lot harder to hide. To compensate, she wore a pair of five-inch heeled boots in the fashion of short-statured aristocratic gentleman of the day. The boots weren't particularly practical for engaging in much activity, in this case climbing a rockery in the middle of a forbidden city in Shanghai. In fact, the tiny nobleman Raquel had swiped the boots from had been passed out drunk when she slipped them off his feet. But at least the high heels helped give her "boy" height (a term that Sadie deemed to have no scientific merit and scolded Raquel for using).

Charlie looked up at the highest point of the rockery. Though little Ingela, who was hopefully sound asleep back on the ship, was the true monkey out of all five of them, Charlie's solid calves and naturally muscular arms made her a decent climber when needed.

"Maybe you like Sadie's cooking more than you care to admit," Raquel chided as she hoisted Charlie up onto the rocks, "because you're heavy." She wiped her brow with the back of her hand.

"Ha! Bet you my heavy ass can make it out of here a lot faster than those prissy princess boots!" Charlie stuck her foot into a crevice and shifted her weight. She looked down at Raquel and whispered, "This will be quick. I don't need to go all the way up to the top. Just until I see the torch." Charlie climbed with ease until she reached a sturdy spot to stand on. From there, she had a bird's-eye view of the sprawling grounds. The aroma of lilies and cherry blossoms lingered in the air. Even in the darkness, it was evident that Yu Gardens, with its pavilions, streams, courtyards, and enormous old trees, was quite magnificent. But they weren't here to sight-see. She turned slowly until she spotted the lit torch. Hurriedly, she climbed back down the rockery to Raquel.

"We need to get across. To a wall with a dragon on it. Follow me." Charlie and Raquel hurried along as quietly as they could manage, aware that besides the crickets, the gardens were unnervingly still and silent. Even the lightest of steps seemed to ricochet through the grounds. To Charlie's surprise, Raquel was able to keep up, despite her ridiculous shoes.

When they reached the dragon wall, they saw a small, cloaked Chinese woman standing with a torch in her hand. "I think whole herd of elephant coming. How can two girl make so much noise?" She surveyed them both severely. "And why two when letter only to one?"

"There was nothing about me coming alone. Plus, I thought I might need help with the language." *And I was way too scared to do this on my own.* Charlie thought better of adding the last part. It was clear by the woman's eagle-eyed stare that if she sensed even the slightest hint of fear, she'd refuse them. Charlie straightened her shoulders and brushed her red hair off of her face. This woman's help was the only lifeline they had.

The woman raised her eyebrow. "You speak Chinese?" she asked, in what sounded like astoundingly perfect Spanish. Raquel cleared her throat. "Not as well as you speak my language, but I know a little," she responded in what sounded like equally good Shanghainese.

Charlie smiled. Her decision to ditch Sadie, who relied on her book smarts way too much, and Ingela, who was completely unpredictable, and instead bring Raquel, was definitely proving to be a good one.

The woman nodded her head with slight approval. "Wear this. And hurry up. Guard coming from break soon." She handed the girls two identical gray cloaks to the one she was wearing. "Not safe for foreigner where we go. Especially foreign girl. Even if foreign girl think she looking like foreign prince with too-high boot on." She extinguished the torch and turned around. The girls put on their cloaks and hurried behind her. Raquel gave her a sheepish grin, but the woman didn't crack a smile.

"Shhh!" she scolded, placing her pointy index finger to her lips. "Like mouse, not elephant! Or you wake up all city!" Charlie and Raquel lifted their feet higher, careful not to even breathe lest it make too much noise. Eventually they reached another gate, on the opposite side of the wall from where they entered. They crossed a bridge. On the other side stood four armed guards, two on each side.

The girls froze.

"Small step like me. Not big foreigner step. And head down!" the woman hissed.

The girls followed, not daring to look up as they baby-stepped behind the woman. One of the guards called out and the woman came to a sudden halt. Raquel silently recited the name of every saint she could think of.

The woman kept her head down while answering back in a dialect neither Raquel nor Charlie recognized. Beads of sweat formed on Charlie's forehead.

The guard called out again. Raquel took a deep breath. The woman began walking, this time with more hurried steps. The girls quickly followed until they reached a giant paifang. The red painted archway seemed to touch the moon. Calligraphy adorned beams on each side while a curling dragon's head snorting smoke was carved on the multi-colored tile roof.

Charlie strained her neck to look all the way up to the top. "Where are we?"

The woman took out a pocketknife, and Charlie instantly reached for her cutlass, which was well hidden under her knee-length coat. The woman deftly knocked Charlie's hand away.

"In this place, bad man very fast. No time for sword." She placed her hand deep into Raquel's cloak. "This better." She tucked the knife far down, next to the girl's hip. Raquel nodded, sure that no one, even her own mother, had ever dared to be so intimate with her.

The woman took out another small knife, piquing Charlie's curiosity. It was hard to tell in the dim light, but a quick glance suggested the woman was carrying at least five different blades. Sailors, seamen, and proper gentleman of the day might arm themselves with a weapon. However, besides panchi warriors, who were a Storm secret all to themselves, only modern-day pirates carried multiple weapons—often as many as eight blades—which they used for cutting rope, getting food, and self-defense. Charlie studied the tiny Chinese lady. Surely, as there was no such thing as female pirates except in the fictional stories the girls spread about the Pirettes, there had to be another explanation as to why this woman packed heat like a buccaneer. Charlie wanted to pry a little further, but sensed from the stern expression on the woman's face that it wasn't a good idea. Instead, Charlie took the knife the woman was about to hide on her. "Thanks, but I can manage this myself." She reached into her own cloak more discreetly than had been done with Raquel and concealed the weapon.

"Stay close," the woman said, as she passed under the paifang. Within minutes, they were assaulted by a barrage of sounds and smells that were a world away from the preserved peace of the Old City. Even the foreign quarter where their ship was docked wasn't as lively as this place. Despite all the hustle and bustle, there was still a seedy undercurrent, and both girls were happy to have their weapons.

"Are we still in Shanghai?" Raquel asked, but a waft of *xiaolong bao*, the perfect Shanghainese soup dumpling they'd been stuffing themselves with since arriving, answered her question.

The woman led them through a labyrinth of streets and alleys. Clusters of dimly lit paper lanterns hung from balconies and rooftops, diffusing the black night sky. Loud vendors advertised their goods, standing in front of wooden shop fronts that sold anything and everything. Across the way were ancient buildings that had roofs with upturned eaves and wall tops flourished with carvings of mythical beasts. They weaved through several crooked lanes lined entirely with looming whitewashed mansions boasting tall red pillars and gold banners hanging from marble balustrades.

On what looked like a main street, locals and sailors ate and drank merrily in cramped watering holes serving mouth-watering delicacies. The rest of Shanghai slept, but in this wild part of the city, it seemed like the party had just started. Raquel passed a heaping plate of *tangcu paigu* and barely stopped herself from reaching out and grabbing a handful of the succulent sweet-and-sour spare ribs. Charlie's stomach growled loudly when she inhaled the delicious aroma of fish heads pickled in soy sauce.

The pungent smell of fermented rice vinegar from dishes like *jiang luobu* and *pai huanggua* lingered in the air. An orchestra of noises ranging from opera singers to barking dogs mixed with the sweat and mad chaos to create an energy that both pulsed and blistered.

The girls were in awe of their strange surroundings as they struggled to keep up with the surprisingly fast woman who no longer baby-stepped but rather strode through the dizzying maze. Still, they kept close, their survival instincts heightening with every dark alley they walked down.

At the end of one of these alleys, the woman stopped in front of what looked like an abandoned store. Though she didn't knock, the front door opened and a man enormous in both girth and height stepped out.

The woman turned to the girls. "Okay, you here. My job done." She reached into her cotton bag and pulled out a flimsy bamboo tiger and handed it to Charlie. "Give to Mr. Chang."

"This thing?" Charlie held the tiger up in disbelief, not sure how a cheap trinket could help her find out who annihilated the Storm. "And who's Mr. Chang?"

But, to no one's surprise, the woman walked away without speaking another word. Suddenly, two fat but incredibly smooth arms yanked Charlie and Raquel inside the building, then dumped them on the floor. The man pointed a chubby finger straight ahead. "Mr. Chang."

"Mr. Chang's there?" Raquel asked in broken Shanghainese, pointing in the same direction. "Are you sure? Because it looks pretty empty. Who is Mr. Chang?"

Much like the woman, the bouncer was also not keen on explanations. He hoisted Raquel onto his left shoulder, and before Charlie could protest, heaved her over his right shoulder.

"Really not necessary! We can walk." Charlie banged on his back with her fists, but it was like hitting iron.

The man dropped them when they reached a staircase.

He handed them each a lantern.

"Mr. Chang," he repeated, while pointing the same chubby finger up the stairs.

The girls knew better than to ask any questions and took the lanterns as they made their way up the steep steps. "Is this really the smart thing to do? I mean, where exactly does this lead?" Charlie asked.

Raquel shrugged her shoulders. "Do we have a choice? It's not like we've been very successful finding out what happened that day on our own."

Charlie raised an eyebrow, but continued climbing the long, winding staircase. "Holy …"

Raquel raced up the remaining steps. "What?" When she reached the top landing, she was also rendered speechless. They stood in front of a gigantic circular archway formed out of what looked like one continuous slab of green jade. Behind the archway, rich bamboo slats offered guarded peeks into a sprawling lair of pure luxury.

"Mr. Chang will be with you when he can. He asks that you wait for him inside," said a baby-voiced, smiling porcelain goddess wearing a flowery *chángpáo*. They had seen many Chinese women of all ages wearing a similar dress, but hers was much more clinging, revealing her long, lithe silhouette.

A set of unseen hands removed the girls' gray cloaks before their hostess led them through the archway. With each delicate step she took, the high slit of her cheongsam, another feature not dared in the everyday cheongsams on the street, exposed her creamy white leg.

After passing another series of bamboo slats, the girls arrived in a dark den layered in splendor. Raquel inhaled a sharp breath. Silk curtains were drawn back to reveal velvet-cushioned Turkish divans and red lacquered Chinese coffee tables. Plush tapestries of suggestive drawings darkened windows, while low-hanging chandeliers cast a crimson glow throughout the entire place.

"Please have a seat here while you wait for Mr. Chang," the hostess smiled as she led them to an empty divan in the middle of the room.

Chinese, European, and Arab men and women mingled together in various groups. Though they varied greatly in size, age, and color, they shared one common feature: shrunken needle-point eyes.

"*Ya-p'iàn,*" Raquel whispered so softly that she wasn't even sure she'd said the word aloud.

Charlie nodded, slightly trembling. She didn't need the translation as she knew exactly what Raquel was saying. *Opium.* They were in an opium den. Or *hua-yan jian,* "flower smoke rooms" as the locals referred to them.

Charlie ran her finger across her necklace, keenly aware of the growing buzz of excitement she and Raquel were generating. Though she had more clothes on than some of the patrons, she desperately wished she'd chosen a higher collar and buttoned her coat closed. She looked around the room. Perhaps it was naïve, but with their glassy eyes and languid poses, they didn't seem to present a threat to the girls. Certainly there was a carnal hunger that hissed in the den, but quite frankly, everyone seemed too intoxicated to do anything about it. Still, Charlie thought as she patted her thigh for yet another time this evening, she was grateful for the weapons she was packing.

"Please," said a glazed-faced grandma lying on the divan across from them. She held out a long ornate silver and green pipe.

Both girls' eyes grew wide, and they shook their heads vigorously.

"More for us, then," the woman laughed huskily as she turned toward an equally elderly man that Charlie assumed was grandpa.

The grandma sucked the pipe until her flabby cheeks were high and taut. Charlie covered her nose as the pungent smoke filled the air. They consumed the stuff as though it were ambrosia, but the sickly sweet smell repulsed Charlie. Her stomach churned.

The first time Charlie had ever used her blade against another human being was in a place like this. She'd drawn her cutlass hundreds of times in training. But up until eleven months ago, she'd never placed her sword against actual flesh with the intent to harm—or worse.

Druggies and drunks were the easiest targets. She'd wait outside of saloons, taverns, and drug houses. Sometimes she'd bring Liu. Liu was a half-decent swordsman, but more than that, she was just good to have around in an emergency. Together, they'd find their marks. Best were fat cat businessmen with too much drink in their bellies and a wad of cash in their pockets, or doped-up society ladies loaded down with jewels.

Usually, their victims were too hammered or ashamed to put up any kind of fight. But once in a while, there was a feisty one, and Charlie would have to draw blood. Then she and Liu would run like the devil with the loot they'd stolen, hoping it was enough to buy them all a few more days of food or get them closer to wherever the hell they thought they were going. But mostly, they just prayed it was enough so that they could stop the thieving.

Eventually it was. But not before a part of Charlie's inside, the part where she wanted to believe she was a good person, had been damaged. She looked around the opium den, studying the faces of its beautifully grotesque patrons. She was in a room of easy marks. Which was why she didn't want to spend another minute in this place. "We shouldn't be here. We need to leave."

Raquel stirred next to Charlie. The memory that had guaranteed she would never again enjoy a peaceful night of sleep flashed through Raquel's mind. The faceless soldier's sword piercing Papa's heart. "This is the only lead we have." She turned to face Charlie, steely determination radiating from her brown eyes. "We're staying."

As the oldest of the five girls and the most authoritative, Charlie was used to giving the orders, but it was quite clear that Raquel wasn't budging. Charlie sighed. She'd lost her own pop on that horrible day, too. Raquel was right, they had no choice but to stay.

Twenty minutes that seemed like an eternity passed before the hostess returned. "Mr. Chang is ready to meet you now. Please follow me."

Charlie and Raquel flew up, thrilled to finally be leaving. They followed the hostess through another series of bamboo slats until arriving at a set of heavy, wooden doors etched with an intricate design of a phoenix.

Again, no one knocked but the doors swung open. The hostess disappeared as two men, both equally as enormous as the bodyguard downstairs, ushered the girls in. To their relief, this time the girls were allowed to walk in of their own accord. The man on Charlie's side held out an enormous hand with sausage-sized fingers. Charlie stared at him in confusion. Did he want a tip?

Raquel rolled her eyes. "The tiger. He wants the tiger." "Oh, right." Charlie exclaimed, having forgotten she'd been holding it in her hand the entire time. She dropped it in his fat palm. He turned the tiger over. It was then that Charlie saw a barely visible image in the shape of an eye etched on the bottom. She frowned. Charlie didn't recognize the eye symbol, but there was no time to think about it now. The man nodded to the other man standing next to Raquel. The two girls were ushered through another series of rooms before reaching an enormous office with floor-to-ceiling windows that were uncovered. With its thick Persian carpets and rich red lacquer, this room was as splendid as the den. But by this point, the girls were too weary to be impressed anymore.

"Are you Mr. Chang?" Charlie asked the stern-looking man sitting behind the enormous dark wood desk, also featuring a phoenix etching similar to the one on the doors. She realized it was highly unlikely he spoke English, but it was her usual m.o. to control a situation by speaking first. He sneered. "Another Western woman who needs to be heard rather than listen. Barbarians." To both girls' surprise, Mr. Chang did speak English, though his choice of words was less than polite.

Raquel stifled a sigh. Charlie really was like a bull in a china shop. Though Raquel would have loved to dangle her knife and show the arrogant Chang just what else Western women were capable of, she knew that in this case, gentility was going to go a lot further than force. Raquel bowed.

Mr. Chang perked up. "I see that at least one of you is a proper lady. Please, come sit. You may bring your companion, if you wish."

Raquel and Charlie approached the desk and sat down on the rigid chairs. Charlie tried to find a comfortable position. With all its ivory bone, this chair felt like it was meant for punishment. After a few minutes of fidgeting, she looked up to see both Chang and Raquel glaring at her.

"Would you like me to bring another chair, or perhaps some cushions to better accommodate you?" Mr. Chang asked, condescension dripping from every word.

"Nope, I'm fine. Thanks!" Charlie flashed him a wide smile, prominently displaying the top and bottom rows of her teeth. Mr. Chang's entire face rumpled in disgust at her blatant vulgarity. Raquel stopped herself from slapping the toothy grin off Charlie's face. The girl was deliberately trying to antagonize him. Couldn't she ever back down from a challenge?

"Mr. Chang, if I may be so bold. We are deeply humbled and appreciative of your kind generosity. Thank you for allowing us to meet you." Raquel looked down at the ground, making sure to avoid direct eye contact. "We know you are a very important man with many things to take care of, so we do not wish to bother you."

"*You* do not bother me," he replied, turning away from Charlie so he directly faced Raquel. "However, I do not know how I can help you."

"Isn't it upon your request that we are meeting?" Raquel asked, trying to hide her confusion.

"No," Mr. Chang replied without elaborating further.

"That short, mean lady who brought us here doesn't work for you?" Charlie shook her head. "Then, who set this up?"

"I was contacted anonymously," Mr. Chang replied to Charlie while keeping his eyes locked on Raquel.

"Why would you agree to a stranger's request to meet to people you didn't know?" Charlie asked.

Mr. Chang didn't reply. Instead, his eyes grew even steelier. Charlie had crossed yet another line. Most likely he had accepted some sort of payment in exchange for this meeting but even a man as shady as Mr. Chang would never admit to such a thing.

"Who would bribe you on our behalf--"

"Charlie!" Raquel stuck her hand up. "Please let us not waste this invaluable opportunity with Mr. Chang asking silly questions." When she felt Mr. Chang's anger subside a bit, she cautiously addressed him. "We are just looking for information. We understand that Charlie's father, Mr. Andrew Drake, provided you with lirium?" Raquel asked.

"I dabble in the lirium business from time to time." Lirium *business*? Charlie shook her head but stayed quiet.

For hundreds of years, their people, the Storm, had found a way to keep water supplies clean all around the world, ridding them of the diseases that had previously killed entire societies. They did this by harvesting and processing lirium, a plant found in the depths of the ocean. They sold or traded it for money or goods that helped them survive, but the price was minimal. The Storm were ancient guardians of the sea; their motto was to protect those in need and destroy those that harm. Providing lirium to people was one of their duties. It wasn't for profit or a business.

However, Mr. Chang, the opium dealer, hardly seemed like he was into charity work.

Luckily, Raquel was thinking the same thing as Charlie. "So Mr. Drake would provide the lirium to you, and you would give it to those in need?"

"Give?" He snorted at the idea. "I did not work directly with Mr. Drake. I only met with him once when he introduced his associate. I work with her."

"A woman? Who?" Charlie blurted.

Raquel discreetly squeezed Charlie's hand, hoping to keep her quiet. "Mr. Chang, please, can you tell us anything about this woman?"

Mr. Chang tapped his fingers against his desk. They were both trying his patience now. "I do not have a name, but I find that despite her sex, she is intelligent. Refined." He waved to one of his security. "Please show them out."

Raquel bit her lip. Mr. Chang's English was heavily accented, but fluent. In fact, how such a well-learned man wound up an opium dealer was probably an interesting story in itself. But right now, what piqued Raquel's curiosity was why Mr. Chang was using the past tense with Andrew, but not when referring to this woman.

The security guards stepped forward, but Raquel planted her feet into the lush rug. "You're still working with this woman. As in the *present* tense. So what's her name?"

Charlie smiled at Raquel. She was definitely proving to be a handy wingman.

Mr. Chang's face turned as red as his lacquer coffee tables. "You stupid girls! You think we use our real names in this line of work and invite one another to tea?"

A tingle ran down Raquel's arm. She'd learned languages from Mama, but the gift of "reading" people was from Papa. Mr. Chang was lying.

Charlie, who just went by pure gut feeling, was again on the same wavelength as Raquel. She leaned in to whisper in her ear. "Do you want to set the little liar's pants on fire, or should I?"

Raquel could see the girl was desperate to draw her sword, but she did want to try to get them out alive. "No need for fires just yet. Let me take a shot at this." Raquel cleared her throat and lowered her voice. It was important not to shame Mr. Chang for his lie, but rather coax him into telling the truth. "Dear Mr. Chang, we are extremely humbled and grateful to be in your presence. Our quest is only to find answers. We were told that an important man like you may have some information. Please, any guidance you can give will be very appreciated."

Charlie tried not to vomit. A blade to Mr. Chang's chest would have been more effective and less humiliating for both her and Raquel.

Mr. Chang sighed. His face slowly started to resume its chalky color. "I only knew Mr. Drake as 'A' up until you two dullards revealed his full name just now. I know her as H."

"And you worked in the lirium *business* with Andrew Drake, Mr. Chang?" Raquel tried to keep the incredulity out of her voice.

"This is what I've said." He pretended to wave a magic wand. "I don't have the time or interest to dispel you girls' belief in the fairytales you've been told."

Though she was still processing what he'd just said, Charlie blistered at the idea of her pop having anything to do with a lowlife like Mr. Chang. "You're a liar! My father would never associate himself with a scumbag drug dealer." Mr. Chang's jaw tightened and his fist tensed. "Oh, so now it's your turn to judge? Hmmph!" he chortled. "Your father might not have been a 'scumbag drug dealer' himself, but he was English, wasn't he? Well, it's the *British* who bring the opium to China. They smuggle it through Bengal and India. You see, you Europeans can't get enough of our Chinese silk, tea, and porcelain, but we have very little interest in your wool and bland spices. So this is your way of balancing the books, as they say." He leered at Charlie. "Sapphire East Trading Company alone imported two thousand chests of opium just in the last year!"

The hairs on the backs of both girls' necks stood up at the mention of Sapphire East Trading Company. As the world's most powerful corporation, SETC had its hands in practically everything, from politics, government, banking, and construction to medical care and food supply. But its main responsibility was insuring ships—particularly big merchant fleets—and keeping them safe as they crossed the seas. When the girls uncovered a secret plan for SETC to ransack one of its own insured fleets, they unwittingly became SETC's sworn enemies. Or to be more specific, enemies of Sapphire East Trading Company's head, Rogers Barrish.

Governor Rogers Barrish was one of the most admired and powerful men in the Western hemisphere—maybe even the world. The girls had never expected to cross paths with him, nor had they wanted to enrage him as they did. Charlie, disguised as a Pirette, had actually been in the middle of mugging a couple of drunken thugs when she'd found out about a scheme to ransack a fleet of American merchant ships. Then it was little Ingela, with her sticky fingers, who'd stolen the map right out of Rogers Barrish's office. Inside the map were secret papers that revealed it was actually Barrish himself behind the scheme. There was probably some kind of karmic lesson in it all against mugging and stealing, but that's not what the girls focused on. Ever since those fateful events over six months ago, they were aware of what a two-faced scoundrel the almighty Rogers Barrish was. What was worse, Rogers Barrish *knew* they knew. This made them the targets of one of the most lethal men around.

Charlie gritted her teeth in disgust. Given her knowledge of Rogers Barrish and Sapphire East Trading Company, it was of little surprise that they were somehow tied up in the filthy opium trade. She sneered at Mr. Chang. "It makes sense that you'd have something to do with a corrupt company like Sapphire, you seedy bast—"

Raquel covered Charlie's mouth with her hand. She really didn't want to die today, which meant shutting Charlie up. "Thank you, Mr. Chang, for your time. We are grateful for your generosity." Mr. Chang ignored Raquel and barked another set of orders to both his men. Raquel hoped it was to show them the way out, but, given the ferocity of his tone, it could just as easily have been to execute them at once.

Charlie threw Raquel's hand off of her mouth, but she got the point. It was better to live than to have the last word. At least, in this case. She remained silent as the two guards escorted them through several dingy hallways until they reached a dark, narrow staircase that, to their relief, led to the outside.

Hidden under their cloaks again, they began to make their way through the maze. What Charlie lacked in social graces, she made up for with an almost photographic memory of streets and maps. Deftly, she led them through the back alleys and side streets. This time, they did not pay attention to the new aromas and sounds. Instead, they walked silently, each deep in her thoughts—unaware they were being followed.

Chapter

TWO

SLOG
Date: August 28
Position: Shanghai, China
Weather: Rainy

This isn't an official slog, since we're still on land. Actually, I'm writing this so there's a written record that I know Charlie's up to something. I know that she and Raquel snuck off somewhere a few nights ago. I know they came back really late. And I know she's been even more tight-lipped than usual. She needs to tell me what her secret is, or else I will put stool-relaxing herbs in her food.

On a happier note, we get Liu back in four days.

Hopefully with the ship!

Signing off for now (SOFN),

Sadie

"Her dress is in my tea!"

Liu evil-eyed her little brother from across the table as she quickly lifted a bell sleeve from her silk brocaded jifu out of the teacup before anyone else noticed. Despite her narrow frame, her brothers knew she had enough muscle to hurt them if she had to.

"What's that, Son?" Zhang Tao asked, beaming with pride the way he did every time he had even the simplest interactions with one of his male children. At nearly 6'2", with broad shoulders and a wide chest, Liu's father was an imposing figure, both in Shanghai society and in his own family. Especially as he sat on his "emperor's throne," an oversized red monstrosity with carved dragons along its base that stood in the very center of his formal parlor.

Zhang Tao turned to face his youngest son. Though he was much too brave a boy to let a girl intimidate him, Fu could still feel the glare from his older sister's stare and decided it was wise to keep quiet. "Um, nothing, Daddy," he replied, as he stuffed his mouth with pieces of dried plum. Liu let out a small sigh of frustration as she struggled to remember the next step in the tea ceremony. Practically every hour she'd spent in her miserable two-week stay with her father and brothers had been dedicated to learning the sacred *Gongfu Cha*. Her hands were covered in blisters from all the times she'd spilled boiling hot water on herself as she tried to perfect each detail of the ten-part ritual. But now her mind was as empty as the teacups in front of her. She surveyed the delicate instruments laid out on the black lacquered drip tray, hoping something would look familiar. *Aaah! That's it.* She was on step #3, *wū lóng rù gong*, which literally meant, "the black dragon enters the palace."

Without even looking up, Liu could feel her father's fiery contempt as he held court at the center of his three adoring sons. *No doubt, the dragon was definitely here.*

She reached for the loose tea leaves inside the *cháchí*, then stopped abruptly. How many times had that nasty tea ceremony instructor yelled at her for using her bare hands? Liu picked up the bamboo scoop and filled the *Yixìng* teapot with Oolong.

When Zhang Tao had challenged Liu to master the art of making a perfect cup of tea in exchange for continued use of his ship, Liu had been amused. She'd excelled at cartography and navigation lessons from her mother, so she was sure to fly through Zhang Tao's latest test, which was—as they always were—based on underestimating her simply because she was a girl.

And though Gongfu Cha had proven to be a bit more intricate than it first seemed, what she hadn't imagined was that she'd have to be doing it wearing a *buyao*. Liu had nearly drawn her cutlass when she was abruptly awakened by six stern-faced ladies' maids at the crack of dawn this morning. For nearly five hours they fussed and mussed over her as they shaped her long, brown locks into a lotus flower, then pinned it with a buyao, a heavy gold ornament covered in dangling jade cranes and strands of cultured pearls. Liu screamed at the top of her lungs, but her protests fell on deaf ears, though she was happy to have gotten in an elbow jab at one of the old grannies who was particularly rough with Liu's sensitive locks.

Liu leaned forward very slowly, careful not to let her hair, which felt like four bird's nests stacked high on top of her head, get too close to the silver candelabras on each side of her. Most Chinese families were lucky to have a few lanterns per room, but multiple sconces and candle chandeliers covered her father's massive mansion, casting a glow throughout the place.

She raised the bigger teapot above her shoulder just as she'd been taught, and started to pour the hot water, creating the illusion of a fountain. Fu's jelly belly jiggled up and down as he erupted into a fit of giggles.

"Look Daddy, it's like magic!" he shouted as he pointed to the stream of water. *Not really, because I'm standing right in front of you*, Liu thought to herself. The kid really was a chump. She stayed silent and continued to smile without teeth so as to appear demure, just like her tea teacher had taught her.

Suddenly, Liu's arm shook under the weight of the heavy clay. The teapot banged into a jade crane, causing the bird to soar across the low table, smacking Fu's eldest brother, Fa, in the forehead.

The room, which had already started to feel nauseating from the cloying stench of cinnamon incense burning on every surface, went sickeningly quiet. Even the yellow songbirds Liu had brought in to liven up the usually stiff atmosphere of her father's house stopped chirping. *Traitors.* Everyone, including Liu, froze, except the red bump on Fa's forehead, which seemed to grow with each millisecond Liu did nothing. Tiny trickles of sweat formed on Liu's brow as she pictured a land-locked life doomed to endless tea ceremonies with these people. She had to act fast.

"These man hands of mine aren't made for holding such precious, delicate things! I beg your forgiveness at my lack of feminine grace," Liu apologized, as she cast her almond eyes to the floor and covered her face with a hand fan. She prayed her act would work while silently begging her mother, who was no doubt rolling over in her grave, for forgiveness.

"It's true, her hands really are like a man's! So big and hairy!" Fa exclaimed, pointing at Liu's hands.

"Her feet, too!" Fu chimed in, pointing at Liu's feet. "Our sister is a big man corpse!" Fu laughed, referring to the nickname they had given Liu for her gangly body and sallow skin, which always looked as though she were infected with the flu.

"Sometimes, she even smells like a man!" added Feng, whose name appropriately meant "silent wind," as he held his nose. Considering all the gas he spread around the house, Liu didn't think he had any place commenting on odors of any kind, but she was willing to let this one go under the tense circumstances.

"I'm so proud to have sons who are so compassionate and forgiving of their sister's many flaws," Zhang Tao proclaimed, his face bursting with joy. He leaned toward his three boys. "After all, it is our duty to make her into a proper lady. Failure to do so will not only bring shame on her, but more importantly, on our family as well," he explained as he patted each son on the head. She wanted to rip off all the jade cranes from her head and pelt them at Daddy Dearest. Instead, she pictured the faces of Ingela, Charlie, Sadie, and Raquel. They weren't related in any way, but those four girls felt more like family to her than anyone in this room. It was Sadie who always mixed up that weird concoction of ginger and valerian whenever Liu got seasick (which was way less often these days). She'd watched Ingela take her first steps and say her first cuss words. Charlie had kept them safe this whole time, protecting them at all costs. And then there was Raquel. They were born in the same year, only a few days apart, but that's not what made them "twins." Raquel knew every good, bad, scary, funny, crazy thing about Liu, and she never made her feel anything but okay about it. They had a language between them that went beyond words. With all four girls, she shared a bond that was stronger than blood. She would do anything for them.

Liu took a deep breath and continued on to the next step.

To her surprise, the rest of the ceremony went smoothly. She poured the last drops of tea from the handmade porcelain *chaichai*, being very careful to steady her shaking hands first. Liu waited for them to finish with bated breath. She couldn't believe that her fortunes, and those of the other girls, rested on a cup of tea. On land, they were all bound to something. In her case, it was a fanatical father and bratty brothers. But on the sea, they were *free*.

Liu anxiously scanned the faces of her family, but the teacups covered their expressions. Three sips were all it took to determine their fate. The first sip was the smallest, the second sip was to truly enjoy the tea, and the third and final sip was to relish the aftertaste. *One. Two. Three* …

Zhang Tao was the first to put his cup down on the table. "Okay."

Liu sprang up in joy, a swirl of jade cranes and cultured pearls twirling around her. "So we've got the ship?"

Zhang Tao pursed his lips before turning to his sons. "Boys, please leave me alone with your sister."

The boys hurriedly slurped the rest of their tea before scurrying out of the parlor. Liu felt like the jade cranes were continuing to whirl around, only inside her head this time. She braced herself for what Daddy Dearest was going to say.

"Our agreement was that you learn how to make a perfect cup of tea. Although that wasn't perfect, it was very good. Especially for your first time."

Was her father actually complimenting her? Liu wondered if she'd already fainted and this was a dream.

"So yes, they may have the ship—" "I can't believe it! Thank y—"

Zhang Tao raised his hand, instantly silencing Liu. "You are much too talkative. You must learn how to speak only when spoken to, Liu."

Liu bit her tongue and nodded. All five girls had lost most of their families on the Day of Destruction. Raquel, Charlie, and Ingela still had mothers out there in the world, but they didn't want anything to do with their daughters. The fact that Liu was the only one to still have a dad not only made her feel incredibly guilty around the other girls, but also made her cling to Zhang Tao in a way she'd never wanted or needed to before.

"I have received news that our fleet has successfully taken off for Japan!" cried a new voice in the room. Ming Hua, a respected elder who had once been an assistant to Liu's grandfather and now served her father, had arrived.

Zhang Tao flashed Ming Hua a look of contempt that stopped the older man from taking any steps further. He squinted his hard, cold eyes. "I am having a discussion with my daughter."

Ming Hua bowed. "I am sorry to interrupt, sir. It's just that you told me to notify you the moment I received any word."

"Now that you've done as you were told, leave us!" Zhang Tao waved his hand without turning his head to acknowledge Ming Hua.

Liu looked away. Ming Hua's status as a trusted advisor to Zhang Tao's father meant he'd always been a kindly uncle to Liu. He had bounced her on his knee when she was just a toddler, and stuffed her with candies. She couldn't believe the way that her father was treating him. Even worse, the fact that he dared speak to Ming Hua like that in Liu's presence only compounded the old man's shame. Her cheeks blazed, but she didn't dare stick up for Ming Hua at this moment, lest it compromise her "good little girl" standing with her father and jeopardize her chances of keeping the ship.

Zhang Tao leaned back on his throne. The blaze from the candles lit him up in full dragon majesty. Though she and her father spent most of their time focused on their differences, Liu realized they shared the same wide forehead (his even more so now that his hairline was starting to recede) and a stubborn streak. She'd always thought of herself as only belonging to Mai, her mother. Now with Mai gone, did she have to accept she was his, too?

He cleared his throat before continuing. "As I was saying, your friends may carry on with the ship. Indefinitely. If you make another cup of tea."

"O—kaaayy?" This was too easy. There had to be a catch. When it came to Zhang Tao, there was always a catch.

Zhang Tao tapped his fingers against the arms of the chair. "For your future husband."

And there was the huge, enormous, gigantic catch. "What؟؟؟" Liu blurted out, not caring if she'd been spoken to first. "Husband؟ Are you out of your mind؟ I'm only fifteen years old!"

"You'll be sixteen in a year, which is the legal marrying age in this province. I might remind you this was the same age as my mother when she was married off. And only a year younger than your own mother when we became husband and wife."

"And look how well it turned out for the both of you!" Tears of rage flowed down Liu's cheeks. Zhang Tao considered his miserable ten-year marriage to Mai his biggest failure and forbade it to ever be discussed. But Liu didn't care how much she enraged him right now. Had Mai been here, she would have chopped off Zhang Tao's head for merely proposing Liu become a teenage bride.

"Your mother had the mouth and mind of a man! She was impossible!" He looked away, running his finger down the five-inch scar that ran from his temple past his ear. It was from a wound that Mai had inflicted, and it signified the end of their treacherous union. Zhang Tao continued to speak with his head turned, this time in a muted monotone which he used when struggling to swallow his rage.

"I have been extremely patient and generous with you, Liu. When you showed up at my door six months ago, begging me for a ship, I took pity. I gave you a ship and let you play your pirate games as you tried to find out who killed your mother. And what have you discovered؟"

Liu shrugged her shoulders.

"Exactly," he smirked. "The only thing we know for certain is that she is dead. Which means the sole responsibility for raising you lies with me. So there is no point in arguing, because you really don't have a choice. Here are my terms. It is time for you to take your rightful place in society as a proper lady, wife, and, eventually, mother. And your little girlfriends, who unfortunately do not have fathers who care about their futures, can take my ship forever while you stay here—where you belong," he said, turning to face her directly. "Now, do you agree to my terms, or should I have the ship taken back in the morning?"

It was their freedom at the cost of hers. The weight of it all was too much. Liu collapsed onto her knees. She would do anything for her sisters. "Yes. I agree to your terms."

***

Sha-kalam. This was what her people named themselves in the African tribal language they spoke hundreds of thousands of years ago. Sha-kalam referred to a powerful disturbance manifesting itself with great force on the sea. Translated directly, sha-kalam meant *stormr* in Old Norse, *sturm* in German, and *sturme* in Middle English. For the last five hundred years, her people simply called themselves the Storm.

Liu brushed her hair gently. After the horrible teatime confrontation with her father the previous afternoon, she'd feigned a headache to avoid seeing him at dinner. However, the headache had become all too real this morning after the stern-faced ladies' maids had shown up to remove the buyao. Much to Liu's chagrin, taking out the buyao apparently required as much hair pulling and yanking as putting the nuisance in. She rubbed at the back of her head where the one lady's maid, who seemed to enjoy inflicting pain, had actually ripped a patch of hair out.

"Sha-kalam," she said to herself aloud. Even after all this time, it still sounded so exotic, so strange, so alluring to her. She'd never heard a thing about the Storm before boarding the *Storm One* nine years ago with her mother, Mai.

Then, all of a sudden, it was like she was immersed in a Storm crash course, as Mai and the other Storm members onboard filled her in on the history, philosophy, and rules. At first, hearing everything, especially her mother's own past as one of the Storm, was like listening to the Chinese myths Mai used to tell her at bedtime, or the crazy superstitions that Zhang Tao had plied her with. None of it seemed real or connected with her in any way.

For centuries, many enemies had fought to control the sea. They'd all been defeated by the Storm, the ancient guardians of the sea. They came from every corner of the world, with ships on all 108 seas, and were as diverse as the seas they pledged their lives to protect. Their identities were only known to each other, and they were united in a single mission to protect those in need and destroy those that harm.

Generation after generation, the powers of the Storm were passed down to daughters and sons. These powers weren't mystical like the flying warriors or fire-breathing dragons in the mythological stories that Liu liked. They were achieved after years of training and pushing oneself to almost superhuman physical and mental limits. With methods designed and perfected through the centuries, borrowing from warriors like the Iroquois, Ninja, the Persian Immortals, and the Byzantine Empire's Varangian Guard, the Storm were taught how to protect the sea at all costs, regardless of the danger.

The Storm had learned how to minimize their need for oxygen so that they could hold their breath underwater for long periods of time, which helped them find lirium, the plant that enabled them to clean water all around the world. They also had techniques to minimize drag and maximize propulsion in the water so that they could float perfectly horizontal, allowing them to swim faster, stronger, and lon-

39

ger than most humans and many sea creatures. They'd developed increased flexibility, agility, and speed, which allowed them to be both expert fighters with weapons and in hand-to-hand combat, all of which came perfectly together in the art of panchi, the Storm's own dagger-fighting method. Along with the physical prowess also came great intelligence. After thousands of years at sea, the Storm had cultivated an encyclopedic expertise of marine life, identifying characteristics of most, if not all, sea creatures and flora; weather and sea conditions; navigational and nautical techniques and equipment.

The Storm were even more awe-inspiring than the mythical heroes in Mai's stories because they were real people. Liu's ship, *Storm One*, held the most elite members of Storm—the best of the best. Even now Liu got chills as she remembered the sheer force of Ingela's father, Knut, who stood as high as a mountain, when he delivered a solid left-hook-and-kick panchi combination. Or how fast Charlie's dad, Andrew, could take down any opponent, most of whom were heavily armed pirates or battle-hungry navy captains, with his two-handed sword fighting. Not to mention her own mother, the ship's cartographer, who had a remarkably precise navigational sense.

Liu put the hairbrush down. At first she'd been so angry at Mai for not telling her about the Storm before. Especially since Liu's first weeks on *Storm One* had mainly been spent in the infirmary because of major seasickness. It all seemed so foreign to her, and like something she would never be able to understand, let alone *be* one day. Informal Storm training began at birth, and formal training started once the kids were four, with basic stuff like learning how to hold your breath for longer periods underwater (since most Storm babies started swimming before they could walk) and tumbling. At age six, Liu felt like she was already late in the game.

It wasn't just the physical training that made one Storm. It was the mental strength, too. Storm was a philosophy, maybe even a religion for some. There were so many ideas, rules, and responsibilities that the Storm were bound to. Storm wasn't something you did, it was who you *were*. It was a new way of life that Liu had never imagined.

Yet, after some time, Liu wasn't just imagining it; she was in fact living the Storm life. She loved it, though it was far from easy. On one hand, the sea was a magic carpet that allowed her to travel all around the globe, experiencing the best and worst the world had to offer. Liu also found that she was good at inventing gadgets. Though none of them were that useful, Mai and the rest of the grown-ups encouraged her to continue. Plus, after being an only child and growing up in a house comprised mainly of adults, Liu now had a whole ship of girls and boys to play with. With more than twelve families living on *Storm One* alone, it was as if she and Mai were part of this great big world that instantly welcomed them. That feeling of belonging was something Liu had cherished more than anything else.

On the other hand, they were bound by the strict Storm code of morals and ethics that Liu sometimes didn't understand. Andrew Drake, Charlie's father, was the captain of *Storm One*, and he ran a tight ship. Days were regimented, beginning at 6am with school lessons, followed by training for the kids that didn't end until 7pm dinnertime. Liu was too young to put it into words then, and maybe even now, but there seemed to be things she wasn't supposed to know about the Storm. Even though Mai was part of the elite Storm Council, there were questions that Liu knew she shouldn't ask. Instead, she went on happily being Storm, because that was what Mai and the rest of her new family was.

However, after the Day of Destruction, when all 108 Storm ships were attacked and the Storm were wiped out, she'd found herself asking questions she hadn't been able to before. What did being Storm mean now that there was no Storm?

Liu looked at herself in the mirror. She winced at the reflection of her shiny fuchsia bedspread. After giving birth to three sons, each time barely surviving labor, Zhang Tao's second wife had forgone her goal of having a daughter. She had, however, fulfilled her dream of decorating a girl's bedroom by filling Liu's room with puffy, overstuffed things in various shades of salmon, rose, blush, and coral. Liu looked around her and wanted to vomit. This "pink hell" was her prison now. She'd be locked up here until Zhang Tao found her a husband who was no doubt going to be better for his business than for her heart. Not that she could imagine any husband would be good for her heart when she was only a teenager.

"Sha-kalam," she said for what seemed like the final time. The Storm was gone. Mai was gone. The sea was gone. Her sisters were gone. Liu stopped getting ready and walked over to the bed. One by one, she plucked off the ceramic dolls, with their glassy-eyed stares and creepy smiles, that the maid arranged on the bed every morning, according to her stepmother's wishes. Some of them made a loud thudding sound as they crashed to the ground, while the rest just cracked without a peep. It wasn't even 8am, but she didn't have the energy to go downstairs and meet Zhang Tao for breakfast. Actually, she didn't have the strength to do anything but sleep. At least today Liu wouldn't need to fake being sick, because everything inside her hurt.

Chapter
THREE

SLOG
Date: August 30
Position: On land, Shanghai, China
Latitude: 31°13.3332´ N
Longitude: 121°27.4836´ E
Weather: Rainy. Wet. Miserable.

Technically we're not required to slog while we're on land, but someone needs to record the activity—or should I say inactivity—while we're here in Shanghai. Liu has never reminisced about her hometown, so I didn't know what to expect. But who could have prepared me for typhoon season on land? (According to "smart aleck" Sadie, I could have prepared myself for this had I bothered to read one of her stupid books.)

Technically, it's not typhoon rain, but still the rain NEVER stops. Every minute it spits, pours, or pelts us in every direction, never letting up. I could have submerged myself in the Yangzi for the last two weeks and I would have stayed drier.

Still, the four of us (Ingela says we look like a pack of mangy mutts with our soaking, matted hair, and I'm afraid we smell like them too, with all the muck, dung, sludge, and filth the rain slings everywhere) venture out from the ship every day, searching for more clues, only to be met with soppy dead ends. Raquel and I have tried to make sense of our conversation with Mr. Chang, but his info has left us with more questions than answers.

We don't know who "H" is. I still don't even know who sent the letter that got me to Mr. Chang in the first place. I have a feeling I might have to tell Sadie about all this, because even I have to admit, she's better at figuring this kind of stuff out than I am. I'm reluctant to share anything with her because she's been snooping around like crazy, which is so typically annoying of her, and because she'll just disapprove of all my actions as usual. Still, anything that can get us closer to knowing what happened to our parents is worth it—even Sadie and her high horse. Because now we've got nothing.

This trip will be a waste if Liu doesn't get us the ship! Speaking of our missing mate, she finally comes back to us the day after tomorrow, no doubt warm and dry after spending two whole weeks in majestic comfort. (She should have at least invited us for tea!). The first break in the rain we have and I plan on getting us the hell out of here!

Charlie

Charlie dove into the water. There was barely a splash or sound—not that it mattered here in this remote part of central Shanghai, which seemed to be a world away from the bustling madness of the opium den they'd visited not even a week ago. Their junk ship, or to be more accurate, Liu's father's junk ship, was a common vessel in Asia, and blended perfectly with the half dozen other junks that had docked in this part of the Yangzi River. But still, five girls alone on a ship, the youngest aged 11 and the oldest aged 17, were marked targets for all sorts of dangers, and so docking in low-traffic areas was essential.

Charlie treaded water to warm up. Though it was only the end of August, it was a bit chilly for a midnight swim. She'd told herself she hadn't wanted to sleep just yet because she was wary of waking up Sadie. But Sadie was a sleeping beast, and usually nothing could wake her. Likewise, Ingela was snoozing away in her usual spot on deck and wouldn't have been ruffled by Charlie.

Curiously, Raquel was on the opposite side of the deck, dancing. Charlie strained to see in the faint moonlight. At least it looked like dancing. Her body was compact, but her legs were long and strong as she did a kick-step combination with her arms moving in accompaniment to the one, two, three of her feet. She followed it with a powerful but graceful full turn. Raquel could be a bit loony at times, with her saints and superstitions, but Embajador's sharp communication skills proved to be invaluable with Mr. Chang.

Charlie dunked underwater. When she came back up, she let out a long, slow breath. For her, the sea was life, adventure, freedom, family …everything.

She'd been born on *Storm One* and had never known anything but the sea. In fact, for as long as Charlie could remember, her father, Andrew Drake, had been captain of *Storm One*, president of the Storm Council and the leader of the entire Storm. Charlie fingered her pearl necklace. Pop had taken care of everything her whole life.

Sadie had come to *Storm One* from another Storm ship on the Caribbean when she was just four and Charlie was five. She was accompanied by her entire family, including her mother, Josephine, who wore long silk scarves in her hair and was the smartest person Charlie had ever met. As the Storm's top chemist, Josephine was always mixing up potions, much like Sadie did now.

Josephine was married to Sadie's father, Henry de Wit, but she never took his family name, preferring to keep her maiden name of Wayo, much to the disapproval of some of the traditional Storm, who saw this as a blatant sign of disrespect for her husband and the institution of marriage. For the most part Henry didn't mind, but that may be because as a physician, his head was perpetually buried in big heavy medical books, and he didn't seem to have much interest in anything else outside of his reading. Sadie was also a big reader like her dad, but much to Charlie's constant irritation, Sadie was the opposite of Henry in that she pried into everything. As impressive as the de Wit-Wayo family was, the true star was their son, Taye. He was the most gifted Storm of his generation, if not any generation.

Charlie's stomach tightened. She flipped onto her belly and started swimming short laps. If there were two things Charlie knew she'd remember for the rest of her life, just because her pop had repeated them so often to her, it was that the Storm were the ancient guardians of the sea, and their mission was to protect those in need and destroy those who harmed. Whether saving an innocent civilian ship from a pirate attack, freeing a slave ship, harvesting lirium, or fighting a royal navy that sought to unfairly control the seas, the Storm were fearless.

Since you couldn't become a Storm soldier until you were twenty-two, Charlie was much too young to participate in any of these missions. Most of the time she didn't even know what was going on until it had already happened, partly because her own pop was so secretive about Storm business. Her lack of actual involvement, however, didn't lessen the enormous pride she had felt for so many years just to *be* Storm. Even if their identities were secret and their heroic deeds went uncredited.

Charlie kicked her legs against the water. After Sadie came Raquel, Charlie remembered, though she couldn't recall exactly where in Spain her family hailed from. She was such a pretty tot, with her ringlets and cherry lips, that she looked more like a precious doll than a real girl. At first, Charlie and Sadie stayed away, sure little Raquel would break easily. But she soon forced herself into their posse and proved that she could hang with the big girls.

Then there was Ingela, who literally popped out of no-where. When Knut—everyone's favorite rebel and the Storm's greatest fighter—brought a baby on board, it was a surprise, to say the least. He already had a son, Axel (and supposedly a few other children spread across the lands). But there was no mother, or ever talk about a mother, except for some crazy story that Ingela was the illegitimate daughter of a member of the Danish-Norwegian royal court.

Charlie chuckled at the idea of their little hellmaker turning out to be a princess. If anything, with all her stealing, fighting, and cursing, Ingela was more like an anti-princess. Though Ingela was a full six years her junior, Charlie sometimes found herself secretly in awe of the little Viking's sense of conviction and sheer courage. Most of that came from Knut and Ingela's older half-brother, Axel, though Charlie remembered a much younger version of herself being much like Ingela. She wondered when she'd lost that. Charlie stopped swimming and floated on her back. The water had become comfortably tepid now. She could stay here all night, and probably would.

The last to join their Storm ship was Liu, who was already six when she and her mother, Mai, just showed up one day. Mai had grown up Storm before she had to give it all up to marry Liu's father. Charlie never really got the full story, but she knew that Mai had been forced into an arranged marriage at sixteen. Ten years later, she rejoined the Storm and resumed her Storm training, quickly earning a place on the Storm Council, and as the ship's cartographer. Charlie always thought there was more to Mai's role. At least it seemed that Charlie's own father, as Storm Council president, was always seeking Mai out for something or other. In fact, Charlie thought she even saw them arguing a few times.

Maybe that was just her imagination. Truth was, she didn't trust her memories anymore, because nothing seemed real. At least nothing before the DD.

The Day of Destruction when soldiers with no faces raided their Storm ship and killed Mai, Josephine, Henry, Knut, and Pop, along with everyone else. At sixteen, Charlie was the oldest of all the kids and the leader of the other girls. That's what Pop had taught her. What he'd trained her for. But when he gave her the signal that day, she wasn't ready. *They weren't ready.* The faceless soldiers with their swords, clinking and clamoring. The screams. The thick black smoke. Even now Charlie's throat tightened as she remembered the suffocating mixture they tried desperately not to inhale.

"Charlie! NOW!" her father had gasped, and, this time, Charlie knew she couldn't ignore him. Did she also know those would be the last words he'd ever say to her? Like always, Charlie followed her father's orders and ran to collect the girls.

The girls held their shirts over their mouths to protect them from the black smoke as Charlie led them to the very edge of the ship. They'd practiced being under attack hundreds of times before, but no one was prepared for the real thing.

"No!" Ingela screamed. "No!" Sadie begged. "No!" Raquel prayed.

Only Liu stayed silent. Then came a loud explosion followed by a roar of fire. CRAC! A huge vibration rocked the ship. Charlie turned around. A red and orange burst of flames rushed toward them. Just ahead of it was a faceless soldier charging forward. A copper helmet enmeshed his head. His mouth was completely covered except for a tiny breathing hole. Two tiny slits were cut into the copper where his eyes should be. Without any warning, he grabbed

Raquel and jerked her away from the girls. Charlie reached for her sword, but Hugo stepped in between them.

"Papa!" Raquel shrieked.

Raquel's father had never been a fighter. Hugo had hardly seen real battle. But that didn't stop him from swiping his cutlass down the soldier's right arm. The soldier released his grip on Raquel and pretended to yield his sword before suddenly lunging at Hugo, pushing the blade directly through his heart. Charlie grabbed Raquel, but not before she saw the sword strike her father dead.

Raquel tried to yank herself away from Charlie's grip, but she didn't have the strength. "Let go of me!" she shouted.

The fire encroached as another herd of faceless soldiers ran toward them. Charlie could feel Raquel trying to free herself, but she couldn't—she wouldn't—let go. After a few more seconds, Raquel relented. They could feel the heat from the fire and hear the final cries of their beloveds. It was only a matter of moments before the faceless soldiers would strike them down, too. All five girls understood that there was no choice now.

Charlie swallowed hard, trying not to let the fear creep into her voice. "One!"

They stepped forward. Liu and Raquel looked at each other, while Ingela focused her steely gaze ahead.

"Two!"

They held hands. Sadie shook so hard that she made Charlie's arm tremble.

"Three!" They jumped.

Charlie's salty tears mixed with the freshwater droplets from the Yangzi as she relived the memory of the worst day of her life. Eleven months later and none of the sounds, smells, or sights had blurred. Nor could Charlie escape the aching emptiness that lurked inside all of them. It too only seemed to intensify with each day that came up fruitless as they searched for clues about who, how, or why.

All they knew was that on the very same day, Storm ships on all 108 seas were destroyed, wiping out the Storm entirely. Except for them. They were the only ones left. Unless you counted those two quitters, Axel and Taye, but Charlie certainly didn't.

They—Charlie, Sadie, Raquel, Liu, and Ingela—had survived. And just like she'd done on the DD, it was up to her to make sure they continued to survive. And yet, she wasn't ready.

Charlie plunged herself underwater and screamed where no one could hear her.

***

Sadie bit into her zongzi. The combination of sticky rice and sweet bean paste wrapped in reed leaves was a typical breakfast food here in Shanghai. Sometimes, after a slow morning, the lady from the zongzi stall down the harbor would offer the leftovers to her for nearly nothing. Though Sadie found them to be a bit cloying for her taste, she could never pass up a good deal.

"Oh, get over it, Sadie!" Charlie balked as she stuffed the last of her second zongzi into her mouth. If she could have her wish, Charlie would eat nothing but bowls of sugar every day.

"Raquel is only fifteen years old! You had no business taking her to an …" Sadie looked around before speaking in a hushed whisper. *"Opium den."*

Charlie chortled. At sixteen, Sadie was only a year younger than Charlie, but her overly cautious nature and constant fretting made her seem more like a grandma. Charlie had never had a grandmother, but she suspected they were all pretty much like Sadie.

"As I've tried to explain, Grammie, I didn't know we were going to end up in a *hua-yan jian*." Charlie tried to pronounce the last word like a local, but instead just ended up sounding like she was coughing up a hairball. Just like her pop, she was hopeless at languages. That was why as captain, he'd ordered all members of his Storm ship to only speak his mother tongue (and Charlie's), which was English. Though the rest of the girls all spoke at least one other language, they'd grown up speaking English, and, to Charlie's relief, it was the language they'd always communicated in. The two girls reclined back and let the rays from the late morning sun warm them. A light breeze brought in the honeyed fragrance of the big golden flowers that were in full bloom all around Shanghai at that time. The river shimmered under the bright sunlight, like a thousand tiny diamonds in the water.

Sadie was a night owl, often staying up till the early hours, which meant she usually wasn't fully functional until at least 10am. But Charlie had too much energy to sleep and was already practicing her swordsmanship or going for a swim by seven o'clock. Today, however, as much as it pained her to admit, Charlie needed Sadie's advice, and so it was best to put herself on Sadie's schedule to get it.

"You have to admit. It was dumb luck that nothing happened to you two! You should have brought me instead, or at least told me about it!" Sadie admonished, swatting Charlie on the arm.

Charlie let out a long, frustrated sigh. She'd been running through the events of the other night, including the stuff Mr. Chang had said about a woman partner, and none of it made sense. Sadie was always reading mysteries and figuring out puzzles. She could see stuff that Charlie couldn't. So Charlie decided she needed to "fess up" and tell Sadie everything, which also meant dealing with her never ending lecturing and judgment.

"No, it wasn't dumb luck. It was because we were smart and cautious. Actually, Raquel held her own." She grabbed the last zongzi from the plate. "I didn't tell you because you would never have let us go. And the only way I would have brought you is if I thought the secret mission was going to involve a spelling test or a book report." Charlie took a gigantic bite, savoring the sugary bean paste. "So now that I need brains, I've turned to you. Figure this out."

Sadie looked away. "Learn how to eat with your mouth closed before you start asking me for favors. You're a savage!"

Charlie opened her mouth, exposing a mishmash of food. "Mr. Chang thought the same thing. He used 'barbarian', though." Getting a rise out of Sadie was so easy, she could hardly fault Ingela for mercilessly teasing her. Speaking of which, she wondered how Squirt was doing, as there'd been no sounds of torture or pleas of mercy yet. Charlie propped herself up on her elbows. Far ahead she could see two tiny figures fishing. She was glad that Ingela hadn't tried drowning Raquel and that the two were actually working well together. Which meant she could focus on Sadie. Charlie nudged her. "Any ideas yet?"

Sadie twirled the anonymous letter between her fingers as she thought about everything Charlie had told her. But no matter how many times she ran it through her head, none of it added up. She read the letter once again.

I know you've been searching for clues about Andrew Drake. I have someone who may be able to give you information. However, you must follow all my rules:

1. *A boat will be waiting for you on White Orchid Pond. Row to the Eastern Gate of the Old City. The guards take their break from precisely a quarter past 10 o'clock to half past the hour.*

2. *Make your way to the rockery. Climb to the highest point and look for a woman in a gray cloak. She will be at the center of Yu Gardens with a lit torch.*

3. *Once you see the lit torch, make your way through the dragon wall. You must complete all of these tasks within the fifteen minutes the guards are on break. The woman will not wait for you past the half hour.*

4. *If you succeed in meeting the woman before the half hour, she will lead you to someone with information. Follow her every instruction precisely or she will not take you to this person.*

5. *If you do not succeed in meeting the woman on time, then I warn you to leave the area immediately, as your trespassing will lead to imprisonment.*

Sadie looked up. "Okay, we were Storm One. Andrew was captain, president of the Storm Council, and basically God on our ship."

Charlie threw Sadie a wry look.

"I'm not bashing your pop or anything, but you have to admit, he was the main guy in control of everything. I mean, EVERYTHING."

Charlie raised a weary eyebrow. "What's your point?"

"Just that everything seemed to go through Andrew.

This made sense since Storm One was central command, and that's where the council was headquartered. Lirium was never a secret, but knowing how to find it, where to find it, and how to process it in order to clean water was a Storm secret." Sadie stopped to make sure that Charlie was following along.

"I get it, Professor." Sadie's condescension infuriated Charlie, but she tried to keep her cool. "Keep going."

"So it would make sense if this 'H' that Mr. Chang mentioned he's working with is Storm. Most likely she—he did mention a 'she', right? Most likely she'd have been on the council if Andrew was working with her." Sadie's brow furrowed. "But we knew the entire council. It was my mom and dad, Mai, Knut, Andrew, of course, and a few other people. All of them are now dead—"

"And no one with an 'H' initial who was a woman." Charlie pounded her fist against the deck. "Dammit! Mr. Chang was the best lead we've had, and all he did was speak in riddles. It's probably all just a pile of lies. I mean, he *is* a drug dealer." "Yeah, but someone went to a lot of trouble to get you to Mr. Chang."

"Which is strange, because I'd never met that Chinese woman who guided us through the Old City ever before in my life. I don't know why she'd send that letter and help us."

"What makes you think that she wrote the letter? First of all, the letter refers to the Chinese woman in third person. See here." Sadie stopped twirling the paper and underlined Rule 2 with her finger.

"'Look for a woman in a gray cloak.' If the Chinese woman who guided you was the letter writer, she'd have referred to herself in the first person, as 'me' or 'I.' Plus, didn't you say her English was broken?" Sadie underlined another passage. "This is written in perfect English." She held it up for Charlie's inspection. "Actually, it's written in perfect *American* English. The writer uses the American spelling of 'center' instead of 'centre.'"

Charlie nodded. "You're right. Good job, Sadie. So we know an American sent this letter. But who?"

Sadie was on a roll now and wasn't ready to stop. She whipped out a magnifying glass from her pocket and studied the letter. Sadie's pockets were always stuffed with a menagerie of curiosities, and it was usually quite a surprise to see what she would pull out of them. "Plus, there is something about the tone. Like they know you or something. Even though the letter isn't addressed to anyone, they tell you rather sternly you must follow the rules as though they know you're the type of person not to." Sadie rested her chin on her hands. "Where did this anonymous letter come from, anyway?"

"A messenger delivered it to the ship. Not like an official messenger, just some boy."

Sadie looked up from the letter but still had her magnifying glass over her eye. "The letter isn't addressed to you. Was there an envelope with your name on it?"

"Yeah, now that you mention it. But I pitched it. Then I got so excited about the letter that I didn't even think about how they knew my name." Charlie squinted against the sun's rays, which had suddenly grown too bright. "Actually, the envelope was addressed to Charlotte." Charlie winced. She'd been named after her mother's hometown of Charlotte, North Carolina, in the newly formed United States of America. Charlie hated her real name, which sounded prissy and formal to her ears, not to mention it reminded her of the mother who'd abandoned her.

Sadie grimaced. "That's strange, since no one's called you Charlotte since we were little." She didn't bother to add that actually no one dared to call her Charlotte anymore after she had knocked out Axel, Ingela's older brother, when he had taunted her about her name. "And Raquel told you later that she had the strange feeling you guys were being followed home after you left the opium den, right?"

"It was just a feeling she had. No hard proof." Charlie fiddled with her necklace. "What are you getting at, Sadie?"

"Even if they called you Charlotte and not Charlie, some-one—"

"Someone knew my name and they knew exactly where to find me," Charlie whispered. A sudden chill went down her spine. Someone knew who she was and how to find her. "But how? We don't even use our names in the Pirette articles that you write and send out to the world." Charlie's mind was running frantically now. "You haven't started adding our names to those, have you Sadie?" Sadie shook her head. "Of course not! What would the point be in that? The stories are purely fictional pieces about our alter egos. I don't use anything that can identify us."

Charlie was only half listening to Sadie's response, as her mind had already moved on. "We're docked in the middle of nowhere. So how did they find me?" She could feel the color drain from her cheeks. "Tell me, Sadie! How did they know who I was and where to find me?"

Sadie held the letter up against the sun and stared at it through her magnifying glass. "Because they're watching us."

"What? What are you talking about? *They're* watching us? Who?"

"I don't know, but look." Sadie kept the letter in the same angle and handed the magnifying glass to Charlie. "Do you see it? You have to hold it up against the sun with the magnifying glass. That's why we didn't notice it before."

All of a sudden, the mixture of sticky rice and sweet bean paste bubbled inside Charlie's belly. Ingrained in the letter, so faint you had to squint even with the magnifying glass, was the symbol of a human eye.

Chapter
FOUR

SLOG
Date: DON'T CARE
Position: DON'T CARE
Weather: DON'T CARE

I HURD CHARLIE & SADIE WISPER ABOUT A LETER AND THAT CHARLIE IS BEING WACHED. A EYE OR SUM THING IS WACHING HER. CHARLIE DESERVES IT 4 GOING ON A SECRET MISSION 2 A OPIM DEN W/ OUT ME. I AM NOT A BABEE.

LIU COMES BACK TUDAY. SHE BETTER HAV THE SHIP.

Ingela

"This isn't a cucumber, Raquel. It's some kind of Chinese vegetable," Sadie calmly explained as she struggled to be heard above the cacophony of shoppers, vendors, and farm animals at the Shanghai market.

Sadie had brought along a book featuring pictures of fruits and vegetables, but had soon realized that a lot of the bushy green stuff and oddly shaped prickly things weren't on its pages. She'd tried smelling a few of them to see if she could identify them that way, but the overwhelming stench of fish filled her nostrils. From spicy anchovies to shredded squid and dried eel, she'd never seen or smelled so much fish.

Still, when Raquel held up a long, yellow something that was clearly not a cucumber, Sadie calmly took it out of her hands and turned to face all three girls. "Haven't any of you ever read an encyclopedia?" She held up her book. "It's a web of information on weather, vegetables, practically anything. And it's right at your fingertips!"

A brown-speckled cow standing next to them mooed loudly in agreement before splattering them all with a light sprinkle of sludge. Sadie failed to mention that the particular volume she was holding in her hands had half the pages missing for fear it would deter their interest. But given the way they were all ignoring her, it didn't seem she'd captured their curiosity anyway.

Sadie sighed. On Storm One, they'd had an actual proper library filled with books about everything from anatomy to Shakespeare. Now, her "library" consisted of the few books she'd managed to salvage from different trash heaps, mostly with torn pages or entire sections covered in goop. Ingela had brought her back a complete copy of *Robinson Crusoe*, and an intact version of *The Anatomy of the Human Body*. Though she'd claimed she'd won them both playing dice, Sadie was pretty sure the anatomy book had been lifted from an unsuspecting physician's office. Still, in this case she was grateful for Ingela's sticky fingers and her own sharp memory, which made sure all those books she'd devoured back on the Storm ship stayed in her head.

She held up her book again. "Seriously? None of you feel like checking out what a lychee is?"

Ingela stopped juggling a trio of lemons, much to the relief of the seller who'd been eyeing her for the last two minutes. "Uh-oh, Fifi's getting pretty feisty over there. Better bite her, Raquel," Ingela laughed as she picked up an orange. The seller frowned.

Sadie stared down the pint-sized menace. "Okay, first of all, you need to stop referring to me as a poodle. It's getting old." She patted her spongy hair. "I know my hair may not be feelin' good in this rain, but I do not resemble a dog. And second, don't you dare throw that piece of fruit at me."

Ingela began barking like a dog, or more accurately, yipping like a poodle. A mother scooped up her toddler and scurried away. But Ingela continued to yip while she chucked the orange at Sadie, hitting her square on the nose. "You mongrel!" Sadie shouted as she ran toward Ingela.

Fast and sneaky, Ingela deftly maneuvered through the crowded lane, hopping over a crate of bunnies and crawling between pairs of legs as though it were a game of "London Bridge." But when she dashed under a peanut stall, the startled peanut vendor turned his cart, pushing Ingela out into the crowd.

"Shoo! Shoo!" he shouted, kicking at her like she was a raccoon trying to eat his goods.

"Okay, okay! I'm going! Stop kicking!" Ingela hollered.

Just then, she felt Sadie's cold, long fingers wrap around her grubby collar.

"Got you!" Sadie yanked her fingers away. "Yuck!" Ingela, who was never particularly clean, was caked in mud from head to toe.

Charlie stepped in between the two girls and let out a long sigh. "Knock it off, you guys! Barking and throwing fruit isn't exactly laying low." She raised her right eyebrow, which already sat slightly higher than the left one. Since cooking was seen as domestic work, there were quite a few unchaperoned women there. The girls could relax a bit, but still, there was no reason to call attention to themselves. "Sadie, you know that daring her to *not* do something is exactly what makes her do it. You were kind of asking for it."

Ingela smirked. Charlie squinted her eyes so hard they practically disappeared into her deep sockets. "And you need to stop acting like such a *baby*."

Now Sadie smiled. At a mere eleven years old, Ingela hated her status as the youngest, and fumed anytime she was reminded of it. She reached for a grapefruit.

"Don't even think about it!" Charlie warned Ingela, backing away slowly. She grabbed a head of cabbage. Or maybe it was lettuce. She'd never really liked vegetables.

"Looks like I got here just in time for the food fight!" said a familiar voice.

"Liu!!!" They all squealed as they ran to hug her. Raquel got to Liu first, practically knocking her over when she reached her.

"Did you get the ship?" Ingela blurted out. She was never good with small talk. Plus, they'd waited on pins and needles for two weeks while Liu's father dangled their fate in his hands.

Liu nodded her head. The girls jumped up and down, surrounding Liu in another group hug.

"You're kidding me? And you didn't have to sell your soul?" Sadie asked. Though she hadn't actually met Zhang Tao, from all of Mai and Liu's stories, he never came off as being a very accommodating man. In fact, they'd all been flabbergasted when he'd agreed to give them his ship six months ago.

"Was it really that easy?" Raquel asked.

Liu fidgeted. Sadie was as curious as a cat, and Raquel could spot a fibber—especially on the rare occasions it was Liu—a mile way. They'd never lied to each other. But right now, Liu couldn't bring herself to tell them her father's horrible ultimatum. "I had to learn how to make the perfect cup of tea."

"Sounds rough," Charlie muttered loudly. "We would have loved a cup of tea in a warm, dry home."

Sadie creased her smooth, mahogany brow. "Ignore her, Liu. Charlie's been on land too long," she said, casting a disapproving look over Liu's shoulder. "Who's the guy with no eyebrows and a permanent angry face standing behind you?"

Liu rolled her eyes. The only way she'd been able to convince her father to allow her to come say goodbye to the girls was if she brought one of his lackeys with her. Though he was also carrying the ship's deed, which Zhang Tao had already transferred to the girls, it was clear his main duty was to make sure Liu returned to her new prison. "He has the deed to the ship."

"Wait—what? Your father is *giving* us the ship?" Charlie couldn't believe her ears. "As in, it's ours?"

Liu knew that if she tried to speak, she'd start to cry. So she just nodded.

The girls began to jump up and down, except for Raquel. She stared into Liu's eyes. "Something's not right here. What's going on, Liu?"

Liu blinked back tears. "I-I-I—"

Suddenly, they all heard Ingela's loud, explosive voice over the roar of the market. "Put down the bag of money and I'll let you go!"

Charlie cringed. She slowly turned to see the young girl drawing a cutlass at a group of boys. All four raced to stop her.

"You know you're not good enough to carry one of those around!" Sadie scolded as they reached her. "Whose is that?"

Ingela glowered at the boys while calmly answering Sadie. "It's one of Charlie's. And I *am* good enough!" Sadie glared at Charlie.

"I didn't give it to her. The little thief must have stolen it!" Charlie stepped closer to Ingela. "Ingela, put it down and let's walk away. There's about ten of them, and we are not ready for this." Charlie surveyed the group of boys. The majority of them looked no older than Ingela, with frozen expressions of terror. But a few, especially the one carrying the dagger, seemed as though they were itching for a fight. "But they're trying to steal the old lady's money! And it's our duty to help!" Ingela argued.

"On sea! Not on land." Raquel corrected.

"And who knows if it's really our duty anymore," Liu tried to rationalize with Ingela.

"You're all a bunch of scared liver faces!"

Raquel, Liu, Charlie, and Sadie exchanged confused looks. Ingela had a habit of making up new curse words without ever explaining what they meant.

"Liver-what?" Raquel asked.

"Are you calling us sissies?" Sadie queried while shaking her head.

"It doesn't matter!" Ingela shouted. Then she turned her head toward the girls and lowered her voice to a whisper. "You don't deserve to be Storm!"

Suddenly the boy carrying the dagger roared as he charged for Ingela.

Sadie shrieked.

Ingela bellowed as she grabbed the cutlass with both hands and swung it around, slicing through his shirt. The other girls watched in stunned silence until they were abruptly forced into action by the angry gang.

Charlie drew her cutlass, which had been conveniently shielded by her coat, surprising her empty-handed attacker into retreat. Sadie began hurling lemons, oranges, grapefruits, and then a rooster at the boys.

All activity in the southwest hall of the Shanghai market ceased as shoppers, vendors, and even the farm animals stopped to watch the brawl that was spreading across the floor. A chorus of bleating sheep and snorting pigs harmonized with the cheers and jeers of the onlookers. Toddlers and babies stopped howling and bawling, completely mesmerized by the unfolding scene.

"Liu! Duck!" Raquel warned before she jabbed her knee into the belly of a boy she probably would have flirted with under different circumstances. She flashed him a wink and a smile right before he collapsed on a pile of garbage.

Liu spotted the boy with the bag of money running for the exit. "Stop him!" she hollered as she elbowed through the crowd. She hurdled over a goat before breaking into a full-speed sprint.

Sadie jumped out in front of the boy with a carton of apples. She dumped them onto the floor, sending both the thief—and unfortunately—Liu crashing into a market stall. The seller, table, and stand toppled over the boy and Liu.

Sadie ran over to them. "Are you okay?" she asked as she bent over Liu.

Slowly, Liu lifted her head. "I think so. What about the robber?"

The boy was sitting up, but judging by the peculiar angle of his ankle and the loud shrieking sounds he was making, he'd broken his leg. "He's not going anywhere soon." Sadie helped Liu stand up. Together, they pried the money bag from the boy's surprisingly tight grip and walked back to the other girls.

With the fight mostly over, the crowd had dwindled. There were still a few cheers and claps as Sadie and Liu returned with the money bag. Charlie and Raquel had some minor cuts and bruises but were thankfully unhurt, but after slipping and sliding around on the putrid ground, they were all as filthy as Ingela. All the boys had fled except the guy with the broken leg and another helpless sap, who was lying under the little swashbuckler's boot.

"We're going to need to stitch that up," Sadie said as she moved in closer to study the gash on Ingela's forehead.

Drops of blood were trickling down her cherubic cheek.

Sadie took out a handkerchief and started dabbing at the cut before Ingela swatted her hand away.

"Or maybe I'll keep the scar as a token of my victory!" Ingela exclaimed as she flung her cutlass high up in the air. The girls rolled their eyes, but Ingela ignored them as she snatched the money bag from Liu and strutted over to the seller. With more pomp than a knight being crowned by a queen, Ingela handed over the bag and smiled proudly at the old lady. There was another faint smatter of applause as the vendor took the money back and grabbed an enormous basket of plums.

"She wants to thank us with a little reward," Liu explained as she translated the woman's words of appreciation to the girls.

"We really shouldn't take it. That's not how it used to work."

Liu turned to Sadie. "I think we should. I'm hungry." Just as they were about to take the basket, a monk carrying a sheet of paper with news printed on it, hurried over to the old woman. He showed her the paper while whispering frantically in her ear. The old woman froze, dropping the basket. Plums rolled all over the ground, but she didn't seem to notice. Her mouth fell open. She lifted a boney, crooked finger and pointed at the group of girls.

"*Xiezi*," she whispered in Chinese.

"What? What did she say?" Ingela asked, turning to Liu. Liu leaned in closer, but there was no longer any need as the old woman and the monk had begun to shout. "Xiezi! Xiezi!" He held his paper for everyone to see. Several of the men in the crowd took out their copies of the local Shanghai *bao zhi*.

There at the top of the page, under the heading "Beware! Armed and Dangerous," was an article about a treacherous group of girl pirates who started brawls, robbed old ladies, and caused all kinds of menace on land and at sea.

Accompanying the article was a sketch of the Pirettes. "You included a drawing of us?" Charlie hissed at Sadie. "Um … Well, Raquel and I thought it was a good idea because I've noticed that some of the newssheets include a drawing or two." Sadie bit her lip. "Obviously we didn't think about the consequences of showing our faces." Sadie peeked at the sketch that was staring them in the face. "Nor did I realize how lifelike Raquel's drawing was!"

Charlie nodded. "Yeah, maybe Raquel's a little *too* good?" The sketch of five girls with torn clothes, vicious expressions, and drawn cutlasses and daggers looked like Raquel had drawn it just several minutes before. Charlie looked around. The canniness hadn't escaped the people at the Shanghai market either.

"Xiezi! Xiezi! Xiezi!" they chanted.

Liu gulped. "Xiezi. Scorpions. That's what they call the Pirettes—I mean, *us*."

"Tell them they're wrong!" Charlie hissed. "Stop them!"

"Seriously, Liu! You gotta do something here!" Sadie cried.

"Xiezi! Xiezi! Xiezi" The growing crowd was quickly turning hostile.

Out of the corner of her eye, Liu saw Zhang Tao's lackey pushing his way toward her. With all the excitement of the past twenty minutes, she'd forgotten this was the end for her. Suddenly, an idea sprang to her mind. She only hoped the girls would be able to run fast enough. Liu grabbed the cutlass from Ingela's hand.

"Hey!" Ingela shouted, but Liu pushed her out of the way. She cleared her throat. She was terrified of public speaking, especially in Shanghainese. But she'd have to give the performance of her life if she wanted to make this work. She gathered all her courage and shouted the most menacing threats to the audience she could think of.

"Are you sure you're supposed to say that?" Raquel questioned. "It doesn't sound right."

Liu shot Raquel a pleading look. Raquel didn't understand what was going on, but she realized that Liu was being aggressive for a reason. Instantly, Raquel followed by flashing her teeth and growling at the crowd.

Sadie turned to Raquel. "What are you doing?" But Raquel ignored her and continued to snarl.

The crowd was growing more frantic by the second. Zhang Tao's lackey had made his way past the people and was rushing toward Liu. This was her last chance. She shrieked one more insult at the top of her lungs.

A man shouted something, and suddenly the horde began to charge.

"What did he say?" Sadie hollered.

Zhang Tao's lackey fell to the ground as throngs of angry people ran past him.

Liu shook her head. "Who cares? Just RUN!!!!"

Tiny sprinkles of rain fell from the gray clouds that hovered directly above. This was a mixed blessing, as it would no doubt help deter the mob,but it also made the stony streets they were running on much slicker. Liu only hoped the girls could keep up. She looked behind her. Right at her heels was Charlie, followed by Raquel and Ingela. Sadie was lagging behind, but, to Liu's relief, she was still in front of the crowd.

The mob had been chasing them through the side streets of Shanghai for the last ten minutes, but seemed to be losing both speed and mass. The mothers who were yelling at them before had realized it was too difficult to run and carry small children. Likewise, many of the pensioners quickly dropped out of the hunt as well. All that was left was a dwindling group of ferocious middle-aged men and a few teenagers. At the head of the pack was the monk who had started all of this in the first place.

Liu scanned the crowd. Zhang Tao's lackey had almost managed to catch up to them. She had to think fast. Liu had been forced to spend many summers in Shanghai with her brothers and father and knew the city quite well. Still, she'd only been to this area a few times. She secretly prayed she was taking them down the right path.

Liu turned the sharp corner. She recognized the green dragon hanging from the candy shop. Sometimes Zhang Tao would take them here for special treats, though Liu was always regulated to half the servings of her brothers so she'd maintain her "slim" figure.

She rushed down the little hill, careful not to slip on the wet rocks. Her stomach was full of knots. All they needed to do was go down this one last street, and then, if she was right, they were home free. Liu sped up.

In no time, the cemetery came into view. Liu swerved past headstone after headstone, delicately avoiding stepping directly on any graves. When she got to the big fountain in the middle, she stopped.

She fell to the ground, both from exhaustion and joy. Her plan had worked just as she'd prayed it would. She propped herself up on her elbows. Charlie, Raquel, and Ingela ran up with Sadie a few feet in the distance. The mob halted at the entrance with the monk shaking his fist in the air, but they did not move forward. Liu's mother had never paid much mind to Chinese superstitions, but her father had, and Liu remembered him telling her many times about haunted graveyards. The mob had decided it wasn't worth waking up the dead to catch the "xiezi" and slowly retreated.

It seemed Zhang Tao's lackey was superstitious as well, as he hadn't followed them into the cemetery either. Charlie, Ingela, and Raquel plopped down on the ground next to her. No one cared that it was muddy from the rain, which was tapering off now.

"Are they gone?" Raquel asked as she tried to catch her breath.

Liu nodded. "They've mostly gone. Chinese superstition says there are ghosts in graveyards, so I was hoping the mob wouldn't go after us here. Though there may be a few courageous ones willing to defy superstition."

Raquel sat up. "It's not superstition, and it's not just the Chinese. We Spanish—"

"We don't care, Raquel," Ingela spat out as she used her shirt to wipe the sweat pouring off her. "Someone get me some water."

"Come with me, Raquel," Liu instructed, reaching out to pull Raquel up. "Don't let them see you," Liu whispered as they both ducked behind gravestones before reaching the big, ominous willow tree at the far end of the cemetery.

"What are we doing here?" Raquel asked.

"Bringing up the dead," Liu answered as she hid behind the tree. "Just follow me."

The cemetery trick had worked on all but two members of the mob. The monk and a balding, middle-aged man were running around looking for the girls. Liu started to shake the willow tree and make low, deep moans. Raquel did the same. Within seconds, the tree seemed to be possessed by every evil spirit that Zhang Tao warned lived in this cemetery. From her hiding spot, Liu saw the monk and bald man stop and stare. Both took a few hesitant steps forward, then the bald man halted, turned around, and ran as fast as he could in the opposite direction, out the cemetery. Whether he was actually afraid, or because he realized he was no match for five knife-wielding girls, the monk retreated as well.

Liu and Raquel made their way back to Charlie and Ingela. Liu was relieved to see Sadie sprawled on the grass next to them. Before she could say "Hi," Sadie spoke.

"What the hell, Liu?" Sadie shouted. Her hair was soaked from either the rain or sweat.

"Let's just make our way back to the ship. I'll explain everything then."

As exhausted as she was, Sadie shot Liu a look that meant they'd be taking care of this now. "You incited an angry mob to chase us down. I need some answers."

Charlie spoke up. "No, the badly timed story that you sent to the officials with an actual illustration incited an angry mob." She shook her head. "Those Pirette pieces are supposed to come out after we leave a place! And they aren't supposed to be accompanied by dead-on drawings of us!"

Raquel smiled. "You really think the sketch was that good?"

Sadie wagged her finger. "Don't try to pin this on me. I admit, I messed up by releasing the story while we were still here, but Liu made that mob come after us!"

Ingela piped up. "It's your fault, Sadie. It's always your fault. Don't forget, I was the one who got the old lady's money back."

"Which was actually how this whole mess started in the first place. Because of your incredibly big, fat ego," Sadie snapped.

Ingela jumped to her feet and glared Sadie down. "Wanna say that again?" She traced the handle of her cutlass.

"Ingela!" Charlie barked. "Put that away! You've already gotten us into enough trouble today with that thing." Charlie reached out her hand. "Actually, give it back to me, thief!" Ingela ignored Charlie's last command, but did sit back down against the fountain. A slight breeze cooled them down. The sun was setting, casting a gloomy orange light onto the cemetery. With its well-manicured grass and big shady trees, the graveyard was actually quite lovely. If one ignored the hundreds of dead bodies buried around them.

Charlie turned to Liu. "Did you really get that mob to go after us?" One look at Liu's guilty expression and Charlie had her answer. "Spill."

Liu plucked a blade of grass and started twirling it between her fingers. "Yes. I told them they'd better catch us before we hurt them."

"And I helped," Raquel looked down. "I growled and stuff. But I knew we had to help Liu even if I didn't know why she was doing it."

Liu took a deep breath and let it out. "Because my father is giving you guys the ship. But in return, I have to go back and live with him. And get married." She could barely make herself say the last word. "That guy who 'chaperoned' me was there to make sure I went back to Zhang Tao."

"What?" All four girls turned toward Liu. "Live with your dad?"

"Married?"

"No way! We won't let that happen!"

After another minute of the girls exclaiming their protests and surprise, Sadie shut them up so she could speak. "You got the mob to go after us so that you could lose Zhang Tao's guy. That was smart. Dangerous if we hadn't all made it. But we did make it, so I'll say it was smart." Her tone softened. "But does that mean you're going to run away? That we're going to have to steal your father's ship?"

"Of course she's going to run away!" Ingela exclaimed. "Liu's not getting married! And we can find another ship!"

The rest of them sat silently. They couldn't just "find" another ship so easily. It had taken them over four months just to get this one, and they'd almost died in the process.

Charlie and Liu had robbed opium fiends and drunks. Ingela had learned how to shoplift fruit, vegetables, and anything else of value, while Sadie and Raquel had become expert pickpockets. They'd perfected a routine of carrying a large, obtrusive basket down busy walking streets. Sadie would profusely apologize as the basket bumped into people while Raquel used the distraction to lift the unsuspecting victim's wallet.

Sadie blushed at the memory of those days, but the truth was that they did whatever they had to do to get by after the DD. They searched desperately for any surviving Storm members, making discreet inquiries at every port they arrived in. Each time they learned of yet another Storm ship being taken out, they were hurled further and further away from their roots, their families, and their old Storm life.

Their new life was about one thing only: survival. More and more, they came to the realization that Liu's father was their only living hope. He was rich, and more importantly, he had ships. So they begged, borrowed, and robbed their way down to Shanghai. They slept in alleys, stowed away on ships, and stole horses when they could. If ships and horses weren't available, then they walked in the blazing sun or cold rain until their blistered feet bled. They went hungry for days on end, to the point where Sadie's restless nights were filled with desperate dreams of food. Then one day, after nearly four months of traveling, when Sadie was sure they couldn't go any further, they finally reached Shanghai.

The other girls had wanted to accompany Liu, but she insisted she approach her father alone. When she came back two days later with the news that he'd given them a ship, at least for six months, no one could believe it. For the first time since the DD, the girls had a real chance to live.

Sadie shook her head. Zhang Tao never quite came off as a good guy in Liu's stories, so Sadie couldn't understand why he'd been so generous then and why he was being so cruel now. "Why did your father give you the ship in the first place, only to turn around six months later and deliver an ultimatum of arranged marriage?"

Liu sighed. She'd been thinking the same thing in the last few days, but she couldn't really bear to face the probable answer, let alone say it out loud. Instead, she just shrugged and stayed quiet.

Sadie put her hand on Liu's shoulder. "That's okay, we don't need to talk about it. But you *do* need to make a decision, 'cuz we gotta act fast. Are we stealing the junk?"

When she'd begged her father to go to the marketplace, maybe somewhere in the back of her head, this had been Liu's plan all along. Surely it was the only result of getting the mob to go after them. But the reality of it all was hitting her. If she did this, there was no going back. The knots in her stomach tightened.

"Yes," Liu whispered. "I'm running away, and we're stealing my father's ship." Liu couldn't believe the words were coming out of her mouth. Raquel and Sadie wrapped their arms around her.

Charlie nodded and sprang into action. Let Sadie and Raquel handle the emotional stuff; she needed to come up with a plan. "Right. The chaperone probably went back to your dad. He's going to send more men." Charlie bit her lip.

Ingela snapped her fingers. "They'll go to the ship! Zhang Tao knows where we're docked."

Liu gently threw Raquel and Sadie's arms off of her. "Then we don't have much time!" She jumped to her feet. "We gotta get to the ship and ..." She stopped. And what?

"And sail away!" Charlie commanded. "Before Zhang Tao and his men catch us!"

All five girls raced through the cemetery, back to the ship.

***

They were too late. Zhang Tao's lackey was standing in front of the junk. Surprisingly, he hadn't gotten more men but was alone. Liu smirked. Of course someone who worked for her father would think that it only took one man to subdue five girls.

She sped up. With enough speed, she could ram her full body into him and at least knock the wind out of him. When he saw her, he waved his arms in the air. Liu tried to stop herself, but there was too much momentum. Within seconds, her entire weight barreled into him, sending both of them crashing backward.

His head cracked against the ground. Luckily, it was not stone here, just dirt. Liu's forehead bumped into his bony chin, causing her to bite her lip and draw blood.

"Didn't you see me surrender?" the lackey spat in angry Shanghainese. He barely stopped himself from hurling an insult at this stupid, clumsy girl.

"You started waving your arms too late!" Liu retorted, dusting the dirt from her front. Not that it made much difference—after all the fighting, running and rain today, she was caked in all sorts of grime. Night had fallen, but this abandoned part of the harbor was well-lit thanks to a full moon above. Zhang Tao's ship, the only home they'd known for the last six months, rocked back and forth in the gentle waves. Liu eyed the lackey. He was the only thing standing between her and freedom. She clenched her fist, ready to do whatever it took to make sure she was on that ship.

Charlie and Ingela ran up to them, their cutlasses drawn, with Raquel and Sadie shortly behind.

The lackey waved his arms again. "There's no need for weapons. I won't hurt you if I don't have to."

Liu nodded and translated his message to the girls. "That's awfully nice of you, but we'll keep these out just in case," Charlie replied. "Tell him we can make this easy or hard for him. Either way, you're staying with us."

Liu conveyed the message but left out the threat. The lackey took out a tin from his pocket while he listened. He tapped the lid then opened it. Liu was surprised to see the tin contained snuff, a mixture of finely ground flavored tobacco leaves that was favored by gentlemen of means. Or at least men who made more money than what Liu assumed the lackey earned. However, a quick whiff of the mentholated odor of the lackey's snuff indicated that it was pretty low-grade stuff. He grabbed a small pinch of snuff between his thumb and forefinger. Then he quickly shoved it up his nostril and inhaled before speaking. "I could take you back and receive my regular, paltry wages from your father. But I have a feeling that letting you stay here is worth more to you than his mere pennies." Liu crossed her arms. Was he proposing to double-cross Zhang Tao? She started to translate, but Raquel had picked up enough to explain to the girls.

"Ha!" Ingela roared. "We could just take you down right here and it wouldn't cost us anything but a few little bumps and bruises." She sliced her sword dramatically in the air.

"You're not a knight challenging someone to a duel!" Charlie hissed. "You're an eleven-year-old kid holding a sword that's too big for her. Seriously, put it away!"

"Shut up!" Ingela yelled. "You're not the boss of me!" She punched Charlie's arm.

"Brat!" Charlie shouted, turning to kick her.

Liu whipped around, squinting at them. "Not now!"

Ingela got in one quick elbow jab before the two girls settled down.

"Really mature," Sadie muttered.

Charlie ignored Sadie and kept her hand on her cutlass, in the ready position. Ingela eyed her discreetly and imitated the same pose.

The lackey grinned, exposing what was left of his few brown teeth. His mocking sneer taunted them now, as though he saw them as nothing but a bunch of clowns.

Liu straightened her shoulders. She needed to regain her credibility after that ridiculous sideshow from Ingela and Charlie. "There's nothing we need from you. It's really just easier to get rid of you."

The lackey reached into the inner pocket of his shirt and pulled out an envelope.

Liu shrugged her shoulders, pretending not to care. "The deed? Zhang Tao will revoke it the moment he knows I've stolen the ship."

The lackey took another pinch of snuff. "Yes, but it takes months to revoke a deed. You can at least use this if you're stopped by Portuguese or English navies."

He was right. Still, Liu didn't want to seem too eager. "So we'll just take the deed after we're done with you."

"Of course, you can do that." The lackey deeply inhaled more snuff. "But then you won't get my important information. You'll need it if you don't want to be found by Zhang Tao or his twenty-five ships."

Liu bit her lip, forgetting it was already cut, which made it sting again. She turned to face the girls, who were just getting the last of the translation from Raquel. They huddled in a circle.

"Who is this guy?" Sadie asked. "I mean, your father is a pretty powerful man. Why's this creep so ready to betray him?"

"Yeah, and what kind of information does he have?" Ingela asked. "I say we beat him up, steal the deed, and sail away."

"We should at least hear him out," Charlie reasoned. "Getting away from a guy like Zhang Tao isn't going to be easy. Did that guy say your dad owns a fleet of twenty-five ships?! We need any help we can get."

Raquel nodded. "I don't think this guy is a model citizen, but he's trying to help us. For his own gains, of course."

Liu took in their advice and thought for a minute before turning to face the lackey. "So how do I know you won't double-cross us like you're double-crossing Zhang Tao?" She lifted a thin, curved eyebrow. "I mean, why would you want to help me?"

The lackey spit a dark, gooey substance on the ground. Liu eyed him with disgust.

"I don't care what happens to a stupid girl like you." His eyes grew dark. "I just want to hurt Zhang Tao."

The pure hate in his voice sent a chill down Liu's spine. Liu looked him up and down. For the first time, it hit her who this young man really was. "Liang?" she croaked. "Is it really you? But I thought my mother had kept you safe?" The knots in Liu's stomach gave way to a burning ache. *The bamboo cane.* All the memories washed over her like the dark, gooey filth Liang had just spat on the ground.

Liu could never say there was a time when she, Zhang Tao, and Mai had been a happy family, but they had lived in one house together. It was an extremely large house, though not as imposing as Zhang Tao's current residence.

At that time, Liu had been Zhang Tao's only child, but the house was filled with servants working round the clock. Old men and women worked alongside young boys and girls. Liu hadn't understood it was their job to be there, and just believed them all to be her aunties, uncles, and friends.

At the back of the house, near the garden where Liu often played, a bamboo cane hung on the wall. The cane was shaped like a regular walking stick, with a thick brass handle. Liu had passed it a hundred times but never gave it a thought. Not until the day she found out what it was really used for.

It was a week after her sixth birthday, and she was playing with a shiny new ball that her cousins had given her.

Since all of her "friends" in the house had chores to do, Liu was playing catch by herself when the ball rolled out of the garden. She knew she wasn't allowed to leave the gates without a grown-up, but she thought that if she was fast enough, no one would notice. She hurried after the ball, tiptoeing past the back door.

At first, she didn't notice. There were no screams, no pleas, not even a whimper. Just the sound of the bamboo cane hitting against flesh and bone. THWACK. She stopped to see where it came from. Not more than twenty steps ahead of her, she saw a young boy with his hands protecting his face as he tried to cower in a corner. Liu recognized Liang, the twelve-year-old who'd just recently arrived at their house.

The tiny room was dark, with only a small window for light, but there was no mistaking the other person in there. It was her father. Liu ducked behind the door. Over and over, Zhang Tao raised the cane over his head, landing it on Liang's legs, back, and arms. THWACK. THWACK. THWACK.

Despite the slight breeze from the early October afternoon, the air coming from the room was stifling. Suffocating. Stale. But Liu was sure that wasn't what was making her sick. From her hiding spot behind the door, Zhang Tao was in full view. His tall, solid frame. The taut, angry cheekbones. The sly grin on his face. All the horror, the fear and the disgust of everything that Liu was seeing, paled against the sight of her father's smile.

Liu didn't know what to do but run. She could always depend on her legs. She ran back through the garden, under the mulberry bush and past the koi pond, until she found her mother pruning a bonsai, a gift from a Japanese friend. Liu had run so fast that she was almost out of breath when she told Mai what her father was doing to Liang. But she managed to get it out, without a single tear, so that Mai could understand.

Mai was an even faster runner than Liu. By the time she reached Zhang Tao, the beating had stopped, though the cracked bamboo cane and the bruised boy lying on the ground was all she needed to see. Mai shouted for Mrs. Wu, the house cook and nursemaid, to tend to Liang. Then she picked up the bamboo cane and locked the door behind her.

Screaming matches between Mai and Zhang Tao were already a regular occurrence. But after that day, when Mai walked out an hour later with a few minor cuts and Zhang Tao was carried out on a stretcher, everything in their lives changed. It would be years later, when Mai recounted the full story, that Liu truly understood what a hero her mother was.

Mai had hated the idea of employing servants, especially children. But Zhang Tao had convinced her it was a way to keep these kids, mostly orphaned, safe, with a roof over their heads, plenty to eat, and decent wages. Though Mai was still reluctant, she gave in on the condition that Zhang Tao would never "discipline" anyone with physical punishment, an archaic treatment that was still being practiced in some wealthy Shanghai circles.

When she discovered he'd broken his promise, she made him pay. While Zhang Tao recovered in the hospital, Mai used her old Storm contacts to relocate all the young servants to safe places. On the day that Zhang Tao returned home, Mai and Liu left for *Storm One*. It took another two years of apologies, remorse, and promises that he'd changed before Mai let Liu see her father again.

Now, as Liu stood in front of Zhang Tao's junk ship, a wave of shame drenched over her. Mai had stood up to Zhang Tao. Liu was running away like a coward.

"Your mother put me with nuns. They were good to me," Liang explained after yet another pinch of snuff.

"So why did you go back to Zhang Tao?" Liu asked, though the steely venom in his eyes told her the reason.

"You know he doesn't even recognize me?"

Liu looked down. This rage-filled man before her was very different from the timid boy cowering in the corner. She'd been looking at him for the last two weeks herself and hadn't recognized him. Though to be honest, her life had changed so much since those days, it had been years since she'd even thought of him. A wave of guilt mixed with her shame.

"There I am, hiding in plain sight, plotting against him, and he doesn't even see me. Maybe that's worse than the beatings he used to give me ..." Liang's voice trailed off.

Raquel tapped Liu's shoulder. "Maybe I've lost something in translation, but what's going on? You're talking about paybacks, nuns, and Mai?"

Liu had been so startled by seeing Liang after all these years that she'd forgotten all about the girls. She turned around to face them. "I'm sorry, we got off track. I'll fill you in later. For now though, we need to pay him so we can get out of here."

All five girls looked at each other and silently agreed. Sadie reached into her bag and took out a handful of small coins.

Before Liu could give them to Liang, he scoffed. "Do you think I'm trying to sell you candy or a shiny new toy?"

"You said yourself you're doing this to hurt Zhang Tao!" Liu retorted.

Liang stepped forward. Charlie and Ingela did, too. Liu raised her hand to indicate that everything was okay.

"And I also said I wasn't doing this to help you!" He let out a waft of hot, sour air directly onto Liu's face. "I'll be a walking target after he finds out I was in on this. *And he will find out.* The joy of seeing Zhang Tao finally lose is sweet, but it's not worth my life. I need money to lay low for a while until I can get away for good. And unlike you, I don't have 'Daddy's' ship to run away in."

With every tobacco-filled breath he let out, Liu could feel the years of spite that had been festering in him. This is what her father did to people. Even if she wasn't courageous like Mai, Liu knew she had to escape Zhang Tao one way or the other. For now, it would have to be this way.

Liu reached into the inside pocket of the long navy blue coat she always wore. She'd sewn this inner pocket just to keep the locket safe. Its thick gold chain had already been pawned a few months ago for supplies and food, but Liu had managed to keep the locket until now.

"No, Liu! You can't! Your mom gave that to you!" Raquel shouted. "We'll find something else for him!"

But there was nothing else. They all knew that. Liu opened up the locket and took out the tiny painting of her mother, which she stuffed back into her pocket. She fingered the smooth gold oval piece one last time. Mai would understand.

Liang snatched the locket right out of Liu's hand.

"Not so fast, Sticky Fingers!" Charlie shouted, pointing her cutlass only inches away from his chest. "You have some papers and information you need to give us."

Liang handed the deed over to Liu. "Zhang Tao sent his ten junk ships to Europe last week. They're long gone. Then he sent the rest of his entire fleet, mostly brigantines, up north yesterday for a massive trade he's working on with Korea and Japan. So head south as fast as you can. By the time he can turn any of his ships around to chase you, you'll be at least a week, maybe even two, ahead of him."

Liu clutched the stolen deed. There really was no going back after this.

Without any goodbyes, Liang turned to walk away, jingling the locket in his hand. "Oh, and one more thing," he turned to face Liu a final time. "He doesn't use the bamboo cane on the young boys anymore."

Liu nodded, feeling a sense of relief. She'd hoped that if Zhang Tao was still beating his servants, she would have noticed.

Liang saw the look of ease that crossed Liu's face. She was as blind as her mother had been. Which made her just as guilty. He was going to enjoy this part. He leaned in close enough so she would hear every word. "It's snakewood these days. Much sturdier. Harder to crack."

Chapter

FIVE

SLOG
Date: September 2
Position: Just out of Shanghai

We set sail almost immediately after parting with Liang. It's never smart to leave in the night, but we couldn't risk Zhang Tao catching us. A full moon brings us sufficient light, and a strong breeze has allowed us some speed.

Like Liang said, we've headed south. I consulted the maps, and we're on the East Sea going toward Zheijiang. I've forgotten a lot of the Chinese mythology that Mai used to tell me, but there's something I can't help but remember now. Donghai Longwag, the "Dragon King of the Eastern Sea," controls the storms and tides here. His dragon palace is located somewhere at the bottom of the ocean, though I think I have narrowly escaped from it, and it's actually in the middle of Shanghai.

At night, it's easy to convince myself this is all just a bad dream. I only fear that as the darkness soon gives way to the harsh morning light, I won't be able to handle what I've done.

All we can do at this point is run. I only hope the real Dragon King, Zhang Tao, does not catch us. Or else it means the end. Not just for me, but for all of us.

L

Raquel snuck onto the main deck. Her body was exhausted. But as it was most nights, her mind was wide awake. Usually, she'd have to tiptoe as quietly as possible so as not to wake up Liu. Tonight, however, Liu wasn't in her hammock either.

The full moon illuminated the entire deck, making it easy to see her daggers as she lined them up, from smallest to largest, just like her panchi instructors, Akule and Hakan, had taught her.

All the Storm kids started panchi training by the age of ten, but learning how to fight bored Raquel to tears. She preferred painting pictures or playing the guitar.

So Raquel spent her panchi lessons pretending to listen while daydreaming about all sorts of other things (a habit she'd perfected now that she was already fifteen). Despite her teachers' constant threats of kicking her out of class, and Liu's prodding, Raquel went on ignoring her panchi for nearly a year. All the other kids, even Sadie, were surpassing Raquel, but she didn't care.

Then one day, Raquel's mother stepped in. Even to this day, Raquel couldn't decide if Rafaella had done this out of a mother's genuine concern, or because she was so competitive that she couldn't stand to see her family lose at anything.

Rafaella had grown up in a family of theater actors who traveled throughout her native Spain, Portugal, and Italy all year long. Until marrying Raquel's father, Hugo, she'd never spent more than a few hours on the water, and that was mostly in gondolas where potential suitors could admire her beauty. Rafaella had never learned the art of panchi.

Raquel stopped sharpening the dagger's blade against the gritty waterstone. It had been years since she'd seen her mother, but Rafaella's fiery eyes, long, unruly dark tresses, and small, stubborn mouth still stood out in her mind. Perhaps through time, she'd even made her mother more stunning, though she doubted that was possible. As a child, Raquel had been proud of her mother's beauty, as though somehow it belonged to her.

Raquel picked up another dagger. Back then, she jumped at any attention her mother gave her. Rafaella often suffered from "dark" periods where she spent days in bed, refusing to speak to either her daughter or her husband. So although Raquel would have preferred singing with her mother, or more accurately, listening to her mother sing, since Rafaella had spent most of her life playing lead in her family's stage productions, she happily took the opportunity to hang with her mom and learn panchi.

Panchi was an ancient martial art developed by the Storm hundreds of years ago. It involved a highly acrobatic style of fighting that combined high kicks, throwdowns, and take-downs along with intricate knife skills. The first year was spent learning each complex leg variation before the knives were introduced to worthy students in the second year. Though panchi could be deadly and was meant to protect the Storm, rhythm was at the heart of the fighting method. Perhaps this is what made Rafaella take to it.

She was a marvelous actress and musician, but at danc-ing, no one could compare to her. Except maybe Hugo. That's why, though many saw how unfit they were as a couple, most suspected that it was being opposites that had attracted them to each other in the first place. After all, many a sin can be hidden on the dance floor.

Like Hugo and Rafaella had done so many years ago, mother and daughter also connected through dance. Of course, Rafaella had taught Raquel—who moved with her own grace—many of the popular Latin dances of their day. But as Rafaella broke down panchi into choreographed movements and rhythms, this was the first time that Raquel could *share* something with her mother instead of just ad-miring her from afar, as she'd always done before.

Those two months when they "danced" panchi were among the happiest of Raquel's life. Her mother didn't suffer a single dark day. Instead, there was a lightness as Raffaella danced alongside her daughter, a happiness that had never appeared before.

Whether it was an audience of one or one thousand, Rafaella needed a stage. So it was little shock to Raquel or most of *Storm One* when Rafaella walked out a few months later to rejoin her family's troupe, which was headed for a grand show in Seville. But just because Raquel had a hunch it was coming didn't mean it hurt any less when her mother left her. Rafaella's abandonment wounded Raquel deeper than any dagger could. A week after Rafaella fled, Akule and Hakan had allowed their most improved student, Raquel, to add knives to her panchi fighting.

Rafaella's betrayal had shattered Hugo, who, despite having the gift of "reading" people, hadn't seen all the signs that the rest of them had. In his final moments four months later, Raquel was sure it was Rafaella who still haunted his thoughts.

Raquel stood up. There was a hefty wind, which allowed the junk to move rather swiftly through the small waves. Her bare feet gripped to the deck for better balance. Then she imagined the music playing. Tonight, it was the simple beauty of the melancholy Spanish guitar. She took out the dagger tucked next to her thigh. Its deep, serrated edges made it a favorite to lead with. *One*, *two*, *three*, she counted off. *Drop. Spin. Kick.* Just like her mother had taught her.

But she didn't dance for her mother. For the past eleven months, every dance was for Papa. She imagined the faceless soldier standing in front of her now. He'd been her only dance partner since the day Papa was murdered. *Drop. Spin. Kick.* And one more move her mother had failed to stick around long enough to learn. *Stab. Stab. Stab.* Over and over, Raquel plunged her dagger into the imaginary soldier's heart.

***

Charlie dunked her hard sea biscuit into the stale "coffee."

It wasn't actually coffee, since only the rich could afford the real stuff. However, Sadie had taken it upon herself to make her own version of coffee by doctoring up some strong black tea with a bunch of herbs to mimic coffee's caffeine jolt. The concoction tasted like sludgy water, but Charlie needed as much caffeine as she could get this morning. She surveyed the other four girls. Judging by the dark circles under their eyes, they probably also needed a caffeine pick-me-up.

She let out a long sigh. It had been a hard night. She'd spent most of it at the helm, trying to get the junk to move as fast as possible. The winds were helping, and luckily, the waters were gentle last night. They'd managed to make good progress in the last twelve hours. If all went well, they'd be in Zheijiang, the next major port after Shanghai, by early evening.

Charlie squinted against the bright light of the mid-morning sun. She put her mug down on the deck floor. They had a proper dining room on the junk where they ate their dinners, but if the weather allowed, breakfast and lunch were eaten out on deck, in the sun and looking out over the sea. It was the perfect way to start your day. If, Charlie thought as she tried to swallow the dry biscuit, you didn't have a massive hangover.

Given her pop's strict rules on *Storm One*, Charlie hadn't had too many occasions to sample spirits. Still, this wasn't the kind of hangover one gets from a night of ale and whiskey, which she understood could be quite terrible. The kind that she and probably the other girls were suffering from was a mental hangover, which was just as painful as the drinking kind, but much harder to get rid of.

Yesterday, with the mob chasing them, Zhang Tao's awful ultimatum to Liu, hateful Liang, and even the creepy "eye" from the letter, it made perfect sense to sail away from Shanghai as fast as they could. But now, in the plain light of day, it was all really sinking in. *They'd stolen a ship.* And not just any ship. Sadistic, revenge-seeking Zhang Tao's ship, a man who beat little boys with canes and forced his daughter into marriage! God, or whoever was in charge up there, had thrown them a major save when they managed to stay alive through the Day of Destruction. She just wasn't sure how many more saves were left. Charlie took another sip of her coffee. They had to come up with a plan.

"This is all I could rustle up from the galley," Sadie said as she set four shriveled pieces of salted pork down in the middle of their circle. "We gotta get more supplies in Zheijiang, 'cuz we're pretty much cleaned out." She took out a small pocketknife to cut the meat. "There's not enough pieces for each of us, so two of us need to share one."

Charlie waved the plate away. "You guys go ahead. I'm not hungry."

Ingela swiped the largest piece and popped the entire thing in her mouth. Then after a few seconds, she realized she couldn't possibly chew it all in one bite, so she spit out half into her hand. Then she began to eat that part. Charlie shook her head. She was no Miss Manners herself, but Ingela acted like she'd been raised by wolves. A quick flash of Knut, Ingela's warrior father, and Axel, Ingela's rebel brother, popped into Charlie's mind. Well actually, you *could* say she'd been raised by a people wilder than wolves—Vikings. Charlie let out another long sigh. It was time to get to business. She toyed with the pearl hanging from her necklace. "Listen, we gotta have a meeting." Everyone turned to look at her. "It's time to come up with a new plan."

Sadie crossed her arms. "I didn't even know we had an old plan."

Charlie grimaced. For the past eleven months, Sadie's favorite pastime was playing a game called "Undermining Charlie's Authority." Luckily, she was yet to win. "Funny, but if you were really that clueless, then let me review. Our old plan was to survive, sail, and figure out who was behind the Day of Destruction."

A spray of saltwater splashed them. The water felt good on Charlie's face. Maybe the salt would even help mask the taste of the bitter coffee.

"Not exactly the most comprehensive plan, wouldn't you say?"

Charlie stopped herself from throwing one of the sea biscuits, which were denser than rock, at Sadie. "You can save your big, fancy words for your super-boring diary, Sadie. And yes, even though you think it's secret, we all know you keep a notebook filled with all your dull thoughts.

But we need real answers now."

Ingela's face turned sour. "Yeah, I stole your diary from your hiding place inside the big science book and tried to read it, but I just ended up going to sleep." She shook her head. "You're a bird turd, Sadie."

Sadie rolled her eyes. "Thanks for the critiques, girls." She was about to explain to the two nitwits that her diary wasn't for secrets, but for her philosophical musings, which she was happy to share with them anytime. However, she realized that this would most likely fly over their heads anyway. Instead, she turned toward Charlie. "Since you need 'real' answers, then I guess we can make our new plan something like: survive, sail, figure out who was behind DD, figure out who sent us that letter and what the 'eye' is all about, and make sure Zhang Tao doesn't catch us."

"Duh!" Charlie shouted. "But how do we do that exactly, Miss Smarty Pants?"

"Guys! Cool it!" Liu yelled, unfolding a map. Actually, it was more like pieces of three different maps held together with fish glue. Maps were expensive, so, as with Sadie's books, they usually resorted to trash heaps to find them. Or they turned a blind eye when Ingela brought home a suspiciously intact one.

"I think we should head this way." She ran her finger down a curvy path that covered Macau, Vietnam, Cambodia, and the Maldives. "It means narrower pathways. Especially here around the Andaman Sea and Malacca." She traced over a tiny strip of land and water. "But that's what the junk specializes in. If Liang was telling the truth, then Zhang Tao's junk ships are headed for Europe, which means they are too far away to turn around and come after us. So he'll have to send his brigantines. Brigs aren't as good in narrow spots as junks." Charlie nodded. Liu had a point; brigs wouldn't be as mobile as the junk, which was both fast and furious when it came to tight spots.

"The Maldives is where we should stop—for a while, at least. That's if Zhang Tao hasn't caught us by then." Liu's face clouded over. It would be something much worse than the snakeskin cane for them if he did.

 Charlie glanced at Liu's sallow face and sunken eyes. By the looks of it, her hangover was the worst of all.

"Hey, you gotta find a way to get straight with this, Liu." Charlie tried to softly pat her on the back, but it ended up being a wallop. Liu coughed. Thankfully, Sadie took over the affectionate part and began stroking Liu's hair. "You made the decision to run because it was the best for you. But we agreed to steal the ship because it was the best decision—really the only decision—for all of us. And at least for now, it seems like Liang kept his word and didn't go running back to Zhang Tao, or else surely there'd be a ship on our tail by now. Liang might have been telling the truth about your father's entire fleet being up north right at this moment." Charlie pointed to the spot near Japan where Zhang Tao was supposedly heading. "A week head's start is a major help." Sadie reiterated the happy thought by giving Liu a tight squeeze.

Sometimes the combined parenting duo of Charlie and Sadie reminded Liu of her parents, constantly bickering and fighting over control. But more often than not, they actually made a pretty good team, with Charlie taking on the role of protective father and Sadie being the nurturing mom.

"Okay, I can see how this could work," Charlie said. "Monsoon winds should begin anytime now, which means we might get some help moving southward. We've got a month and a half of sailing to make it here." She put her finger on the Maldives. "But I'm curious—why'd you choose this spot to end up?" On *Storm One*, they'd sailed to so many regions of the world, but never to the Maldives.

Sadie looked directly at Charlie. "I chose the Maldives. If you ever read one of my 'boring' books, you'd know that the Indian Ocean is very warm there."

Charlie gave Sadie a blank stare. She was always speaking in riddles. "So? Did you want to take some long swims and work on your tan?" Charlie chuckled. Everywhere they went, it seemed that fair skin was the standard for feminine beauty. However, all the girls reveled in their outdoor life and the healthy glow that came with it.

A flock of seagulls overhead swooped down low. The girls instinctively placed their hands over their biscuits. Growing up on the sea, you learned how to protect your food from scavenging gulls. Though, since the birds seemed to have a higher culinary standard than most sailors, they would probably find the sea biscuits inedible.

Once the menacing seagulls had moved on, Sadie spoke. "No, we should go to the Maldives because lirium thrives in warmer waters. It will be easier for us to find it there."

Charlie's jaw tensed. They'd been over this a dozen times, yet Sadie still refused to listen. One of the Storm's jobs was to harvest lirium so they could process it to provide clean water to communities. But actually finding lirium required an extremely difficult and dangerous method called gilling.

Gilling meant diving down into the depths of the ocean, all the way down to the dark ocean floor and staying there through the use of controlled breath. It took years to perfect. Storm members began their gilling training at age sixteen and completed it at age eighteen. Which meant that out of all the girls, only Charlie had begun to gill, and that was only for a few months before the DD.

"There's not a 'we.' It's just a 'me.' Like I've said a hundred times before, it's too dangerous for you guys to gill!" Charlie herself had never gilled alone. Lirium was harvested from October to January, so gilling season was a mere three months long. This time last year, they didn't even have a ship, and having just lost their parents, they were not in a mind to gill.

"You're such a butt belly!" Ingela stomped her foot. "Liu's a better swimmer than you, and I'm pretty much as good as you in everything. Or at least, I will be by the time I'm your age. So we should gill with you."

They all looked at Ingela. Her confidence was admirable but her logic made no sense.

"Charlie, we could all start gilling even before the Maldives. Even as early as Malacca. The more the better." Liu looked down. It was so difficult to bring it up but someone had to say it. "We need the money."

The weight of that last sentence was like an anchor chaining them to the bottom of the sea. It was definitely the reason for the dark circles under Charlie's eyes. They *did* need money. Not just as in enough coins to get them some food and supplies for the week. They needed serious, cold, hard cash. They were on borrowed—or more accurately stolen—time with this junk ship. It wasn't a matter of *if* Zhang Tao caught them, but *when*. If they were smart, they might be able to elude him for some months, maybe even a year. But the faster they could ditch the junk and get their own ship, the better their chances of survival (or at least escaping whatever horrible fate Zhang Tao had waiting for them).

But gilling wasn't going to be the fix. "Even if we picked up loads of lirium every day of the entire gilling season, we still wouldn't make enough moolah to buy a ship." Storm traded lirium for supplies or sold it for pennies so that everyone could have clean water.

Raquel, who'd slept less than all of them, had been wavering between consciousness and sleep during most of the discussion. But she decided it was time to say something now. "Well, maybe it's worth more. Mr. Chang *did* call it a business."

Sadie furrowed her brow. "I've been thinking about that a lot, and I still don't know what he means. As Storm, it wouldn't be right to sell lirium for profit."

"Storm?" Liu looked around her. "There *are* no Storm left! We tried to find survivors, but there were none. We are alone in all of this! Which means we're on our own when Zhang Tao finds us. Do you understand that I will be lucky if all he does is force me into marrying someone at this point? He broke Liang's arm for stealing a piece of chicken. A piece of chicken. Imagine what he'll do to the five of us for stealing an entire ship. Not to mention shaming him in front of all of Shanghai's high society!"

Charlie was going to say something, but decided against it. The usually level-headed Liu clearly needed to have this freak-out moment. She was usually so cool and calm. They'd never seen her express so much in one sitting. Except maybe Raquel, since the "twins" shared everything.

While Raquel hugged Liu, Charlie eyed Ingela, who looked like she would be the next one to erupt. Though she'd been Storm for the least amount of time, the little one held fast to their Storm roots. She didn't question being Storm at all, and got pretty huffy when any of them did. "We're Storm. We'll have to decide what that means ourselves," Charlie said, raising an eyebrow at Ingela, "another time." To her surprise, this satisfied Ingela, who remained quiet.

Charlie continued. "The fact is, the sooner we find a new ship—one that's legitimately ours—the sooner we can give this one back to Zhang Tao. But in the meantime, we still need to survive, and thanks to our predicament, lie low while doing it. Harvesting lirium lets us do that. It's not the golden ticket, but it's all we have for now."

Raquel tapped her nails against her cold tea mug. "And lirium is the only link we have to the DD." She'd replayed that conversation with Mr. Chang a hundred times, and it still didn't make any sense. But she had a growing suspicion that her father's murder was connected to lirium.

Charlie gave Raquel a quizzical look, expecting her to elaborate on her statement. Raquel just smiled back. Charlie made a mental note to pick that one up later with Raquel. Right now, there were more pressing issues.

Puffy white clouds dotted the baby blue sky. A steady breeze kept the junk moving rapidly and cooled them off in the growing heat. It was shaping up to be a beautiful day so far. Who knew if it would end with them under siege by Zhang Tao's fleet, or continuing to sail southward?

Charlie took a deep breath, letting the salty air fill her lungs. It wasn't the best plan by far, but they really didn't have a lot of choices. She fingered the pearl on her necklace. Pop. What would Pop do right now? Charlie came to a decision.

"To the Maldives we go!" she exclaimed, mustering all the enthusiasm she could.

***

"Hey, I know! Say that I bit the little baby. That'll scare ,em!" Ingela exclaimed.

"Oh, yeah! We haven't had a biter before." Sadie scribbled ferociously on a sheet of paper. "That's a good one!"

As far as Sadie was concerned, she was the editor-in-chief of the Pirette Chronicles. This wasn't an actual newspaper, but what they'd jokingly come to call the set of Pirette stories that Sadie had put together.

Ingela, who was a pretty big fibber in her daily life, was unsurprisingly imaginative when it came to making up Pirette stories, especially the parts where violence was necessary. So she and Sadie had collaborated on dozens of stories in the seven months that the Pirettes had existed.

All five girls got into the fun of making up the stories, but in actuality, the Pirettes were serious business. After Zhang Tao had allowed them to borrow his ship seven months ago, they'd found themselves faced with the reality of being a group of girls all alone on the sea. This made them targets both on land and in the ocean. In most of the world, girls weren't even allowed to leave the house without a chaperone. Here they were, five teenage girls living by themselves! So, in order not to be messed with, they made up the Pirettes.

"And you're sure there are no screw-ups this time?" Charlie twirled her pen around. She preferred making up the stories and then letting Sadie do the actual writing. "We can't afford another Shanghai market scene."

Sadie flipped around so fast that she nearly knocked over a candle. After dinner, they'd decided to spend the rest of the evening on Pirettes stories. Now their dining table looked like a massive study, with papers and quill pens spread all around. Throw a poetry reading session in and this would be Sadie's dream night. However, at this very moment, Charlie's micromanaging was about to make her lose it.

"I've been over this a dozen times with you! Yesterday, after we picked up supplies in Zheijiang, I dropped off two anonymous letters to the local newspaper, and one letter to the local police about the Pirettes going head-to-head with a band of pirates, robbing a bunch of taverns for both ale and money, and inciting an angry mob in Shanghai. Obviously the last one wasn't fiction." They were still working out their system, but basically all the girls updated the Pirettes' status with letters to local newspapers and lawmen. Each of the girls (except Charlie) knew at least another language, so collectively they wrote in English, Spanish, Chinese, Norwegian, Italian, Portuguese, and French. In the letters, they'd pretend to be concerned citizens reporting some criminal act they'd witnessed the Pirettes commit. Then, just before they left any locale, Sadie was in charge of making sure the letters got to the right places. If everything went as planned, the letters would be turned into newspaper articles, or otherwise find their way to the public, which helped grow the Pirettes myth.

The girls also wrote letters making up Pirette sightings in different parts of the world. Sadie had collected the mastheads of many newspapers, which she used to get the addresses for the editors whom she mailed the letters to. That way, there would sometimes be stories about the Pirettes before they'd even reached a port.

"You promised, no more sketches," Charlie said to Sadie. For the most part, she saw the upside in doing all this Pirettes stuff. Plus, Sadie was doing a great job of keeping it all running. But it was still a delicate balance between laying low versus protection.

Sadie shook her head adamantly, slapping her spongy locks against Ingela and Liu, who were on the other side of her. "No, I didn't. The sketches are staying." She shrugged her shoulders. "But we'll make sure they aren't so real."

Raquel stopped drawing and looked up. "I just spent the last two hours drawing this. And believe me, it's not easy capturing your weird-shaped eyebrows or Ingela's snaggletooth, so we'd better use it!"

Liu leaned in closer to get a better look at Raquel's work. She lifted the candelabra to get better light. "Hold up, Raquel! Ingela's fangs aren't that big! She looks like a vampire," Liu giggled.

"Well, we all know little diablo is a bloodsucker!" Raquel snorted.

Ingela hurled her body across the table to inspect the drawing. Clearly approving of the vicious appearance that Raquel had given her, Ingela flashed her crooked smile proudly.

Sadie turned toward Charlie. "The sketches are useful. Newspapers like having a drawing—we get closer to the top of the newssheet when we include a sketch. Which means more people read about the Pirettes. The sketches won't hurt us as long as I make sure they go to papers on the other side of the world."

"I guess you know best." Charlie put her pen down. "Sadie, I'll tell you stuff and you write it down. My hand is starting to cramp," Charlie complained, though she hadn't written more than four lines. She let out a massive yawn.

"Pew! Maybe cover your mouth before you do that!" Raquel hollered, trying to clear the air with her hand.

"Or brush your teeth once in a while," Sadie scoffed.

They all began to laugh, especially Charlie. Neither Zhang Tao nor the Day of Destruction existed in the world of the Pirettes. In that world, nothing harmed them, and they were free to do whatever they pleased. Maybe it was all made up, but after the drama of the last few days, the girls desperately needed the escape to "Pirettes Land," even if it was just for a few hours. Charlie recognized this. She handed her pen to Sadie. "Write or I'll breathe on you some more!"

***

Sadie walked up to the helm of the junk ship carefully, steadying the tea mug in her hand. The waters were smooth, but Charlie was sailing over them so fast that it made balancing difficult. Sadie squinted from the late morning sun, which was shining brightly down on them. Slowly, she handed the tea to Charlie. "Hey, you look like you're dragging this morning. I thought maybe you could use this."

"Did you make it?"

Sadie smirked. "No. Raquel did."

"Okay, then I'll have it," Charlie replied as she took one hand off the steering wheel.

"You know, I'd rather just pour this on you!"

"Just hand it over." Charlie grabbed the cup and set it down next to her. "You're right, I'm definitely dragging. Ingela and I stayed up most of the night taking turns at the wheel." She took a long sip. "We'll probably have to do it again tonight if we want to get some distance between us and Zhang Tao."

"Well you should at least get a nap in," Sadie admonished. "Liu, Raquel, or I can take over for a bit."

Charlie nodded. "After lunch, maybe. Now tell me what you're really up here for, because I know it's not to bring me tea."

Sadie smiled sheepishly. "You really do look haggard, but you're right. That's not the only reason I'm here. I was thinking …what if we ask my big bro and Ingela's brother to help us?"

Charlie felt the hairs on the back of her neck stand up. "Ask Taye and Axel to help us with what, Sadie?"

Sadie shrugged. "Help us get away from Zhang Tao."

"And how do you propose they do that? I mean, the Castaways aren't magicians that can just make us disappear," Charlie reasoned. Castaways was the nickname they'd come up with for Axel, Taye, and their posse. She tried to make herself sound as calm and reasonable as possible.

"Yeah, you're right. I was just thinking that it would be nice to have some help. But I'd never want Taye to know I'd stolen a ship! He'd worry so much!"

Sadie continued on with this line of thought for a few seconds while Charlie tuned her out. The last thing they needed on top of all this mess was a visit from Taye.

Suddenly Liu came bursting into the helm. She looked bewildered and was mumbling something. "He found us."

"What did you say, Liu? Speak up." Sadie leaned in closer to hear the dazed girl.

"Zhang Tao's men are here," Liu finally spat out. She turned away from the helm and pointed.

"What? Where are they?" Sadie shouted as she took the spyglass from Liu. She gasped. Sure enough, not far on the horizon was a massive brigantine that was quickly making its way toward them. "Are you sure that's them behind us?" Liu, who was now visibly trembling, nodded her head.

"The dragon on the flag. It's his emblem."

"But how did he catch up to us so quickly? We've been making such good distance!" Charlie slammed her hand against the wheel. "That damn Liang must have ratted us out as soon as he left us!"

The junk was sailing so fast that there was a steady breeze cooling the girls from the hot sun. Yet Liu found her hands were clammy, and she was sweating. "Who cares if Liang told? The point is that Zhang Tao's men are here. They've come to get us. Do you know what he's going to do to us?" Images of her father's cold eyes, his slow grin, and the bamboo cane flashed before Liu. She couldn't stop shaking or sweating.

Sadie grabbed Liu by the shoulders and spoke calmly. "Liu, where are Ingela and Raquel?"

Liu tried to concentrate on what Sadie was saying. "The weapons room."

Calling it a "room" was a bit of an exaggeration, since most of their weapons fit on one expansive wall below deck. Like everything else on the ship, the weapons were second-hand and often patched together with odds and ends, but the girls had managed to stock a decent arsenal that held a bow and arrow, a few different cutlasses, daggers, dirks, and a couple of flintlock pistols.

"Okay, Liu. I gotta help Charlie steer. You stay up here and tell us everything you see with the spyglass," Sadie commanded in a reassuring voice.

Liu nodded. Sadie turned back to Charlie and grabbed the helm. It only made sense that Liu was more terrified than all of them, given what the consequences would be for her with Zhang Tao. Still, it was rare to see Liu so shaken.

The junk continued to skip through the waves at breathtaking speed, but Zhang Tao's ship was getting closer.

"They're catching up!" Liu shouted. The ship was close enough now that Liu didn't need the spyglass to make out Zhang Tao's dragon emblem on its flag. There was no doubt now that this was her father's ship. He'd found them. The thought of what would happen once he caught them made her knees weak. Liu steadied herself against the railing.

"We're in open water. There's nowhere to hide. We gotta try to outrun them!" Charlie responded, wondering just how they were going to do that. If there were some coves or inlets, they might have been able to maneuver into the shallow water safely and get away from Zhang Tao's brigantine. She gripped the steering wheel tighter. According to her and Liu's calculations, it would have only been one day more of constant sailing until they would have reached those shallow waters. But here in the middle of the open sea, they were essentially sitting targets.

"They're pointing their cannons!" Liu shrieked.

"What?" Sadie screamed back. "Your father gave his men orders to shoot us?"

Liu nodded silently. Of course, Zhang Tao wasn't on the ship that was chasing them. He was tucked away safely in his home planning whatever torture he had in store for them. Liu knew he'd want revenge, but she'd never imagined that he'd send a ship after them with orders to shoot. Her father really didn't care if she died.

"We have to abort!" Charlie shouted. There were no swivel guns or cannons on the junk ship, so there was no hope for retaliation or defense. The only thing they could do was hide. "We need to take cover below deck!" Charlie took the spyglass from Liu. She wasn't a guns expert, but it looked like Zhang Tao's men were getting ready to shoot a carronade. The carronade was less powerful then a long gun cannon, but as it only weighed one ton, it was much shorter and faster to load. "We don't have long before those guys are ready to lock and load, so it's time to get out of here! NOW!"

Charlie and Sadie began running down the bow, half-dragging and half-carrying Liu with them. Liu heard the loud roar of the explosion before she saw the cannon fire and closed her eyes. When she opened them a second later, all she saw was the ship ablaze in flames. But to her astonishment, it wasn't *their* ship. It was Zhang Tao's ship!

From out of nowhere a third ship had appeared. Was it a pirate ship? Liu lifted her spyglass, but it was impossible to see anything through the smoke. Liu wasn't even sure if what she'd seen was real. Had a third ship come racing from behind and blasted Zhang Tao's ship out of the water? Was that possible? Where had the third ship come from? And why? "Wh-what just happened?" Liu asked, feeling her knees go weak again.

"I don't know, Liu!" Charlie called out as she climbed back up to the helm. "But we need to thank our lucky stars and get out of here! FAST!"

Chapter
SIX

SLOG
Date: October 14th (43 days at sea)
Position: The Maldives
3.2000° N, 73.2200° E (Unlike the others, I actually consulted the almanac, so I know this is correct.)

After hightailing it out of Shanghai with our lives (barely) intact, then (barely) escaping from cannon fire, we've been lost at sea for the last 43 days or so. Well, maybe lost at sea is a bit of an exaggeration (for now), since Charlie claims we're following her plan.

#1. The plan wasn't that good to begin with. It was something like: survive, sail, figure out who was behind DD, make sense of Mr. Chang's info and make sure Zhang Tao doesn't catch us. And there was something about gilling in there, too. Little vague, don't you think?

#2. Who made her captain all of a sudden? Just because Charlie's the oldest at 17, doesn't mean she's the automatic leader. I'm only five months younger than her.

#3. Maybe we should evaluate Captain Charlie's progress so far to see just how well she's doing.

Let's start with a brief recap. We know it was Zhang Tao's ship that almost got us, but we don't know who fired at it. We don't know if Zhang Tao sent more ships after us. We don't know why the mystery ship that shot down Zhang Tao's ship turned around and headed off in the opposite direction! It was hard to tell through all the smoke and flames, but we could have sworn we saw what looked like a band of pirates on its deck. So why didn't they ransack Zhang Tao's ship, or take his men as prisoners? Why did they save us and then leave?

We've been following Charlie's plan all the way down from Shanghai through the Bay of Bengal to the Maldives, an archipelago in the Indian Ocean (I've included a map I found in Singapura highlighting our route). The monsoon winds began a couple of weeks back, giving us a steady breeze as we head south. We got out of Shanghai so fast that we didn't get to buy our supplies. (Really, we had no choice as there was an angry mob chasing us!) Luckily we were able to stock up at the next port, Zheijiang. Not as much as we'd liked, though, since Shanghai money is worthless in Zheijiang, with the two cities being rivals. So we couldn't buy as much as we needed. This would have been okay if the fishing had been good, but it wasn't.

In fact, our Shanghai money turned out to be completely worthless outside of China, and things started looking a bit bleak. Supplies got dangerously low, and it could have been a disaster, except that we sailed into Sumatra two weeks after we left Zheijiang. The locals there were so generous! They gave us fruits, fish, and even jars of salted meat.

But that was already a couple of weeks ago, and our pantry is almost bare again. The Indian Ocean seems to be fishless! We just reached the Maldives and are hoping for better luck here now.

Charlie's grade for surviving: B-

We've almost run out of supplies twice. If not for the good people of Sumatra, we'd be eating each other right now. On the other hand, we haven't run into any of Zhang Tao's men again. Yet. Charlie has expertly maneuvered the junk through some pretty shallow waters, maintained a fast pace, and kept us out of trouble.

Charlie's grade for sailing: A

Like I wrote above, thanks to Charlie, we're still out here sailing. There's been no sighting of Zhang Tao in almost 40 days. But we're still far from safe.

Charlie's grade for gilling: D-

As Liu suggested, we've stopped along the way to gill. Or to be more specific, we've stopped along the way so Charlie can gill, since she refuses to let anyone else try because it's too dangerous. I personally am relieved not to be gilling, because the whole thing seems pretty scary to me. But Charlie's insistence that no one else can try, despite the fact that she hasn't found anything yet, is starting to anger the others. To be fair, as of this writing, Charlie has only been gilling for 30 days. She's been a trooper and began gilling even before we got to Malaysia, just to get the practice. Maybe I shouldn't grade her so harshly, but she still hasn't found anything, which means we have no lirium to trade. Which means we're no closer to saving enough cash to buy a ship (if that's even possible) than we were 43 days ago.

Charlie's grade for finding clues to the DD: F

We haven't discovered anything new since Shanghai. Granted, we couldn't exactly stay there longer, but maybe if we'd been able to figure out who or what the "eye" in the letter was, we'd have gotten some real answers, rather than just the nonsense Mr. Chang fed Charlie & Raquel.

So Charlie's got a Caverage, which means she's seriously underperforming. I know I'm being mean here, but I'm frustrated with her! I can see the worry on Charlie's face, but honestly, she needs to stop acting like our captain and realize we're all here to shoulder the burden together.

Something's been bothering Raquel and Liu, too, but I don't think it's about our supplies. They've been in their own heads for a while now. To be honest, the fact that we actually stole a ship is always on the back of my mind, so I can just imagine how it weighs on Liu. But I'm not sure what's going on with Raquel, exactly. Just that the bags under her eyes grow every day. Think I'll do some investigating (for medical purposes, not gossip).

Better go now—the other girls always complain I use too much space (Maybe that's because I'm the only one with anything useful to say).

Signing off for now (SOFN),

Dr. Sadie de Wit - Wayo

(If Charlie can appoint herself captain,
then I'll be the ship's doctor!)

Rogers Barrish waited a full minute on the other side of the door. He had all the time in the world and liked to keep her waiting. When he finally decided to enter the dark room, she was standing in her usual spot, deep in the shadows, her body partially turned away from him. Though he preferred to think of their roles as a strategic partnership, they'd essentially been working together for nearly four years, and he had yet to see her face. In his dreams, where he was choking her to death with a heavy looped chain, he imagined that when he ripped her hooded cloak off, she'd be horribly disfigured. But he guessed her need to enshroud herself had to do with something other than a gross deformity.

He didn't know how she'd found the rickety old house on the cliffs that was their meeting spot. It was more like a cave thanks to its dank stench and hollowed rooms. Even the view from the window she always stood at was mundane. Seashore, waves, and birds—made for the kind of stuffy old landscape painting that hung in bleak old castles.

Barrish preferred the view from his fourth-floor residence in the center of London. From there he could admire all the fashionable ladies preening and sashaying up and down the busy streets while he simply sat back and stalked his next prey. Perhaps after this dreary meeting, he'd treat himself to some hunting.

"Do we have a problem?" she asked.

Barrish felt a shiver running down his back. She never yelled, but her hushed tone belied a chilling rage that was far more intimidating. He suspected that, given another set of circumstances, they could have had quite a bit of fun together. If she didn't mind being dominated, that is. He studied her rigid posture from afar. A tiny smirk crossed his face. She'd probably like it.

"*Again?*" She held up a newssheet.

He stifled a sigh. Like all women, she spoke in riddles. He had no way of knowing what she was talking about without getting closer to her. When he'd tried to approach her in the past, she'd reacted ferociously and with the reflexes of a cat. He now knew to remain standing where he was. "Pardon me, Countess?"

She flung the paper in his direction. It landed next to his feet. He refused to bend down and retrieve it. It seemed like she was in one of her moods today.

"They already outfoxed you once, Governor Barrish."

Barrish snarled. He was a decorated navy war hero who'd led the command to kill dozens, both friend and foe. Now he was a highly respected governor and the head of the most prestigious company in the world, Sapphire East Trading. No one who was still living dared speak to him in that tone. But he especially would not tolerate it from a member of the weaker sex.

Women were decoration. Pretty dolls one displayed and played with on occasion. When they spoke, which he preferred them to do as little as possible, they said silly things and weren't so fun anymore.

That's certainly how he saw this mere housewife standing before him, who'd been lucky enough, or had the physical assets, to marry a count. Or at least, that's how he assumed she'd managed to get her title. Though again, it was hard to tell what was happening under that thick cloak. She'd had the greater fortune of becoming a widow and inheriting all of her husband's riches, which, in Barrish's eyes, had made her far too powerful for any bitch to be.

The only reason Barrish indulged her was that in the last four years, she'd managed to make him heaps of money. Otherwise, she'd certainly be chained in his chamber with the rest of them.

"*Who* outfoxed me once, Countess?" "Those scavengers. The pirates."

He tried to recall the last time he'd been outfoxed by a group of pirates. Usually it was the other way around. But if she wanted to continue to speak in riddles, it was no problem for Barrish. He was in no hurry.

"Could you be more specific?" he asked in a deliberately calm voice. Though she was much too cool to be riled, he did notice the slightest nervous twitch. She rubbed the pearl ring around her wedding finger. Curiously, Barrish had met many nobles in his life, and the women were always laden with jewels. Even an afternoon tea required baubles of some kind. But he'd never seen the Countess adorn herself with anything but this single ring, which appeared to be just a natural pearl set on a simple gold band. It was something a schoolboy would have given a first love. Barrish had never been close enough to her to inspect it further, but he couldn't understand why she wore it.

"The Pirettes, Governor!" She looked out the tiny window in the corner. "Besides reading every city, regional, and community paper that I can get my hands on within a hundred-mile radius, I receive news from all over the world by way of the ships that dock each day at the local ports. Even if the information is months old, I need to know what is going on in as many parts of the world as possible. As I'm sure you do in your position with Sapphire East Trading Company. In the last two weeks alone, I've come across at least five stories about these girl pirates causing all kinds of menace. They even incited a mob in Shanghai! Though I don't know how they managed to be in Peru, Paris, and Shanghai in such a short time." She tapped on the window with her ring finger. The pearl scraped against the glass. "The point is that they are definitely out there. And they can catch you again."

Barrish felt every muscle in his body grow rigid at the mention of those damn Pirettes. The last thing he needed was the Countess meddling in it. They were just a group of girls! He'd already sent a little "explosion" their way, and would handle them further if necessary.

The Pirettes are not a problem," he answered, mustering as much cordiality as he could.

She turned slightly, her face still carefully shielded. Once, he'd caught a glimpse of a tiny wisp of her red hair. He'd always had a thing for gingers. But that wasn't going to save this one.

"I will not tolerate another mistake like what happened with the Americans, Governor Barrish. That ended up costing both of us far too much time and money."

It took every bit of control Barrish had not to rip every red hair from her head. His hand trembled. Who did this *woman* think she was speaking to? When he finally got her down in his chamber, she would be given no mercy.

Since Sapphire East Trading Company insured 95% of the legitimate ships out on the sea, Barrish had access to every ship route, itinerary, and manifesto imaginable. When information about a particularly valuable or reasonably unguarded fleet crossed his desk, Barrish hired a group of pirates to attack the ships, providing them with details to the exact routes the ships would take during their journey. The deal with the pirates was that they could keep half of the plunder and give Barrish the rest. However, since pirates weren't exactly known for their honor, Barrish also contacted the Countess, who would send a ship full of her own private guards to finish off the raid, and, more importantly, steal the entire loot from the pirates and the merchant ship. This ingenious scheme that Barrish had concocted with the Countess not only ensured that he received his fair share of the treasure, it also meant that the whole attack was virtually untraceable back to him.

No one but the Countess knew of Barrish's duplicity until those bothersome twits stumbled upon his scheme. Apparently, the Pirettes were in the middle of mugging a lowly member of the pirate crew that Barrish had hired to ransack the American fleet, when the pirate spilled the beans on the planned attack. Being the standup citizens they were, the children warned the captain of the fleet about the looting, completely foiling Barrish and the Countess's plans for what seemed like an easy capture.

At that time, however, the fools had no idea of Barrish's involvement in the scheme, so when the bighearted American captain brought the Pirettes to Barrish's office as a show of appreciation, Barrish played his role as the kind and dutiful governor, thanking them for being such good citizens and for helping Sapphire East Trading Company do its job of keeping the seas safe. They'd seemed to buy the whole phony act, and everything should have been fine. However, before leaving his office, the conniving thieves had swiped a prized set of maps from his desk. How they'd managed to do this without him noticing was still astonishing. While the maps had their own value, what was especially troublesome was that he'd hidden all his plans for the attack on the American merchant ships in those maps. It was hardly enough evidence to go to the authorities, but it was certainly enough for the Pirettes to discover Barrish's secret.

He admitted that the silly crooks were a minor irritation, though he hardly believed that they'd cross paths again. Actually, Barrish was already making sure they wouldn't, so it was outrageous for the Countess to dare threaten him with the prospect of the Pirettes "striking" again. Sure, she'd been livid that a group of girl pirates had thwarted her plans and cost her a few gold coins, but the bounty from the American merchant fleet wasn't big enough to have her second-guessing his abilities. Barrish was one of the most esteemed men in the world. Neither a group of savage girl pirates nor an aging countess were any type of match for him.

For the time being, he needed to focus on the money the Countess was going to bring in with their next plunder. The sultan's fleet would be their greatest raid yet. Every year, the Sultan of Marrakatra, one of the richest men in the world, took a religious pilgrimage that was so grand it had become famous throughout the globe. His two ships, *Haman* and *Shamana*, made the journey from the port of Marrakatra, filled with the finest jewelry, teas, artwork, ceramics, silks, and spices to sell at the port of Mecca. These goods had much value on the open market. On the return home, both *Haman* and *Shamana* were laden with blocks of gold from the sales of these goods. Despite a few failed attempts, no pirate had successfully captured the sultan's ships, because they were among the most heavily guarded on the seas. Sapphire East Trading Company provided extra security to ensure the safe passage of the sultan's fleet. However, this year the security would be arranged by the Countess and Barrish, who would raid and loot the sultan's fleet, stripping it of all its treasure. They'd spent two years planning every detail of this attack, and finally, they were ready.

The spoils were immense, and the Countess was essential to the raid's success. Though what Barrish should do is slap her across the face for her insolence, there was no point in angering the beast just yet. He'd have his time.

"The situation has been taken care of, Countess." He looked out over the water. Maybe after he was done with her, he'd throw her out into her beloved sea. Then he quickly decided against it—she didn't deserve any leniency.

"I trust then that everything will be fine, Governor Barrish." Trust was such a ludicrous idea to the Countess. The last person she'd trusted was the boy who'd given her the pearl ring on her finger. She wore the ring as a constant reminder never to trust again.

Trust was one of those silly ideas like love and honor that polluted the minds of young girls who dreamed of living in a castle with their darling prince. The Countess had learned early in life that the only way to have your own castle was to get rid of the prince, or in her case, the count. There was no place for love or trust in her fairytales. Not any more. The Countess slid the ring up and down her finger. The raid on the sultan's fleet was far too important to risk any sort of complications. But for now, she would leave the Pirettes to Barrish.

Without any further discussion, she turned around and disappeared down the long, black corridor.

***

Ingela scurried along the ship's deck. Both of her hands, which were surprisingly large for an eleven year old, were gripped around a bamboo fishing rod. Blisters were starting to form on her palms, but she had no time to attend to them and tried to ignore the burn. The first jerk on the end of the line sent her stumbling forward. She caught herself, repositioning her stance so that her legs stood slightly apart. Bright rays of early morning light shone directly into her line of vision. If she could free one of her hands, she could use it to shield her eyes or make obscene gestures at the sun, but instead, she decided to keep both hands around the fishing pole and squint hard.

When she'd won a set of four fishing rods in a card game off the coast of Ceylon, she was sure she'd been conned. In fact, Ingela had conveyed her fury at the perceived deception with a right hook to the losing sailor's chin and was about to land a hard kick to his knee before Charlie yanked her away. Now, as Ingela prepared to catch her seventh fish of the morning—and this one felt like a real whopper judging by the vibration at the end of her line—she hoped she hadn't knocked any of the sailor's teeth out.

Compared to the ash rods she'd used before, the bamboo rod was much stronger and more flexible, allowing her to bring in the bigger, heartier fish by herself, without help from any of the others. This would hopefully go a long way in proving to the girls that she could do more than they ever gave her credit for.

Ingela surveyed the sky. Clear blue without a cloud in sight, which meant she might be able to keep this up the whole day. No seagulls yet, either. But once those pesky birds came flying around, it would be a fight to the death for the fish. Gulls were ruthless with their prey. Good thing for Ingela that the seagulls around the Maldives liked to sleep in. She quickly took one hand off the pole to wipe her brow with the back of her sleeve. The sun was getting hotter by the minute. Tiny beads of sweat lined her forehead. The smell of salt lingered in the air. It was her favorite scent in the entire world.

Ingela kept her arm muscles taut as she continued to grip the fishing pole, but relaxed her shoulders under the cool tickle of the light wind. She smiled to herself. Who knew that fish liked pickles? Liu would probably be miffed that Ingela used her last jar, but she'd hopefully get over it after seeing all the fish it helped catch. On the other hand, Liu refused to eat any kind of animal (she even turned down salmon, which was Ingela's favorite). Ingela, who prided herself on her practicality and her adventurous appetite, thought Liu's "no animal" policy was stupid considering they spent most of their life out at sea. Still, Ingela felt bad about the pickles and decided she'd give Liu an extra helping of rice tonight to make up for it.

Water splashed on the deck as the fish wriggled on the line.

"Whazafuz!" Ingela exclaimed as the fish flashed its sharp-edged fangs. She'd have to look closer, but judging by the small, smooth scales covering its body and its nasty face, this was a barracuda. Not one of the massive barracudas that were as long as humans, but still, even catching a small barracuda all on her own was quite impressive.

Knut would be proud. Her father, whom she'd always called by his first name, descended from the Norwegian Vikings and was a great hunter, fighter, and fisherman. He'd been the best out of all the Storm. Having said that, even he didn't know the pickles trick!

Knut had been the quartermaster on Storm One. Quartermasters maintained order, settled disputes, and doled out punishment on board. They were elected by the crew to serve the crew's interest, and, on some ships, had equal power to the captain. Not on Storm One, though, as it seemed that Captain Andrew Drake was unwilling to share control with anyone. Still, Knut, who'd gained much respect within the Storm for his years of experience, strength of character, and sheer excellence as a soldier, was a formidable opponent to Andrew on many occasions.

Ingela knew this not because Knut had told her. Quite the opposite—her father was never one to boast or spill secrets. Instead, Ingela had come to learn this through her mopping duties. At age eight, when Knut had put a mop in her hand and told her to go clean the ship, she'd obliged, as she usually did with Knut, but she wasn't happy about it. Until she discovered that cleaning gave her the perfect excuse to hide out in all sorts of corners on the ship and eavesdrop.

Like Charlie, Ingela had lived on *Storm One* her whole life, so she didn't have any other ships to compare it to. Still, when she thought of how it sat out on the water against other ships, it truly was a superior vessel. Of course, there'd been many *Storm Ones* through the centuries, but the ship that Andrew and Knut constructed was the vision of two exemplary Storm soldiers.

Ingela didn't tolerate Knut's modesty when it came to the building of *Storm One*, and made him tell her the story of its "birth" so many times she could recite it in her sleep. Given her penchant for sleep-talking (which was strange, since she barely spoke when she was awake), she probably had recited it a few times already.

Storm One was a 200-ton frigate built in England sometime around 1759. Originally named *George I* after the British monarch, the triple-decker vessel was the length of a standard "ship of the line," 52 meters long on the gun deck and square-rigged on all three masts. She was big yet fast, and easy to maneuver, which was probably why she was stolen by the French and modified into a slave ship they renamed *La Nantes*.

When Knut and Andrew were only a few years older than Axel, Ingela's older brother, and Taye, Sadie's older brother, were now, they'd become commanders of their own Storm battalions. Given that Knut was three years senior to Andrew, he should have become battalion commander earlier, but his animosity toward authority (a trait he handed down to his children) was a sore spot with the higher-ups on the Storm Council, and therefore, Knut's promotions were well-deserved but greatly delayed. When the time came to elect the new leader of the Storm, the captain's spot went to his Andrew, who was a natural bureaucrat and politician.

However, when they received the intel on *La Nantes*, both Knut and Andrew were command officers hungry to prove themselves. They led their battalions straight into battle, refusing to surrender as they fought for eight straight days off the coast of Martinique. It was in that battle that Knut almost lost his right knee. The ship's carpenter, who doubled as the ship's doctor, was able to forgo amputation, but Knut would permanently walk with a slight limp from the wound. Andrew sustained a permanent back injury which would continue to flare up from time to time, especially during rainstorms, causing him great pain. Still, despite their wounds, both men and their battalions prevailed, and they captured *La Nantes*. After freeing the slaves and executing its vicious crew, Knut and Andrew soon realized the power and force of the vessel herself. She was big enough to hold an entire Storm crew, yet still fast and agile on the water.

Seeing yet another chance to make their mark on the Storm, the two friends and their battalions got to work modifying the frigate. They disguised her as a merchant ship, but mounted her with forty cannons, turning her into the ultimate warship. On her three vast decks, they built communal living areas, private living quarters, training spaces, meeting spaces, secret chambers, a jail, a library, an infirmary, and even a small general store. There was enough space for children to run freely, and there were hidden corridors and passages for all kinds of covert adult activity. By the time *La Nantes* had been rechristened *Storm One* two years later, Andrew and Knut's vision had been fully realized, in that they'd essentially built a self-contained city on the sea.

Sunday nights at nine o'clock, when the Storm Council had its weekly meeting, was Ingela's favorite time to grab a swab and start mopping. Sure, she was supposed to be in bed by that time, but Knut was never a stickler for that kind of thing, plus he was too busy arguing with Andrew at the meetings to notice that she was still up.

They didn't always argue. In fact, most of the meetings that Ingela eavesdropped on were pretty boring. They'd discuss routine business like maps, missions, and violators. Violators were the people who had broken a Storm rule or were somehow straying out of bounds. As quartermaster, it was Knut's job to see that the punishment was carried out. He was always on the soft side of the law, though, preferring to let these infractions, many of which seemed minor, go without much penalty. Andrew tended to be sterner, believing that even petty violations should be dealt with swiftly and severely so as not to encourage greater "disruptions" in the future. "Disruption" was a word that Andrew liked to throw around a lot, and that ten-year-old Ingela was unfamiliar with, until she'd asked Sadie to tell her what it meant.

At first when she'd started to listen in on conversations, she'd tried to lean her ear against a door. Sometimes she'd use a drinking glass for better hearing. But Ingela quickly found out that this was amateur stuff. The best way to really snoop was through the walls. *Storm One* was built impeccably. However, no matter how outstanding the craftsmanship, most ships had gaps in the paneling. These gaps were ideal for a little ear to listen through. In the case of *Storm One*, Ingela had found a spot in the storage room next door to the Storm Council meeting room, where if she crunched down on her belly, she not only could hear most of what was being said, but also make out faces.

It was during one of these evenings spent on her belly in the cramped, dark, and damp storage room, that Andrew announced the latest and biggest disruption. To this day, Ingela still didn't know what it was, as a sudden draft in the storage room caused a crate to fall over just as Andrew spoke. The noise from the falling crate had startled Ingela so that she'd turned around, missing Andrew's one-word announcement. By the time she returned her attention to her spy mission, Knut had erupted, but over what she wasn't sure. He rambled on for a few minutes until Josephine, Sadie's mother, calmed him. For the rest of the meeting, they spoke in hushed whispers, something they'd never done before. Knut's posture was rigid, as though he were on high alert, while Andrew was slumped over, like he'd already been defeated. Josephine was ashen, and given the red of her cheeks, Mai, Liu's mom, was livid.

The following week, there was no Storm Council meeting, because an army of faceless soldiers managed to compromise their city on the sea and kill Andrew, Knut, and the rest of the Storm Council. Ingela replayed the moment in her mind, sometimes even in her sleep, over and over. What had Andrew said in that last meeting? Was it "hell," "her," or a name? Or had she imagined it all? Ingela shook her head. She would never know.

The smile on Ingela's face faded. It hurt to think about Storm One, especially Knut. It was easier to concentrate on fish, she thought, as she hoisted the barracuda with one final yank of the rod. A wave doused her as the fish flipped and flopped onto the deck.

Ingela licked her salty lips. Tonight, they would have a feast.

***

After spending the last half-hour trying to convince herself she could still sleep, Charlie conceded defeat and opened her eyes. She pulled the thin knit blanket up around her, exposing her feet to the cold draft that went through the sleeping quarters. Finding a blanket long enough to fit her was always such a hassle, she thought, as she tucked her ankles underneath her.

"RRRRggggrrrrrhhhhh!"

Charlie jumped, catching herself before she fell out of her hammock. Even after all these years, Sadie's thunderous snoring could still startle her. When they were little, Charlie had spent many a night wide awake, sure that it wasn't Sadie in the bottom bunk making all that noise, but a loud, vicious creature. She dug into her right ear and pulled out a small, rounded piece of clay. These days, these makeshift "snore busters" that Liu invented helped block out the tiger on the bottom bunk.

"RRRRggggrrrrrhhhhh!"

Charlie chuckled. Sadie usually kept vampire hours, reading by candlelight or mixing up crazy herbal concoctions well into the first light of dawn. By the sound of her snores, she'd probably pulled another late night, and it would be a few hours before she was up and about. One thing Charlie had learned the hard way was that waking Sadie up before she was ready was like swinging a stick at a hornet's nest—you were bound to get attacked.

Usually, Charlie was the first one to rise, but judging by the ruckus up on deck, it seemed the little monster had already awakened. She didn't even want to think about what trouble Ingela could possibly be up to so early in the morning.

The sleeping quarters on the junk were the tightest that Charlie had ever slept in. Built as a classic Chinese junk ship, it was cramped below deck, even for a small crew of five. However, its magnetic compass, stern-mounted rudder, and watertight hull section, features that none of the Western ships had, more than made up for the lack of leg room.

Charlie thought that if you were going to steal a ship, this one was totally worth it.

However, during the very first night on board, Ingela complained that she felt like she was sleeping in a coffin and hitched her hammock up on deck. Besides the worry of strong winds carrying her off, Charlie wished Ingela would sleep down below with them so that they could keep an eye on her.

Granted, she and the girls probably shouldn't let an eleven-year-old gamble, but Charlie had to admit, Ingela really had a knack for cards, dice, and anything that required outwitting people into giving you their most treasured items. And, as Charlie reminded herself while tracing the etching of her prized pocket watch, most of the stuff that Ingela brought home really had helped them out.

Since it seemed that queens in royal Scandinavian courts weren't too keen on keeping in touch with their bastard daughters, none of them had ever met Ingela's mother. But they all carried cherished memories of dear old Knut. He was the feistiest, strongest, bravest man she'd ever known, which was a big admission for Charlie, considering she felt something short of hero worship for her own beloved pop. Though it meant that all kinds of chaos was thrown their way, Charlie was happy to see that Ingela was growing up to be every bit like Knut—and her rebel brother, Axel.

Charlie smiled to herself. Axel was only two years older than her, but it seemed like everyone, even the adults, had looked up to him on *Storm One*. Not just because he was so good at all things Storm, but because he was his own person, no matter what. He didn't give a damn about pleasing anyone. So it wasn't much of a surprise when at age fifteen, he just packed up and left. He had a quick little chat with Knut and Ingela over breakfast, and by lunch he was gone. Four years later he was sailing the seas with his own group of hellions. Though they didn't have an official name, the girls "lovingly" referred to them as the Castaways.

Over the years, the Castaways had had a few incarnations, as different members would turn up then disappear because of jail, hospital stays, or even death. Now they were a solid group of four guys, including Sadie's older brother, Taye. Charlie felt a pit in her stomach. She couldn't think about that now.

What the Castaways were up to was always a mystery. They seemed to have been everywhere, and possessed a worldly confidence that the girls didn't have. the boys reveled in living a completely carefree life where they avoided tying themselves to anything or anyone.

Her brow furrowed. She needed to concentrate on what was important: finding lirium. Charlie had just begun learning how to gill, the Storm's technique of deep diving for lirium, when her father was killed. With only three months of training, she was the most experienced of the girls. Charlie shuddered. She was fearless with her sword, but all alone in the deep, dark depths at the bottom of the sea, she was surrounded by terror. The fear of drowning, suffocating, being eaten by a shark or strangled by an octopus. The horrors were endless.

Her fear prevented her from finding the lirium. Without the lirium, they wouldn't survive. And without them, no one would ever find out what happened to their families.

Charlie wished she could lie in bed forever. But just like she had every morning since the Day of Destruction, she thought of Knut, Sadie's parents, Raquel's father, Liu's mother, and her own pop.

"RRRRggggrrrrrhhhhh!"

Charlie nodded. "You're right Sadie, I gotta get up." Funny how they could agree on things more easily when one of them was practically unconscious.

Charlie took a deep breath and hoisted herself out of the hammock. Captains didn't have the luxury of fear.

***

The rope tied around the rowboat bobbed up and down.

Liu grabbed the long rope line out of the water and started pulling up. In less than ten seconds, Charlie's fiery red head popped to the aquamarine surface. She gasped for air while resting her upper body weight on the buoy, an empty basket floating on top of the water, secured by the rope tied around Charlie's waist.

"Anything?" Liu asked with more optimism than she actually felt.

Charlie didn't even bother to answer, instead concentrating on getting as much oxygen in her lungs as she could. Though it was already October, the water around the Maldives was comfortably warm. She rested her head on the buoy, letting the sun warm the back of her neck.

"Charlie, you've been doing this for almost two hours!" *For over a week here, not to mention thirty days before this*, Liu silently added, but knew better to say out loud. "Why don't you let me try gilling?"

Charlie lifted her head abruptly.

"You know I'm a better swimmer! And a better diver!" Liu argued.

Charlie readjusted the white cloth scarf tying back her long hair into a ponytail. The Japanese believed the color white scared off sharks. She wasn't sure how true that was, but when it came to preventing a shark attack, Charlie was happy for any tips. "These really help!" she exclaimed, retying the knot on the "sea glasses" that Liu had just invented that morning. She'd replaced the bottom of a small, oval basket with glass. Charlie was sure the added advantage of swimming with her eyes open would help her find lirium, but it wasn't turning out that way.

"Charlie, did you hear me? I think you should let me gill. I'm a stronger swimmer and diver." Liu had been too young to learn gilling before the Day of Destruction, but she'd been out with Charlie enough to realize that all the sea glasses in the world weren't helping her.

Small waves swayed the rowboat softly from side to side. This part of the water was so clear that you could see almost ten meters down from the surface. Schools of red, white, yellow, purple, and black fish mixed with pink, green, and orange coral, creating a swoosh of colors below them.

"I think I need a few more stones." Charlie opened the leather pouch tied to her hip. She hadn't weighed it, but she figured it had about ten kilos of weight in it. The heavier the pouch, the faster she could descend.

Liu reached into the sack at her feet and counted out five midsized stones. She dropped them into Charlie's hands. "I know you heard what I said."

Charlie let out a long, deep sigh. Out of all the girls, Liu was the strongest in the water, but she'd never even had one proper lesson! Allowing her to gill would be reckless. "Liu, it's too dangerous."

Without any further discussion, Charlie dove back into the water. With the added stones, she descended so fast she hit the bottom of the sea floor with a crash. There was no warm sun lighting her path anymore. It was just cold and dark here.

She tried to ignore the pressure in her head and the tightness in her lungs. What she hated most was the sense of two big hands choking her neck. The shrill ringing in her ears began. Instinctively, she patted the knife on her right hip. Down here in the dark, where you couldn't even scream, you never knew what hungry predators were lurking around.

She took a few steps toward a big rock. Lirium liked to grow in cool, dark places. Charlie started to bend down, but the tightening feeling in her lungs was getting worse. She couldn't bear it any longer. All she wanted was air. She dumped the stones out of the pouch and hurriedly pulled on the rope.

Liu let out a loud, frustrated sigh. The minute hand on Charlie's pocket watch hadn't even passed the "12" once before the rope bobbed up and down.

Charlie gasped for air as soon as her head popped through the surface.

Liu let her regain her breath and took a deep breath of her own before speaking. "Charlie, don't go back down there."

Charlie was draining the water out of her ears and strained to hear Liu. "What?"

"Don't go back down."

Charlie looked up at the sun. "It's still pretty bright out. I think we can get another hour in, at least."

Liu shook her head. "That's not what I mean. Listen, Charlie, everyone knows you're the bravest girl around." She tried to ignore the wave of panic that was flowing through her. "But this isn't about there not being any lirium. It's about you being too afraid to stay down long enough to actually get it." Liu had been holding on to her sentiments for so long it almost felt good to get them out, but she knew how much they would hurt Charlie's pride.

Liu's words stung Charlie harder than a slap across the cheek. Her neck blazed from the shame. She wanted to slug the girl. But Liu was right. "What else can we do?" Charlie asked, feeling the humiliation of her failure with every word.

"Well, Ingela's got us enough fish to keep us going for a while." She could see Charlie about to protest and held her hand up. "I know that's just for right now. And you're thinking about our future. Believe me, we're all worried about it." They'd managed to outrun (or outsail) Zhang Tao for exactly fifty-two days. That first initial shock when he'd almost caught them had sent Liu reeling. But now, with each day that passed, Liu found herself waking up hopeful. Then, after a day spent gilling with Charlie, she'd go to bed even more defeated. Something had to change, or they would end up in Zhang Tao's hell very soon. They'd risked too much to let that happen. "We need to figure something out. But this just isn't it."

Liu felt the knot tightening in her gut. She looked around her, half expecting to see another one of her father's ships on the horizon. The constant fear that Zhang Tao was finally going to catch them was its own kind of hell as well. Liu didn't have the stamina to be out here a second longer today. She grabbed Charlie by the elbows and hoisted her up.

Charlie gladly fell into the rowboat. She wasn't going to give up on gilling that easily, but for now, she was too exhausted to argue with Liu. And, though she wouldn't admit it out loud, she was relieved to be out of the water.

Chapter
SEVEN

SLOG, clog, bog, fog, dog ... ruff ruff
Date: October 31st
Position: In Hell

Sadie is makig me start all over. Sadie suks.

Date: October 31st
Position: Still in Hell

We r in Maldiv. Hav so much fish that Sadie is getting 2 fat. Been here for 2 weeks and still no lirium. We should all be gilling. If we aren't finding lirium then what's the point of being here. We got no mula and we can't just live off my fish for the rest of our lives. We r Storm. We need to fite! But hey one good thing, Liu's Dad hasn't found us agan.

Sadie's fancee calendr sez it is Octobr 31, so tuday is Day of Dead. Will cover myself in fish gutts n blud n scare Raquel 2nite.

ha ha ha

Ingela

"Full moon!" Sadie exclaimed.

"Yuck!" Raquel shouted, covering her eyes.

"No! A real full moon!" Sadie pointed ahead as the moon peeked through a set of clouds, casting a silvery light on the sea.

Raquel took her hand off her face, happy to admire a full moon that didn't involve Ingela's bare bottom. "*Hermosa luna,*" she muttered, letting the gentle breeze lull her. A full night's slumber wasn't an option since Raquel would inevitably wake up for her nightly "dance" with the faceless soldier, but maybe she could doze for a while.

Waxy and luminous, the moon looked like a giant pearl in the sky, Charlie thought, as she fingered the single pearl hanging from the silver chain around her neck. Pop would have been so ashamed of her. Charlie was so used to being good at things. She'd never failed this badly.

It had been over two weeks and she didn't have a single lirium plant. Their plan was hopelessly failing, and she didn't know what to do. The defeat hung over them almost as heavily as the fear of being caught by Zhang Tao. She'd let them all down so miserably.

"Hey, I made us some tea." Liu walked onto the deck holding a tray with wooden cups. To their happy surprise, the junk rig had come equipped with enough plates, cups, and cutlery to accommodate all five of them. A luxury on land and sea.

"Shhh," Sadie whispered, putting her finger to her lips and then pointing to Raquel, who'd drifted off to sleep. Judging by the dark circles under the girl's eyes, she was in definite need of a serious siesta.

Liu nodded, wishing she could also doze off for a while. But there was just too much to think about. The stolen ship, of course. Escaping Zhang Tao. Leaving her family. But now, it was gilling. Obviously Charlie wasn't going to come out and admit to the girls that she couldn't gill. Probably because she still couldn't face it herself. But it was time for everyone to get real, and it looked like Liu was going to have to do it. She took a deep breath. It was best to start with Sadie, who always had a way of knocking sense into Charlie. "Sadie, Charlie, I think we need to talk about the gilling thing."

Sadie stretched her legs out. "Yeah, this place is no good for lirium, huh? Should we head a little more south?"

Liu focused her eyes on Sadie. "No, I don't think it's about there not being any lirium. It's because Charlie—"

Charlie popped up. "What about me?" She eyed Liu.

Out of nowhere, Ingela dropped down in the middle of their circle from what seemed like the heavens. Though heaven was probably not the place the little hellion came from. Her skin was pallid, and she wore a grim expression.

"Oh, so you've been hiding up on your perch, huh?" Sadie teased, looking up at the main mast.

Ingela ignored her. "They're climbing on board!!! They've got hooks and ropes! I don't know how many!"

Charlie reacted with lightning speed, drawing her cutlass. "Positions!"

In case of a sneak attack, they'd practiced their fight strategy plenty of times, but they'd never actually had to use it up until now. Zhang Tao had found them! This was it. Charlie immediately ran to the far end of the junk, while Ingela and Liu, both holding their cutlasses, ran to the opposite side.

Sadie stood dazed. "We're being attacked! Wake up!" She shouted across to Raquel, though she seemed to be saying it for her own benefit as well.

"Que?" Raquel asked, her hand on her dagger before she opened her eyes. She had more daggers strategically placed on other parts of her body as well. "Sadie, get your bow and arrow!" She tried to keep the panic out of her voice.

"It's-it's d-d-downstairs," Sadie replied sheepishly. She knew she was supposed to have it on her, but she'd never actually thought she'd need it on board. Her whole body began to tremble.

Clearly Sadie wasn't ready for this. "Go downstairs! I'll cover your post!" Raquel began running toward Charlie. "Now, Sadie!" she shouted, without looking behind.

"I can't get this!" Liu shouted. The breeze had picked up to a gust, which made lighting the torches difficult.

Ingela stood in front of Liu, acting as a block for the wind. "Try again," Ingela said, as she held the first torch steady for Liu's match. Lighting up the ship signaled to the attackers that they'd lost the element of surprise, though to be honest, they were all startled.

On the other side, away from the wind, Charlie and Raquel had lit all six torches. The ship was ablaze in light, which was necessary considering that the pearly moon Charlie had admired earlier did very little to illuminate the ink-black sky.

Raquel remembered her father's warning that it was easier to keep pirates, or any attackers, from boarding than get them to leave the ship. The attackers had hoisted ropes over to climb aboard on. Immediately, Raquel began cutting the first rope with her dagger. "Help me!" Raquel ordered Charlie, wondering why she hadn't already taken the lead.

Charlie hurried over.

Raquel fiercely cut away, relieved to see the rope tearing apart. "Adios!" she shouted as she watched the man attached to the rope fall in the water. Just then, she saw a massive hulking mass behind Charlie. "Watch out!" Raquel screamed.

Charlie whipped around to witness a giant hoisting himself onto the junk. Maybe he wasn't a monster, but he was certainly equal to, if not larger than, the sumo wrestlers

Charlie had seen in Osaka when she was a child. Only, unlike the sumo wrestlers, whose layers of fat flopped over the *kesho-mawashis* they wore, the giant standing before Charlie was a solid, heaving mass. His enormous torso, arms, and legs looked as though they'd been cut out of granite.

He straddled the ship's railing, glowering at her with beady eyes sunken so far back into his head that the sockets seemed hollow. His large, bald head was like a misshapen boulder sitting on top of a mountain. It was hard to tell exactly where such an odd mix-and-match of features came from, but Charlie didn't think he was Asian. Zhang Tao probably had all types of guys in his employ, so there was no way to rule out if this was one of his men. Whatever the giant's reason for invading their ship, it was clear to Charlie, by the way his large nostrils flared and drool fell from his heavy, fleshy jowls, that the beast was hungry.

If she was going to have any chance of taking him down, it was best to strike while he was still unsteady. She backed up a few steps and then charged with all her might. He shook but didn't fall. Charlie backed up again, this time with her cutlass out before her, preparing to ram it into his chest. But now he was steadier and gripped the cutlass by the blade, barely flinching as it ripped through his hand. With his bloody hand he threw the cutlass aside as though it were a mere pocketknife. Then he grabbed Charlie, flipping her around and ramming her back into the rail. She reached for her other sword, but he was too quick for her and placed her in a chokehold.

Raquel held a dagger like a dart and aimed it at the beast. She focused on her target and threw it with all her might. She managed to cut the guy on his upper shoulder, but it didn't faze him. There was no dancing with this guy. If she got too close, he could easily take out both her and Charlie. To Raquel's horror, Charlie's face was turning the same tomato color as her hair. She needed to win this with precision throwing. She pulled out another dagger. She also needed back up.

"He's got Charlie!" Raquel yelled.

Liu and Ingela heard Raquel's shouts, but were too preoccupied with a man holding two flintlock pistols, each aimed at their heads. They'd made it over to the other side of the ship just in time to see him climb over. He was of average height and build. From his brown hair to his pale skin, the rest of him was equally nondescript except for the long, deep gash that extended from his hairline all the way to his left ear, dividing his face in asymmetrical halves. Charlie and Raquel were the knife experts, but if Ingela had to put her money on it, judging from the jagged edges of his wound, she'd bet it was from a serrated double-edged blade.

"Oh, look at that, girls! It looks like you've managed to get right in the way of my pistols." Scar Face smiled, revealing a mouthful of tiny razor-sharp teeth.

Whether he'd been born with the deformity or had chosen to have it done, Ingela recoiled at the sight of his dagger mouth—no doubt his most lethal weapon. She wondered why he wanted to shoot her when a bite would clearly cause more damage than a bullet. Ingela hoped he wouldn't get the chance to do either, and curled her fingers into a solid fist.

Liu kept her eyes fixed on the man's face. The violent scar was old, but it seemed to have a life of its own, pulsing and bubbling with each angry breath he took. Zhang Tao usually used locals as his henchmen, but maybe he'd thrown a Westerner into the mix for fun. After all, Daddy Dearest was proving to be so unpredictable.

The last time that Zhang Tao's men had come for them, Liu had been paralyzed with fear. She was equally as terrified now, but this time she wasn't going to go down without a fight.

She took a deep breath and tried to calm the hysteria running through her. "Don't fight like pirates. Fight like the Storm," Liu said to herself and Ingela.

"Did you say something about a storm?" the man chuckled. "A little rain won't stop me from killing you."

Ingela had heard Liu loud and clear. She also took a deep breath. Stealth and speed. Mind over body. In unison, they took a wide sidestep out of the weapon's firing line. Scar Face fumbled around as he attempted to regain his targets. Each girl took the opportunity to strike the back of his arms, putting as much weight as possible in the hopes his hands would twist inward. Ingela's fingers slipped before she managed to get a firm grip, but Liu felt his bone snap.

He wailed, dropping the gun to the ground. As Scar Face instinctively cradled his broken wrist with his other hand, the second gun fell. With a final elbow to the gut and a crushing kick to the knees, he buckled under.

From a corner at the top of the stairwell on the main deck, Sadie went over the archery instructions again in her head. Like most things in her life, she hadn't actually shot a bow and arrow, but had spent a lot of time reading how to do it.

"Mind over body," Sadie mumbled, but, at that moment, the words felt as useless as all those archery books she'd read. First, focus your dominant eye on the target. She aimed it at the chest of the giant. Second, place your feet shoulder-width apart and stand up without tension. She tried to do this as best she could, though watching her best friend being choked to death in front of her was causing tension. Third, point the bow toward the ground and nock your arrow. To her surprise, she did it correctly on the first attempt. Fourth, raise and draw your bow. She held the bow so she could see straight down its spine. Fifth, aim and release. This seemed easier on paper. She took a deep breath and let go. Sadie watched as the arrow flew through the air and landed in the mammoth's left shoulder.

Raquel felt something sharp graze her cheek and turned around. She hadn't seen Sadie until that moment, and was astonished to see her holding a bow and arrow. Raquel looked up to see the monster grip the arrow with his left hand and pull it out. Blood squirted from his shoulder, but he didn't seem to notice. The beast released his hold of Charlie, hurling her into Raquel. Both girls went soaring across the ship's deck. Then he turned his head in the direction of Sadie.

The assault of arrows in his general path, none of which came even close to hitting him, didn't deter him as he slowly made his way across the deck to the dark spot in the corner where the arrows were coming from. There was no need to hurry, because it seemed his one step was the equivalent to four steps of a normal person.

Sadie watched in wide-eyed terror as the beast approached. A loud, pounding vibration reverberated every time his feet stomped the ground. Or maybe that was just the heavy pounding of her heart. "Fee-fi-fo-fum," Sadie mumbled to herself, thinking of the giant in the fairytale her mother would tell her when she was a little girl. But this monster wasn't imaginary. With every step, he became more real.

Sadie wanted to run, but her feet, which were still shoulder-width apart, felt glued to the spot. She hastily shot arrow after arrow, each landing further away from the moving target. When he got close enough for her to smell the ripe stench of rum on his breath, he lunged toward her. Gripped with nothing but fear, her mind and body stopped. With the force of what seemed like a dozen men, she toppled to the ground.

Charlie gasped for air. It seemed that no amount of deep breaths could satisfy her lungs. She squinted. Through blurry eyes, she could see the giant grab Ingela by the collar. Ingela thrashed and kicked while Liu punched him and Raquel tried to get close enough with her dagger. *Mind over body.* She took one more gulp of air before drawing her cutlass.

"WATCH OUT!" Liu, Raquel, and Ingela turned to see Charlie wildly wielding her cutlass over her head. Raquel and Liu jumped out of the way just as the sharp blade slashed the back of the beast's billowy shirt. A mound of fur sprouted through the tear. He dropped Ingela, who landed with a thud, then turned to face Charlie. Her pulse raced. Exhilaration and rage were coursing through her veins. How *dare* this monster hurt her girls?!

Charlie raised her sword and swung again. Her blade dug into his thick flesh and sliced all the way down. Blood spattered on her face, but she didn't stop to wipe it. Now that the full weight of her fury was unleashed, Charlie couldn't stop. She swung her sword and cut and cut and cut.

***

"We were just looking for some coins, jewels, even some rum or salted meat," replied Scar Face, whose name turned out to be Seth. He cradled his broken wrist with his other hand and looked up at all five girls standing in front of him like a firing squad. Much to his relief, none of them were carrying guns. Though, much to his unease, the crazy lass with the wild red hair was still holding her cutlass.

After Sadie tended to the prisoners' wounds, the rest of the girls tied them up for the night. Now, in the sharp early morning light, the extent of the men's injuries, not to mention their own cuts and bruises, looked quite gruesome. Len, the hulking giant, had come off worst, and resembled a butchered piece of meat. His cuts were, thankfully, only superficial, but just the sight of his sliced-up arms, legs, torso, and face turned Sadie's stomach. Liu, Raquel, and Ingela looked pretty nauseated by his appearance as well. Charlie, who seemed to take pride in her handiwork, was fine.

"Except that you said you were going to kill us," Liu responded. "It was when you were holding the gun to my head. Remember?"

"I was just trying to scare you." Seth smiled, revealing his tiny dagger teeth again. Sadie and Raquel jumped. Liu looked away. The guy gave her the full-on creeps.

Storm One had spent a lot of time on both sides of the American continent. Charlie was willing to bet by the way Seth pronounced his "r"s that he hailed from the southern part of the United States. She didn't know for sure, but she didn't think Zhang Tao would have an American goon working for him. But then what was this guy doing here?

Charlie looked over at Len. Seth had shared his name in exchange for a sip of ale. Len had been tight-lipped all morning, apart from an occasional low groan of pain. Charlie had to admit, she'd thought that her blade had done a lot more damage last night than the morning light had proven. She shivered.

"You're lying," Raquel declared as though it were fact rather than opinion. "About coming on our ship to steal stuff." She knelt down and touched the collar of Seth's knee-length coat. *Plush.* Though she rarely had an opportunity to wear them, she knew everything about the finest fabrics. She reached in and ran her hands through the inside. So *soft.* "Cashmere wool with a real silk lining. Hmmph!" The mere thought of a criminal wearing such elegant threads enraged her. She gestured wildly. "You weren't trying to steal from us! You don't have to! If anything, we should be stealing from *you!*"

They already had stolen from him, Ingela thought, as she tugged at her flimsy jacket, hoping it concealed the bulge of Seth's coin bag. *Finders keepers, losers weepers*, she reminded herself. Though, to be fair, he'd only dropped the coins after she'd kicked him.

Seth chuckled to himself. He could never afford these designer duds on his own henchman's salary. But the "guvnah" insisted they dress fancily, and furnished them with an entire wardrobe. "Glad you like the threads. Feel free to touch some more," he grinned. Raquel took several steps back. Seth liked making her squirm. "You should come over sometime. Would love to show you what else the boss bought me—" Seth stopped; he'd said too much.

"Shut up!" Len wheezed from his makeshift cot in the corner. Apart from the moaning, these were the first coherent words they'd heard from him.

Charlie snarled at Len. "Ignore him, Seth!" she said, doubting either Seth or Len were even their real names. "Unless you want to end up like him." She circled Seth slowly, pointedly dragging her cutlass. "So you're working for someone? A boss who likes you to wear fancy clothes and kill innocent girls?"

Seth scowled. He didn't like the crazy one so close.

"If we were going to kill you, we would have," Seth sneered. He glanced over at Len, who was lying there like a big, wounded beast. The black girl who'd taken care of them, the only one out of all these loonies with any sort of feelings, said Len would live. And she reset Seth's wrist so that it would heal properly. But he wasn't sure how much you could trust the medical skills of a girl Negro.

"If you're not gonna talk, we can always keelhaul you," Ingela threatened in a low, steely voice.

Seth stared incredulously at the pint-sized thief with his coin bag bulging underneath her clothes. She was far from the flower-picking, doll-playing little girls he knew.

A chill ran down Sadie's spine. Charlie was turning into a maniac, but Ingela too? Keelhauling was the torturous punishment of dragging a prisoner under the keel of a ship. Not only did they usually drown, but the barnacles attached to the hull ripped their skin to shreds. She'd never wish it on her worst enemy. Sadie hoped—no, prayed—that Ingela had only meant it as an empty threat.

Charlie was taken aback by Ingela's keelhauling suggestion too, but she did notice it had irked Seth. "Seth, just tell us who you work for and why they sent you here to *not* kill us and we can spare your skin." She lowered herself so they were face to face and pulled out a tiny pocketknife. Charlie lightly grazed it over the scar across his face. "What's left of your skin, that is."

"Charlie!" Sadie scolded, but Charlie ignored her. Liu and Raquel stepped to the side.

"Besides the fact that they're white guys, Seth sounds American. And I think Len's English, though he hasn't said enough for me to really know," Raquel whispered, darting a glance over at Seth and Len. "Do you think they're your father's guys?" she asked doubtfully.

He'd already tried to shoot them once, so there was no doubt that Zhang Tao was out for blood. It was pretty clear that Seth and Len would have killed them last night if it wasn't for Charlie and her courageous swordsmanship. But Liu still felt her dad would be more into capturing them, doling out some sadistic punishment, then watching them suffer. It wasn't his style to just hire two hit men to take them out. Besides, Zhang Tao had a lot of guys working for him, but the Westerners were usually part of management, the classy guys. Not the henchmen.

Seth and Len's clothes also told a different story. Liu walked back over to the two men and stooped down. Raquel was right. Seth's jacket was impeccably tailored, with double-stitched silk thread. These weren't the clothes of a common thief. They were the clothes of a criminal masquerading as a gentleman ...

"Sapphire East Trading Company!" Liu shouted, then regretted saying it out loud. She wasn't sure it was wise to reveal her realization to the men. A sense of relief instantly overcame her. These definitely weren't her father's goons.

"Rogers Barrish!" Raquel and Liu exclaimed at the same time.

The others jumped at hearing the names, while Liu and Raquel stared at each other in horror as they realized what they'd just discovered.

***

"I fed them some hardtack," Sadie announced as she climbed down the teak wood ladder into the "dining hall." As junk rigs like this one were mainly used to carry expensive cargo, they'd been built with internal watertight compartments or bulkheads. The bulkheads were watertight because they had no doors, just ladders. Since junks were the only ships to have this design, it was a bit strange for the girls at first. But now, they got up and down in a flash. "It looks like they're too tired to eat, though," she finished reporting as she crossed the galley to the long wooden table the other girls were sitting at.

Charlie was displeased by Sadie's constant updates on the two men, as if they were invited guests rather than prisoners. Trust Sadie's bleeding heart to sympathize with the enemy.

Ingela burped up a stinky mouthful of turtle stew in protest. "Why do the prisoners get better food than us?" Hardtack was cheap, tasteless crackers often referred to as "dog biscuits." Ingela picked up her nearly full bowl of Sadie's leftovers. "Forcing them to chow on this cat piss would be better punishment."

Ingela's jutted chin cast a long shadow on the wall. Since they could only afford to light two of the ten candelabras down here, the room was full of dark corners and dancing shadows.

"Oh, so you don't want to shred their skin anymore?" Raquel asked, feeling both sad and angry. She was proud of how they'd protected themselves, but sad over the relish that Charlie and maybe Ingela had for it all. She'd known her sisters to be courageous, not cruel.

Ingela shrugged her shoulders. "I just said that to scare him." Her eyes grew big. "And you saw how spooked he got!" "Cariña," Raquel gushed. Ingela wasn't the warm and fuzzy type, but Raquel wanted to believe that under all the tough stuff, there was still a genuine heart. She reached out and rumpled Ingela's greasy golden hair. To her surprise, Ingela didn't slap her hand away.

"Maybe the keelhauling was taking it a bit too far, Squirt?" Charlie asked.

"Look who's talking! You're a maniac!" Sadie shouted across the table. That hadn't come out as eloquently as she'd imagined, but at least it had been said.

Now it was Charlie's turn to be taken aback. "Maniac? I saved your life!"

"At nearly the cost of another man's! You know how easily you could have cut open an artery? Then he would have bled to death!" Sadie hollered.

"We were defending ourselves. We had the right to do whatever it took!" Charlie looked around the table, searching for some supporters.

"But you took it too far. You *enjoyed* it!" Raquel couldn't even look at Charlie.

Raquel's words sucked the stale air out of the room. Charlie felt as though Len were choking her all over again. She tried to recall slicing him with her cutlass, but it was all a haze. Tears brimmed from the corners of her eyes, but she wasn't sure if she was crying because Raquel was wrong, or because she was right.

"You just kept on going and going—"

"Stop it! Both of you!" Liu banged the table with her fist. She'd been so down on Charlie for not finding lirium, but last night, she proved once again that she was the only one who could really keep them safe. "Charlie was a warrior who fearlessly protected all of us! She shouldn't have to justify her actions or her motives." Liu understood the insecurity that Charlie struggled with in the water. She wasn't going to have her confidence undermined on the ship, too. Liu turned to face Sadie. "Especially you! You were useless last night, and Charlie saved you!"

"Liu!" Raquel jumped to Sadie's defense. "That's not fair. Sadie tried!"

Ingela jumped in. "Tried? We could have died from her trying!" She looked at Sadie. "Have you ever even shot a bow and arrow before?"

"Okay, maybe she wasn't a perfect shot, but she managed to get one in him. Right in the shoulder," Raquel explained. "No, Ingela," Sadie whispered, glad to have the darkness to hide the shame she felt. "I hadn't ever shot a bow and arrow. I mean, not for real." Charlie was the swordmaster, Raquel was panchi, Liu was guns and all sorts of weapons she invented, and Ingela was simply born to fight. Sadie had wanted to be useful, too, so she picked up archery. The problem was that the few times she'd practiced, she'd been so bad that she never bothered to try to get better. She'd been too embarrassed to admit that to the girls.

"What?"

"Huh?"

"Qué? But what about all those times you took off to practice?" Raquel asked gently. None of them had thought that Sadie had become an expert archer, but they presumed she at least knew how to shoot an arrow. Although now that Raquel thought about it, before last night, she'd never actually seen Sadie do it.

Sadie's voice trembled. "I read a book about bow-and-arrow shooting. *A Midsummer Night's Dream, Gulliver's Travels* ...I know I say it all the time, but you really can learn a lot from reading."

"Stop trying to turn this into a sappy learning moment!" Ingela barked. "I hate books!"

"That's because you can't read—"

Liu cleared her throat loudly. "Really not the point, guys!" She pointed at Sadie. "You were saying?"

Sadie wiped away her tears. "I know I put us all in grave danger, but I honestly didn't think we'd ever have to rely on my bow-and-arrow skills!"

"Why didn't you just tell us you don't like archery?" Liu asked. "We wouldn't have cared. I just don't get why you lied about it, Sadie."

"My mind is razor-sharp. Maybe it wasn't completely there last night, but I can always rely on this." Sadie tapped the side of her head. "But I don't have the physical prowess you guys do." She saw their blank faces. "The physical *skills* that you guys have."

"Oh, Sadie! Don't say that! It just takes practice. We're all learning." Raquel reached out for Sadie's arm, but to her surprise, Sadie pulled away.

Sadie put her hand up. "I don't need Embajador right now. Don't coddle or condescend to me, Raquel." She didn't care how many fancy words she was using now, she needed to get her point across on her terms. "I'm not saying you guys are ninjas. You have a lot of improving to do, too. I mean, we all barely got out of that fight alive. But even if I practice and train as hard as you all, I'll never be as good as ..." Her voice faded. "As the Storm."

Charlie, who'd been quietly listening the whole time, finally spoke up. "So that's why you made up the bow-and-arrow stuff? So you'd be good enough?" Charlie blinked back the tears, both for herself and Sadie. "None of us are good enough for the Storm, Sadie." She put her hand on the pearl that hung close to her heart.

Liu was filled with remorse for what she'd said to Sadie earlier. "How do you know what you could have been? How do any of us know? Our parents were trained until they were twenty-two, and they still kept on practicing after that! We'd just begun when it all ended ..." They'd lost so much. Not just their parents. But their futures. Liu choked back a sob. "Charlie's right. None of us are good enough for the Storm." They sat quietly, allowing themselves a rare occasion to mourn. Unsurprisingly, Ingela, who hated discussions but also loathed emotional anythings, cut through the heavy air. "But we *are* Storm." Ingela looked each of them in the eye. She lingered on Sadie. "All of us." She could feel their doubt, but she didn't have the patience for it. "We were attacked by guys from Sapphire East Trading Company, and it's time to find out why."

***

The five girls who came to face down Seth and Len the next morning were different than they'd been the previous day. They were determined.

It was early, but the sun was already hot and bright. This day was definitely going to be a scorcher, which would only add to the prisoners' discomfort, Charlie thought. But all the girls, including Sadie, agreed that unless these scumbags started cooperating, there would be no mercy.

Charlie wielded her sword in Len's face, not caring how "maniacal" she looked. "Remember what I did before? I'm ready for another round if you don't start talking."

They'd been going at Len for nearly a half-hour, but he hadn't given an inch. Though his stubbornness was frustrating, Charlie somewhat admired it, even if he was the enemy.

"Forget about Len. 'Specially 'cuz Seth seems like he's just dying to talk," Ingela hollered, stressing the word "dying."

Charlie grimaced. It was a bit disturbing how much Ingela got into the whole thing. Though she shouldn't talk. She knew she was going to do whatever it took to get some answers today. She untucked her shirt. The air was sticky and humid. She could see that Seth wasn't doing too well under the sweltering sun either. Beads of sweat were running down his face. Charlie pointed her cutlass directly at his chest. "Seth, we know you work for Sapphire East Trading Company, and we know Rogers Barrish sent you. Why?" Charlie circled his chest with the tip of her blade.

Seth sneered. The crazy one was definitely the most unhinged out of all of them. But these broads were all talk and no bite. He ran his tongue underneath his razor-sharp teeth. He was all about the bite.

Len moaned. He was still in pretty bad shape. The cuts were deep and throbbed endlessly. Some of them even ripped further when he moved. Still, despite his physical state, he remained threatening, watching the girls like he was stalking prey. He gave Liu the jitters. It seemed that Seth could be intimidated by Len, too. Though he was trying to hide it, the menacing glare that Len was throwing Seth's way was making him uneasy. Liu stood in Len's line of vision. "Seth, you don't need Len's permission to answer a simple question," Liu said calmly.

"Thanks for the tip, China Girl," Seth scoffed.

"If you want to play it that way, then maybe this will help you talk." Raquel unscrewed the cap on a bottle of rum. "It's time to clean your wounds, Seth." Simply looking at the degenerate made her uneasy, but she forced herself to get closer to him. Raquel lifted up the sleeve of his shirt and looked for the deepest wound. When she found it, she doused it with the rum.

Seth shouted.

"Sorry, I'm not as careful as Sadie."

His arm was flaring up with red, flaming blisters. "Enough!" Seth shouted, bristling with so much rage that the scar across his face looked as though it were about to re-open.

Raquel stopped. "Okay, so can you please answer my friend Charlie's question now?"

Charlie smiled. "Let's try this again, Seth. Why did Rogers Barrish send you to kill us?" She continued to let the tip of her blade touch him.

"He didn't send us to kill you. He just wanted us to hurt you real bad." Seth leered at the blade the crazy one held to his chest. He didn't add that now he was more than willing to hurt them, even without Rogers Barrish's orders. He looked up at the red-headed bitch. He couldn't wait to sink his teeth into her. Bet she tasted as sour as she looked. "Okay, but why? As revenge for uncovering his dirty scheme? That Sapphire East Trading Company insures huge fleets of ships and then sends pirates out to raid them?" Charlie pressed her blade a bit more firmly into Seth's flesh. Maybe warning those American captains was the noble thing to do, but now she really wished she hadn't gotten involved.

When they'd first gotten the junk from Zhang Tao, they were thrilled to finally be on the sea again. But they still needed money, food, and supplies. Which meant that Charlie was robbing drunks.

One night, when they were in London, which was a haven for barflies, she waited in her Pirettes disguise for drunks to stumble out of the pubs. Maybe it was because he was sloshed, or because he genuinely thought that Charlie was going to take his life, but one guy confessed that he was part of a plan to raid a fleet of American merchant ships an-

143

chored in London's harbor later in the week. He offered to split his share of the loot if Charlie let him go.

After taking his wallet and pocket watch, Charlie wrestled with her conscience about the confession. She discussed it with the other girls, and they decided to tell the captain of the American fleet about the planned attack. So the next day she set off for the harbor with Ingela, who demanded to come along. The American captain was so happy to receive the information he insisted on taking Charlie and Ingela, who'd introduced themselves as the Pirettes instead of giving him their real names, to meet Governor Rogers Barrish. Sapphire East Trading Company's headquarters were there in the center of the city, and the captain wanted Barrish to be immediately aware of the Pirettes' good deed.

When Charlie met Governor Barrish, she had no reason to believe he was anything but the upstanding guy he presented himself to be. She would have gone on happily thinking that, never planning on seeing him again, had it not been for Ingela's sticky fingers. It was only after they came home that Charlie learned of the map that Ingela had stolen from Barrish's office.

When Ingela unrolled the map, both she and Charlie were shocked to find a set of papers hidden along with it. Among them was the itinerary of the American merchant fleet, along with Barrish's notes on the planned raid. That's how the girls found out that Barrish had been in on the scheme himself. So not only were the Pirettes responsible for botching up Barrish's plan, but when he noticed his map and papers had been stolen by them, he would know that the Pirettes knew his dirty little secret. A secret that he would probably go to painstaking lengths to cover.

Seth looked down. The sword's tip was getting closer to breaking skin, and his arm was on fire, but he kept his mouth shut.

"Seth, don't make Raquel have to clean another wound," Charlie threatened.

Raquel opened the rum bottle again. The smell was nauseating, but Seth stayed tight-lipped.

Charlie looked at Sadie. She nodded. Charlie took a deep breath. It was the only choice. She dug her sword in the spot directly under his heart, just like Sadie had explained to her. Then pushed down, piercing the flesh. She could feel her blade ripping his skin open.

Blood gushed out of Seth. He shrieked from the sheer agony and from seeing his chest ripped open. "She's killed me!"

Sadie stood over him. "No, Seth, she hasn't killed you. Not yet. We can stop the bleeding by applying pressure, which will save your life. But you gotta tell us everything first."

Seth's shirt quickly became soaked in blood. Len tried to say something, but Seth ignored him. "Okay! I'll tell you what you want. Just don't let me die!"

"Help him, Sadie," Charlie commanded. Sadie stooped down and put a heavy rag against the gushing wound. "Now talk, Seth."

He took a deep breath. "Governor Barrish has a raid planned. We were supposed to make sure you guys didn't get in the way."

"Where? When?"

Seth shook his head. "I don't know the details!"

"Okay, Seth, if that's how you want it." Charlie looked down. "Sadie, I think the prisoner is being uncooperative." Sadie nodded and removed the rag from the wound. Instantly, blood squirted out. "No! Put it back. Please!"

Charlie looked at her pocket watch. "Better talk fast, Seth. You don't have much time."

Seth looked at Len, scowling at him. Then he looked down at the blood spouting out of him. It was going everywhere. "I gotta tell these broads somethin' or they're gonna off me any second now." Len furled his lips, but Seth turned away. "I overheard Len and the governor talking. Didn't get everything, but they were discussing the raid. It's got something to do with a religious trip. A sultan. From Marrakesh? Marra—"

"Marrakatra!" Sadie jumped in. "The Sultan of Marrakatra's yearly hajj to Mecca!"

As one of the richest men in the world, the Sultan of Marrakatra was famous. His yearly trip to Mecca was renowned for its luxury. Sadie had even seen an article about it that described ships filled with solid blocks of gold. She also remembered reading about the elite royal soldiers who guarded the fleet. How was Barrish planning to pull off such an enormous attack?

"Yeah, somethin' like that. The Sultan of Marrakatra," Seth seethed. He didn't think these girls had it in them to take it so far. There would definitely be repercussions for his spilling the beans, but right now, his bigger concern was making sure the crazy one didn't kill him.

Charlie beamed. Sadie really was good at solving puzzles. She wasn't so bad as an assistant punisher, either.

"Who are the pirates that Barrish is using to attack the fleet?"

"I-I dunno," Seth's eyes began to roll back in his head. His face was turning ashen. Charlie gave Sadie the go-ahead to save him. They'd gotten everything they needed from him. For now, at least.

***

The girls had decided to eat all their meals below deck, away from the prisoners who were tied up on the main deck. They devoured their lunch. The morning had really worked up their appetites.

146

Charlie knew that she should probably feel guilty for taking it as far as she had, but right now, she didn't care. They'd gotten exactly what they needed. Besides, it wasn't like they'd killed anyone. Seth was still alive and recovering from his latest injury. She mopped up the last bits of fish stew with her sea biscuit. It was Liu's turn at galley duty this week, and Charlie had to hand it to her: though Liu didn't eat animals, she sure knew how to cook them. "Got any more?"

"Half a pot." Liu was just sticking to the stew broth herself, without the fish. The way that Raquel could "read" people, Liu connected with animals. She believed they had souls and couldn't bring herself to eat them, despite life on the sea as a vegetarian being far from easy. She took another sip of her soup. At least when she cooked, it had flavor.

"Okay, so are we gonna talk about it?" Charlie couldn't help but be in a celebratory mood. Seth's news was the golden ticket they'd been waiting for. She wondered if the others thought the same.

"There's nothing to talk about. We gotta save the sultan's ships," Ingela said, handing her empty bowl to Sadie. "I want more soup."

Sadie stopped eating. "First of all, get it yourself, Squirt. Especially since you're always shouting that I'm not your mom. Second, there's a lot to talk about."

Charlie rolled her eyes. "We can discuss it for hours, like I'm sure you'll make us. But here's the bottom line: we need a ship. One that's not stolen. And if we save the sultan's fleet, with all its loot, then he'll give us a big reward so we can buy our own ship." Charlie took a big bite of her stew. She didn't follow what happened in the world like Sadie, but even Charlie was aware of the Sultan of Marrakatra's vast wealth. Stories about the enormous treasure on board the sultan's ships *Hamman* and *Shamana* were part of sailor

147

folklore. "And then we can give the junk back to everyone's favorite daddy, Zhang Tao."

Liu clinked her bowl against Charlie's. They were both on the same page, though she didn't think it was going to be that easy. "Exactly!" They still had to give it a try.

Ingela banged her fist against the table. "No! I want to do it because we're Storm. And the Storm protects those in need and destroys those that harm," she shouted, reciting the motto. "Saving the sultan's fleet is our mission."

Ingela had been raised on her father's Storm stories about freeing slave ships and saving merchant fleets from pirate attacks. It was their obligation to help the sultan.

"Okay, then we'll do this mission because we're Storm."

Charlie beamed. "Storm that gets a reward."

"It's not that simple, Charlie," Sadie began.

Charlie sat back against the wall. This was going to be one of Sadie's lectures, and she wanted to get comfortable. "Do tell, Professor."

Sadie didn't miss the sarcasm, but decided not to retort. "As I was saying, we're talking about facing off against a band of pirates, Rogers Barrish, and Sapphire East Trading Company, the most powerful company in the world! Just the five of us! You don't think that's a bit too dangerous?"

To Charlie's great surprise, Sadie had actually managed to get her point across in less than ten thousand words. "It's not facing off against a band of pirates. We're going to warn the sultan's fleet before the pirates get to it. Yes, that will piss off Barrish, but we're just gonna have to get out of there before he finds out it's us." She fidgeted in her seat. "What happened to all that stuff yesterday about not being scared anymore?"

"This isn't about being scared. This is about not being stupid." Sadie shook her head. "It's suicide."

Charlie's shoulders fell. Sadie's words had taken the happy out of her. She'd been so excited to finally have a real way out of all this that she hadn't considered the danger involved. As much as she hated to admit it, Sadie had a point, even if, like usual, she'd jumped to the most extreme scenario.

Raquel put down her spoon. "But what about gilling and lirium? Shouldn't we keep on trying that instead of risking our lives for this mission?"

Any joy left was instantly erased at the mention of lirium. In all the frenzy of the last two days, Charlie had gladly forgotten about her lirium problem.

Sadie nodded. "Raquel's right; why don't we just gill? Obviously there's no lirium here or Charlie would have found it. We should head further south to even warmer waters—"

"It won't help." Charlie felt her cheeks get hot. "I can't gill."

Ingela stopped eating. She couldn't believe what she'd heard. Raquel's mouth opened in disbelief. There were no words she could find in this moment.

Sadie had never heard Charlie say she couldn't do something. "What do you mean, you can't gill? You've been doing it for nearly two months. We just have to get somewhere where there's lirium, Charlie."

Charlie was happy they could only afford to light two candles so most of the room was dark. She didn't want them to see her. "It won't help. I suck at it, okay?"

"Then teach the rest of us to gill!" Raquel exclaimed. "If we're all doing it, we're sure to find lirium."

Liu pushed her bowl away. "Then what? Are you guys listening to me? Even with three months of gilling, we won't find enough lirium to buy a ship. If we even have that much time. Rogers Barrish found us, so how long do you think it will be before Zhang Tao catches up to us again?" She slammed both hands on the table. "We need to get a new ship. And this mission to warn the sultan is our only way. I agree it's dangerous, but do we really have another option?" She looked around the table. "I mean seriously, do we?"

The candles flickered. They knew they were far from ready, but they also knew there was no choice. In the near-darkness, they nodded in silent agreement.

***

"What the *Hajj* are you talking about?" Ingela rubbed her temples. With all the charts, maps, and books that Sadie, Raquel, and Liu were showing them, this was feeling like school. And Ingela *hated* school. Wasted hours spent in a classroom reading, writing, and learning math. Things that she had no use for then or now.

Charlie sighed. "Okay, go get us some fish. We'll give you the rundown later."

Ingela grinned, then jetted out of the dining room. Charlie turned back to Sadie. "Alright, take it from the top. I want to make sure I get all of this."

"Right, as I was saying," Sadie cleared her throat. "Hajj is a religious trip that Muslims take to Mecca. It's made during the end of the year. Since the Islamic calendar is a lunar calendar, it's about ten to twelve days shorter than our calendar. So, I checked my almanac and figured out that this year Hajj will be between November 25 to 27th and Eid, which is a major feast at the end of Hajj, will be between November 27 to 29th."

Charlie stifled a yawn. She really did want to understand this stuff, but Sadie did not know the meaning of summarizing. "I don't need every detail, Sadie. There's too much info to get through. Just focus on the main points."

"Right." Sadie didn't really appreciate getting a teaching lesson from Charlie, but she bit her tongue and continued on. "I found this article from a few months ago talking about the Hajj that the Sultan of Marrakatra takes every year." She held up a yellowed newssheet.

"Actually, I kept it because it mentioned Sapphire East Trading Company and ever since that mess with the planned raid on the American ships, I've been trying to save anything I find on SETC or Rogers Barrish. But we'll explain SETC's part in all this later. Now I'll just go back to the Hajj stuff.

Charlie was spare and organized, while Sadie had the annoying habit of saving everything "just in case it may come in handy," which it rarely did. Now, as Sadie stood next to a pile of old newspapers, Charlie realized it would be impossible to ever convince her to throw anything away in the future.

"The Sultan of Marrakatra is the richest sultan in the world. His yearly Hajj is major. He sends two ships: one filled with his guards, the other with members of the royal court and his family. According to the article, one of the sultan's daughters will be making her first Hajj this year. Her name is Princess Imera, and she's said to be known for her beauty and kindness. Other than that, there's not much on her. But there are pretty good details on the ships. The guards' ship is pretty fancy compared to our standards. However, the royal ship is ultra-lux. It's loaded with jewels, silks, tea, paintings, spices—everything rich people like. While the main purpose of the trip is religious, the crew will also sell the goods that the ship carries. When they get to Mecca, there are lots of travelers on similar religious pilgrimages who are hungry for the famous silks, jewels, and other things that come from Marrakatra."

Charlie gave Sadie a look that meant she needed to get to the point a bit faster. Sadie nodded and continued to talk. "So when the sultan's ships make their return journey from Mecca to Marrakatra, that's when they carry nothing but stacks of solid gold bars. That's the treasure that everyone wants to get their hands on."

"Right." Without missing a beat, Liu picked up where Sadie left off, as though they'd practiced this. "So given that the sultan's trip takes place every year around the same time and is known all over the world, you'd think that it's probably pretty easy for pirates to figure out when and where the sultan's ships will be." Liu walked over to the map that she'd tacked to the wall. "Well, it is. Marrakatra lies here, near India. So there's basically only two routes the ship would take to and from Mecca." She traced her finger from Marrakatra to the Red Sea and around a small island called Perim. "The pirates would probably be waiting here in Perim to attack the *Haman* and the *Shamana*, which is the ship that carries the royal family. As Sadie said, they would attack after it's loaded up with all its gold, on the way back from Hajj." Liu took a brief pause to check and see if Charlie was still with them. To her slight surprise, she was. Charlie squinted as she studied the map. The "map" that she was currently looking at was a compilation of other map scraps that Liu had pasted together like a jigsaw puzzle. For the most part, it worked well, except that the tiny kingdom of Marrakatra, which was located on an island just outside of India in the Arabian Sea, had an ink splotch on it. Still, one could vaguely make out that it was in fact Marrakatra. "Okay, so if this is such major loot, then lots of pirates have probably tried to raid these ships and are most likely going to try this year, too." They'd splurged for this presentation and lit four candles, but the dark room still could have used a half-dozen more. Charlie walked over to the map to inspect it closer. "Yeah, it would probably be a central target for pirates, except that it's also famous for being one of the most highly insured and highly protected fleets in the world. Not only does it sail with a special ship for the sultan's guards, but Sapphire East Trading Company sends a ship of its own with security. They were bragging about it in the same article that Sadie mentioned. With all those armed guards protecting it, most pirates don't dare attack the sultan's fleet."

There it was again. Sapphire East Trading Company and Rogers Barrish. Charlie shook her head. It seemed that all things always led back to SETC and the governor.

Raquel tapped Charlie on the shoulder. "It's really much better if you sit down for this." She had inherited a flair for drama from her mother and was waiting for the perfect moment to give the big reveal. But Charlie, like Ingela, looked like she was about to walk out, so she hurried her performance. "The only way Rogers Barrish can pull this attack off is if it's an inside job. More specifically, he'll use men working for him as the SETC extra 'protection.' They'll be right there on the *Haman* and the *Shamana*, and they'll provide all the necessary access because *really* they're helping the pirates."

It wasn't for certain, but they girls were pretty sure they'd figured out Barrish's scheme.

"So what's next?" Raquel asked, barely able to contain herself.

"We get to the princess and warn her about the plot!" Sadie sang out. She was thrilled they'd pieced this all together. "We just have to get to her before she leaves."

"Today is November eighth." Liu pointed to a calendar. "We're going to be sailing upwind, which will take longer. We stock up in Malé, which is the capital city of the Maldives and about a one-day sail away from our current location, if my calculations are correct. From Malé, it takes about twenty-two to twenty-four days to get to Mecca. Or technically, Jeddah, because that's the closest port to Mecca and where the princess's ship will be. So if we finish preparing in the next few days and stock up in Malé, then we can make it to Jeddah before the sultan's fleet leaves." Liu wanted to dance on the table. For the first time since they'd left Shanghai sixty-seven days ago, she actually had hope. They might really pull this off. "It'll be tight, but we can do it."

Charlie chewed on her lip as she studied the map and graph again. Ten minutes passed before she turned to face the girls. "So we go to Jeddah and warn the princess about Barrish's scheme. She'll get rid of the SETC ship and take the route back to Marrakatra that will avoid contact with the pirates. Which means we'll also avoid any contact with the pirates. Then we'll collect a generous reward for saving the sultan's ships."

All three girls nodded in unison. Charlie smiled. Of course, it wouldn't be that simple. There were a hundred things that could go wrong, all of which could very easily end with them dying. Still, their plan was pretty good. As Charlie thought about it, her guilt at not finding lirium was slowly giving way to something else. Fear, of course. But also excitement. They might actually make this work.

"How are we going to make the princess believe us? We don't have proof unless we take Seth with us and torture him into admitting everything again in front of her."

Sadie waved her hand. Of course she knew that Charlie was being sarcastic, but even she, the most cautious of them all, actually thought this plan to warn the princess was viable. "When the time comes, we'll do everything we can to make sure she believes us. If this all goes well then we'll have our own ship, and we can stop running from Zhang Tao. We can also get back to what's really important, which is finding out what happened to our parents." Sadie put her arm around Charlie's shoulder. "Come on, what do you say?"

Charlie's stomach filled with butterflies. Some good butterflies, but some bad ones also. When she'd forced them to jump off the ship on the DD, she'd been scared, but she'd been sure she could protect them. In the months since, especially the last two with the lirium, all of that had changed. Failing as badly as she felt she had was causing her to question herself in all sorts of ways.

She knew how important this mission was to their futures, but she needed to believe in herself completely if she was going to lead them. Charlie fingered the necklace from her pop. She didn't. She turned to face the girls. Staring back at her were the hopeful, shiny faces of Sadie, Raquel, and Liu. Above her, she could hear Ingela stomping about. The butterflies fluttered wildly. She believed in her sisters. Charlie silently prayed that this would be enough.

"Well?" Liu asked.

Charlie broke out into a huge grin. "Looks like we've got a princess to save!"

Chapter
EIGHT

SLOG
Date: November 12
Position: The Maldives

We careened the junk on Ari Atoll, meaning we put it ashore so we could clean the hull. Keeping the hull smooth is key to speed, and we can't afford any setbacks. We have to time it perfectly with Hajj, so everything's gotta be precise down to the details. Now it's time to go to Malé to stock up on supplies. Ingela won a bag of coins from gambling, and it will be enough to get the basics, plus a few extras.

This is a huge mission, and we're all scared, but if we can pull it off, then we're saved! It's strange to finally feel hope again. Yet I still keep on looking over my shoulder, expecting to see one of Zhang Tao's ships coming to take us away. Yesterday, I was sure I saw a ship with his dragon flag. My heart dropped. I know that as each day passes, my father gets angrier. My punishment will be the harshest, but he will make all of us pay. Knowing that I'm to blame for whatever horrible retribution Zhang Tao has waiting for them causes so much worry inside me. Almost as much worry as the constant fear that he has finally found us.

"Where the hell are we?" Seth shouted as Charlie and Liu pushed him onto the tiny raft.

Charlie let out a long, exasperated sigh. The girls had tended to their prisoners' wounds, fed them, even bathed them (well, Sadie wiped a wet cloth on their decent parts), and now they were complaining about being let go? The girls had tried to squeeze more info from Seth, but he had nothing, while Len remained tightlipped. They were totally useless to them. "Well, maybe you should have thought about all this before you tried to *not* kill us!" Charlie nudged the raft along.

"Hey!" Seth scowled at Charlie. He grabbed onto the girl's rowboat. "We'll go when we're ready."

Liu shook her leg impatiently. "You'll go *now*." The rain had held off, and there was a steady late morning wind. She'd studied the map again last night. There was still half a day of sailing before they got to Malé, and they needed to arrive before sundown in order to stay on schedule.

Len laughed to himself. These twits were stupid to let them live. When it was his turn, he wouldn't be nearly as nice. That was why girls, with all their feelings and morals, didn't belong at sea.

Len leered hungrily at Raquel one more time. She was his favorite, with her shapely rump.

"It's time for us to say goodbye," Raquel waved her hand. Charlie groaned. Raquel was always trying to use her diplomacy skills, like everything was some big peace treaty. "Hey, Embajador, these guys aren't our friends. They tried to kill us."

Raquel was about to retort when she noticed the way Len was ogling her. Gross. She shifted behind Charlie.

"Oh, one more thing!" Liu turned to Ingela, who nodded happily.

Ingela reached into her pocket and pulled out a round rubber stamp. It looked like those found in fancy offices to authenticate official documents. However, when this one was pressed down, tiny spikes appeared. Ingela had brought the idea of the device to Liu, who had then been working on

157

its design for the past few days. They'd decided not to tell the other girls until they had a working prototype. Now, Sadie, Raquel, and Charlie looked on in confusion as Liu lit a match to the bottom of the stamp.

"What are you going to do to us now?" Seth barked. He was so eager to lay his teeth into one of them that he could feel himself frothing at the mouth like a rabid dog.

"It's just something to guarantee you guys won't talk." Liu pressed the stamp against Seth's forehead, being careful to keep enough distance so that he couldn't touch her. Even if he was tied up, his mouth was lethal. She applied pressure. Instantly a cluster of tiny circular cuts, each no bigger than the tip of a sewing needle, formed a "P" in his skin. Tens of tiny droplets of blood formed in the holes. "Ingela."

Ingela nodded solemnly and placed a damp cloth against the cuts, wiping away the blood that was now trickling down Seth's face. Seth growled, exposing his killer canines. Liu watched closely. "That's enough," she said as Ingela sponged up blood around Seth's eyebrow. Given that Ingela was never this thorough with her own cleanliness, Liu was impressed at the attention she was paying now. "Ink, please."

Ingela reached into her back pocket and took out a small bottle of pen ink. She unscrewed the top and held it out for Liu. With the solemnity of a priest performing the last rites. Liu dipped the round stamp into the black ink. She tapped it against the side of the bottle to remove the excess ink before placing it on Seth's forehead. He didn't say anything, but she could feel his fury mounting. It was best to get this done as quickly as possible. Liu tried to line up the stamp with the previous cuts, but her nerves were making it difficult. *Stop shaking*, she thought to herself.

Sadie was fascinated by Liu's newest device and stepped forward, then took a step back. Cuts and blood of any kind fascinated her, but she didn't want to trample on Ingela's turf. "Squirt!"

Ingela glowered. She didn't like being called by her nickname when she was in the middle of serious business.

Sadie corrected herself. "Ingela! Make the forehead taut so Liu can re-stamp easier."

Ingela's scowl turned from annoyed to confused.

"Like this," Sadie directed, using her hands to show how to move the skin back.

Ingela nodded, and maybe even smiled a little, as she followed Sadie's instruction. Liu realigned the ink-stained stamp, then pressed it against Seth's forehead.

Charlie and Raquel looked on in bewilderment while Sadie smiled approvingly.

Being careful to remain out of biting distance, Liu moved closer to inspect the mark on Seth's forehead. "It's called scarification, and it's been around forever. There's lots of ways to do it. But this method is the least painful." She eyed Seth. "You cut the skin open, then you fill it with ink. As the cuts heal, the ink stays."

Raquel nodded in awe. Liu was a master at inventing crazy gadgets that were remarkably handy.

Liu turned to Len now. "You're next." She waved Ingela over. "I'll let you do the honors. Can you guys help me hold him?" Though Len's arms and legs were roped together, she didn't trust him to sit still.

Charlie and Sadie grabbed one side of him, while Liu and Raquel took the other.

Ingela imprinted Len with the same stamp. She stepped away to admire her work.

"You tattooed us?" Seth asked, studying the blotch on Len's forehead. He would make them pay for using him as their lab experiment.

"Sort of. The 'P' is for Pirettes. Now everyone will know a bunch of girls beat you." Liu stared Seth and Len directly in the eyes. She couldn't help but admire her handiwork. The single letter "P" was bold and black, which made it stand out prominently on both men, but it was starkest on Len's waxy forehead. "That should keep you quiet. Especially when it comes to Rogers Barrish, who surely has some kind of punishment waiting for those who fail his orders."

Len nodded in spite of himself. He had to give it to China Doll—she was smart. Next time, he'd get her out of the way first. Then slowly exact his revenge on the crazy redhead. Maybe save his favorite for last.

Or should he reverse the order? He wasn't sure yet. There was a different flavor for every appetite. And Len was hungry.

As the raft drifted away, he was already making plans for his return. He eyed Seth. First, he needed to get rid of some deadweight.

***

"I told you to stop fidgeting, or we're going to have to start all over again!" said Raquel, admonishing Charlie. She dipped her brush into the gray pigment.

Charlie huffed. "Why do I always get stuck playing the guy these days? I thought we were supposed to be taking turns being the chaperone."

"Well, you don't have boobs, hips, or a butt to speak of," Sadie giggled. "So you're really the most natural man out of all of us.

"Ha-ha." Charlie chucked one of Raquel's brushes at Sadie.

It was much too scandalous for young "ladies" such as themselves to walk around without a male to escort them, which meant they each took turns dressing up like a guy at different ports. All except for Ingela, who, ironically, was the most boyish out of all of them, but with her short stature and chubby cheeks, she didn't look old enough to be walking them about.

"If I just wanted someone with no boobs or butt, I could use Liu," Raquel explained, as she blended white into Charlie's jawline. She stepped back to inspect her work. Though it was always best to use natural light, the late afternoon sun was throwing a dark pink haze on everything. Raquel added more white. "But Charlie's skin makes her my perfect canvas."

"What's wrong with my skin?" Liu asked. In the distance, a set of drums was starting to beat. It sounded like the evening market was opening in Malé. She checked her pocket watch. They'd made it here in good time but Raquel's art project was starting to delay them. "Hey, we need to get going soon."

Raquel ignored Liu. She didn't want to be hurried when she was "creating." "Liu's skin is way too creamy and soft." Raquel wagged her finger. "But Charlie's is ruddy, like a man's. Sometimes, in a certain light, she even looks like she has a tiny mustache."

Charlie started to get off the stool. "Okay, I think like Liu said, it's time to go."

"Embajador!" Sadie jokingly scolded. "Not exactly your most diplomatic moment."

Ingela put her index finger above her lip to form a mustache. "Yeah, way to go, Embajador. Captain Mustache over there doesn't think that's funny."

"No, Charlie, please!" Raquel blocked her from leaving. "I didn't mean it like that. The girls are just being mean." She eased Charlie back onto the stool. "I love painting you." Charlie was still irritated, but decided it was easier just to sit back down and get this over with. Despite what the rest of them thought, faking as a guy hadn't been that easy for her.

It got easier about a month ago, when Raquel had started using her as a human canvas. Encouraged by how good she was getting with her sketches, Raquel had wanted to start "drawing" on people. More specifically, she'd begun experimenting with make-up to create elaborate disguises. Not make-up as in prissy girls dolled up with tons of rouge and powder, but ruses that looked like they belonged in a theater play and were actually pretty cool. She'd painted Ingela into a frightening sea monster, Sadie into an evil crow, and Liu into a warrior. But her favorite was turning Charlie into all sorts of different male characters: a farmer, a banker, or a deadly pirate (which wasn't much of a stretch).

As a rule, Charlie couldn't stand even having the tiniest bit of lip balm on. Being forced to sit still while being poked and prodded with different brushes and things she didn't recognize was certainly not ideal. Since real cosmetics were expensive, Raquel came up with her own compounds and shades from all kinds of stuff she found, most of which were cakey, greasy, or sticky. Charlie did enjoy seeing what fantastical mask Raquel created, and Raquel seemed to have fun doing it. So for the time being at least, Charlie was a good sport.

"I know you hate this part," Raquel said as she brought out a goatee made out of Charlie's hair trimmings that she'd sewn together.

Charlie groaned. "Not the fish glue!"

"It's all we have!" Raquel scrunched up her nose at the smell. "I won't use more than is absolutely necessary." She dotted the top with tiny circles of glue. Then she placed the entire goatee directly under Charlie's chin, carefully positioning it straight. She took out a tiny comb and delicately smoothed it out. "Okay, we're done!" Raquel beamed. She held up a hand mirror for Charlie to see.

"Wow!" Charlie barely recognized herself. She studied her face from the side.

"Hey, great job, Raquel!" Liu exclaimed.

"Looks nothing like Charles!" Sadie walked closer to get a better look. "So who is this guy supposed to be?"

Raquel thought for a moment, then she smiled. "I'd like to introduce you to Mr. Graham Blakely. The new headmaster at St. Mary's School for Young Ladies. He will be our chaperone today, girls."

Sadie and Liu curtsied, while Ingela just gave a quick wave. And with that, the four ladies and their gentleman escort were off to Malé.

***

"You have been kind to listen to the ramblings of an old man like me," the toothless man smiled at Raquel.

"It has been my pleasure to hear your wise words," Raquel smiled. As the Portuguese were avid explorers and sailors, it was useful to speak their language. She used it often in their travels. However, she was surprised to find a native Maldivian who was as fluent as she was here in the Malé market.

The market was small, but abuzz with locals and some foreigners all milling about. The old man had been selling beautiful pieces of beaded jewelry that instantly drew Raquel's attention. She couldn't afford anything, but the old man had been kind enough to let her try on many of the pieces.

"I would like to give you this," said the old man, turning behind him and reaching for a linen pouch. He handed it to Raquel. "Make good use of them."

Raquel looked into the pouch and saw that it was filled with lovely seashells. She reached down and touched the egg-shaped shells, with their porcelain-like surfaces. "Thank you, Sir." She hugged the old man. "I know exactly what to use these for!" She wasn't sure how many were in there, but hopefully enough to surprise each of the girls with her own seashell bracelet. A favorite hobby of hers was collecting seashells, along with other things she found, and fashioning them into unique pieces of jewelry. Anything could be made into something beautiful with a few swings of a hammer.

Loud drums started to play, signifying that the market was closing. Raquel gathered her things, ready to leave. She tucked the bag of seashells inside another bigger bag. "Shukuriyaa," Raquel said again to the old man, this time testing out her Divehi, the language of the Maldives.

The old toothless man smiled and waved. "Dhanee." Just then, Liu sidled up to Raquel. "Ooh, found yourself a Maldivian boyfriend?"

"Funny. We just fell into a very nice chat."

"You speak Maldivian?" Liu asked incredulously.

Raquel shook her head. "It's Divehi, and of course I don't. Except for shukuriyaa, which means 'thank you'." She raised her voice as Ingela, Charlie, and Sadie joined them. "Speaking of thank-you's—I think we should all give one to Ingela for being so kind and sharing all her money with us."

"Thanks, Squirt!" "You're awesome!" "We love you!"

Ingela shrugged her shoulders and sped up. The girls walked out of the Malé market, bogged down with brown packages of different sizes, all tied up with string. The main market, which only had a handful of stalls and no farm animals, was relatively calm compared to Shanghai. And luckily, there was no angry mob chasing them out this time.

"What's bugging Ingela?" Liu asked the girls in confusion. Usually Ingela demanded praise for the littlest gestures. It wasn't like her to shun adulation.

"Maybe she's hungry?" Charlie mused. A little patch of her goatee had fallen off, but for the most part, Raquel's disguise had managed to fool the people of Malé.

"I don't think that's it," Sadie replied. "But I am ready to chow down!"

"Uh-huh!" Raquel responded in excitement. She was lightheaded from her shopping high. Or maybe it was the heavy humidity that lingered in the night air. But even after buying all their supplies, they had enough to enjoy a meal out, which was definitely a rare treat.

"This looks like a good spot. Leave the packages here with Ingela and Sadie. The three of us will go and get the grub," Charlie instructed. "We can get food from up there and eat it here." Charlie pointed to a man cooking over a fire up ahead.

Charlie had never been to Malé before. They weren't going to spend much time here, since they had to get going on the mission, but this was what she loved about sea life—the freedom to explore all kinds of places. *Storm One* had sailed to North America, South America, Europe, Asia, and Africa. Charlie had swum in every type of water there was, from tiny streams to vast oceans, seen every kind of sea creature, including massive blue whales and killer sharks, and had explored bustling harbors in the biggest cities as well as tiny inlets on faraway islands. She loved seeing new spots and learning new things, soaking up all the sights and sounds they had to offer. What made it even more exciting was that there were still so many more places she had yet to discover.

Charlie, Raquel, and Liu made their way up the beach.

Sadie and Ingela sat quietly, watching the waves crash on the shore. The sea was calm tonight. Huge white palms lined the beach. It was a moonless night, but the stars lit up the sky. Up ahead were the party sounds of a drum, joined by a guitar. Ingela found a stick and drew figures in the sand.

"Okay, spill."

Ingela ignored Sadie and continued to draw.

"Come on, Squirt. I can tell something's wrong." She took one of the lighter packages and chucked it at Ingela.

"Don't!" she shouted.

"I'm sorry! I didn't think it would hurt you!" Sadie reached out toward Ingela, but she pulled away.

"The money wasn't from my gambling!" Ingela's lip trembled. "I took it from Seth." Ingela was confused. She'd hustled people, especially sailors, out of stuff in poker games, but that was different. Whatever she'd picked up in those games, it was fair and square. After all, they'd tried to hustle her, too; she was just better at it. But she'd outright stolen this bag of coins when Seth was down, and they'd ended up being way more valuable than she'd imagined. In fact, Ingela had never stolen so much from one single person.

Sadie nodded. "I figured as much."

Ingela cocked her head. "You did? But you didn't say anything."

Sadie shrugged. The Storm always had such a definite line between right and wrong.

It was easy to know when you'd crossed it. But now, in this new life, it was getting harder to tell where that line was.

"Stealing is wrong. And you stole. Let's be honest. We *all* stole wallets and purses off of pretty innocent people more times than I care to remember. So is it wrong that you stole from a very bad man to help us?" Sadie shrugged her shoulders. "I don't know that it is. There's a new set of rules these days. I mean, we agreed to this mission because it might bring us a reward!" Sadie traced her finger along the package string. "That would never have happened back in the Storm days."

Ingela blinked her tears back. She felt some of the guilt go away. On the other hand, there was a new feeling that she didn't like. Sadie was the biggest goody-two-shoes out of all of them. If she didn't know what was right and wrong anymore, how was Ingela supposed to figure it out?

Charlie, Liu, and Raquel returned carrying what looked like a feast.

"You guys ready to chow down on some of this?" Raquel squealed excitedly. A half-hour watching the intricate preparation of the food had certainly convinced her that this was good enough for her "sophisticated" palette. She held out a steaming hot banana leaf filled with big chunks of tuna. "The man called it *mas riha*."

Sadie opened up her banana leaf and inhaled all the aromas. "Mmmmm … I definitely smell coconut and curry leaves. Did you know that the curry tree grows in—"

"Can we please skip the teaching lesson for today and just eat?" Charlie asked through a mouthful of food.

Ingela took a bite proportionate to a teenage boy. She was hungrier than she thought. Emotions did that to her. Sadie was right about the good and bad stuff being all mixed up. But she was wrong about the mission. Ingela didn't care about any rewards. She was doing this for the same reason Knut would have if he'd been here. They were Storm, and this was their duty.

***

"Shhh!" Liu looked around. "Do you hear something?"

The girls continued chitter-chattering as they boarded the junk.

"Guys!" Liu stepped in front of them. "Listen!" She pointed downstairs. It sounded like muffled voices. Liu strained to hear. Maybe male voices?

"¡Dios mío!" Raquel exclaimed. "Not again!"

"We shouldn't have all left together!" Sadie crossed her arms. "Someone should have stayed with the ship."

Charlie rolled her eyes. "Glad you mentioned that now."

"Seriously, shut up!" Ingela scolded.

They finally quieted down enough to all hear the faint sounds coming from below. It was hard to tell if they were indeed male voices, given how muted they were. They must have been whispering. "How many of them do you hear?" Sadie asked, dropping her packages in a pile with the rest of them. "I think there are about four."

Charlie drew her cutlass. "It's hard to tell from up here." She huddled them together. "There's no element of surprise if we go down those ladders."

Liu nodded. "We need to lure them up on deck."

"And then what?" Raquel asked, reaching down at her feet for the tiny dagger wrapped around her ankle. "We can't take out four men!"

"What's our plan?" Sadie whispered.

"How 'bout if we grab our weapons and stand around the doorway? We'll make noise and when they come up, we'll charge them," Ingela stated, as if it were the most natural thing in the world.

Liu lowered her voice to a hush. "Better if we make them think there's only two of us up here."

Charlie looked up. "No moonlight, but the stars are pretty bright. Let's get into position." She couldn't help the giddiness that was running through her. The adrenaline was already kicking in, and she was anxious but excited about what could be waiting for them. It was terrifying, yet it was that terror that made it so thrilling.

The girls took out their cutlasses and daggers. Though Sadie had been practicing with the bow and arrow since the last attack, she wasn't nearly ready to begin using it and opted for a knife instead. They tiptoed quietly to the doorway.

"That was really some party! I think the others will stay on the beach all night. Guess it's just the two of us for now." Charlie announced loudly, overemphasizing the word "two."

"You're a horrible actress!" Raquel hissed. "Let me handle this." She cleared her throat. "Yes, it is only the two of us, and I feel a terrible cold coming." She began with a light cough that became more and more violent as it continued. "A cold, Raquel! Not tuberculosis! Take it down a notch,"

Sadie derided.

Raquel took Sadie's direction and ended her performance with a diminuendo of spluttering fake coughs. Sadie nodded in approval. Raquel beamed like a stage star receiving a standing ovation.

Suddenly, there was a loud thunder of boots climbing up the bamboo ladders.

"Aaaargh!" Ingela shouted as she threw her body against the first one that flew out the doorway. To her surprise, he wasn't much bigger than her.

"Hey!" the second guy shouted. He tried to go toward his partner, but was quickly thwarted by Sadie and Raquel. The two girls pushed him to the ground, neither noticing that he didn't have a weapon.

"Stop!" the third man shouted before he reached the doorway. He waved a grimy, grayish handkerchief in the air. "Truce! Don't hurt us!" He laughed wildly.

All the girls froze. That chortle could only belong to one person.

"Axel!" Ingela shouted, releasing her innocent victim from a headlock. She ran to the tall figure in the doorway.

"Squirt!" he cried, lifting her up and wrapping his wiry arms around her. Anyone else attempting to bearhug Ingela would receive a swift kick in the gut, but Axel was given a reprieve from almost anything by his adoring little sister. "Glad that this is still your junk! Things could have gone very awry if some people came home to find a group of strange-looking dudes just sitting on their ship."

Raquel looked down to see smoldering dark eyes and a chiseled jawline. "Javier! *Buenas noches.*" She smiled, hoping there was no banana leaf stuck between her teeth.

"It is not a good evening with you sitting on me," Javier seethed through gritted teeth. He heaved Raquel off of him. Sadie, who was sitting on his legs, quickly jumped off. "*Idiotas!*" Javier yelled, as he brushed himself off. "Out of nowhere they start hitting, biting, spitting! And I don't even have a weap—"

"Now Javi, you better not be callin' my lil' sis an idiot!" A deep, low baritone threatened from the doorway.

The weight of her sword became too much as every muscle in Charlie's body quivered. She discreetly lowered the cutlass to her side.

"Taye!" Sadie shrieked so loudly that the sound might have carried halfway across the Indian Ocean. She ran into her brother's strong embrace.

Taye lifted Sadie off the ground and whirled her around, pretending not to see Charlie trembling in the corner. Charlie looked away. If Taye was going to avoid her, then she was happy to stay as far away from him as she could.

The Castaways were back. Again.

***

Charlie simmered in a corner. They always showed up just at the wrong time, she thought. Though deep down, she knew that wasn't true. She pulled at pieces of her beard, mortified that she was seeing Taye for the first time in six months while wearing facial hair. She stopped scraping the red fuzzies off her face, angry at herself for even caring about how she looked to Taye.

Axel had left the Storm at the tender age of fifteen to "do his own thing." He'd put together a merry band of misfits that raised havoc both on sea and land. Through the four years, the boys changed and the numbers varied, but the themes were the same. Sail hard, party hard, fight hard, and live hard.

Charlie chuckled to herself. This was a bit of an oversimplification, but basically Axel and his boys were the Robin Hoods of the sea. They didn't just steal from the rich and give to the poor. They bucked traditional systems in every way so they could help the "everyman." As a result, they'd managed to become beloved folk heroes throughout Europe and many parts of North America. They also found themselves constantly on the run from a government, lawmen, or a navy. However, much of the actual lawbreaking had calmed down a bit since Taye joined Axel and his gang two years ago.

Charlie surveyed the guys. Axel and Ingela were the children of Knut but had different mothers. It was hard to tell what Ingela would end up looking like since she was only 11, but she shared the same wide shoulders and tree trunk shape of her father. On the other hand, Axel was tall and strong like Knut, though his frame was sinewy. Both brother and sister had comically similar golden hair and pale blue eyes. But Ingela, with her plump cheeks and sunkissed locks, resembled a cherub, no matter how much she scowled. Whereas Axel, with his wiry frame and dirty-blond spiky hair, looked more like a junkyard dog fresh from a fight.

There had never been any big fanfare or drama about Axel leaving the Storm. It was clear that he marched to his own beat and Knut took it all in good stride. Though curiously, Charlie's pop was taken aback by his departure, as Axel, despite his troublemaker tendencies, had always been a favorite of Andrew's.

Not even a year after he left, Axel had fallen in with Javier. The two couldn't be more different in terms of looks and attitude, but they were obviously incredibly tight. The Storm was a secret, and ex-Storm were expected to keep it that way. But Javier would often accompany Axel on his visits to *Storm One*. Charlie always wondered if Javier knew anything about who they really were.

"Javi" wasn't easy to warm up to. He usually gave one-word answers and always seemed pissed off about something. Charlie realized that despite having met him on several occasions, she barely knew anything about him. Except that he was from South America, the same age as her, and seemed to hate everyone. She sighed. Though he was too pretty boy for her taste, with his dulce de leche color, muscular chest, and dark, curly locks, he was what Raquel called "caliente."

At the other end of Raquel's *caliente* scale was Jimmy. At a mere fifteen, Jimmy was the baby of the group. Granted, a loud, mischief-making baby who seemed to spend his entire life hustling or planning his next elaborate prank. He stood shoulder to shoulder with Ingela and had bright, ginger hair that one could spot oceans away. Charlie smiled.

With his big horse teeth and dorky laugh, there was something "little brotherish" about Jimmy. His past was vague too. Charlie had heard something about him running away from his home back in New York when he was only twelve. Axel found him hiding as a stowaway a couple of years ago.

The last member of the gang was Taye. Charlie yanked the rest of her beard off her face, convincing herself it was because it itched. The smell of fish clogged her nostrils. There was no way she was ever going to let Raquel use that putrid glue on her again. She stole a quick glance at Sadie's older brother.

It was funny to think of him that way. As Sadie's older brother. Axel's best friend. Josephine and Henry's only son. Taye was always just hers. At least until two years ago.

Charlie traced the pearl hanging from her neck, her mind suddenly a world away. Sadie had been four and Taye six years old when their parents brought them to live on *Storm One*. With Charlie being exactly five years old, she seemed to fit in with them perfectly. Charlie and Sadie had to share bunk beds from the start, and they fast became friends, although their arguments, which involved more hair-pulling and biting back then, were fierce.

But Taye and Charlie were inseparable. At first, it was purely based on competition. Charlie was the best swimmer, diver, and swordsman (with a blunt piece of wood) next to Axel out of all the kids under eight. Until Taye came around. He'd been born Storm, living on a ship in his native Caribbean prior to joining the elite *Storm One*. From the get-go, Taye started everything early and excelled—swimming, diving, and swordplay, to name a few. By the time Charlie and Axel met him, it was like he was already years ahead.

Prior to Taye, Charlie had never met anyone who was as good at being Storm as her. Axel was an awesome athlete and fighter, but his unruliness meant that he would never quite fit into the structured, rule-oriented Storm. But while Axel kicked ass, Taye was simply *badass*. It wasn't just his physicality, which was at times awe-inspiring. He had impeccable reflexes and a natural athleticism, which meant he could swim faster, dive deeper, and fight better, making the adult Storm members take notice of him when he was a child. It was also his mind. Charlie went from tracing the pearl to running her fingers along the chain it was attached to. Taye was sharp, strategic, and daring. In short, Taye was the perfect Storm. At first, all Charlie wanted to do was beat him. She often found herself throwing kicks and punches his way. Then all she wanted to do was be with him. She'd found someone who loved the Storm just as much as her, who wanted to be the best just like she did. That's why it was so crushing. Charlie could still feel the ache in the depths of her chest as she thought back to when Taye just quit the Storm three months before his seventeenth birthday and joined Axel's gang. No one, especially Taye's family, could make heads or tails out of his abrupt decision. They were devastated.

For Charlie, her world shattered. She was always fierce, strong, and stubbornly independent. Losing a boy wasn't going to change that. But it was like one half of her had suddenly died.

Charlie took a deep breath, inhaling as much of the salty air as she could in one big gulp. A wave of overwhelming sadness rushed over her. After he left, it was nearly a year before any of them saw Taye again. They knew he was with Axel's crew but he never joined Axel on his *Storm One* visits. Then one day Axel, Javier, Jimmy, and Taye came around.

Charlie spent most of that time trying to avoid Taye, and was thankful his stay was short. In fact, all the boys left just a mere week before the DD. An image of the faceless soldiers flashed through her mind. Charlie couldn't help but think that things would have turned out differently had Taye been there. She wondered if he felt the same way.

In those months after the jump from the ship on the DD, when things got so dire for the girls, Charlie looked, hoped, prayed for Taye to show up. She never said it out loud to anyone, even Sadie, who of course wanted the same thing. Then, one day, out of nowhere, he did.

The Castaways had been jailed for some kind of reckless stunt in Turkey, or maybe it was Greece, during the DD. Only when they were released a month later did they even hear about it. They searched desperately for survivors. Axel couldn't bear losing Knut, but the thought of Ingela dying made him frantic.

Then one day, Taye read an article about the Pirettes. From the very first Pirette story, Sadie had insisted on hiding subtle clues for Taye or Axel to find. To everyone's utter amazement—especially Charlie's—they did. The boys showed up when they'd gotten Zhang Tao's junk ship for the first time.

At first, Charlie had to admit, it was comforting to have them so close. Then after a full month of them tailing the junk, no matter how good their intentions, it was downright annoying to have them so close. Not just for Charlie, but for the rest of the girls, too, as the Castaways were acting a bit too overprotective. So, with some diplomacy from their dearest Embajador, Raquel, and tough love from Sadie, they were finally gone. Until three months later, when they returned. Then again two months after that.

In fact, Charlie thought as she watched the Castaways talk and laugh with the girls, had they really ever left? A mixture of grief and anger hit Charlie. Taye had. Years ago. And that was all that mattered.

Thousands of stars lit up the black sky, while a beautiful breeze rolled off the massive palms lining the beach around them. The junk swayed gently back and forth, like a mother rocking a cradle. It would have been a perfect night to join Ingela and sleep up here.

Charlie looked again at the Castaways laughing with the girls. It was going to be a long night. Taye was practically at the other end of the deck, but that didn't seem far enough. The fresh sea air had become suffocating. She desperately wanted to escape and got up to leave.

"We just followed the trail right to the Pirettes." Axel walked his two fingers up Sadie's arm. Then he swiftly removed them, looking to see if Taye had noticed. To his relief, Taye hadn't.

"Really?" Sadie clapped giddily. After the Shanghai fiasco, they'd made sure the Pirette stories appeared only *after* they'd left a town. But she'd still placed tiny clues in each one.

"You got the reference to the Iroquois' favorite ocean? The Indian Ocean. That led you right to us!" Sadie grinned from ear to ear. Axel lingered on Sadie's perfectly straight white teeth. "And may I say, Sadie, it was quite good reading." Axel took a sip of his ale. No one else was helping themselves to any drink, but he didn't see the harm in having a beer or two. "Poppycock! *This* is how we found you." Jimmy pointed to bright strawberry-red marks on both Axel and Javier's necks. "The Mermaids."

Ingela made loud retching noises at the mere mention of the name "Mermaids." The rest of the girls were a bit more subtle with their disapproval. Sadie threw a dose of stink eye, while Charlie pretended not to hear, and Liu crumpled her face in disgust. Embajador forgot her usual diplomacy and hurled an expletive Javier's way.

The Mermaids weren't actual mermaids, as in the legendary sea creatures with fish tails. It was the name that mariners called girls from the island of Mer. Every year, a new crop of heavily chaperoned Mermaids was sent out to sail the seven seas in search of husbands. In fact, there were so many fathers, uncles, and brothers on board to protect the Mermaids' honor that it was a testament to the girls' pure ambition that they managed to meet any new men at all. Still, those that succeeded in finding marriage were rewarded with a happy life in Mer. Those that didn't were shamed as old maids. Perhaps it was this pressure that made the Mermaids so jealous, vicious, and downright mean to other females.

Javier grinned proudly, while Axel turned as red as his love-bite. He thwacked Jimmy's arm away.

"So the Mermaids told you where we were?" Sadie's face fell. They'd briefly run into the snarky girls last week in the

176

Maldives. As the gossipmongers of the sea, the Mermaids could be bribed to give up any secret for a few shiny baubles. Or, it seemed, a few worthless kisses.

"No, Sadie! It was your stories, really!" Axel readjusted his shirt to cover his neck. "They led me right to you!"

Taye, who was only half-listening to the conversation up until this point, perked up. He didn't like all the attention Axel was giving to his baby sister. Or the way he was touching her hand. "Don't you mean they led *us*, Ax?" Taye said, lobbing a brown package at Axel.

Axel sprang his hands up in the air, catching the package before it nailed him in the face. "Chill! Was just trying to pay your sister a compliment." Still, Axel thought as he inhaled the smell of annatto oil wafting from Sadie's hair, he hadn't expected for Taye's geeky sister to grow up to be so … Axel decided it was better not to complete the thought. He turned his back on Sadie and instead focused his attention on Ingela, who was a safe distraction. "Wanna arm wrestle, Squirt?" Raquel ignored the arm-wrestling match to chastise the rest of the boys. "So you boys slummed it with the Mermaids." She turned her nose up in disgust, making sure to give Javier a big dose of stink eye as she spoke. "Then you thought it was a good idea to surprise us on our ship? We could have killed you!"

"Yeah, right!" Javier scoffed.

Raquel put her hands on her hips. "We had you pinned to the ground, Javier!"

Javier waved her away with his hairy arm. "Oh, please, I didn't even have my weapon!"

"Yeah! You fight like girls!" Jimmy balked.

"That's right, we do!" Liu barked. "And Javier, you were down. Weapon or not!"

"Not to mention that Ingela almost made you cry, Jimmy!" Sadie yelled.

Charlie, who looked like she was in the middle of a hasty exit, stopped. "You Castaways are nothing but a bunch of liars and cowards!" she blurted out, her words aimed directly at Taye.

Taye was startled. Not by Charlie's silent hate, which he'd almost become accustomed to these days, but because this was the first time she'd spoken to him all evening. He cleared his throat, "Um, what was that name you called us?"

"Liars. Cowards."

Taye suppressed a giggle. He'd always teased Charlie about the fold of skin that appeared between her eyes when she'd get angry. Even in the dim starlight, he could see it. He wished he could walk over and pinch it, just to make her laugh like he used to. Taye sighed. But those days—their days—were over. Now, all that was important was that Charlie would never know why. He shook his head. "No, the other name. Cast-somethings?" They didn't have an official name, or even a nickname, they used for their gang. Maybe it was time they did.

"Castaways!" Raquel exclaimed.

"What does it mean?" Taye asked, not really caring about the answer as he continued to look in Charlie's direction.

Charlie bristled, not wanting to look at Taye, but unable to take her eyes off him. For most of her life, she'd stared into his face every day, knowing it better than she knew her own. The tiny scar on his chin from the time Axel accidentally cut him when they were practicing sword fighting. The way his left iris was more rounded than his right. The patch of skin on his forehead that started to itch if he accidentally ate raw apples. Then, suddenly, without any warning or reason why, that face she'd loved so much disappeared. Now it was back. She glared at him from her dark corner. And now that face belonged to a stranger.

"Charlie? Charlie?"

Charlie was suddenly aware that Raquel was speaking to her. "Huh?"

"I was explaining that we started calling them Castaways because they don't belong to anything. I mean, you know, how they pride themselves on having no commitments. And no one wants them. Right? You were the one to come up with the nickname."

Charlie nodded her head absently. "Yeah, whatever."

Axel was the first to burst out laughing, but soon the rest of the guys joined him.

"Better than what most people call us," Jimmy chuckled.

"Gotta admit, it fits," Axel added.

"Especially the part about no one wanting you!" Ingela chimed in, thumping Axel on his arm.

Charlie couldn't stand another minute of all this cheerful camaraderie. Taye didn't deserve any of it. Suddenly the mas riha curry started doing flips in her belly, as though the fish had come back to life. When she finally got to the other side of the upper deck, she bent over the railing and vomited.

***

"Rogers Barrish." Axel pounded his fist on the table.

Sadie giggled. His tall, spiky hair seemed to grow even taller when he was irritated. It was cute in a cartoonish way.

Axel walked around the table, then paused. "So let's go over this again."

Taye let out a long, drawn-out sigh. "Axel, we've been over it enough already!" The thought of anyone trying to hurt the girls sent fire through his veins, but they'd rehashed the story multiple times since last night and no new insights had been gleaned.

Axel shielded his face from the sunlight. Though it was already close to 1 pm, he'd only rolled out of bed a half-hour ago. It had been a late night on *Holy Tide*. Judging from the pounding headache he was having, it had been a good night, too. Still, he wasn't going to let a little thing like a hangover dampen his spirits.

Axel broke out into his goofy, lopsided grin. "Humor me!"

"Okay," Liu began. "A few months ago, the Pirettes discovered a plan to plunder an American merchant ship."

"Maybe not discovered so much as stumbled upon," Sadie corrected.

"Whatever!" Charlie waved her hand. She ended up the hero in the story, but even she was sick of hearing it so many times. "The Pirettes found out—no *stumbled upon* a plan to plunder an American merchant ship. The Pirettes warned the Americans and they were grateful. Rogers Barrish was scared that the Pirettes knew his wicked little secret—"

"That he secretly raids ships that his company, Sapphire East Trading Company, insures and are supposed to be protecting," Sadie interrupted.

"Right," Charlie nodded, though she really didn't need Sadie's help in telling the story. "And he sent a couple of guys to get them out of the way before his next plunder."

Sadie butted in again. "It was a little more complicated than that. Charlie was really the one who got the message to the Americans, and that wasn't easy—"

"Who cares¿!" Ingela blurted out, cutting off Sadie mid-sentence. She didn't like discussions much as it was, but she'd puke if she had to hear the tale of Charlie's heroics again. "The point is that I got the bad guys to confess to Barrish's new plan, and now we're all going on a mission to stop him."

Sadie raised an eyebrow. "Seth confessed that Barrish was planning on sending a group of pirates to plunder the sultan's ships on his Hajj."

"So Sapphire East Trading Company insures these ships for tons of money. Then Rogers Barrish secretly plans pirate attacks on them so he can get all their booty. And he's actually the *head* of Sapphire East Trading Company?" Axel asked Sadie. He liked the way she looked with her hair up. He shook his head. Sadie wasn't just a girl, he reminded himself, she was his best friend's little sister.

"Snarky!" Jimmy chuckled in admiration. He never faulted anyone for trying to make a buck, honest or otherwise. "Hey, why do you girls always talk about the Pirettes like they're other people? I mean, aren't you girls the Pirettes?"

"Yes."

"Sort of."

"I think so."

"It's complicated."

The girls looked at each other, puzzled. Jimmy furrowed his reddish-orange eyebrows.

Taye put a hand up. "Okay, let's not complicate this further with philosophical ponderings about the Pirettes." He looked around the table, carefully avoiding Charlie's permanent stink eye. "Let's stay on topic, which is this mission."

Charlie bristled from head to toe. After she'd left them last night, the girls, or should she say Liu, had the bright idea of telling the Castaways about the mission with the sultan. Actually—Charlie's face grew hot—not only had Liu told them their plan, but the rest of the girls thought it would be a great idea for the Castaways to join them, reasoning that they could use the extra ship and people. When they'd filled Charlie in on the latest developments this morning, she'd had to stop herself from drawing her cutlass on all of them.

Now that she'd had several hours to get used to the idea, she still felt like lopping their heads off. Yes, of course it made good sense to team up with the Castaways, especially on a mission as dangerous as this. Charlie clenched her fist so tightly her knuckles hurt. The idea of accepting help—accepting *anything*—from Taye infuriated her. And she certainly wouldn't give him the satisfaction of seeing how pissed off she was about it. So she swallowed her rage and pretended like the idea was a great one. Or at least *tried* to pretend.

"Right," Liu responded. "The sultan sends a special fleet for Hajj every year. And Hajj is the Muslim pilgrimage to Mecca that takes place at the end of the year. Right, Sadie?" Liu stopped. "Aren't I right? That Hajj takes place at the end of the year?"

Sadie shook her head. "Yup. The meaning behind Hajj—" "Ladies!" Javier bit his knuckle. It was impossible to spend more than fifteen minutes with these girls and not want to throw one of them overboard. But he knew he had to play nice for Taye and Axel's sake. "Stay on topic, *por favor*!" He forced a smile.

Liu tried to ignore the look Javier was giving her and continued. "So Hajj takes place at the end of the year. But the Islamic calendar is a lunar calendar, so the year is about eleven-to-twelve days shorter than our solar calendar. So Sadie figured out that this year, Hajj will be around November 25 to 27th."

The group nodded back, though only a few of them actually understood the part about lunar and solar calendars. "Eid, which is a major feast, takes place at the end of Hajj. Again, Sadie figured out that Eid will be between November 27 to 29th." Mostly blank faces stared back at Liu decided it was best to simplify everything. "We need to warn the sultan's daughter about the pirate attack before she begins her return journey."

"From Mecca?" Axel closed his eyes, trying to remember. "No! In Jeddah. Because Jeddah is the closest port to Mecca, and that's where her ship will be. Right?"

"Right, Axel!" Sadie cheered. Axel smiled.

Taye rolled his eyes. "You're going upwind." He looked down at the meticulously detailed sea chart that Liu had created. "Against monsoon winds, so that's going to slow you down a bit. But it should take about twenty days." He unrolled a long piece of parchment paper, holding it open on one side, while Sadie held the other. All the months and dates had been printed on the same sheet, making the type very small and hard to read. Taye leaned in toward the calendar. "If everything is really ready and you take off the day after tomorrow as planned."

"The junk isn't going to be slowed down. It specializes in sailing upwind." Charlie made sure to point her comment away from Taye, but plastered a cheery smile on her face as she said it.

"Right," Taye responded, keeping his eyes down on the calendar. *Holy Tide* is just a regular sloop," he explained sarcastically while bringing up the Castaway's powerful ship. "She hasn't mastered upwind like the all-superior junk rig."

"Well, don't expect the junk to slow down just because *Holy Tide* can't keep up!" Charlie focused her eyes straight ahead at the bamboo wall.

"Okay! Thanks for that friendly bit of team spirit, Charlie. I think you've made your point that *Holy Tide* better haul ass. Now, can we move on, Prickles?" Axel couldn't resist giving the jab.

The entire group cracked up. Even Charlie broke out in laughter. Sadie wiped a tear from her eye. She admired the way Axel could always lighten a tense situation. "Okay, so are we all in this together? We've got a lot of work to do if we want to set sail in two days."

"It's just that this one thing keeps bothering me." Javier chewed on the tip of his finger, deep in thought. "How do we know this information that Seth gave you is reliable? I mean, what if it's a trap set by Rogers Barrish?"

"Given the circumstances, I don't think Seth lied," Liu said, thinking back to Charlie and her sword-slicing.

Axel looked at Taye. They were both thinking the same thing. They didn't really have a choice. The girls were determined to do this.

Suicide mission or not, they were all in this together. "Okay, we're in!" Axel announced.

"Yup," Taye nodded, tapping his fingers against the ship rail. "We're in."

The rest of the girls cheered, while Charlie's heart dropped to the bottom of the sea.

Chapter
NINE

SLOG
Date: November 14, 15, or 16 (Liu knows)
Position: Still in Malé

Dear Stolen Ship,

Are you really ready for this? Because I don't know if I am. Tomorrow we set sail. We have to end up somewhere called Jeddah. Liu knows.

You're going to have to go superfast and do stuff you're not used to. That we're not used to. Luckily, we have the Castaways with us. Not lucky like we can't do anything without boys. But lucky because the more people there are, the less likely we're gonna end up dead. That's a real possibility, Stolen Ship. Dead. I thought of Papa all night and prayed extra this morning. But it doesn't feel like enough right now.

On a slightly different note, Charlie's furious. She's not acting angry. In fact, she's making a point of being really nice and cheerful, which is creepy in its own way. But inside, you can tell something is really pissing her off. (Am I allowed to write that in the official slog?)

Buen viaje, Ship!
Kisses,

Raquel 💗

Rogers Barrish raced down the corridor, sweat trickling from his brow. When he reached his office, he slammed the heavy mahogany door and poured himself a stiff glass of single malt scotch. He drained it, then poured himself another.

Had he actually just lied to the Countess? Barrish was accustomed to lying. In fact, it came so easily that he hardly thought of his untruths as anything but "necessities." While he and the Countess certainly weren't in the habit of sharing everything, he'd never straight-out lied to her.

He paced back and forth, aware his military boots were wearing out the precious silk threads of the Turkish rug he'd received as a gift from the emperor upon the signing of the Treaty of Küçük Kaynarca. A miserable man with surprisingly good taste.

Normally, Barrish forbade anyone from entering his office wearing shoes (except himself, of course). This wasn't only because of the rug, which he generally didn't allow anyone to walk on anyway. He also found that people were more vulnerable with their feet exposed.

Barrish plopped down on the aged leather sofa, replaying the events of the last ten minutes in his head. She'd brought up the Pirettes. No, no. Actually, she'd commended him. Yes, that was it. The cold, wretched woman had actually paid him a compliment! That's what threw him off. He didn't know how to react other than to lie.

She'd been pleased to see no Pirette stories in the papers of late. He told her that, rest assured, there wouldn't be any in the near future.

Barrish took another unsteady swill. He hadn't actually heard from Len yet, but he assumed that everything had been taken care of, and that the Pirettes were, in fact, out of the way.

So maybe he hadn't actually lied to her. He'd just been prematurely optimistic. Yes, that's how he would frame it if it ever came back. Everyone needed a dose of optimism. Especially her.

***

"So you think it should take two months to reach Europe?" Sadie asked. There were still so many errands to run before they left Malé. She was already late getting back to the ship, but Sadie wanted to be as careful as possible about ensuring the latest set of Pirette articles wouldn't reach their intended destinations before the girls did. It had taken Charlie a long time to forget the disaster at the Shanghai market, and Sadie wasn't planning on allowing any more mishaps like that to happen. She handed the stack of letters to the postal worker behind the desk. "You're sure it's two months?"

The man nodded sternly. She was going on and on in words that he didn't understand. Yet she smiled as though they were speaking the same language. Maldivians were known for their politeness, and he didn't want to be rude and tell her that he didn't understand the never-ending stream of gibberish coming out of her mouth.

This girl's incessant questions were making him late for his dinner. His wife had prepared dhon riha with the fresh mangoes he'd picked yesterday. They would be so juicy and ripe now. In fact, if the girl's enormous hairdo wasn't in the way, he'd have a bird's-eye view of his wife stirring the pot of fish.

But here he was, letting the girl just go on and on, while his dhon riha got cold, nodding his head every time it seemed she wanted an answer. He didn't know what he was saying "yes" to, and quite frankly, he didn't care. It seemed that the more he nodded, the more she smiled. Which might mean that she would leave soon, and he could finally close the office for lunch.

He looked at his pocket watch. Her mouth just kept going and going and going.

"Okay then, thank you!" Sadie collected her change. She was utterly surprised to find someone at the local post office who understood English. Still, she thought she should try speaking his language, and said the one word she knew in Maldivian. "I mean, *shukuriyaa*," she smiled, remembering that was the way to say "thank you."

The man ignored her and collected his things. The problem with having a wife who cooked so well at a home directly across from where he worked was that between the hours of 9am to 1pm, he was easily distracted with thoughts of his lunch.

Earlier in the morning, he'd noticed his wife setting the dhonkeyo kajuru on the window to cool. There was nothing like a slice of fried banana cake after a hearty meal. He smacked his lips. Maybe two slices. The man threw the girl's letters in the express mailbag and hurried out of the post office.

***

Both Axel and Taye stormed onto the junk ship to find the girls taking a late-afternoon break. The girls were relaxing out on the deck. The sun blared down on them while the hot, sticky air cast a lull.

"Hi!" Sadie called out.

"The Blood and Bone Brothers!" Axel shouted, unable to keep it in any longer. Beads of sweat formed along his hairline.

The girls were jarred awake.

"What?" Ingela asked, scowling either because of the bright sun, or just because.

"What about the Blood and Bone Brothers?" Liu asked, sitting up. She pulled the wide-brimmed hat down over her face, trying to shield her face from sunburn.

"They're the pirates that Rogers Barrish hired to plunder the sultan's ship!"

"What?!" Sadie's mouth dropped open. "How do you know?"

"Intel," Axel responded without giving any other information.

Sadie discreetly studied Axel's neck to see if "intel" meant sucking face with the Mermaids again.

Axel noticed and shook his head. "No, not gossip from the Mermaids. I know some people here in Malé . Word on the street is that Rogers Barrish hired the Blood and Bone Brothers."

Charlie sat against the wall, feeling the butterflies explode inside her. Axel had lots of contacts in the highest and lowest areas of life. Most were pretty solid, which was why he always seemed to know things no one else did. If it was true that the Blood and Bone Brothers were Barrish's hire—which it most likely was—this mission was *screwed*.

There had been so many stories about Clive and Gunnar Vaughn, and their reputations had reached such mythic proportions, that it was hard to know which were true and which were just sea tales. Their savageness was even known on land, as newspapers frequently published sketches of the mangled corpses they left behind. No one could really say where they came from, or if Clive and Gunnar were actually their names. For the most part, they were called Brother Blood and Brother Bone. Brother Blood liked to make deep, painful incisions until you slowly bled to death, while Brother Bone crushed your bones one by one.

Most of their slaughter was done on the sea. They weren't really pirates though; more like murderers on a ship. Their method was to seize a crew, hold it hostage, and exact their torture one member at a time.

Charlie rubbed her belly, trying to soothe the growing nausea. The thought of being in the hands of the Blood and Bone Brothers was absolutely horrifying. But the thought of going to jail or worse once Zhang Tao caught them was just as bad.

Axel cleared his throat. He knew they didn't want to hear it, but someone had to say it. "We can't go through with this mission. We need to call it off."

The hot sun bore down on them from above, giving them no reprieve. Now they were all sweating as they sat in silence.

"We can't," Liu said, barely able to speak past the growing lump in her throat.

"Why?" Taye asked. "Is this about the Storm? Or does it have something to do with the DD?" He was determined to find out just why this mission was so important to them. He'd even left Jimmy and Javier back on *Holy Tide* so the girls could speak freely.

The girls collectively shook their heads, except Ingela. "It's always about the Storm."

"What do you mean?" Taye asked quizzically. "I mean, it's our duty."

"We can't gill," Sadie responded, avoiding eye contact with Charlie. She used "we" so as not to single Charlie out, but she knew the girl would still be pissed.

Taye whipped around. "Lirium?" He sat down, carefully selecting a spot far away from Charlie. Just his mere presence seemed to make her sick these days. Though it seemed this conversation, mixed with the clingy air, was creating a kind of nausea cloud over all of them. "You're doing this because you can't find lirium?" Taye asked, not sure how that made any sense.

"No, we're doing this because we can't gill," Sadie clarified, once again emphasizing the word "we."

"Gilling isn't that hard," Axel said as he continued to pace. He'd calmed enough to sit down and chose a spot next to Sadie. He flapped his loose shirt to cool him down, unaware of the musky stench that was coming off of him. "We can teach you how to gill."

Sadie discreetly turned away. Apparently hygiene wasn't a priority for either of Knut's kids. "How do you know how to gill? You left the Storm when you were fifteen."

"Yeah," Charlie followed. "Storm rules were specific in that no one learned how to gill until they were sixteen."

Axel shrugged his shoulders. He'd always thought all of the Storm's rules and procedures were a joke. "We've been gilling since we were fourteen." Axel looked over at Taye.

"You too, Taye? You gilled for over two years?" Charlie asked Taye, temporary lifting her ban to not make eye contact with him.

"Yeah, something like that," he answered, trying to blow off the question. He'd dreaded this moment and needed to make it stop.

Charlie shook her head, incredulous. Why had he kept that a secret from her? And what else was he hiding?

"Seriously, guys, if you've got a good teacher, gilling is easy," Axel explained. "Charlie's dad taught us, and he was the best."

"What?" Raquel asked, feeling a tingle in her neck. "What?" Charlie shouted, raising her right eyebrow so high it almost disappeared into her hairline.

Taye wanted to clock Axel, or at least gag him. He had to manage this before it went somewhere none of them wanted it to. "Chill, Charlie," he flipped his hand. "It's history. Get over it." Taye felt his insides shrivel. He didn't have to look at her to know what he'd done. But he had to think fast, and being a jerk was usually the most effective way, even if it did earn him another year of silent treatment.

"This isn't about gilling or lirium," Liu said firmly. "Then what is about, Liu?" Taye asked. "I mean, will someone please tell us why you guys would even consider going on this mission now that you know the Blood and Bone Brothers are involved?" Taye was brave, but he wasn't stupid. He didn't want to end up anyone's lunchmeat.

Sadie shook her head behind Taye. She couldn't bear to let her big brother know what they had done.

Charlie saw Sadie shaking her head furiously, but decided she'd ignore it. After all, even if Sadie hadn't identified who exactly couldn't gill, she'd still spilled Charlie's secret. Plus, she was furious at Taye for telling her to "get over it." It would be worth it just to see the look on his face. "We stole this ship from Liu's dad."

All the hot, sticky air circulating about was sucked right out with Charlie's admission, leaving them all feeling suffocated.

"What?" Axel and Taye both said. For a few seconds, neither of them could find words, until Axel finally spoke up. "I thought Zhang Tao *gave* you the ship."

Liu sighed. Might as well get the whole sordid story out now. "Only for six months. Then, when I returned to 'renew' our lease, Daddy Dearest said the girls could keep the ship forever. But I'd have to stay and get married."

"No way were we ever going to let that happen," Raquel said, putting her hand on Liu's. "So we escaped with Zhang Tao's junk."

Taye sighed. He'd never in a million years think his nerdy little sister was capable of stealing a ship. Nor that she'd be so dumb about it. "Is your dad a forgiving type of guy, Liu?"

"What do you think?" Liu responded.

Taye nodded. "Exactly. So you guys stole a ship from a guy who wants revenge."

Charlie rolled her eyes. "Oh, get over it. It's not like the Castaways don't know a thing or two about stealing ships." "Which is exactly why we know that you're not supposed to steal ships from people who can find you!" Axel yelled, jumping up again. The heat was making his blood boil. Or maybe it was the frustration of finding out such smart girls could be so stupid.

"We didn't have a choice!" Ingela screamed. She hated looking dumb in front of her big bro. "He was going to take Liu away, and we couldn't lose our ship and—"

"Okay, we need to take this down a notch," said Sadie, putting her hand on Ingela's shoulder to calm her. To her surprise, Ingela didn't swat her hand away. "Yes, we stole a ship. Zhang Tao will probably find us. And we were stupid. Now what?"

Taye sighed. "When did you steal it?"

"Almost two months ago," Raquel said. "And we haven't gotten caught yet." Axel stopped pacing and looked down at Raquel. "You will."

"Then you know that we have no choice." All the girls turned to look at Charlie. She was right. The Blood and Bone Brothers or Zhang Tao.

"We have to do this," Liu said. The choice was clear for her. "Telling the princess and the sultan about the planned raid will save the gold treasure. Saving that gold treasure gives us a very good chance of getting a reward from the sultan, which would allow us to buy our own ship. Then we can give this one back to Zhang Tao." Ingela nodded her head.

"And once we can stop worrying about Zhang Tao, then we can go back to focusing on the most important thing—finding out who or what was behind DD," Raquel added. She looked at each girl, eagerly hoping to get reassurance that this was still their shared goal.

"Of course, Raquel. Without a ship of our own, there's not much we can do for ourselves or our murdered parents," Sadie responded. She turned to her brother. "With or without you, we're in."

Taye and Axel looked at each other. This was family. They didn't have a choice either. Taye nodded.

Axel tried to erase the terrifying images of the Blood and Bone Brothers massacres that were running through his mind. "We're in, too."

***

For the last minute, Liu had been watching Raquel twirl and kick with two daggers in her hand. She was doing panchi, but the way she glided across the deck was really more like a beautifully choreographed dance.

"Raquel?" Liu asked, standing on the main deck in her pajamas. The hot day had led to a sticky night without much in the way of sleep. The fact that their mission started the next day didn't help either.

Raquel jumped, nearly dropping a dagger. She turned around. "Don't you know you shouldn't surprise people holding knives?" The bright moonlight splashed across them.

"Don't you know it's weird to be dancing with daggers in the middle of the night?" Liu shrugged. "Seriously, Raquel, what's this all about?"

Raquel tucked the knife next to her hip. "I don't know. I couldn't sleep, was all."

Liu cocked her head. Was she really going to play her? It was true that Raquel had a way with people, but Liu wasn't a dummy either. Especially when it came to her "twin."

Liu had willingly fled with Mai on *Storm One*, but she'd never been good with change, then or now. The rest of the girls had been friendly enough to her, except Ingela, who was then in her "terrible twos" and was going through a painful biting stage as well. Apart from Liu, they'd all grown up on the sea. In Liu's six-year-old eyes, the other girls were masters, expertly maneuvering their way in, on, and around the water. Sometimes, Charlie even shared the helm with her dad. Meanwhile, Liu's water experience until that point had been swimming in the local lake and an occasional Sunday afternoon boat ride.

Mai, who'd lived on a Storm ship from her first waking moments on earth, had deliberately kept her daughter away from the water, more for her own protection than Liu's. She'd never accepted the landlocked life her arranged marriage had forced her into and was perpetually afraid that any prolonged contact with the sea would tempt her into abandoning her husband, and maybe even her child.

To make matters worse, Liu suffered from debilitating seasickness. During those first few weeks on *Storm One*, she saw more of the infirmary than anywhere else on the vast vessel. She spent days and nights isolated from the other kids, who were becoming better sailors, soldiers, and swimmers, while Liu disintegrated into a hopeless, pukey mess. Then there was the fear. Liu had been so afraid of the sea. It was huge, monstrous, untamable—Liu was sure it would swallow her whole at any moment.

It was during one of her nights in the infirmary that Raquel, the Spanish girl with the eyes that danced even when she was sad, snuck into her room. She'd explained it was to escape her mother, who was having one of her "fits." After spending a brief time hospitalized for her dark days during her youth, Rafaella abhorred anything associated with medicine and fastidiously avoided the infirmary wing of *Storm One*. That's why Raquel often escaped there, sometimes spending entire nights alone in the darkness. Hugo, who'd been too preoccupied assuaging his wife's rage to tend to his daughter, would then wait until the liquid opium he gave Rafaella took effect before retrieving Raquel from her hiding spot and bringing her back home.

From the beginning, the two girls talked about everything. It was strange for Liu, who found she didn't have much in common with two-legged creatures, and therefore preferred animals. It wasn't just about talking to someone, though. Sadie was always talking to Liu about something or the other. It was the *way* Raquel and Liu talked. At first it was about regular stuff; favorite colors, favorite animals, life on land, life on sea. Then it turned into something else. Mai had been teaching Liu English from early on, but her language was broken then. And yet, she found herself able to express herself to Raquel like she'd never been able to, even in her native tongue with Mai. They talked about why Liu hated her father and why Raquel feared her mother. How Liu was scared, and so was Raquel. They talked so much in those first few weeks that they stopped needing words.

Though Liu still suffered from seasickness worse than the rest of the girls, after about a month-and-a-half on *Storm One*, she'd finally been well enough to join the other kids. It was Raquel's hand she held the first time she dove into the sea. When she popped back up to the surface seconds later, she found Raquel hadn't let go. Soon enough, with Raquel by her side, Liu's fear turned into excitement and exhilaration. Her strong running legs became expert swimming legs. The faster and deeper she swam, the more new creatures she met: dolphins, otters, eels, and so many more. With Raquel, a whole new fascinating and limitless world had opened up. Even more than Mai, Raquel had given Liu her life.

Liu guessed you could call them twins, but it was more like they were reverse twins. Instead of starting from one egg, then splitting into two, they were two that became one.

Liu looked past Raquel to the ocean. Slivers of moonlight sprang along its dark waves. These days, the endless sea was beauty, strength, love; it was Mai. Raquel had helped her see that, by always being there for Liu. She'd been ignoring Raquel's pain for a while now, too wrapped up in her own stuff to deal with anyone else's. But when Raquel suffered, so did Liu. It was time to get to the bottom of all of this night-time dagger-dancing. "I know this has been happening for a while. I just figured you'd tell me when you were ready." She yawned. "But it's time to come clean. What's all this late-night panchi practice about?"

Raquel watched the sea. It was calm and lifeless tonight. Besides the Castaways ship, it was like there was no one else alive but them. That's how it felt after DD, too. There was no point in lying to Liu. She had to come clean.

"Revenge." "What?"

Raquel pulled out the dagger hidden in the waist of her skirt. "I want revenge for Papa."

Liu shook her head. "We *all* lost our parents that day. We all want revenge."

Raquel stopped what she was doing and looked Liu directly in the eyes. "No." She shook her head. "Some of you want justice. Some of you want peace. Some of you want truth." Raquel squeezed the handle of the dagger she was holding. "I want blood. I want to take this blade and stick it into the heart of the man who murdered my papa."

Liu sat down. The same steely hate she'd seen on Liang's face was now on Raquel's. Liu shivered, remembering the darkness that was inside Liang. It rotted and festered in him. Would Raquel's hate do the same to her?

They locked eyes. The green speckles in Raquel's eyes danced somberly but with determination. Liu was wary of Raquel's vengeance, but she understood it. She even wondered why she didn't feel that kind of wrath for the person who killed Mai.

"Okay, I get it. Kind of. This mission is all about our dads." Raquel cocked her head. "What?"

Liu made a place for Raquel to sit next to her. "I mean, you're doing this to avenge Hugo. And I'm doing this to save myself from Zhang Tao."

"What I don't get is why Zhang Tao even gave you the ship in the first place if his plan was just to trap you into a marriage? I mean, he could have just given the same ultimatum the first time we asked."

Thoughts about Zhang Tao, the bamboo cane, and his wicked games had been whirling around endlessly through Liu's head as well. She smiled. It seemed that no matter how much time she spent analyzing, the reasons behind her father's madness remained vague. "I'm not quite an expert on Zhang Tao's tactics and techniques of manipulation, but I have been subject to them for many years," Liu said. "That whole thing with lending us the junk is pretty standard Zhang Tao. He does you a favor, makes you drop your guard, ensures you're indebted to him, and then *pow*!" Liu punched the air. "Just when you're vulnerable and have no other option, he goes for the kill. Or in my case, the arranged-marriage thing. I was stupid for trusting him in the first place."

Raquel listened but didn't say anything. She couldn't imagine having to run away from your own father. Hugo was a fool when it came to Rafaella, but he'd loved Raquel with an honesty that poor Liu would never understand, thanks to Zhang Tao. She felt an ache deep inside her. *Her* mission would end with bloodshed. An eye for an eye. A heart for a heart.

Liu waited for Raquel to emerge from her thoughts before speaking again. "Do you realize that we could die on this quest? Die for our dads? I mean, I'm talking pirates, treasures, cannons, guns, monsoons, warships, enemy waters—real stuff." Liu had factored in all of these dangers when making her plan, but it wasn't until this very moment that she realized how tangible they were.

Raquel nodded slowly. It was hitting her, too. The two girls stopped talking. They didn't need words. Instead, they sat quietly in the thick night air, arm in arm, both imagining what that lay ahead. There was no going back. Liu locked hands with Raquel. Together, they would move forward.

***

The next morning, the girls kept their fear at bay by focusing on the tasks that needed to get done.

Ingela slid down the mast. Each batten had been raised. Charlie nodded in approval. The battens were trimmed as tightly as possible so that they could sail close to the wind. Without, hopefully, entering the "no go" zone.

Ingela ran and grabbed the helm. Charlie, Raquel, Liu, and Sadie followed. They would all need to help steer the junk out of the port.

"Fair winds," Sadie began.

"And following seas," Ingela finished.

The girls looked toward the horizon, each lost in her own thoughts, hopes, and fears about what lay ahead.

Slowly, their ship sailed forward.

Chapter
TEN

SLOG
Date: November 22
Position: Middle of the Indian Ocean (11.2847° N, 49.1825° E)

According to my reading, we're currently sailing on the third largest ocean in the world. The Indian Ocean makes up 20% of the Earth's water and has year-long warm temperatures that make it susceptible to monsoons, tsunamis, cyclones, and strong winds. Sometimes I wish I didn't read so much.

When we were on the Indian Ocean before, it didn't bother me. Now, as we speed along, sometimes even going up to 12 knots, I'm frighteningly aware of everything that's out here.

With each smooth sail, I get happier. We all do. We started this mission over a week ago in a bummed mood. However, now that we're almost a third of the way through it (we'll reach Jeddah in about 12 days), we're startin' to feel good. Knock on wood. No, don't even knock on wood. I don't want to jinx anything.

Quick update: I think I've given up on archery. It's too hard. Turns out I like books about bows and arrows more than the real thing. Maybe I can become a poison expert. SOFN,

Sadie

Liu stirred the ground lime into the tung oil and added the cut-up pieces of hemp fishing net. The sharp, pungent smell of the oil filled her nostrils. She pinched her nose with one hand as she whipped the mixture with the other.

This was the caulking mixture that had been used to waterproof junks for centuries. Liu had to hand it to her people—they really knew how to protect a ship against flooding. The lower part of the vessel was built as three separate decks, with planking edge nailed on a diagonal. Then limber holes were placed on the bulkheads so that water drained to the lowest level. This way, one could pump the water out easily without having to worry about flooding the other decks. Kind of ingenious, Liu thought, as she scraped the caulking mixture in between the planks.

Still, there were thousands of these planks all over the junk. Water was bound to seep through somewhere. As an extra measure of precaution, she'd spent the last two days applying caulking. It took about eighteen hours to set, which meant that the bilge deck was probably already dry. She'd go and check after she was done up here. Liu blew her nose into a dirty rag. The scent lessened as it dried, but when it was still wet like this, it was pretty potent. Though anyone who'd eaten Sadie's cooking knew that there were much worse stenches in the world.

She heaped the mixture onto her spatula, scraping the excess on the side of her bucket. Liu imagined she heard the trill of a dolphin's whistle, followed by clicking noises. *Wait.* She dropped the spatula back in the bucket and ran over to the row of portholes on the other side of the deck.

Liu pressed her face against the glass but couldn't see anything. She moved to the next porthole, but it was too small to give her a good view. Then she heard a low moan that sounded like a creaking door. She wasn't imagining anything. That was unmistakably a dolphin. Or more likely, a pod of dolphins.

Hurriedly, she climbed up the two sets of ladders until she was on deck.

"Whoa!" Sadie shot her hands out, narrowly avoiding a collision with Liu. "What's the hurry, speed demon?"

Liu didn't respond, and instead pulled Sadie by the arm. "Liu, I gotta go downstairs and—"

"There! Do you see that?" Liu pointed to a spot a few meters in front of them.

"Aaawww!" Sadie's whole face lit up. "Dolphins!" They were so close she could almost touch them. She thought she saw at least three of them frolicking back and forth with one another. One jumped in the air doing a full somersault, while the other nudged the third. "I think she's trying to get the other one to chase her!" Sadie said, pointing to the dolphin in the middle. "I didn't know they did that!" It had never come up in any of her books. The third dolphin took off after the second. "Oh, look at them go!"

Liu ignored everything Sadie was saying. "Bottleneck dolphins."

"Okay, if you want to be specific. You're the animal expert—"

"No, they're not supposed to be here." Liu shook her head. "Something's wrong."

***

"So you're saying that just because you saw some dolphins, I made a mistake?" Javier shouted.

"I'm trying to tell you that probably because of the high speeds that we're going, we've veered off course." For the last twenty minutes, Liu had tried to convince Javier of what she was saying. But he couldn't seem to get past his massive ego to even listen.

"But everywhere you look there's a dolphin!" Jimmy started doing a jig, which made his shaggy red hair swing from side to side. "Dolphin here, dolphin there. Dolphin everywhere!"

Sadie pretended he wasn't there, and Liu counted to five before speaking. "Yes, but they aren't all alike. The dolphins that hang out around the Indian Ocean and the Red Sea, where we're supposed to be heading, are smaller, with gray spots on their bellies." She waited a moment, hoping her information sank in this time. "The dolphins we saw were a lot bigger and are found more south than where we're supposed to be."

Javier slammed the heavy almanac shut. Since he was a child, he'd learned about maps, charts, and compasses from his uncle. Together, they would locate the North Star and calculate the distances for longitude and latitude. "I use science to navigate! Not some kind of crazy animal logic!"

Javier turned to Axel and Taye. "Are you going to listen to me over this dolphin psychic?"

"Can you just put your ego aside long enough to hear me? I didn't say the dolphins spoke to me, you idiot! I said the dolphin's lack of spots indicated it was the wrong kind of species—"

"Chill." Sadie put her arm around Liu. "There are enough hotheads in this room already, and we're not getting anywhere."

"Sadie's right. Let's just calm down and think this out." Axel turned to Liu. "We've read the compasses, checked the maps, and everything shows that we're going in the right direction."

Liu suppressed a sigh. Contrary to what Javier claimed, navigation was not a science. Liu's mother had probably been the best cartographer out there. She'd taught Liu everything she knew about currents, winds, speeds, and even dead reckoning. But the most valuable lesson she'd passed on to her only daughter was that, in the end, none of this stuff was as reliable as instinct. Liu couldn't place it, but she knew, deep down in her gut, that something wasn't right.

Taye looked down at the map. "Do you know how far off we could be, Liu?"

She shook her head. "No."

Javier gestured wildly. "Then how can we correct our course?"

"I-I have to study the map! When I saw the dolphins I came running!" Liu gulped. "I haven't had time to figure it out yet."

Javier really wished he could throw each and every one of these girls overboard. "So then this is all really based on dolphins. Loca. Garotas estúpidas!"

It was good that Raquel wasn't there to translate Javier's rant, or she would have most likely ripped out every strand of his prized shoulder-length hair.

"Cool it, Javi!" His shipmate's arrogance quickly tired Taye. "Liu was reading sextants before she was out of diapers. And her mother was the best navigator I've ever known."

Javier lifted his brow.

Taye nodded. "Yes, even better than you." He turned to face Liu. "How long will it take you to figure out our correction?"

Javier started to protest, but Taye quickly silenced him. "That is, if we even need a correction."

"A day, day-and-a-half. I'll get started now."

"Okay, see what you can find out and come back to us. Sadie, can you help Liu? So she can get it done faster." He surveyed the rest of them. When Charlie wasn't present, making eye contact with the group was easy. "If Liu's theory is right and we need to change something, then we'll do it." Everyone nodded except for Javier, who skulked away.

***

"I can't get this!" Liu shouted, slamming the book shut.

Sadie rubbed her eyes. They'd been working on finding the correction for the past few hours, and neither of them had been able to do it. Something wasn't working. "I don't get it either. And we actually have full maps this time."

Holy Tide, the Castaways' ship, was stocked with all sorts of detailed maps and reference books. Sticky fingers seemed to run in the Ingela-Axel family. But at least the boys were generous with sharing their goodies.

Suddenly, the ink pot tipped over, dripping ink down the long wooden table. Maps and charts followed, sliding to the ground. The ship jerked to one side.

"What the hell?" Sadie yelled.

Before Liu could respond, the maps, charts, and spilled ink slid to the other side, as the ship jerked in the opposite direction.

"All hands on deck! All hands on deck!" They heard either Charlie, Ingela, or both of them shout from above.

"We'd better go!" Sadie said to Liu, and they both shot up. The two girls rushed to the ladders. Liu jumped up first.

She made it up two rungs before another jerk yanked her back and she toppled onto Sadie.

"Are you okay?"

Sadie got up, then fell back down again. "I can't get any balance!"

Liu tried to stand up but the ship took a hard left. Books and papers came flying at them. Both girls stayed low. "We need to crawl!"

They got down on all fours and made their way to the ladders, avoiding being hit by enough books to make a library. Sadie hoisted Liu up.

"Here, take my hand!" Liu called, but a hard right sent Sadie crashing to the ground again.

Liu held on tight to the ladder. After a few seconds, Sadie managed to stand up. Liu turned and reached her arm out again. This time Sadie caught it, and they both managed to get on the ladder. Carefully they climbed up.

"What the hell?" Liu asked as she reached the main deck. The sky was black except for an angry swirl of clouds directly above. A frenzy of wet winds whistled around them. Liu's stomach dropped. Yesterday, Javier had been right. They hadn't veered off course. The dolphins had traveled north to escape a storm brewing in the south. A storm that had apparently grown and moved right in the path of the junk. Ingela and Raquel started down the mast. A gust of wind plastered them to the pole. They held on as tight as they could, both acutely aware that they were very, very high up. So high that Raquel felt she could reach up and burst one of the dark clouds that hung above them, but she didn't dare let go.

Needles of rain stung Ingela's eyes. She looked down. Sometimes, when she was this far up, she liked to imagine the girls as tiny ants below. Now all she wanted was to get off this slick pole and be an ant herself.

Together, they'd reefed the mainsail. Reducing the size of the sail made it easier to manage the ship in this choppy weather. But judging from the increased gust coming at them, it didn't seem like it would be enough.

"Should we go bare poles?" Raquel asked.

Ingela shook her head. "If we take all the sails down, we won't have enough control if the waves get bigger."

Raquel nodded, relieved. Though the girl was four years younger, Raquel was happy to trust Ingela's sailing intuition. Besides, Raquel was the worst climber out of all of them (except Sadie, maybe) and was overjoyed to be heading back down.

Sadie and Liu rushed around the deck, securing anything that might shift in the rough storm. The last thing they needed on top of the wind, waves, and rain was heavy objects flying at them.

"Got it?" Sadie asked Liu.

Liu finished tying the rope into a bowline knot around the railing of the ship. She pulled at it to make sure it was tight. "Yup." She nodded to Sadie. The two girls ran the course of the rope along the rail, slipping every few feet. The slick deck and large waves were testing their centers of gravity. "Drop down, it's easier," Liu instructed. She went down on all fours like they had below deck and began crawling on her hands and knees. Sadie followed suit.

When they reached the other side of the railing, Sadie stood up to tie the rope in a bowline knot, like Liu had on the other side.

"Tight enough?"

The two girls pushed down on the rope line, making sure there wasn't any slack. This would give them something to hold onto as they tried to make it from one side of the deck to the other.

Restless waves shattered against the vessel, unleashing a surge of fury with each hit. Liu steadied herself as the ship catapulted …forward? Back? It was hard to tell where it was going.

Knowing the edge was the worst place to be, Sadie tried to hurry away from there, but it was too late. A squall blasted both girls, launching them through the air. Like bowling balls into pins, they crashed straight into Raquel and Ingela. From her position at the helm, Charlie was already caught in the storm. "Help! Help!" she shrieked, ringing the alarm bell, unaware the rest of her crew was lying in a heap below. The girls untangled themselves from each other as fast as they could. They crawled along the deck to the helm.

"The winds are pushing us too close to the rocks!" Charlie had no time to acknowledge or even notice the bruises and cuts the girls were sporting. The roar of the storm was so deafening, she had to shout despite them all standing inches apart. "Can *Holy Tide* pull us?" The ship was considerably bigger than the junk, and therefore stronger.

Charlie, Ingela, Raquel, Liu, and Sadie all grabbed onto the helm of the ship. They looked at each other. Sadie's heart dropped, and Ingela turned ashen.

"We were just up on the masts and there was no sign of *Holy Tide*." Raquel heard the shaking in her voice. "We're alone out here."

Charlie tried to keep the ship steady, but wave after wave pounded at it, their frothy tops dangerously close to touching the main deck. The water line was rising too quickly. They had no time to worry about *Holy Tide*. The girls had to move fast.

"With these waves, bilge water is already gotta be getting deep down there," Sadie yelled, referring to the water that was collecting on the lowest deck. "We need to start pumping now!" The weight of the water threw the stability of the entire ship. The faster they got it out, the better their chances of not sinking.

"I caulked the planks down there two days ago. They should be dry." Liu informed Sadie.

Sadie nodded. "Good." She turned to Ingela. "Come with me."

Without a word of protest, Ingela began to crawl down from the stern and make her way below deck.

Liu finished the quick calculations running through her head. "We don't have the sea room to leeward." Of course, she couldn't be sure there wasn't enough room for the ship to turn against the wind, but her gut told her they were already dangerously close to land. "Our steer power can't counter the current, waves, or the wind!"

Charlie's and Raquel's arms tensed against the wheel. They knew what was coming next, but neither of them were ready to hear it. A violent gust of wind ripped through them. They ducked, each keeping their hands to the helm.

Liu stood up cautiously with the other two following. "We need to run off!"

Charlie swallowed hard. For all her years helming a ship, she'd never "run off" in a storm. Running off was essentially sailing straight into the storm. It was a move only experienced captains like her pop attempted, because it required constant steering, or else the winds would make the ship go too fast and wipe out. Essentially, running off in this kind of storm, with their combined lack of experience, was committing suicide.

"We can't!" Raquel cried. "We'll die!"

Charlie and Liu nodded solemnly. They knew they had no choice.

Raquel nodded, too. All three gripped the helm and prepared themselves.

Ferocious winds and stiff waves clobbered them over and over. Charlie was gripping the steering wheel so tight her hands cramped. They were losing this battle. Charlie could see from the bleak expressions on Liu's and Raquel's faces that they knew it as well. The ship had not sunk, but facing the eye of the storm was proving to be too much for the junk. Charlie knew the ship would not be able to survive much more of the nonstop battering from the waves and the winds.

"We're going too fast!" Liu shrieked. "We have to slow down!"

A windy shower had suddenly started to accelerate the speed of the ship.

Raquel shook against the gusts. "We can't! It's out of control!"

"Over there!" Charlie screamed. "Look!"

"What?" Liu shouted. The visibility was so low they could barely see past the ship's bow.

"It's a clear spot of land!"

"Are you sure it's not rocks, Charlie?" Raquel's head was spinning, and her stomach was sick from all the violent thrashing about. She tried to focus on the horizon, but there was no horizon. Only angry waves and endless sea.

"I can't see, but it's our last shot!"

Their final hope rested on the storm that might kill them rescuing them instead. They all turned the wheel. Even that slight effort took up too much of Raquel's dying strength. Then, one by one, Raquel, Liu, and Charlie took their hands off the helm. Depending on what nature had in store for them, the strength of the winds would carry the junk with full force and speed as far onto shore as possible. Otherwise, the storm would swallow them whole right here.

There was no time to warn Ingela and Sadie, who were safer below deck. A massive wave drenched them in salt-water. Raquel slumped down and vomited. Charlie closed her eyes. Liu said a prayer to any god that would listen.

The junk moaned and groaned as she catapulted forward. Charlie opened her eyes to find she was being hurled through the air toward the bow of the ship. To her horror, they weren't headed for a patch of clear land but straight toward a reef of tall, jagged rocks.

The junk crashed onto the rocks, with its bow standing upright at nearly a forty-five-degree angle. Charlie lost her grip and slipped down the entire length of the ship, crashing into its stern. Her legs hung over the waves, which were battering her already bruised and beaten body, while wind and rain lashed at her from every side. An earth-shattering boom filled her ears. She looked up to see the vessel crack in half. The bottom part of the ship slid back from the slippery rocks and into the furious sea.

Charlie struggled to break free of what remained of the capsized ship, but its heavy bamboo batten slammed down onto her. She thrashed against the relentless waves, struggling for air. The ship she'd loved and admired was now drowning her. Charlie punched, pummeled, and jabbed her way back up to the surface. She opened her mouth and took a huge breath of air before being wrenched under again.

She plummeted deep, deep, down. Maybe she'd find lirium, Charlie thought to herself, half-smiling at the irony. Down here the storm couldn't reach her. No more clobbering waves. No more vicious winds.

Down here, everything was calm and peaceful. The warm water caressed her tired muscles as her exhausted mind drifted away. Where were Sadie, Liu, Ingela, Raquel … Taye? She imagined giving her final captain's orders: "All hands lost."

Down here, she could stop fighting. Her body went limp.

***

Liu paddled and kicked. She'd been hurled from the junk before it had landed on the rocks. And, if her salt-filled eyes weren't playing tricks on her, before it had cracked in two and sunk.

Waves crashed into her, throwing her this way and that, but the adrenaline pumping through her made every aching part of her body revolt against nature's wrath

"Bring it on!" she shouted, either aloud or in her head.

Today, she wasn't going to die.

Raquel lunged for the sail mast floating in the water. This was the only thing she could see of the junk or the girls. She relaxed her body against it, letting it keep her afloat. Her boots were making it hard to swim. Actually, the giant waves and sinister winds were making it hard to swim. The heavy boots weren't helping, though.

She'd been thrown out of the junk shortly after they'd decided to shoot for land. She remembered sailing through the air. But she couldn't remember anything else. Even the image of the man stabbing Papa was slowly fading away.

The blood trickling down her face mixed with the salt-water. Raquel choked a little. She desperately wanted to lift her head to see if she could find anyone else, but it felt too heavy to lift. Instead, she closed her eyes.

***

Taye burst to the surface of the water. He could still hear the guys and Sadie shouting for him to come back, but he continued to ignore their pleas. There was no waiting until the storm broke.

At first, it had been a perfectly clear day, with the junk safely behind them. Then, without any warning, a twisted storm had separated them yet again.

He launched himself into the wave, letting its force propel him further in the water. He kept his body taut, with his arms and legs bent.

They'd tried to turn the ship around the moment they realized the girls weren't there, but it seemed Mother Nature had other plans for them. Eventually, *Holy Tide* fought her way back, but it was already too late by then.

They'd found Ingela sleeping on Sadie's lap, the two tucked deep inside a dry, safe part of the collapsed junk rig. Liu swam to them, dragging Raquel's tired body with her. But no one had seen *her*.

"Charlie!" Taye roared above the winds whirring around him.

An enormous wave heard his call and answered by rolling over him. He choked, gasping for air. When he caught his breath, Taye dove deep down. Lirium deep. He forced his eyes to stay open, despite the burn, while he searched for her.

After many minutes, when his head popped back up, he let out a sigh of relief. She wasn't down there. From a distance, he spotted the floating debris from the sunken ship. Taye swam forward.

Waves clobbered him, threatening to swallow him whole. His body was pulled under. Taye thrashed until he reached the surface. He gulped for air but was thrown under too fast. Again, he fought. He had to find Charlie. This time he came back up and was able to breathe.

He swam to the flotsam. With every few feet, he wrestled against the storm. Winds lifted pieces of the junk and sent them crashing down on him. A wooden board slammed against his cheek. Taye threw it forward and continued looking. He dove down into water, searching desperately for a glimpse of her red hair.

In the middle of the wreckage, between the battens, he spotted Charlie's listless body. He raced toward it. An angry wave dragged him back. He struggled against it before breaking free. Another wave ripped into him, this time chucking him in another direction. He thrashed against it, beating it to a pulp. He swam with total determination, focusing all his concentration on getting to the center, being careful not to get tied up in the rigging from the sails.

When he reached her, Taye wrapped his arms around Charlie as he had so many times before. He pressed his body against hers, shielding her from the waves. Her body was cold and limp, with no life in her limbs. Her head flopped to the side like an old rag doll. A blast of wind hurled a tide surge at them. He cradled Charlie's lifeless head to his chest while he battled the swell, ready to fight whatever lay ahead. Anything to save her. Again.

Chapter
ELEVEN

SLOG

RIP Junk

RIP Pirettes

RIP Storm

Without a ship, we're not Storm or Pirettes. Without Charlie, none of it matters.

Ingela ✗

"Coffee?" Axel's lopsided grin was slightly irritating this morning, Sadie thought, as she reached for the steaming cup. "Be careful! It's hot!" he called out as she turned her back to him.

Java was just one of the luxuries here on *Holy Tide*. Sloops like this one were already the vessel of choice for sailors and pirates because they were fast and compact. With a bowsprit almost as long as its hull, a sloop could run circles around larger ships, as well as maneuver in shallow water, allowing it to hide from enemies. Sadie perched herself on a deck chair away from the rest of the group. She'd never dared ask her brother how they'd managed to own a sloop, nor had he ever volunteered the information, but she suspected it wasn't exactly through legitimate means. Regardless of how they acquired the ship, the Castaways had truly turned *Holy Tide* into their own custom-made, souped-up ride.

Though they'd upgraded the ship with lots of features, the most impressive were the stripped interior bulkheads and forecastles, designed to add extra speed. Likewise, the standard rig, with its fore-and-aft mainsail and jib, had been enhanced with additional sails for more power. Whatever the Castaways were chasing, you could be sure they'd catch it with the swift, strong *Holy Tide*. Last night, they'd been lucky it was the junk.

The scorching coffee burned against the roof of Sadie's mouth. She didn't know where they would be if the Castaways hadn't come back for them.

"Come join us!" Liu called, waving Sadie over to where Ingela, Taye, Axel, and Jimmy were sitting.

Leave me the hell alone! Sadie wanted to shout. Instead, she faked a smile and said, "No, thanks! I'm gonna sit here for a while. I'll join you all in a bit!"

Rather than sitting out here drinking coffee like everything was fine, Sadie wished she could walk over to the main deck and turn the eight swivel guns and four cannons on the sun, the clear blue sky, and the calm, fluffy clouds overhead. The peaceful morning weather enraged her. Like a father using the light of day to erase his drunken rage of the night before, Mother Nature was showing them her best behavior to make up for yesterday's wrath.

Sadie took another long, blistering sip of coffee. Her mother had always told her to be fair and forgive her father's drunken outbursts. If Josephine were here now, she'd remind Sadie of the unpredictability of nature and ask her to forgive it, too.

Sadie turned the deck chair around, which she suspected Axel had conveniently placed in the opposite position. Straight ahead of her, the bow of the junk rig lay beached on a rocky reef while, below deck, Charlie lay battered and bruised.

Just as the hateful words her father spewed were forever etched in Sadie's memory, the cruelty that nature bestowed upon them would stay with Sadie for as long as she lived. Tomorrow, she would forgive and go back to being sensible Sadie. The girls depended on it. But today, as she lifted her hand to block out the sun's powerful rays, she thought she was allowed to be pissed off.

***

Taye sat down on the chair next to the bed. The infirmary already smelled like Charlie—sea salt mixed with lemons. He picked up the book that lay on the floor. *The Iliad & The Odyssey*. This had to belong to Sadie. Taye chuckled. Despite having grown up like sisters, it was always remarkable how little Sadie and Charlie knew about each other. Or was it more like how much they ignored about each other? The only thing Charlie hated more than reading was to be read to. Taye closed the book and laid it back on the floor. Judging from its thickness, Sadie wasn't too optimistic that Charlie was going to wake up anytime in the next century. He looked at Charlie, with her long red hair fanned out around her, and leaned in closer. Was that a mermaid-shaped barrette in Charlie's hair? It seemed Raquel was feeling better. Regardless of her tacky accessories, with her hair properly brushed and her mouth shut, Charlie could almost pass for a proper lady.

But that's not who she was. Charlie was opinionated, feisty, and sometimes downright surly. Most of all, she was a fighter. Taye shook his head. That's why this didn't make sense. Sadie had explained to all of them that nothing was medically wrong with Charlie. There was no great blood loss or misplaced organ keeping her asleep. She just wasn't ready to wake up.

Taye kicked the side of the bed. Charlie wasn't some delicate princess locked in a sleeping spell. She didn't just give up. Not *his* Charlie.

He grabbed her hand. "Hate me. Spend the rest of your life wishing I were dead." His voice broke. "But don't leave me."

The sound of glass shattering against the ground stirred Taye out of his thoughts.

"*Chica*!" Raquel shrieked. "I asked you to be careful with my things!" She bent down to pick up the remnants of the glass turtle that Ingela had shattered into dozens of tiny pieces.

"It was stupid and ugly!" Ingela screamed back. The storm had wiped out the junk, which pretty much left the girls useless. Charlie still hadn't woken up after three days, and yet, somehow, out of everything, Raquel's kitschy glass turtle survived! Ingela was glad she'd smashed it. She searched Raquel's wooden trunk, looking for more things she could break.

"Girls!" Taye opened the door to the infirmary. "Keep it down or you'll wake up Charlie!"

Ingela crossed her arms and looked up at Taye while still holding Raquel's glitter headband, the next item she was planning on ruining. "Don't we want Charlie to wake up?"

Raquel tried to grab the headband out of Ingela's grasp, but she just raised it higher over her head and smiled.

Taye sighed. "Obviously we want her to wake up." He didn't have the patience for these two today. "Just don't make so much noise." He seized the headband from Ingela and handed it back to Raquel. "And stop fighting over dumb stuff like this."

Ingela smirked. "See, Taye thinks it's ugly, too."

"He said 'dumb,' not ugly!" Raquel countered, raising her voice.

"It's dumb and ugly—" "Guys!"

Taye whipped his head around. "Charlie?" He rushed to her bed, with Ingela and Raquel right behind him.

"Ingela's right." Charlie said in a low, hoarse voice. "That thing is ugly and dumb." Her chapped lips cracked as she half-smiled at the gaudy headband that Raquel was holding. "Wouldn't you know it—even after such a long sleep you still wake up the same old Prickles!" Raquel whooped as she jumped onto the bed. Ingela followed immediately. Taye stepped forward. "Girls! Don't overdo it! Charlie needs her re—" He couldn't finish the sentence without his voice cracking. It didn't matter anyway, as it was clear that the girls weren't listening.

Raquel and Ingela engulfed Charlie in an enormous hug. Instead of tensing as she usually did, she relaxed and hugged them back, ignoring the ache in her muscles as she squeezed them. "How long was I out for?" The last memory she had was the sense of sinking deep, deep down. Shivers ran down her spine.

"Three days," Ingela said, nuzzling up even closer to Charlie.

"Whoa, Squirt!" Charlie howled, but she didn't stop her. Ingela and Raquel cuddled up as tightly as they could to Charlie. They felt so warm and safe that Charlie couldn't resist the snugness of the embrace, nor did she want to. Another memory came flooding back to her. Taye. His arms pulling her up. His arms wrapping around her. His arms holding her as he swam them back to the ship. Charlie looked up and past Raquel, but Taye had apparently left the infirmary.

She reached up around her neck and let out a deep sigh of relief as her fingers grasped the pearl. Both the necklace and she had survived the storm. Salty tears flowed down Charlie's face. It was good to be alive.

***

Ingela marched into *Holy Tide*'s main cabin and dumped the contents of the bag directly on the floor.

Raquel leaped from the sofa. "Those are my shells!" She rushed over to Ingela. "I told you not to go through my things, *pequeño diablo*!"

Sadie's mouth dropped open. She looked across the long room at her brother to see if he was as stunned as she was by Ingela's discovery. To her dismay, Taye was looking down at his guitar, trying to distance himself from the drama unfolding in front of them all.

Ingela pointed to Raquel in an accusatory way. "I found these hidden in the fussy hussy's wooden chest."

Raquel scowled at Ingela. "Fussy hussy" was unusually harsh, even for her foul mouth. "I was going to surprise you all with seashell purses!" She began to pick up the shells and put them back in the bag. "But the nosy *mocosa* has gone and ruined the surprise!" She stopped to polish a seashell with the front of her dress. "I guess I can make them into necklaces and bracelets for myself." Her eyes lit up. "Maybe I can make a whole set with a headband, too!"

"No, Raquel!" Charlie shouted from the silk-covered divan. Her words echoed in the spacious cherry oak sitting room, which was lined with leather-bound books and intricate wood carvings. "Those shells aren't for handicrafts!"

"Do you know how much those are worth?" Sadie asked, finally getting her speech back.

Jimmy's eyes glistened. "What did you do to get all of those?"

Liu shot Jimmy a dirty look. "Raquel didn't *do* anything, Jimmy!" She stopped and cocked her head. "How did you get them, though?"

Raquel rubbed the bandage on her forehead. She was completely confused by all the nonsense going on around her. "What are you guys talking about?" She held up a shell. "The old Maldivian man gave me these."

Ingela turned around. "The man from the Malé market?

He just gave you this whole bag of shells?"

Raquel was still too peeved at Ingela to address her directly, so she turned to the rest of the group. "I told you we had that nice talk about how he was super old and his life was over? Then, at the end, he gave me this bag and said to do something good with it." She rolled her eyes.

"That's why I wanted to make seashell purses for all of us, but Ingela—"

Ingela raised her arms up in disbelief. "Are you for real? Now I'm gonna go through the rest of your stuff for sure, and see what other treasure you have hidden about!"

"Treasure?" Raquel shook her head.

"These are valuable, Raquel." Sadie picked up a shell.

"What?"

"These are cowry shells." Liu turned an egg-shaped, porcelain like shell in her hands. "People use these as money in Africa, India, China—"

"They do?" Raquel's face lit up. "So we're rich?"

"Not rich enough to buy our own ship." Charlie pointed out. She couldn't believe she survived a killer storm just to end up roomies with the Castaways. It had only been a day-and-a-half since she'd woken up, but already being around Taye this much was messing with her head, even if he was sitting so far away from her he was practically in another room.

Javier stopped playing his game of cards. Besides the fact that he was losing, this seemed like a perfect opportunity to serve his interests. "They could definitely help us get our ship fixed up," he said, winking at Raquel.

Raquel ignored Javier's wink in favor of dreamy visions of sparkly dresses with real lace crinolines, not the itchy stuff she had to put up with, and petite sugar-frosted cakes from fancy patisseries. Or a new set of daggers. Sharp enough to kill.

"First of all," Sadie eyed Javier, "the shells belong to Raquel, so she decides what she wants to do with them." Sadie understood this potentially meant watching their second chance fizzle into satin bows and fur muffs, but it was only fair to give Raquel absolute say. "Supposing she does share them with us. Is it enough to fix your ship?" She turned her question to Axel and Taye, whom she trusted.

Axel sneered at Javier for throwing the card game just as he was about to win. "The damage to *Holy Tide* is minimal. We could fix it ourselves in a day or so if we got the right supplies. It wouldn't cost more than half those shells." He called out to Taye. "Do you think we could make it to Bosaso with our torn sail? That's a pretty big port—they'll have the stuff we need."

Taye was pretending to learn a new chord. He strummed his guitar.

"Hey, Maestro, I know you can hear me."

Taye sighed and put his guitar down. "You're seriously thinking about continuing with this mission?"

"Yes, now that we can." Sadie relit a candle. Unlike on the junk, light was plentiful here. No dark shadows loomed on *Holy Tide*, which made everything easier to see, including her big brother's messy feelings for her best friend.

She stared into the flame. The others didn't suspect anything, except maybe Raquel. Sadie had had her suspicions for a while, ever since Taye came back six months ago.

The way he'd risked his life to save her, without a single thought to his own safety. The look on his face when he carried her lifeless body. Not to mention the state of panic he'd been in until she woke up. Sadie didn't know what exactly had gone down between Taye and Charlie. Though, again, her instinct told her that it was major.

"Sadie, be sensible! We had a snowball's chance in hell before, but now, with one ship and a broken crew—!" Taye was too frustrated to even finish his thought.

Sadie balked. If anything, she was always sensible! When Charlie woke up, she made amends with Mother Nature. But like the candles lighting the room, there was a flame inside of her that grew hotter and hotter. "Taye, we can't live here forever. This mission is our only hope of getting our own ship."

They'd both had enough loss. She'd do anything to spare her brother the pain of losing his sister or Charlie, except sacrifice the one thing none of them could live without—*freedom*. "We still need to do this," she said, not to Taye, but to her sisters.

Liu couldn't believe what she was hearing. Especially from Sadie! The same adrenaline that had kept her kicking and paddling through those killer waves pumped through her again. "We've lost too many days. We'll never make it to Jeddah now."

Sadie's face fell.

"But we could make it to Djibouti. Near where we think the pirates are staked out. Still, we'd have to race to get there, but—"

"Liu! Are you saying we should go head to head with the Blood and Bone Brothers?" Axel ran his hands through his spiky hair. "Taye's right. That's worse than suicide! It's just plain stupid." He stood up and started to pace.

The Blood and Bone Brothers got their jollies from inflicting torture on their captives. Axel wasn't a coward by any means, but one of his main strategies for staying alive was choosing which battles to fight and which ones to stay as far away from as possible. Before, when it just meant warning some princess about an attack, the mission was dangerous. But going directly against the BBB was out of the question.

"No, there's another way." Liu walked over to the globe standing in the corner and began to drag it to the center of the room.

"Hey, be careful with that!" Jimmy cried, running over to help Liu. "It's not a toy!" He bent his knees and gently lifted the three-legged pedestal base as though the globe were a sick child. When they reached the center, he set the globe down with the same attention. "Don't leave any smudgy fingerprints," Jimmy commanded, pointing to its shiny patina finish.

Liu nodded. Although Jimmy seemed a bit overprotective, the thirty-two-inch-diameter globe really was magnificent. She spun it against the solid mahogany meridian, watching as the rainbow of colors swirled together. Since coming aboard *Holy Tide*, she'd already spent many hours studying its magnificently detailed cartography. Now, however, was not the time to get lost in geography. Liu could feel all eyes were on her, which suddenly made her palms sweat. Sadie was much better at playing the teacher. "Sadie, do you want to explain?"

"You know this stuff better," said Sadie, nodding encouragingly. "Just focus on the facts."

Liu swallowed. They'd followed her right into the storm. What if she was leading them to another catastrophe? *Just the facts.* If she focused just on what she knew, then it was up to them to decide their fate. She cleared her throat. "Most likely the Blood and Bone Brothers will hide out in Murad waiting for the sultan's royal ships, because the waters are smoother. We could take this route, on the other side of Murad, past Djibouti, which *avoids* the pirates but lets us reach the princess before they do."

"It gives us a good chance of avoiding the Blood and Bone Brothers, but it doesn't guarantee it." Jimmy countered, shaking his shaggy head. "It's still too risky."

"No, it's not." Ingela stuffed a handful of sweets into her mouth. She'd found almost two full tins of goodies in the *Holy Tide* kitchen and promptly helped herself, not bothering to share with the others. "Liu just explained how we're going to do it." She grabbed another bonbon.

Raquel spoke. "We'll pay to fix the ship and give the Castaways a sixty-forty share." Pretty things were always nice, but the sea allowed them to control their own lives. That freedom was the only treasure truly worth having.

"Liu's plan could work." Javier wanted to support his new friend Liu. He appreciated the respect she'd shown by staying silent for their entire two-hour conversation yesterday. "It could work for seventy-thirty, that is." Still, he couldn't let friendship get in the way of profit.

"Sixty-forty, and we'll give you the whole bag of shells." "It's a deal!" Javier started to walk over and shake Raquel's hand.

"No, it's not a deal, jerk!" Axel shouted. "We don't hustle our family!" He stood in front of Javier. "If we do this, it's fifty-fifty, and we'll pay the girls back for fixing the ship."

Axel leaned against the table. "Liu's plan is good if we don't face the Blood and Bone Brothers." He chewed on his thumbnail. "But it's damn dangerous!"

"We don't have a choice, Axel!" Charlie leaned back against the soft pillow, avoiding eye contact. "Taye was wrong. *We're* not broken. *I'm* broken." She was aware that Javier and Jimmy could never know about the Storm or gilling, so she kept her words vague, but she hoped the others would understand her. "This is the only chance we have left to survive. To escape Zhang Tao. To find out what happened to our families." Charlie took a deep breath. "What I want to say—"

"It doesn't matter, Charlie. None of it matters, actually." Taye's words were terse. "This isn't some democracy where everyone gets an equal vote." His eyes smoldered. "I'm the captain here, and I decide where this ship goes. And it's not going on this mission!"

Taye stood up and walked out.

***

"Hi, Big Bro! Have a second to chat?"

Taye groaned. "Not you too, Sadie! Raquel can't stop looking at me with sad puppy dog eyes, Ingela stomped on my foot this morning, and Liu barged into my cabin with a brand-new sea chart." He sighed. "My decision is final. We're not going on that mission."

Sadie leaned against the rail. The bright moonlight cascading over the sea spilled onto the stern of the ship. "What about Charlie? What did Charlie do?"

Taye looked away. "I haven't paid attention to Charlie." "You always pay attention to Charlie. Especially when you're not paying attention to Charlie." Sadie put her hand on Taye's arm. "It's because of Charlie that you're not letting us go on this mission."

The sloop, which had been anchored in the same spot since the storm, swayed back and forth against the gentle waves. Holy Tide, just like its crew and its new guests, was getting restless.

Taye stared out at the water. "You don't know what you're talking about, Sadie."

"Yeah, I do. You know I do. And I'm not here as your pesky little sister trying to get dirt on your secrets." She turned to face him. "I'm here because I know you're scared about losing her. This isn't the way to keep her, though."

"It's not just her! I need to keep you safe, too! All of you." He gripped the railing tightly. "That storm made it real for me. You guys are alone—no families, no Storm to protect you. And you're not ready."

"I know—we know we're not ready. What choice do we have, though? Here's what made it real for us. Our parents were killed on one single, horrible day, and now we have nothing." She tried to keep herself calm, but that flame was starting to grow again. "But there's no way Liu's ending up the wife of some rich old man, Ingela sure as hell isn't going to an orphanage, and I'm not ending up picking cotton in a plantation—"

"Sadie! How can you even think I'd let that happen!" "Because you can't protect us all the time, Taye! Only this can!" She pointed around her. "The sea. This is where we're safe from forced marriages, orphanages, slavery, and all the other wicked things that society does to girls like us." Her voice softened. "And those things, Taye, are a lot scarier than storms and pirates."

Taye turned away. He flashed back to the storm, fighting to stay above the massive waves that crashed down on them relentlessly, over and over. Choking on the saltwater that stung his eyes so that he couldn't see. Holding Charlie's limp, cold body as he struggled to make it back to *Holy Tide*. Waiting, praying to whatever cruel god would dare play with a life so young, so strong, so needed by everyone—by him—to let Charlie live. She was awake now, and though she avoided him, at least she was still here, in this miserable world where they were forced apart.

Taye slammed his hands against the rail so hard there would be a bruise tomorrow, forgetting Sadie was standing behind him. He allowed himself a rare moment to think about the things he buried deep inside. Not just for Charlie, but for his own survival as well. He'd never make it out here without her if he let himself think of everything he'd sacrificed. The Storm, his family, Charlie.

His jaw tensed. He saw his parents. Josephine in the lab wearing the parrot-colored dresses that stood out against the black, white, and gray starkness of *Storm One*, and Henry, a bastard when he'd had too much whiskey, but still a beloved father who tried to do right by Taye. *He could have saved them.* Taye's right arm, the arm he held his sword with, trembled. It was too painful for him to ever admit out loud, but the thought burned at the back of his mind. If he'd only been there for the Day of Destruction. If he hadn't been a stupid, lovelorn kid who'd abandoned his family and his duty, he would have been on *Storm One* when the faceless soldiers attacked. He would have killed every last one of them. And his parents would have lived.

He'd lost it all because of Charlie. He hated her, yet he didn't. Now, the weight of nine lives crushed down on him, their mass pulling him under like the waves in the storm.

Sadie, Axel, Jimmy, Javier, Raquel, Liu, Ingela. His. And hers …

"Taye?" Sadie whispered.

He was too lost in his thoughts to respond. Sadie walked up behind her big brother and gave him a hug. Then she left him alone.

Chapter
TWELVE

SLOG
Date: Dec 3
Position: 11.2847° N, 49.1825° E

We've fixed the torn sail and are leaving Bosaso. We have less than two days to get to the sultan's ship, and we're literally racing against the wind. We're following Liu's plan and going through Djibouti. Fingers crossed.

It's been over three months since we left Shanghai, and it seems like a lifetime ago. We're different. All of us.

I don't know what changed Taye's mind, but I'm glad something did. I'm ready to fight again. There's nothing like almost dying to make you want to live.

Charlie

"Bloody hell!" Axel shouted out loud, voicing the sentiments most of them were thinking at that exact moment.

They'd already heard the cannons as they were approaching, which should have been an indication of what lay ahead. Now, while Holy Tide hid near a cove no more than ten miles from the gruesome scene in the distance, there was no escaping what Charlie had previously deemed the worst-case scenario. Directly ahead of them, a battle was being fought in the open water. At the center was a large sloop, which was most likely the princess's ship. In front of it was one of the most enormous vessels Charlie had ever seen.

Nearly 70 feet long, the royal guard's ship had 16 nine-pounder guns and probably weighed close to 150 tons. This wasn't just any old sloop; the sultan had outfitted his warship to be an impenetrable fortress on the sea. Yet, by the looks of the black smoke rising from it and the enemy pirates on board, the ship was desperately compromised.

"Looks like you were wrong!" Javier yelled, quickly turning on his new friend Liu. "The Blood and Bone Brothers were already waiting for them in Perim, not Murad!" He crossed his arms. "Now we're screwed."

"There's no way we're going up against the BBB." Axel crossed his wiry arms.

"We need to turn this ship around before they see us," Taye commanded.

"NO!" All five girls yelled in unison, each equally surprised by the other's response.

"Look." Charlie held the telescope out. She wasn't sure what she was going to say exactly, but she had to try something. "I don't know what happened, but the Blood and Bone Brothers only have one ship and not a lot of men. And they can't see us from this cove, so we have the benefit of surprise."

"It also looks like quite a few of the sultan's royal guards are still fighting," Raquel added.

Liu took Raquel's spyglass. "Most of the fighting is taking place on the guard's ship. Only a handful of the BBB men have actually made it onto the princess's ship. Probably because of the musket fire and cannons they're shooting."

"Musket fire and cannons? That's not exactly a welcome for us to climb on board!" Jimmy exclaimed. Strands of his wild red hair seemed to quiver with fright. He didn't need a telescope to see the giant in front of him. "How are we even going to penetrate that thing—it's like a hundred blue whales stacked up on top of one another!"

Cannon fire exploded against the bright blue sky. A shower of reds and oranges shot up toward the fluffy white clouds before falling down into the dark blue water. One could almost mistake this for a fireworks show if it wasn't for the bodies being thrown overboard. "Oh, and I forgot to acknowledge the gunfire and cannons," Jimmy added, steadying himself against Ingela as the powerful explosion sent *Holy Tide* rocking back and forth. They all held onto something for balance.

Sadie stood against the wall and pointed forward. "We don't need to get onto the guards' ship. Instead, we can just go directly to the princess's ship! There's an opening on the far northwest side, away from the Blood and Bone Brothers' ship. There's no gunfire or cannons shooting there." She eagerly held the spyglass up for Taye's inspection.

Taye nodded. "Sadie's right. Check it out, Ax."

Axel walked over to the bow of the *Holy Tide* with his telescope. "It's narrow. We'd have to be really fast and squeeze ourselves as close as we can to the princess's ship. Then we'll jump from our gunwale." He faced the entire group. "I mean, we gotta be in and out, people! Before Brother Blood or Brother Bone has time to retaliate. Otherwise, we're gonna end up with our mangled bodies drawn on the front page of the newspaper." Axel didn't have a hint of irony in his voice.

Charlie shook her head. "No, there's no way we could get that close without the BBB spotting us. It's best if we keep *Holy Tide* hidden here and a few of us row out there on separate dories and climb on board." She pointed to the ropes and grappling lying in the corner. "A ship that size may even have side steps we can climb."

"Charlie's right. Rowing out there is our best option," said Axel as he looked around. "But what's our plan once we're on board?"

Taye, who had been deep in his own thoughts, spoke. "We need to save the princess's ship, because that's where the treasure is." He looked at Sadie. "What about Sultan Musef? Are you sure he's not on board?"

"There wasn't a lot of information, but from what I could find, he doesn't take the journey himself. He just sends members of his family and his royal court."

Liu stepped forward. "Right, Sadie. So our plan is that we take over the helm of the princess's ship and sail it away." She held up a makeshift map she'd drawn very hastily, laying out the route between *Holy Tide* and the battle scene ahead. "If we row all the way down the length of this cove we're in, then we can stay hidden, and we'll only need to be in open water for a few minutes before we reach the princess's ship. It's a lot rockier, and it will take more time, but it's safer."

Taye glanced at Liu's map. "Good plan." Then he addressed his entire crew. "We weren't expecting to engage, but now we're going to have to. The Blood and Bone Brothers are outnumbered, but still putting up a good fight. Once we climb on board, there's no avoiding them. We don't have the manpower to combat them one-on-one for very long. *Stealth and speed.*" Like the Storm taught us, he would have added if Javier and Jimmy hadn't been there, but the girls fully understood. "Charlie, Axel, and I will take the helm."

He turned to face them. "The Blood and Bone Brothers will have stationed most of their men around the wheel, so if we want to take control of the ship, it's going to come down to good old-fashioned hand-fighting. Be sure to take extra daggers and swords with you." Taye pointed to Raquel and Liu. "You two need to make your way to the princess and let her know we're here to help her." Then he addressed Javier, Jimmy, Sadie, and Ingela. "You all stay and guard *Holy Tide*. The moment you see us take off on the princess's ship, we'll need you close behind in case the Blood and Bone Brothers chase us." Then he turned to face the whole group again.

"I know we've had to change our mission twice already, and we need to improvise once again. But the goal is the same: to save the treasure so we can earn ourselves a big, fat reward." Taye tried to deliver the last line with a sense of excitement, but the danger loomed so heavily over all of them that no one really responded to it.

Everyone nodded silently. Another cannon fired up ahead, creating a series of shock waves. *Holy Tide* swayed back and forth again. Sadie's stomach plunged as memories of the storm came rushing back. Had they survived that only to die now?

Taye closed his eyes. His sister's words sat heavily on his shoulders. *They needed this.* Still, he wouldn't risk any of their lives just for a reward. They hadn't been expecting to walk into a battle. At nearly nineteen, he was a young captain, so maybe he was just being foolishly optimistic. He believed they could pull this off, but he sensed not all of his crew agreed.

"Do you trust me?" he asked, startling everyone out of their own thoughts. One by one, they each nodded. When he got to Charlie, he didn't avert his gaze. Neither did she. Charlie nodded, too. Taye shouted out his last command before the group dispersed. "We're ready."

***

Holy Tide was well-equipped with smaller vessels, which meant that Charlie, Liu, Raquel, Axel, and Taye had the luxury of not just one, but two dories. This was incredibly useful, because if something went wrong and they had to exit the princess's ship, then they probably weren't going to be doing it together and would need more than one boat. Dories were lightweight and compact, which made it easy to row fast. They followed Liu's plan and stayed along the cove. The six minutes they spent in open water seemed endless and terrifying, but the dory containing Charlie, Liu, and Raquel, as well as the boat that Axel and Taye were on, managed to make it to the princess's ship without being spotted by the Blood and Bone Brothers. As Charlie had predicted, there was a set of steps on the side of the ship, so they didn't even need to use the grappling hooks and rope they'd brought just in case.

The stairs were surprisingly under-guarded with only four men. They proved to be easy to throw overboard, after which Charlie, Liu, Raquel, Axel, and Taye made their way onto the main deck. Charlie bounded up the stairs. "I think the princess's quarters are through there!" she called out, pointing down the carpeted hallway. Who had ever seen rugs on a ship before? "Do you want me to come with you?" Before she could hear the answer, a pirate lunged toward her. With her razor-sharp reflexes finely in tune, Charlie lifted up her cutlass with two hands and swung. Her adrenaline was already pumping, and she was elated to be back in action.

"Can someone give me a hand here?" Taye, who was fighting two guys at the same time, shouted.

The sky was bright blue, and the sun was shining, but the winds were picking up, sending heavy gusts their way. All around them there was mayhem, with swords, daggers, and pellets sailing through the air. One could hardly decide whether to duck for cover or run away. Except for Charlie, that is, who ran right into the heart of it without a second's hesitation.

"Coming!" Charlie yelled, as she turned her back against the draft. She ran to help Taye, but paused at Raquel and Liu, who were still standing at the top of the staircase. "You guys okay?"

Liu nodded. "Go help Taye! We'll find the princess." Raquel covered her ears. The banging of the blades, thunder of the cannons, and cries of the wounded were deafening. She'd only seen this once before, on the day her father was murdered. She backed into a corner, trembling from head to toe.

"We got this, Raquel." She looked Raquel directly in the eyes. "*Mind over body.*" Liu helped Raquel get on her feet.

Raquel nodded, and drew a dagger in each hand. Together, Liu and Raquel ran down the hall. Liu carried a sword in her free hand. Her long navy coat held two flintlock pistols she was terrified of using.

They passed down several thickly carpeted hallways, all of which were surprisingly free of any Blood and Bone crew members, and lined with paintings in gilded frames. The girls didn't have time to study the artwork, though it was like being in the world's most exclusive museum.

"¡Dios mío!" Raquel blurted as they both came to a full stop.

Never in their lives had they seen so much bling. Huge trunks spilling silver, gold, diamonds, sapphires, rubies, and a variety of other gems lined the cabinet. Chests stuffed with pearls, silks, and spices were stacked almost to the ceiling.

"Shhhh!" Liu warned Raquel, though it seemed both of them had been rendered temporarily speechless.

After a few more seconds of silent awe, Raquel whispered. "I think we found the treasure. Unless there's more hidden somewhere else."

Liu pointed ahead of her. "We can figure that out later. I think the princess's suite is probably over there."

Raquel shook her head. "But shouldn't there be guards here? You'd think the Blood and Bone Brothers would have someone watching over this stuff."

"They do." A gruff voice answered as two hands covered each of the girls' mouths.

***

"Watch out!" Charlie shrieked as she charged into Taye, sending both of them flying.

A cannonball flew through the air, barely missing them. "Thanks!" Taye called out, dumbstruck. He'd been standing directly where the cannonball landed.

"Now we're even!" Charlie answered, glad she'd paid Taye back for saving her life. She hated being in debt to anyone. Especially him.

Axel ran over to them and ducked under an awning. "The mainmast has been hit! This ship is stuck! And they're getting ready to fire another round of muskets!"

Taye's brow furrowed. This wasn't going well. He needed to think fast and come up with a new plan. Before he could, a man put a gun to his head.

***

Princess Imera crossed her arms, which were lined up and down with bright jeweled bangles, and shook her head vehemently, causing her enormous emerald earrings to jangle angrily. Dressed in an ornate silk robe, with baubles hanging off what seemed like every limb, the princess was a glittery, sparkly vision. However, at closer inspection, her rather pointy head and angular chin gave her a sharp edge that enhanced her intimidating manner.

Raquel bit her lip. This was her first time meeting an actual, real-life princess, but her awe was quickly turning into annoyance. When the two big brutes had stupidly dumped Raquel and Liu in the same room as the princess, the girls were ready to escape with her in tow immediately. Instead, they'd wasted the last three precious minutes trying to convince her that she was in imminent danger.

Princess Imera half-yelled, half-whispered something that sounded like a combination of spitballs and a bad cough. The language was foreign to Raquel's well-trained ear, but she suspected it was the princess's native Marrakatran.

The older woman standing next to the princess responded to her in the same language. Out of her mouth, the words sounded smoother and less guttural. Raquel studied the woman. Gray hairs were forming at her temples, and her eyes were lined with crow's feet, but she retained a rather bright, sandy-colored complexion and a full, round face with high apple cheekbones that made her appear younger than she probably was. Yet something in her honey-colored eyes told Raquel this was a woman who'd been around for a while and wasn't so easily messed with. If Raquel had to guess—and she was usually pretty good with her guesses—she'd say the woman was in her forties. As for Princess Imera, Raquel would have placed her around Charlie's age, though her childish behavior made her seem younger than Ingela.

"Princess Imera says she will only go with you if you have been sent by her father, Sultan Musef," the older woman explained, cradling her injured arm. Blood soaked through her makeshift tourniquet. "I have explained that this does not matter, as we do not have any other options."

Both Raquel and Liu looked at the woman in surprise. They had not expected either woman to speak English, especially so fluently. Raquel melted at the lilts and sharpness of what her trained ear told her was a highly educated accent, with distinctly English roots. She would have loved to sit down and let the woman read her a story, but there were more pressing matters at hand, like the guards returning.

The knots in Liu's stomach were growing tighter with every precious second that passed by. "Okay, so tell the princess we've been sent by her father. And that we're in a hurry." The woman grimaced. "Of course, it is not that easy. She will want official proof that you are following the orders of Sultan Musef." Her brow furrowed. "I am suspecting you do not have this proof?"

Raquel shook her head. They didn't have any proof, but what she did have was her panchi. They'd been stripped of all their weapons by the two guards, but she could still land a pretty powerful punch to the princess's egg-shaped head, which would surely help to knock some sense into her. Instead, she restrained herself and tried diplomacy first.

"Princess Imera, I understand you may not trust us. My name is Raquel, and this is Liu. We can help you get out of here if you please let us. But we need to move fast."

"I am Amsha," the older woman smiled and was about to extend her right hand before remembering her injured arm. The princess, however, did not bother to acknowledge either Liu or Raquel. Raquel couldn't tell if the blasé expression on the princess's face was because she was in a state of shock, or if she was actually indifferent to the danger they were in.

"Princess, listen to Amsha. I think it's best if we leave now—before those scary men come back." Liu shook her head in frustration. Surely if all princesses were as obstinate as this one, there wouldn't be so many folktales dedicated to them. Why did they have to end up with the ornery one? "Princess Imera believes her royal guards are handling the situation. Would you mind giving us a detailed report on what is happening out there?" Amsha asked. "Also, Princess Imera requests that you address her as 'Your Majesty'," she added with an embarrassed smile.

Raquel crossed her arms behind her back to stop her from socking Her Majesty in the eye. She took a deep breath. "Your Majesty, as we have been trying to explain, your royal guards have lost control of the situation. The Blood and Bone Brothers have pretty much captured your warship— the ship that your royal guards were on. Our friends are taking over the helm of this ship before the Blood and Bone

Brothers capture it. But we all need to go to a safe place where their crew can't find us." She was not going to end up anyone's torture toy tonight. She turned to Liu. "We have no weapons to fight them with."

Raquel and Liu waited for Amsha to translate the information to the princess. An animated discussion followed for another minute or so, then everything seemed to calm down, with the princess turning her back to them all.

"There is a hidden tunnel there. I am not certain where it leads, but I believe it is to the main deck." Amsha pointed with her good arm toward the other side of the cabin. "Unfortunately, I was unable to move the armoire by myself, and Princess Imera was not cooperative." She tried to hide a smirk as she said the last sentence, but couldn't. She wiped it off before the princess noticed.

"It looks heavy, but it's our only chance." Raquel turned to Amsha. The gash on her arm was quite deep. "Your bandage is pretty bloody. Should we change it before we go?"

Amsha shook her head, spilling curly black locks out of her bun. "No, it will hold for the time being. We need to get out of here before those men come back."

Liu looked Amsha over. She was tall, with wide hips and solid calves. Even with one good arm, she seemed more useful than Princess Imera, who at least had stood up but had yet to move any further. Liu, Raquel, and Amsha ran to the armoire while the princess watched. They stood on one side and tried to push it, but it wouldn't budge. Then they put their backs against it.

Liu wiped the sweat off her brow. "This thing is impossibly heavy, even if there were four of us to move it!" She eyed the princess, who had scurried to a jewelry box and was busy loading up her arms with more bangles and shoving more rings on her fingers. Liu cursed the princess under her breath.

Raquel stood up and waved for them to clear the way. She ran and high-kicked the armoire. Another classic Rafaella dance move, though Rafaella would have kept her toes pointed for good form.

"Brilliant!" Amsha quietly cheered as the armoire tipped slightly.

"I hear them!" Liu cried out. "The men are coming back." Raquel backed up and ran into the armoire, landing another solid kick.

"One more, Raquel! Before they get in!"

A key was inserted into the lock on the front door.

"Princess—Your Majesty—get the hell over here!" Liu commanded. Without a fuss, the princess ran over to her.

The key turned in the lock. Raquel delivered one more kick to the armoire, which toppled over with a loud thud. Raquel leapt over the hunk of wood. Liu grabbed Amsha and helped her to the other side.

A bangle slid off the princess's arm. She bent down to grab it, but there wasn't enough time. Amsha yelled out sharply. The princess looked at her, startled. The front door opened. Without another second to lose, Liu yanked the princess into the dark tunnel. She drew her pistol and shot at the brutes charging toward them before turning around and running as fast as she could.

***

The man held the gun to Taye's head while Charlie watched in horror. She wanted to lunge toward him, but her feet felt as though they were glued in place. He pulled the trigger. To his shock—and Taye's relief—the gun failed to go off. Flintlock pistols were notoriously finicky, often malfunctioning because of too much salt or wind in the air. Luckily, today was a particularly gusty day. Still, most pirates, like this one, carried a few guns on them just in case of glitches. The man reached into his coat for his second pistol, but Taye was too fast for him. He kicked the gun out of his hand and threw a right hook straight into his jaw.

Charlie, who'd watched as the man put the gun to Taye's head and pulled the trigger, was still temporarily stunned. However, a swift kick to the back of the head woke her up. She leapt around with her cutlass in the air. Before she laid eyes on her opponent, she felt her blade cut through his flesh. He used one hand to cover the wound on his thigh that Charlie had inflicted. This was where he was vulnerable, Charlie thought. A better look at her opponent revealed a baby face underneath his shoddy beard and thin mustache. He was probably no older than her. Still, he was the enemy, and she had to get him while he was down. She lunged forward, plunging her sword directly into the gash, cutting it open even further. He shrieked as he fell down on one knee.

**

Around the corner from where Charlie was battering her opponent, Raquel, Liu, Amsha, and Princess Imera made their way through the tunnel. The two brutes, who despite their massive size were proving to be quite swift as they navigated the tight corners and sharp turns of the passageway, were fast behind the girls and quickly catching up.

Liu was too busy running away to know for sure, but she didn't think the two brutes chasing them now were the same two who had locked them in the room. Brute One, who was so close to nabbing her she could feel his fat, sausage fingers skim the back of her shirt, was more squat than the previous guys, while Brute Two was much fatter. So much so that Liu could hear his blubbery hips scraping against the walls of the narrow tunnel they were all trying to find their way out of.

"Help! Help!"

***

"That's Raquel!" Charlie shouted. She ran toward the sound of the familiar voice.

Raquel ran out of a dark tunnel first, with the others following. As soon as Liu reached the open air, she turned around and pointed the barrels of her two guns at Brute One. She fumbled with the trigger, hesitating long enough for the brute to plow straight into her, knocking both Liu and the guns to the ground.

Taye and Charlie wielded their swords.

"Axel, use the dory and take them to *Holy Tide*! We'll follow!" Charlie called out.

The other brute, the one with the enormous belly, lunged his dagger at her. She swerved out of the way, narrowly missing him.

As though they'd been choreographed, the two brutes turned around simultaneously. With the force of a pair of elephants, they ran backward, knocking the cutlasses out of Charlie and Taye's hands, and slamming them against the wall.

Charlie felt her insides squish together as the fat brute smothered his considerable weight against her.

"Daggers," Taye choked out while trying to push the smaller, but much more muscular, brute off his diaphragm.

"Double Cross." Charlie looked at Taye. He nodded solemnly.

She'd practiced this move with the Storm dozens of times but never actually used it. Charlie slowly lowered her arms and grabbed the daggers on each side of her hips. Then, she lowered herself so that the blade tips were at the bottom of the V that shaped the groin on the brute. His gut hung so low that she could feel it set against the top of her head.

"Now!" Taye instructed, with his shanks positioned identically to Charlie's on the other brute. "Fast and deep!"

Charlie plunged the knives in and cut along the V, slicing along the femoral artery at an angle.

The two brutes shrieked in unison, but it was too late for them.

Blood gushed out of one of them immediately. He fell to his knees. Then he dropped directly over, his potbelly crashing into and surely smothering the other brute.

Charlie and Taye bent forward and took a deep breath. "We gotta—" Charlie sucked in more air. "We gotta go," she said as she picked up her cutlass.

Taye nodded and reached for his sword.

The ship rocked as a cannon exploded on the main deck. Charlie went crashing against the wall. Flames ignited behind her.

"Come on!" Taye shouted, as he grabbed Charlie's hand. Raquel watched as Axel hoisted the princess over his shoulder and made his way to the side stairs. "Follow me!" he shouted through the pandemonium.

"Got it!" shouted Raquel, who was only a few steps back with Liu and Amsha in tow. She turned the corner right behind Axel when she spotted him. At first, Raquel thought her mind was playing tricks on her. Amid the thick black haze of smoke, she could barely see her own hand in front of her. But she stopped anyway, oblivious that Liu and Amsha had run ahead. After a second, he appeared in full sight. As clear as the first time she'd met him.

The faceless soldier.

Raquel kept her eyes fixed on him, ignoring the roaring fire that was quickly engulfing the main deck she was standing on. His entire head was enmeshed in a copper helmet that extended past his chin down to his shoulders. His ears and nose were made out of the same copper, while his mouth was completely covered except for a tiny breathing hole. His eyes were merely two tiny slits cut into the copper.

Raquel drew her daggers. The faceless soldier had not seen her. She would have the element of surprise. He was too far for her to throw her knives. Besides, she'd been waiting for a dance.

Raquel was about to run through the fire when something pulled her to the ground. "What the hell?" she screamed, as she landed on her butt.

Liu had doubled back after noticing Raquel was no longer by her side. "What are you doing?" she shouted as she grabbed Raquel by the wrist.

"He's *here*!" Raquel cried in a rushed panic. She started to move, but Liu didn't let go.

The black smoke hung in the air, stinging her eyes and tickling her throat. "Who?" Liu asked, coughing. Tears ran down her face. "Don't you see the flames? This ship is on fire!" Liu coughed again. "We gotta go before it sinks!" She held her hand over her mouth to stop inhaling the smoke, which was suffocating her.

"The man who killed Papa!" Raquel struggled to break free of Liu's grip, but Liu's long, bony fingers were clasped tightly around Raquel's petite wrist.

"What?!" Liu squinted, trying to see through the layers of black smoke. It was impossible to make out anything but outlines of figures. She shook her head. "I don't see any faceless soldier!" Liu held on hard to Raquel and pulled her toward her. "We don't have time! We gotta go or we'll die!" "I don't care about dying!" Raquel shrieked as she raised her free hand. Before Liu could stop her, Raquel's blade came down on Liu, slicing her arm. "¡*Lo siento!*" she cried, before running away.

"Dammit!" Liu saw the blood before she felt the deep sting of the blade. But there was no time for pain, as Raquel had taken off again. The black smoke was seeping into Liu's lungs, making it hard to breathe. Though it felt like a flesh wound, blood gushed from the cut, leaving her whole arm bloody. Liu ignored it all and covered her mouth with her left hand. As she'd done so many times before, Liu depended on her legs to get her through this.

Up ahead of her, Liu saw Raquel. Or to be accurate, Liu spotted the tacky, brightly colored vest that Raquel had insisted on wearing for the mission. Raquel had worn the magenta and fuchsia piece for the specific reason that Liu would be able to find her if they separated. The clown vest now served to the detriment of Raquel and the advantage of Liu. Liu ran forward, deftly maneuvering her way around the sword fights that were still going on despite the fact that the ship was about to go down. A man staggered into Liu's path. She used both arms to push him out of her way and back into his opponent's line of fire. Liu didn't notice the man fall onto his enemy's sword, because her eyes were focused on finding Raquel in the cloud of black smoke.

When she glimpsed Raquel's vest just ahead of her, Liu reached out to grab a piece of it, but couldn't. She struggled to keep her eyes open in the thick haze. Liu looked up to see Raquel seconds away from stepping into the fire. Sheer momentum pushed Liu forward. She reached out for a strand of Raquel's long, brown hair, which had come out of its ponytail and now fell loosely down her back. She twisted her hand around Raquel's hair and yanked as hard as she could. "¡Santo Cielos!" Raquel cried, as Liu ripped a handful of her hair straight from the roots and sent her toppling backward.

Liu dropped to the ground and sat on Raquel's chest, pinning her arms to the ground. Suddenly, everything felt hotter, as the fire was dangerously close.

"Let me go!" Raquel squirmed under Liu's weight. "NO!" Liu shouted, digging her weight further into Raquel. Drops of blood from her arm fell onto the gaudy vest and smeared Raquel's cheek. "Get up, let's get out of here!"

Raquel didn't respond. Instead she lifted her leg and delivered a wallop of a kick directly into Liu's kidneys. Liu fell forward, releasing her grip on Raquel's arms. Raquel pushed Liu off of her and began to get up. Liu stuck her leg out, sending Raquel face-first to the floor.

A cannon exploded, followed by the bow of the ship falling into the sea. Liu had been through this with the junk and knew it was only a matter of minutes before they were all in the ocean with it. She grabbed Raquel and lifted them both up.

"I have to kill the faceless soldier!" Raquel shrieked, while delivering another perfect panchi kick, this time to Liu's groin.

Liu hunched over in agony. She took a deep breath and collected herself quickly. *Mind over body.* The fire blazed only a few feet away. Another loud crack echoed through the air. The stern dangled loosely, sending the ship rocking. Liu and Raquel crashed against the handrail. Liu steadied herself. She and Raquel were getting off this sinking ship one way or the other. She grabbed her "twin" by the tails of her vest and whipped her around. "For your papa!" Liu shouted, then cold-cocked Raquel with a blow to the head. Instantly, Raquel fell to the ground.

Despite the shooting pain in her kidneys, groin, and arm, Liu lifted Raquel's thankfully light body and hoisted it over her shoulder, like Axel had done with Princess Imera. *Mind over body.* Praying her legs could keep up with the urgency of the situation, Liu ran as fast as she could to the dory.

***

Charlie and Taye sped to the opposite side of the main deck. The side stairs had collapsed only moments before. Charlie looked over the edge of the princess's ship to see the second dory, along with the ropes that they'd hastily left inside it, burning up in flames. The fire on deck roared, growing closer.

"We gotta jump!" Charlie shouted. "Then swim back to *Holy Tide*. We've got a couple of miles in open water before we make it to the cove."

To the left of her, Charlie saw another pair of thugs quickly making their way toward them. If they stayed to fight another battle on the ship, they were sure to go down with it. There was no time.

Charlie and Taye backed up. The last time she'd had to escape a burning ship was on the Day of Destruction. But this time, it was different. Despite the imminent danger around her, she felt safe. She and Taye briefly glanced at each other before locking hands and leaping into the air.

***

"Everybody get below deck!" Axel shouted as he ran up the plank to the main deck of *Holy Tide* with Amsha and Princess Imera. He'd left Liu in the dory to manage Raquel by herself, because he needed to get up to *Holy Tide* as soon as possible and assess the situation. They hadn't saved the treasure, which made this whole mission a failure, but now there was something much more dangerous at hand. Axel needed to get *Holy Tide* out before the Blood and Bone Brothers found them. Axel turned toward the princess, who seemed glued to her spot. He pointed his finger downward.

"I said get below deck! NOW!"

Jimmy raced down first, pushing Princess Imera out of the way. His tiny legs took two stairs at a time, ensuring he was under cover well before anyone else, including the royalty on board.

"The Blood and Bone Brothers spotted us!" Liu yelled as she raced up *Holy Tide*'s gangplank, her entire right arm covered in blood. "They're turning the guard's cannons on us!"

Sadie jumped. Was that Raquel over Liu's shoulder? "Did she get hit with a gunshot or a blade?"

Liu dropped Raquel to the ground and hunched over, panting for air. The girl was deceptively petite and had much more solid muscle mass than Liu had thought. Liu's arms and legs ached, and her groin and kidneys were sore. "Neither." She answered between deep breaths. "I coldcocked her."

Sadie's eyebrow shot up, but there was no time for explanations. "Just get her down there and stay with the others." Liu nodded, too exhausted to speak anymore. Using all the strength she could muster, she flung Raquel over her shoulder and made her way downstairs.

Just as Liu descended, Charlie and Taye ran up the gangplank and fell onto the deck in exhaustion and sopping wet from head to toe.

"What happened to you two?" Sadie asked. "Did you swim back?" She was about to ask what happened to the second dory, but Taye cut her off.

"No time to explain." He hoisted himself up, leaving a puddle where he was standing. "The Brothers are about to shoot."

"Javier and I will go get the swivel guns ready!" Charlie said while she lay flat against the ground. She'd never swum so fast in her life. Those minutes out in the open had seemed like hours, as Charlie had forced herself to swim underwater for as long as she could, severely limiting her breath intake. Her head was pounding from the lack of oxygen, and every part of her body wanted to collapse. She desperately wanted to lay here for the rest of the day, but she knew that wasn't remotely possible. She and Taye had just fought like hell to make it back to *Holy Tide* in one piece, and there was no way she was going to let the BBB take them down now. "It'll take about ten minutes to load up our guns."

"Sadie, is everybody else below deck?" Taye extended his arm out to Charlie.

She took it and stood up on two very wobbly legs. "DUCK!" Axel shouted.

They all quickly dropped down on their bellies as the other ship blew a volley of musket fire. Thankfully, due to the infamous inaccuracy of the musket, most of the shots landed in the water.

Sadie stood up slowly. Muskets also had long loading times, so they still had a few minutes before the next round. She counted in her head. *Taye, Charlie, Axel, Jimmy*—

Taye and Axel used the pause in gunfire to run to the helm, while Charlie and Javier took over the swivel guns. Up ahead, a round of cannon fire bombarded the princess's sloop. The ship swayed to the left one more time before completely sinking into the Indian Ocean. Men slid down the deck and plunged headfirst into the water. Half a dozen had managed to jump off, but for the twenty or so men on board, their fates were sealed. Javier, Axel, Taye, and Charlie watched in stunned amazement, while Sadie turned away. Waves rippled through the water, sending *Holy Tide* rocking.

"The ship sank!" Javier shouted, stating the obvious. "Yeah, but the Blood and Bone Brothers have the massive guns from the guards' ship turned our way!" Charlie shot back. She squinted. Had another ship joined the attack? Where had it come from?

"Javi, do you see that ship?" Charlie pointed to the right of her.

Before Javier could turn around, another volley of musket fire rained down on them. Just as before, they all ducked to the ground.

"Here!" Charlie yelled, after the shots had ceased, to let the rest of the crew know that she had survived the attack.

"Here!" Javier followed.

From the distance, they heard Axel and Taye shout "Here" as well.

"Here!" Sadie called out, unable to keep the nerves out of her voice. She desperately wanted to get below deck and hide. Let Taye, Charlie, Axel, and Javier play battleship. When she saw muskets and cannons, she ran in the opposite direction. Quickly, Sadie resumed her counting. *Taye, Charlie, Axel, Jimmy, Liu, Raquel (sort of, since she was currently passed out, thanks to Liu), princess, princess's friend, her …*

"Ingela! Ingela!" Sadie shouted. She wasn't surprised that Ingela hadn't gone below deck yet—she loved the action too much to do that. But it was too dangerous to let her stay out here. Sadie decided it was better to just go and get the girl herself. She stayed down on the ground a few more seconds to make sure there were no delayed shots. When she was convinced the musket fire had temporarily ceased, Sadie scurried around the corner.

As she turned, Sadie saw Ingela's legs sticking out from behind the extra rigging. "Squirt!" Sadie whispered. "You can get up! They're reloading the muskets." Her legs didn't move.

"Squirt!" Sadie said louder as she ran over to Ingela. Just before she reached her, Sadie slipped on something slick. "What is this?" Sadie muttered as she landed on her bottom. She looked down at her palm, which was covered with blood.

"Where's this from, Squirt?" Sadie looked around, then ahead. Directly in front of her, Ingela lay face down in a pool of her own blood.

Chapter
THIRTEEN

SLOG
Date: December 6
Position: Leaving Perim

It's chaos on Holy Tide, and I don't know why I'm taking the time to write this except that I want a record of today to survive in case we don't.

The sultan's fleet is gone. His navy ship has been captured, and the princess's ship has sunk. Charlie mentioned seeing another ship join the attack, but none of us saw it, and it hasn't come after us. Instead, the Blood and Bone Brothers sent a smaller ship to chase us. Holy Tide is practically flying through the water, but the other ship remains fast behind. They shoot at us and we shoot back. The blasts of the swivel guns pound in my ears.

Princes Imera is on board Holy Tide. But all the jewels, coins, and other valuables are gone with the loss of her ship. We have forsaken any chance of a reward.

Maybe it's because of our greed that we're being punished. Ironically, Ingela was the only one of us who wasn't doing this for a reward, but from a sense of duty.

I've never seen so much blood.

They're calling for me—I must go.

Sadie leaned over Ingela's body. In between whiskey bottles, or during those futile occasions when he'd decide to dry out,

Sadie had learned anatomy and science from her father, a medical doctor by trade. From her mother, a chemist, she'd soaked up everything about compounds, elements, and even herbs. But her schooling had been cut off before she could get to this part. Surgery. Her mind struggled with something it wasn't accustomed to feeling—not knowing what to do.

"Sadie! Do something!" Axel screamed. "Save her!" The scalpel shook in Sadie's hand. "I-I can't!!!"

Amsha, the princess's friend, burst open the door to the infirmary. "I only now received news of the gunshot!" Sadie put the scalpel down. "And who are you exactly?"

Her nerves were already frayed, and she didn't need this lady to push her to the brink.

Amsha slowly made her way through the room, which was dark and cluttered. She bumped into a cabinet, or perhaps it was the wall, before deciding it was best to use her good arm to feel her way. Someone, maybe Raquel, pulled her forward to the table where the body lay. Under the dim light that surrounded the table, Amsha studied the victim, first taking note of her small feet and working her eyes upward to the cherubic cheeks. She stifled a gasp.

Raquel, Liu, all of them were young—too young, but this poor soul who'd been mercilessly shot and was now losing her life was nothing but a dear, sweet child. "I am Sultan Musef's royal physician," Amsha whispered, trying to keep the tremble out of her voice.

Raquel cried out something in Spanish, but no one was really paying attention. With the aid of smelling salts, she'd come to a while ago with a major headache and an even bigger gripe with Liu. That would have to wait. Ingela's life was more important than paybacks.

Amsha took a deep breath. They had to take action immediately. "Fetch me more light!" she ordered Axel. She looked at Raquel. "Grab clean bandages. If you do not have them, then get the cleanest cloths you can find. What about antiseptic?"

Sadie shook her head. Despite all the other luxuries on board *Holy Tide*, the infirmary was hopelessly basic. This was probably because of the Castaways' bloated sense of invincibility. Sadie's own antiseptic compound, a mixture of wax, oil, turpentine, and St. John's wort, had been lost in the storm, along with most of her medical supplies.

"I think all we have is liquor," Sadie answered haughtily. *Who was this woman pushing her way into their business?* Under normal circumstances, she'd be elated just to spend time around a medical doctor, but now Sadie was irritated by the presence of this know-it-all "royal" physician.

Amsha looked at Liu. "Find a bottle of the liquor with the highest alcohol content." Then she turned her attention to Sadie. "Your instinct was right. The first thing is to apply pressure to stop the bleeding. This rag is soaked through, so you will need to get a new one."

Perhaps it was Amsha's snooty accent, or her condescending tone, but Sadie found her voice grating. She reached for the old rag. "Obviously I should take this one off first."

Amsha gently stopped her. "No, keep it. Taking it off now risks contaminating the wound. Just place the new rag on top of the old rag."

Sadie stopped. She'd never known that before. Sadie ran to the corner for a roll of cloth, tore a piece off, and hurried back to Ingela.

Axel rushed in carrying two standing candelabras. He placed them directly around Amsha and Ingela. As *Holy Tide* skipped through the waves, the ship rocked back and forth. Axel lit the candles and held onto the candelabras to keep them steady.

"Much better," Amsha commended Axel as he repositioned the candelabras closer. "Now I have a closer inspection of the situation."

Liu came running in carrying a large bottle of rum with her good arm. Her other arm had lost a lot of blood, but thankfully Raquel's cut turned out to be a flesh wound that she had managed to clean and bandage up by herself. However, Liu had already pissed blood once from the kidney kick. Or maybe it was the groin kick. Either way, Liu was nursing her wounds and intent on not speaking to Raquel, and Raquel seemed to be doing exactly the same.

Raquel's head throbbed as she followed Liu in with a bagful of clean bandages. She handed the bag to Amsha, then steadied herself against the cabinet, feeling dizzy, either because of her head wound or the fast pace of the ship.

Ingela's eyelids fluttered as she drifted in and out of consciousness. The ship swayed to the left, then quickly back to the right.

"Instruct the captain to slow down at once!" Amsha directed. "I need this vessel to steady!"

The group exchanged worried looks. They were on a high-speed chase with the Blood and Bone Brothers' crew.

They couldn't afford to slow down.

Amsha didn't wait for a response to her request, and bowed her head further to examine Ingela. Her brow furrowed. "This is worse than I thought." Whether Amsha muttered the next part to Ingela or just to herself, the rest of them heard her clearly. "We do not have much time."

***

It took several minutes of scolding, followed by threats, before Jimmy eventually climbed back up to the main deck. He loaded the swivel gun with a chamber pre-filled with gunpowder.

"Jimmy! Over here!" Charlie yelled.

Jimmy crawled as fast as he could from Javier to Charlie, his shaggy red hair flopping back and forth like a troll bounding through the forest. He grabbed another chamber. The other ship was so close, he could easily make out the snaggle-toothed leer of the Blood and Bone Brothers' quartermaster. Since most of what they knew about the BBB's crew was rumor and legend, he wasn't sure the information was to be trusted. Jimmy had heard that the quartermaster, who went by the name Snake, wasn't as sadistic as his bosses. However, he was known to keep cages of deadly pythons that he released on his captives, which Jimmy thought was pretty gruesome. He was doing his best to make sure he wasn't snake food tonight.

"Let's both shoot at the sail!" Charlie instructed Javier.

He nodded and rotated his swivel gun upward. Only one meter high, with a diameter of three-and-a-half meters, swivel guns were actually more like small cannons. Their portability made them ideal weapons on pirate ships, as they could be easily mounted on the deck railings. Their limited range and tiny caliber didn't make them capable of sinking ships, but they could still cause a hell of a lot of damage.

The sun was setting now, casting a bright pink glow on the water and the crew. A strong gust of wind was helping to push *Holy Tide* forward, but the same wind also helped the other ship move fast.

Javier hesitated. "You think we can make the main sail?" His dark brow furrowed. "We need to make this ammunition count." He shook his head. They should have traded in the whole bag of Raquel's shells for more gunpowder. Actually, they never should have listened to these girls and gone on this mission in the first place.

There was a loud boom. A round of musket fire landed directly next to him. Javier dropped flat on the main deck. "Here!"

he called out, though he remained on the ground. "Here!" Jimmy shouted, crouched down and shaking next to Charlie.

The enemy ship knew nightfall would greatly limit their visibility, making them all sitting targets. That's why they were getting more aggressive with their fire. It was hard to gauge accurately, but judging by the rapid and steady rounds they were firing, it seemed that the Blood and Bone Brothers weren't worried about running out of ammunition anytime soon. *Holy Tide* needed to strike hard and fast, or they were sure to be dead in the water.

"Here!" Charlie shouted, as she tried to ease Jimmy off of her. When he wouldn't budge, she threw a hard elbow jab into his ribs. "Get into position, Jimmy!" she commanded. Jimmy skulked away. Charlie peeked over at Javier, who was still lying on the floor.

She cleared her throat. "Get up, Javi!"

Reluctantly, he sat up behind the swivel gun. "We only have one or two good shots!" he shouted in protest, or defeat. His wavy hair sagged across his forehead.

"Then we gotta focus, Javi!" Charlie shifted her gun slightly. She would have liked to say something to rally her "troops," but given her penchant for sticking her foot in her mouth, Charlie decided it was best to ditch the pep talk and just stick to business.

"Javier, count us off!"

He took a deep breath. "*Um, dois, três,*" Javier counted off in Portuguese. He always found it hard to speak in English when he was frightened.

Together they fired a round. A shot ripped through the enemy's mainsail. Almost immediately, the ship slowed down before stopping dead in the water.

Charlie jumped up and down. "We got it!" she cried.

Once they knew the coast was clear, Javier and Jimmy stood up and joined Charlie. Together, they all cheered.

Snake and his crew continued to shoot their guns, but *Holy Tide* was already too far away.

***

"Who has the steadiest hands?" Amsha asked, tucking her grayish-black hair behind her ear.

Everyone in the room pointed at Sadie.

"I cannot do this with my injured arm, but I will talk you through it," Amsha explained in a tone that was strong and direct, but still friendly. Her flawless English was distinctly educated and aristocratic, yet her demeanor was warm, though urgent, given the immediacy of Ingela's situation.

Sadie's eyes opened wide. "No! I-I-I can't." Except for some toads in her father's biology tutorials and the fish they ate, she'd never actually cut anything up before. Especially a human!

Especially Ingela.

"I can see you have good instincts," Amsha spoke in a calm, reassuring voice. "Now you have to put them to use." She turned to the group. "I need someone to hold the little one's—what is her name?"

"I-I-Ingela. She's my sister. Half-sister …sister." Axel tried to keep himself together, but just seeing her tiny body covered in so much blood was too much.

Even when Ingela was asleep, she was full of life. Or at least mischief. One could watch her snooze and feel the schemes she was dreaming of and the devilry that was in store. Often, she'd yell out nonsensical words in her sleep, much like she would while awake, and her fingers and toes would wiggle in delight as though she was fighting her way through some wild, crazy nighttime adventure.

Axel checked her toes. They were more still than he'd ever seen them. It wasn't just all the blood. It was seeing her so lifeless. He turned away.

"Okay, why don't you come here and hold her head steady?" Amsha asked Axel. She saw him hesitate and smiled softly. "Please? Your sister needs you."

He nodded and walked over to her. Axel cradled Ingela's head between his hands.

"That's a good brother. Raquel, you hold down her arms, and Liu, please take the legs. And whatever you do, do not let her move!"

They all took their places, each grabbing a different part of Ingela.

"First thing, carefully remove the rags." Sadie followed the doctor's instruction.

"Good job, Sadie." Amsha smiled. "Now, you see the tear in her clothing where the bullet went through?"

Sadie nodded, secretly basking in the glory of Amsha's approval. She felt guilty for hating Amsha less than twenty minutes earlier, and because she should only be concentrating on Ingela now.

"The ball round probably tracked bits of her clothing as it went in. That is why we need to remove the bullet immediately, before the cloth starts to cause an infection." Amsha used her good hand to reach into the inner pocket of the flowing cotton gown she wore over a pair of pants that tightened around the ankles. She pulled out a small black bag and handed it to Sadie.

"I always carry an emergency kit on me, in case of times like this. A habit of being a physician," she said. "Take out the surgical scissors to cut her shirt so you can see the wound better."

Sadie opened the bag and grabbed the scissors. She cut along the upper right corner of Ingela's shirt, noticing for the first time that the girl hadn't even gotten properly dressed this morning. She was wearing a man's undershirt, and to no one's surprise, a badly-patched pair of trousers.

Her blond hair, which usually fell into her eyes, had been clipped back off her face with one of Raquel's barrettes, something that Ingela would never forgive them for if she found out. There was a thick layer of grime covering her skin that most likely had been there for at least the last few days, and a rank smell seeped out, which was also due to a lack of hygiene. Sadie could handle the dirt and odor because they were innately Ingela. What wasn't natural was the grim, lifeless expression she wore. Ingela's usual scowl was serious but always spirited, while the bleak look she had now looked more foreign on Ingela than the gunshot that had caused it.

The shirt was cut open, fully exposing Ingela's right shoulder. Amsha lightly patted her finger around the bloody area. "Here, this is the bullet." She pulled Sadie's hand to where hers was resting. "Do you feel it?"

Sadie followed Amsha's lead until she also felt the round object inside Ingela's skin. "Are we …are we going to have to amputate?" Sadie sucked in her breath.

Axel grimaced. At nineteen, he was fortunate to have all of his parts, something that was increasingly rare among seamen. He'd heard some pretty gruesome amputation stories during his years on the sea. A few years back, he'd even witnessed a guy get his foot cut off. Blood loss and infection were the greatest threats after a shooting or a stabbing, and surgeons were often forced to amputate limbs. With the invention of the screw tourniquet, a device as excruciating as the name suggested, amputations had become even easier, and were therefore the most popular surgical procedure out on the sea. That is, easier for the physician, but not for the patient, as there were no anesthetics available stronger than rum to numb the agonizing pain. To make matters worse, if the vessel didn't have a proper doctor, the ship's carpenter was tasked with using his tools to cut straight through an injured crewman's flesh and bone.

To everyone's great relief, Amsha shook her head. "No, amputation is something Western physicians use as their first option. In the East, we use it as our last." She pressed her finger around the wound with more pressure this time. "It feels like a surface wound," said Amsha, turning to Axel. "I know it looks like a lot of blood, but I do not think the bullet hit any major organs or arteries."

Axel nodded, grateful for any bit of light in this darkest of hours. He tightened his grip around the candelabra, then turned away. He'd allowed his little sister to get shot! He could hear Knut cursing him from the grave.

Ingela murmured something, but it was difficult to decipher if she was actually coherent and making up curse words, or just speaking gibberish. Her head rolled from side to side, her eyes flickering open, then shut.

Amsha picked up the rum bottle. "It would be better if Ingela was sedated for this, because this is where it will really begin to hurt." Amsha handed the bottle to Axel. "Raquel, soak some clean rags with this. Axel, pour some of the liquor into your sister's mouth."

They both obliged Amsha. Axel took a swig for himself as well.

"Sadie, you need to clean the area with the rag. Get as far into the wound as you can without pushing the bullet further down. It is crucial that we sterilize the area as thoroughly as possible."

Sadie brushed the rum-soaked rag over the blood. The sharp, pungent smell filled her nostrils and made her eyes wet. Her father had preferred whiskey, but he'd gladly help himself to some rum once the whiskey was finished. Sadie shook her head, trying to get the images of her father out of her head and concentrate on Ingela. As the alcohol touched the outer edges of the bullet hole, she could almost feel the sizzle herself. Goosebumps ran up her arms.

"Cut you!" Ingela called out, as her left foot jerked forward.

"Keep her steady!" Amsha warned.

Liu put more of her weight on Ingela's legs.

Amsha looked around and found a random wooden spoon. "Poor darling, it looks like she is still slightly awake." Amsha handed the spoon to Axel. "Give her this to bite down on." She inspected Ingela's right shoulder area. "It's clean. Next step, take the scalpel and cut along here." Amsha pointed to the gash.

Sadie picked up the scalpel and pressed it against Ingela's flesh. She began to slit open the wound.

Before Sadie proceeded any further, Ingela's entire body flinched. She shouted. This time it wasn't gibberish, her scream was clear, even with the spoon in her mouth.

Sadie put the scalpel down. "I can't!" Tears sprang from her eyes.

Amsha placed her good hand on Sadie's shoulder. "Sadie, we do not have time for second-guessing!" Her voice was firm. "Stop crying and pick up that scalpel, or Ingela is going to die on this table!" She turned to Axel. "Give us more light."

Axel tilted the candelabra forward, careful to make sure no hot wax spilled. Without another second of hesitation, Sadie wiped her eyes with the back of her sleeve, picked up the scalpel, and sliced further into the wound.

"Exactly. Open it wider, wider. That's it." Amsha soothed. Her words were being drowned out by Ingela's shrieks. There was no doubt that she was fully awake now.

Ingela's left arm shot up. Raquel held it down but looked away, reciting every prayer her father had ever taught her.

Axel wanted to cover his ears from the sound of his sister's flesh being ripped open, but his hands were busy holding Ingela's head steady, as well as the candelabra. His salty tears fell upon her forehead, which he kissed. "It's almost over, Squirt. We love you. We love you. We love you," he repeated over and over.

Ingela chomped down harder on the wooden spoon. "Do you see the bullet, Sadie?"

Sadie drowned out everything around her except for Amsha. "Yes."

"Good. Take the tweezers, steady your hand, and then pull it out. Sadie, it is critical to Ingela's survival that you take out the whole thing. Do not leave any part of it inside." Sadie took a deep breath and waited until her hand was stable. When she was ready, she inserted the tweezers into the gash. After a few excruciating moments, Sadie clenched the bullet.

"Have you grasped the entire bullet?" Amsha asked. Sadie nodded.

"Extract it slowly."

With the same steady hand, Sadie took the bullet out with the tweezers. Bits of white cloth from Ingela's shirt were stuck to it. She plunked it in the bowl next to her.

"Bravo, Sadie!" Amsha cheered.

They all breathed a collective sigh of relief.

"Now, we must cauterize the wound to stop it from bleeding further."

Amsha handed a knife with a wide blade to Axel. "Clean this with the rum. Then, heat it over the candles." She turned to Sadie. "Have you ever cauterized a wound before?"

Sadie gulped. "Yes, one short burst? To close up the injury but not burn any healthy tissue."

"Exactly."

After a few minutes, Axel handed the hot knife to Sadie. She pressed the flat side of the blade against Ingela's open wound. It hissed against the damaged flesh. Ingela's body went slack as she passed out from the pain.

Axel staggered out to the deck railing and vomited.

If he'd bothered to notice, he would have been surprised to see that it was already nighttime, with a full, glorious moon hanging low in the sky.

"Ax?" Sadie called.

Axel waved her away. "Go away, Sadie! Leave me alone!" He held the railing. "I mean, thanks for saving my sister's life. But I can't be around anyone right now."

Holy Tide skipped along the waves, moving especially fast now that it was traveling downwind. They weren't being chased anymore, but they were still in a race. Sadie's life-saving surgery had gotten Ingela out of the woods for now, but she needed to get to Amsha's clinic in Marrakatra before her condition worsened.

"That's just it, Ax. I was supposed to be watching her!" she shouted, her voice trembling.

Axel whipped around. "I'm her big brother. It's my responsibility to protect her!" He crumpled to the ground. "She's only eleven!" He punched the ground. "She's just a kid. I forgot that because she's so …"

"Tough?" Sadie asked, slightly smiling through her tears. "Yeah." His little sister idolized him and mimicked everything he did. What a useless hero he'd turned out to be. Axel buried his face in his hands. He'd never forgive himself for this.

Sadie dropped down beside him. She looked up at the brightest star in the sky and made a pledge that if Ingela made it, Sadie would never neglect her again.

Together, side by side, Axel and Sadie cried.

***

Len sat in silence. The silence was almost as terrifying as when she spoke. The doctor took out a long, thin needle.

Len smirked. They would need something a lot bigger than that to put him down.

The doctor walked around to Len's chair. "Forward, please," he said in the same jovial tone he used with his patients, most of whom were children. He liked playing with grown-ups, too, though he found they usually cried more.

Len obliged. Not that he had much choice, considering his hands and feet were shackled together and a henchman stood only a few feet away armed with a mighty big hammer.

The doctor ran his finger along Len's spine. With so much excess mass on the patient, the spot was difficult to find, but the doctor didn't dare disappoint the Countess. He felt along the bony groove on Len's lower back. "*Cauda equina*," he murmured to himself. Too far. He ran his finger back up along the spine. There, he found it! Inside *conus medullaris*, between the L2 and L3 vertebrae. This was always a favorite for him, the doctor thought to himself as he inserted the needle a third of the way in. He was honored the Countess had listened to his suggestion.

Len let out an involuntary snicker at the tickle of the needle. What was next? A hot bath?

"You stab me in the back," the Countess said. "And I'll have to stab you in yours."

Len looked up, down, to the left, to the right, but still he couldn't figure out where she was. His head had been covered in a potato sack, but he knew they'd taken him from his stuffy jail cell down several sets of stairs before arriving here. The air had gone cooler, danker, and mustier. He looked around the damp, dimly lit dungeon for a woman, but all he could spot was a strange-looking man with a peculiarly sordid grin wearing a white doctor's coat, a henchman, and the weaselly Rogers Barrish, who was standing a mere few feet in front of him.

The doctor nodded to the henchman. Len relaxed even further as the henchman put down the oversized hammer. Then, he walked over to the chair. He grabbed hold of the needle sticking out of Len's back and twisted it slowly.

"What the—!" Len shrieked. An excruciating pain shot through his body, like a thousand knives plunging into him at once.

The doctor watched. As he'd explained in great detail to the Countess, the spinal cord consisted of millions of nerve fibers. The point he'd chosen for the patient controlled the lower back and legs. It was incredible how one tiny spot could radiate so much agony. He sighed. The wonders of science.

"Stop lying," she ordered, her voice calm and still over Len's loud wailing.

Barrish winced. He'd never been a needles kind of guy. His preferred method of torture was chains. "Just tell her what she wants and she'll let you go!" he whispered.

Len grimaced. Every word out of that rat was a lie. Although he couldn't see her, Len knew this lady was merciless. In the last minute-and-a-half, he'd become aware that for the first and last time in his life, he wasn't going to get himself out of this. The only thing left for him to do was to make sure he took it all like a man.

The henchman pushed the needle in further.

Len's manly resolve broke instantly. "Okay!" he cried through gritted teeth. Despite the chill in the downstairs dungeon, sweat beads rolled down Len's forehead.

The doctor nodded to the henchman, who retreated back to the corner.

Len waited for the sharp, stabbing sensation to subside before speaking. After a few moments, he spoke. "They captured us." Len motioned to the tattoo on his forehead. He still had to give it to China Doll for coming up with that brilliant move. It had ensured his silence. He'd be wearing their stupid scar to his imminent grave. "Me and Seth." He flashed to his old pal flailing up and down in the water, begging Len not to drown him. To Len's dismay, the skinny bastard was more buoyant than he'd counted on and had cost him almost a whole day out on that sea.

"How did they manage to get you both? Are these Pirettes expert fighters?" Barrish asked. Len and Seth had been some of his best goons. In fact, it had taken his men an entire month to track down Len, who'd been hiding out in a remote part of Scotland after botching up the Pirette mission, and bring him back to the dungeon here in London. Once he'd found Len, though he refused to talk, it wasn't hard to figure out that Seth was still somewhere in the Indian Ocean.

Len grunted. The same question had been haunting him for a month now. He thought about how the crazy one, the maniac redhead and her sword, sliced and diced him. There was a slow, steely ruthlessness that seethed inside her. Similar to the invisible woman talking to him now. He'd regret not getting to administer his own special brand of suffering on the crazy one. Still, he decided he'd keep his memory of her to himself. After all, he had a legacy to think about now, and it couldn't be tarnished with stories of a girl beating him up. "No, they were clumsy. Like you'd expect a bunch of lasses to be. Dumb luck, really," he answered. "They had some kind of strange way about them."

"What the hell do you mean, 'strange way'?" Barrish asked, the disgusted expression on his face further enhancing his rodent-like features.

"They kept on mutterin' some nonsense." Len didn't even see the doctor nod this time. He just felt the henchman twist the needle, and then the shooting, paralyzing pain.

"STOP! STOP!"

The doctor was deaf to Len's cries. Instead, he pondered whether it was time for another needle. Maybe in the eye? There were so many nerve endings there, too. Then he thought against it. The Countess was a woman of controlled restraint. After a few more seconds, he nodded to the henchman, who retreated back to the corner.

Len was dizzy from the pain. "Over and over," he muttered, whirling his index finger. "Then they did a bunch of sword stuff." He dropped his head. "'Mind over body'."

Mind over body. The words were like a punch directly to her gut. The Countess's mind reeled from the implications. It was impossible. *She'd made sure of that.*

The Countess leaned against the wall. The stone cooled her. She needed to attend to this business first. "Take him."

Two armed guards walked into the cell and lifted Len out of the chair.

"NO!" Len shrieked, suddenly becoming very alert. "I-I-I can find them again! Give me another chance!" he begged. His pleas were met with cold silence.

Barrish straightened his coat. He checked his pocket watch. There was an important board meeting he had to get to, and he'd already been delayed enough by the Countess's silly games. A few thrashes with a chain and he would have gotten Len to sing.

He made his way to the door. The henchman blocked the exit. Suddenly, out of nowhere, another henchman of equal size appeared. The two men restrained Barrish. He thrashed against them, but they were too powerful. One picked up the giant hammer.

The doctor clapped giddily. Two in one day! The Countess was always spoiling him with her surprises!

From somewhere deep in the dark shadows, the Countess spoke in that low, icy tone. "Please stay, Governor Barrish. We still have some business to attend to."

Chapter
FOURTEEN

SLOG
Date: December 9
Location: 3°15´N 73°00´E / 3.250°N 73.000°E

It takes one week to sail from Djibouti to Marrakatra.

Amsha says we have five days to get Ingela to her clinic. I don't want to add maps, wind conditions, and weather reports. Because we've been here before—on the Indian Ocean, racing against all hopes to get somewhere, then POW! Last time it was the storm. I learned then (the very hard way) that all the sea charts and maps in the world won't make this ship go faster, keep deadly storms at bay, or keep Ingela alive.

SOFN,

Sadie

Holy Tide stopped behind the massive gated wall. Charlie looked up to see an enormous blockade made of gigantic sheets of iron and stone. Its sheer size was intimidating enough, as if it could touch the fading moon up above and spanned as far as the eye could see across the ocean. Charlie shivered.

Amsha yelled at the guards in a language none of the girls could understand, though it was safe to assume by the fierceness in her tone and rapidity of her words that they weren't exchanging niceties. Axel stood next to her, holding Ingela's limp body in his arms.

Strong downwinds had let them reach Marrakatra in six days instead of seven. But this was still a day late for Ingela, whose condition had worsened. Despite her Scandinavian roots, Ingela always held a healthy tan, perhaps because she refused to ever go inside. Now, however, her skin was drained of all color, sallow and pale like the moon was tonight. Worse yet, she'd stopped speaking in gibberish or saying anything at all. Ingela had always been loud in everything that she did, so her becoming silent felt as strange and lonely as a carnival without music.

All that stood in the way of her possible chance of survival and Amsha's clinic was the impenetrable mass in front of them. Axel lowered his ear to Ingela's chest. His little sister's heartbeat barely made a sound. "Open the bloody gates!" he roared. "She's dying!"

Amsha turned around and shot a furious look at Axel. "I am trying to convince these guards that you are not an enemy ship and that the princess and I are not your prisoners. Your outbursts are only serving to weaken my argument!" She looked over at Sadie, who'd become her unofficial apprentice these last few days at sea. "Sadie, take care of him. And keep wiping the damp rag over Ingela to keep her cool."

Sadie continued to rub the rag over Ingela's blistering body. "Axel, chill," she whispered.

He nodded while shaking his leg in his usual jittery fashion. Just then, Princess Imera burst onto the main deck, much to everyone's surprise. Except for her constant demands for better accommodations, food, and bedding, she'd deliberately kept herself away from the crew for most of the six-day journey. The first hints of dawn coincided with the princess's appearance. The round sun, with its rosy glow, was in sharp contrast to the princess, who seemed too angular and stern against the warm morning light.

Charlie studied her from afar. With her pointy head, ears, and nose, and triangular shaped frame set upon two stubby legs, Princess Imera resembled one of those Christmas tree drawings Ingela had made as a small child.

She placed her heavily bangled arms on her hips. Ignoring the fact that she'd actually been rescued by *Holy Tide*, Princess Imera refused to take off any of her jewelry for the entire duration of the trip back to Marrakatra, apparently fearing that the crew would steal them. Now her jeweled bangles jangled loudly as she shook her arms at the guards. She shouted in a high-pitched shriek that unfortunately had become an all-too-familiar noise on *Holy Tide* this past week. The guards straightened.

Amsha balked. "Oh, Princess! Please help us. They saved our lives and brought us back home! You—"

Princess Imera raised her hand, instantly silencing Amsha. She turned around and sneered at the mismatched group of vagabonds surrounding her.

"What did she say? What is she doing?" Axel whispered at Amsha, his anxiety and growing anger dripping off of every word.

Amsha shook her head vigorously as a warning to Axel to keep quiet. The princess had the power to arrest them all and, judging by the snide expression on her face, it looked as though she might do just that. It was imperative to placate her with their silence.

Amsha watched as Princess Imera shouted a succession of demands—underlined with threats—to the guards. Once the princess had finished, the guards immediately rushed off. Amsha let out a sigh of relief. Even if it was for her own selfish purposes, Princess Imera had managed to get them inside. The gates slowly began to open, and *Holy Tide* started to make its way into Marrakatra.

***

It was past seven o'clock in the morning now, and none of them had gotten much sleep the night before. Despite their exhaustion, no one wanted to leave Ingela until they knew she was all right. Everyone, that is, except Javier and Jimmy, who were happily tucked away in the second of Amsha's two guesthouses. For as liberal as she seemed to be, Amsha just couldn't accept unmarried or unrelated males and females sleeping under the same roof, and therefore had assigned one guesthouse for the Castaways, and another for the girls. This, after having been roommates for several weeks now, was fine for all of them, especially Charlie.

After the gates had opened, they'd managed to bypass the guard's interrogation (with no help from Princess Imera, who'd gone straight to her royal chambers) and rushed Ingela to Amsha's clinic. Charlie sat back against the plush divan and wrapped the cashmere throw around her bare feet. Despite Sadie's protest at Charlie removing her boots, she'd gone right ahead and done so anyway, and was now waving her offensive feet in Sadie's face.

"You have ten seconds to get your putrid hooves away from me!" she said as she slapped away Charlie's malodorous tootsies.

Charlie chuckled. Since Ingela wasn't here to do it, someone had to get a rise out of Sadie. Being that person made Charlie feel a little better. She fluffed her silk pillow. She'd never been in a hospital as fancy as this. Come to think of it, she'd never been *anywhere* as fancy as this! Having spent their lives on the sea, with only sporadic visits to the ship's infirmary, none of them were too familiar with hospitals. But the few they'd had the misfortune to visit were disease-infested, filthy ratholes.

Amsha's clinic, however, was a world away from those "gateways to death." She'd explained her healing philosophy on *Holy Tide*, but truthfully, only Sadie had paid attention. It was something about celebrating life and bringing dignity and beauty to the patient. With its domed ceilings, beautiful whitewashed walls, and marble floors, this hospital clearly embodied Amsha's compassionate approach to medicine. This place even had twenty-four-hour meal service, though none of them had much of an appetite to take advantage of it.

Charlie re-fluffed her pillow, this time punching it a bit too hard. As comfortable as this place was, they'd been waiting anxiously for some kind of news about Ingela for the past couple of hours. She sighed. It was the not knowing that was unbearable. Multitudes of horrific scenarios involving the little one's fate were playing themselves out in Charlie's head. That, mixed with the helpless feeling of knowing a loved one was suffering and she was helpless to stop it, was excruciating.

Everyone was pretending to be calm, but their worried expressions and Axel's nonstop pacing back and forth indicated they were all having similarly terrible thoughts. Charlie looked at Liu and Raquel and decided they'd be a good distraction. "Spill," she said as she pointed to Liu.

"What?" Liu took a sip of sweet tea. They not only liked milk in their tea here, they also loaded it up with lots of honey as well, turning it into a candied goo.

"Your arm's all cut up, and Raquel has a knot the size of Sadie's ass on her head," Charlie replied. She'd tried to have a cup of that tea, but she found it too cloying, despite her enormous sweet tooth. In fact, just watching Liu drink it now made her a bit nauseous.

"Ha, ha. At least I *have* an ass," Sadie said, giving Charlie the stink eye. "But Charlie's right, what happened between you two?"

Charlie grimaced. Sadie went mad over a good piece of gossip, and she was a relentless hound when it came to sniffing it out. She looked at her pocket watch. Twenty-two minutes had gone by since the last time she'd checked it. At least this was going to help make the time go by faster. "Sadie, in your best medical opinion, what caused the gash on Liu's arm?"

Taye, who was sitting next to Sadie, took a sip of his mango lassi and looked on with mild amusement. Guys were so much easier to deal with. Just give them some ale and they'd brawl it out. But these girls, especially Charlie and Sadie, loved to play torturous mind games. Sadie also had the annoying habit of always wanting to talk everything out. Taye slurped the rest of his drink down, then he rang the bell to order another. Whatever happened between Liu and Raquel, it wasn't over just yet, judging by the bruises and blood.

"I didn't have the chance to actually attend to the wound, Charlie. However, in my best medical opinion, it was a flesh wound along the radial artery caused by a serrated blade found on—" Sadie reached into her pockets and took out her magnifying glass. Adopting her best detective impression, she continued. "As I was saying, caused by a serrated blade found on a dagger like Raquel's."

Liu set her empty teacup down with a little bit more force than she intended, clinking it loudly against the saucer. "Whatever. Just leave it alone, guys."

Axel jumped out of his chair and stood in front of Sadie and Liu. "No, please continue," he said. "Any more impressions you guys want to try out? I mean, let's make this amateur comedy hour at the expense of my little sister who might be dead ..." Axel stopped speaking.

"What? No!" Sadie sat down next to him. "We were just trying to let off some steam. It's so tense, and we're all a ball of nerves. We're sorry," she whispered.

Axel shook his head and plopped back down next to Sadie. "Yeah, me too. I shouldn't have blown up like that."

He smiled apologetically while playfully squeezing her shoulder.

Taye's jaw clenched. He would have liked to throw his lassi at the two of them, but he clearly saw that Axel was a wreck and that, much to his displeasure, Sadie had a way of calming his best friend. Taye would have to ask about this growing *whatever* between Axel and Sadie soon. More specifically, they'd have to drink a couple of beers and throw a few punches over it. She was his little sister, after all! Taye stole a glance at Charlie. Good thing she never had any older brothers, he thought, though Charlie did have a miserable father.

Charlie looked at Sadie and Axel and wondered when they had gotten so close, before refocusing her attention on the topic at hand. "Okay, Embajador. Try to talk yourself out of this one," Charlie said, licking her lips. "Why'd you cut Liu?"

"I saw the faceless soldier," Raquel announced.

Charlie nearly fell out of her chair in shock, while Sadie, Axel, and Taye sat in stunned silence.

Raquel took a breath. She was a master at dramatic timing. When she was ready, she spoke again. "He was on the princess's ship. I tried to kill him," Raquel glared at Liu. Her eyes were like cold steel. "But Liu got in my way. So I cut her. Obviously, that wasn't enough."

Sadie gasped. "You mean the faceless soldiers from the DD? They were on the princess's ship?" She felt her heart pounding loud and fast.

Charlie, Axel, and Taye exchanged puzzled looks.

"But we scoured that ship from one side to the other and we didn't see them." Charlie shook her head. Raquel had been known to say some pretty kooky things before, but mostly about saints and superstitions. She was theatrical, but not a liar. Still, how had they missed the faceless soldiers?

"Exactly!" Liu shouted, pounding her fist against her leather chair. "And it wasn't a 'them,' it was a him. As in Raquel only saw *one* faceless soldier. Who I didn't see. And Raquel was trying to literally walk through fire to kill him, so I cold-cocked her to save both of our lives."

Raquel lunged at Liu. "*Bruja!*"

Liu sidestepped her. The two girls circled each other.

"I know what I saw!" Raquel shouted. "He was there! And you robbed me of my chance to avenge my papa! I will never forgive you!"

Charlie gulped. This stuff was heavy. No way had she thought that she was stirring up this much trouble. She jumped up and stepped in between Liu and Raquel. Taye got involved, too, and managed to coax Raquel into sitting down.

"Even if you didn't see him," Raquel yelled, angry tears falling down her face, "what about the black smoke? You know it was the same kind of smoke."

Liu's voice trembled when she spoke. "Yes, it was the same black smoke. It made me choke." Liu turned to Charlie. "This was at the end. Right before the ship went under." Charlie nodded. "Which explains why we didn't see any of this. I think we'd already jumped off." She looked at Taye, then again at the group. "I saw another ship." Raquel perked up. "With the faceless soldiers?"

Charlie shrugged. "I don't know. I couldn't see who was on it. I only noticed it as we were leaving. But it wasn't there when we first arrived."

"Before we get ahead of ourselves," Liu said, looking at Raquel, "admit that you had a freak-out when we first got on the princess's ship." They'd fought in the past, but never like this. Still, she had to get it all out before they started down the wrong path. Raquel scowled. The last person she ever thought she'd have to convince of her honesty or sanity was Liu. "Yes, I had flashbacks to the DD. Didn't all of us? But that doesn't mean I hallucinated seeing the person who murdered my father!"

Except that you've been obsessed with the faceless soldier, practicing how you are going to kill him, every night since the DD! Liu wanted to shout, but she wasn't going to betray Raquel's secret just to win this argument. She crossed her arms and resolved to remain silent for now.

Sadie nudged Axel's head off her shoulder and sat in the chair next to Raquel. "You were under a lot of stress. We all were," Sadie said, stroking Raquel's back. "Is it possible that you don't really know what you saw?"

Raquel smoldered at the condescending tone in Sadie's voice. She jumped back up so fast her boots scraped against the marble floor. "I dream about revenge for my papa! I flashed back to the DD when we got on that ship. It doesn't mean I'm *loca*! I saw the faceless soldier!"

Charlie pondered the revelations of the last few minutes. The black smoke, the mystery ship, and the possible faceless soldier meant something. She just wasn't sure what yet. As she was about to speak, Taye jumped in.

"Raquel, no one's saying you're crazy. This is just a lot to take in. Especially if it's linked to the Day of Destruction. We're all going to have to go over what we saw and sort this out." Taye sat back in his chair, unable to hide the smug smile on his face for "saving the day."

Charlie glowered. Just because they didn't have their own ship didn't mean she'd stopped being the captain of the girls. She'd been exhilarated after the run-in with the Blood and Bone Brothers. Even if the mission hadn't been successful, *she'd* been successful. She'd managed to protect her girls, just as she'd done on the DD. It had restored her—invigorated her, actually. Sure, Taye had helped, but they'd been a team in a way they hadn't been in years. Both parts equal. Now, here he was, stomping on her territory. She was about to put him in his place when Amsha came rushing out of the double doors.

"Ingela is losing too much blood!"

***

They stood in the operating room together. This room, which was triple the size of the spacious waiting room, lacked any of its bright cheeriness. Though there was still a lot of light, strange medical devices lined the walls. Liquids, solids, and odd substances labeled with unrecognizable text covered every shelf and flat surface. This could easily be a place of medicine or a house of horrors.

"As I was explaining, Axel, the procedure is called a blood transfusion. I transfer blood from you to Ingela." Amsha turned to Sadie. Her dark bushy eyebrows, which sat like angry caterpillars on her forehead, didn't match the soft, warm glow of her coffee-colored eyes. "Please take the vinegar from the bottom shelf and soak a few bandages in it." Sadie nodded, slightly in awe. Blood transfusions were crazy operations mentioned in her adventure books about the future. But here they were, actually about to do one!

The only woman she'd met like Amsha was her own mother, Josephine. Both women were smart, bold, and unafraid of their brains or voices. But Amsha had followed a path her mother had never dared travel. For better or worse, Amsha had never married or had children. Sadie couldn't quite tell how old Amsha was, given her kefir-colored skin was wrinkle-free except for a few lines across her wide forehead, and the silver slivers in her hair only made her black mane shine brighter. But she was probably well past the age to be a bride or bear a child. Instead, Amsha had devoted her entire life to her career. *By choice.* Sadie dipped the last bandage in the vinegar. Before meeting Amsha, Sadie had never known women could do that.

"We still have a lot of learning to do before we perfect this procedure. They do not even attempt it yet in the West. Perhaps those European physicians might learn a thing or two from their Eastern brothers *and* sisters." Amsha flashed a slightly superior smile. She pushed up Axel's shirtsleeve. He looked at her with a dazed expression. "I began transfusing blood from dogs, then sheep, and only started with humans two years ago," said Amsha, anticipating Liu's question. "All the animals survived."

"So what are the results? For the humans, I mean," Axel asked shakily. He'd do anything to save his sister, but, given they were both gamblers, he thought it best to know the odds.

"Six were successful, and two were not."

"You mean two have d-d-died?" Axel asked quietly.

Maybe Amsha should just stick to sheep.

Amsha nodded matter-of-factly. "This procedure is still very much in its early stages, and we have much to learn before it is perfected. I would not risk it except that it is your sister's only chance now."

Forget odds. This was his baby sister. "Do whatever you need to," Axel said solemnly.

Amsha walked over to another table holding a large ivory syringe. "I will need to take blood from you five times with this right now. It is a significant amount, but I am afraid that Ingela needs it."

"Can't the rest of us give our blood?" Raquel asked. Amsha hesitated a moment before answering. "My colleagues are rather free about exchanging blood, sometimes even using their own blood for a transfusion. I do not have any scientific evidence to support me, but I believe there is such a thing as blood compatibility. So I try to limit blood transfusions to family members." Amsha straightened Axel's arm. She pointed to a spot above the inside crux of the elbow. "Sadie, this is my incision point. Clean this, please."

The sour smell of apple vinegar filled the room. "I'd rather do this with rum."

"Sorry, Axel, liquor in your system is not conducive for a successful blood transfusion." Amsha held his arm out while Sadie wiped the vinegar-soaked rag over it. Amsha unscrewed the cap of the syringe.

Axel flinched. "You're going to stick that entire thing into me? It's huge!"

"Yes." Amsha tied a tourniquet around his arm. She ran two fingers up and down the skin, looking for a vein. "Found it." She stuck the needle all the way in, pressing the wooden plunger until it was no longer visible. Axel flinched hard.

Sadie's eyes were transfixed, while Raquel turned away. There'd been too much blood lately.

"Sadie, prepare Ingela's arm in the same spot."

When the syringe was full of Axel's blood, Amsha walked over to Ingela. Then she injected the same blood-filled syringe into the little girl's arm. The whole procedure was finished in ten minutes.

"That's it?" Axel asked. He couldn't believe his sister's entire life hung on a method that took less time than Raquel did to curl her hair. Suddenly, his head felt like he'd drunk a few too many beers. Sadie jumped to steady Axel, easing him down on the bed he was sitting on.

"Now we wait twenty-four hours to see if Ingela's body accepts the blood."

Amsha placed her ear against Axel's heart to listen for any abnormal sounds. "Everything sounds okay with you. For now at least." She patted Axel on his hand. "You were very brave."

No one wanted to ask the question, but someone had to. Liu stepped up. "What happens if Ingela's body doesn't accept the blood?"

Amsha's calm expression clouded. She ran her hand through her big messy hair, getting it stuck in a tangle. "An integral component to a patient's recovery is positivity, so we will not entertain any thoughts about rejection now." She pointed to the exit. "Ingela and Axel need their rest. I suggest you all get some sleep, too."

One by one, each girl gave Ingela and Axel a peck on the cheek. When it was Sadie's turn to kiss Axel, she blushed profusely. Luckily, he was too dizzy to notice.

After they all left, Axel closed his eyes. He didn't put too much faith in the idea of gods. But he sure as hell believed in the power of their old man. So for the hundredth time this week, Axel called upon Knut and begged him to save their girl.

***

"You're not even trying!" Taye shouted at Charlie. They'd only been gilling for a half-hour, and he was already tempted to row the boat back to shore and leave Charlie stranded. The only thing was, it would be unfair to Raquel and Liu, who were actually trying to learn how to gill. Though not together, as they were only speaking to each other if necessary.

"Then *you* go down there and do it!" Charlie yelled back as she hoisted herself into the boat.

Taye wrung his hands in frustration. He really wished Axel was here. The guy always had more patience when teaching smartasses like Charlie. When they'd visited the hospital this morning, Axel had regained his cheery mood. Ingela's body had accepted his blood, and he was preparing to give her another five units, but much to Taye's dismay,

Axel had requested he take the rest of the girls (except Sadie) out and teach them how to gill. Sadie was conveniently assisting Amsha. That was probably a good thing, Taye thought, as his sister was another know-it-all who was impossible to teach.

Liu's head popped out of the water. She reached into the boat for her pocket watch. "I stayed down for over two minutes!"

"You're a natural at this! Great job!" Taye complimented. Liu smiled. "Thanks. You're a good teacher!"

Charlie rolled her eyes. "As much as I enjoy this sweet little lovefest between you two, I'm done."

"No, you're not," Taye said. "You're scared. That's why you can't stay down there long enough."

Taye tried not to notice the drops of water glistening off of Charlie's curvy midriff. He thought back to how her alabaster skin would glow underwater when they used to swim together with much less clothing on than they had on now. The way the white cloth stuck to her thighs, revealing their firm, muscular shape, was still something Taye really wished he could stop staring at.

Charlie's cheeks turned red. It was humiliating to have Taye know she was scared of anything. "No, it's too dark to see anything down there. This isn't a good spot to gill." Even as she said it, Charlie realized how weak she sounded. The part of the Indian Ocean where Marrakatra sat was even better for gilling than the Maldives. The water was so crystal clear you could practically see all the way to the ocean floor. Besides that, there was no frightening current, and the area wasn't known for sharks, though jellyfish, with their stingers, were something to look out for. Still, Charlie shouldn't be afraid here. But she was.

Raquel swam up to the surface "How long was I down?" Taye checked his watch. "Almost two minutes!" he replied.

"Good job! Did you go all the way to the bottom?" "Yeah, but by the time I touched, I was running out of air. I need to get better at holding my breath." Raquel rested her body against the boat, kicking her legs against the warm waves. In the entire week they'd already spent in Marrakatra, they hadn't seen much except the clinic and their guesthouse. Raquel was anxious about Ingela and the whole thing with the faceless soldier, but it was relaxing to finally be outside and in the water. They were spending the entire afternoon swimming and gilling, which was turning out to be better than she'd thought it would be. But she could see how dangerous gilling could get, especially in rougher seas. "So now we can all gill, right? With all of us doing it, we'll be able to save money toward a faster ship."

Charlie whipped around. "What do you mean, 'We can all gill,' Raquel?"

Raquel shrugged her shoulders. "I'm just saying that since we messed up with the treasure and won't be getting a reward, we'll need to gill harder. That'll be easier with three of us now instead of just one."

"You've had a single lesson, and though you seem to have caught on pretty well, you're hardly ready to be out there gilling every day like I was."

"Charlie, calm down," Liu said. "All Raquel was saying was that now the reward is out of the question, we need to find other ways to buy a ship." Liu gave Raquel a smile, hoping she'd appreciate that she'd come to Raquel's defense.

Raquel glowered. "I'm perfectly capable of speaking for myself—in more languages than *you*, I might add, Liu!"

Charlie rolled her eyes. "Maybe before you two take on the responsibilities of gilling, you should drop this stupid grudge!" She undid her ponytail. "Anyway, we're stuck in Marrakatra until Ingela gets better. So there's really nothing we can do about getting a ship for the time being."

Raquel slapped her palm against the water. It wasn't just Liu who was infuriating; Charlie was getting on Raquel's nerves as well.

Taye, who'd been quietly listening to what had turned into yet another heated discussion between the girls, decided to shift the conversation back to gilling. "If you do the whistling trick I showed you, it'll help you suck in more air," he said to anybody who would listen.

Raquel nodded.

"Should we go another round?" Liu asked, eager to get back down. She hadn't found any lirium yet, but she loved gilling already. Plus, she welcomed the distraction that gilling provided from her endless worries over Zhang Tao. "In a few minutes. Can you guys hold the line for me?" Taye replied, taking off his shirt and tying the rope around his waist. Charlie tried to look away but couldn't. He'd always had a lean, athletic physique, but in the last two years, his muscles had become more chiseled and defined. He looked like a real man. Or, as much as she hated to admit it, like an Adonis standing in the middle of a fountain. Instead of just her cheeks, her whole face was now red.

Raquel openly stared at Taye's ripped abs. "Does Javier look like this, too?"

Taye's face scrunched up in a confused expression. "I don't know what you're talking about, Raquel. Maybe you stayed down too long. Just chill for a bit and get some air." Taye turned to Charlie. "I'm gilling." He tied another piece of rope around her waist. His fingers fumbled as they skimmed over her soft skin. Taye concentrated on securing the rope. "And so are you."

"What? Together?" Charlie could feel her heart beating out of her chest.

"I need to see what you're doing wrong in order to help you." He couldn't even look at her directly now that they were so close. "We don't need the rocks. I want to see how far down you can go without them."

Charlie tried to untie the pouch around her waist, but her fingers fumbled with the knot. Her cheeks, her neck, every part of her body burned. Taye was taking control like he always did, treating her like a child. Or worse, an incapable girl. But that's not why her body trembled. She was going to be down there with him. He'd see her fear. How weak she was. Charlie tried to fan herself. Not gilling with him would make her look like a high-maintenance wuss, which was even worse than just being a regular wuss. She had to go down there with him. In the next ten seconds, she needed to toughen up. She finally untied the pouch and left it in the rowboat. "Okay, I'm ready."

"One. Two," Taye counted off. They each sucked in a huge gulp of air. "Three." Then they dove into the water together. As soon as they were underneath, Taye swam to Charlie, wrapping his arm around her waist. The arm was more muscular these days, but the familiarity of the touch felt better than Charlie would admit. Her muscles relaxed against the weight of his firm body. His chin rested against her shoulder. She didn't think about the darkness, her breathing, drowning, or the creatures that might lurk around the corner. Instead, all her thoughts disappeared, and all she could do was feel. She felt every part of Taye over her.

Which made her feel safe.

They swam deeper and deeper together, their fingers intertwined. Four giant spider crabs crawled along the sandy bottom. Taye led Charlie to a large rock.

Exploring the ocean had been "their thing." Since they were kids, they'd swum for hours, together uncovering the mysteries that lay below. Down here, they'd seen their first shark, raced their first eel, escaped their first octopus, and shared their first kiss. All of this had taken place when they were much younger than Liu and Raquel were now.

By the time Charlie was twelve and Taye was thirteen, they'd been fighting, playing, and swimming with each other for so many years that they shared an intimacy that neither of them questioned. They burped, farted, cried, and peed in front of one another. Although, since entering adolescence, they didn't do so much of the last thing around each other anymore. Maybe this was because they were both becoming aware of themselves in a way neither had ever had to care about before.

Charlie hated the musky scent from her underarms, and the red hairs that were growing in patches all over her stark white legs. Taye was suffering through his own growing pains, with a voice that seemed to shift octaves, like an orchestra performing a symphony. So, without ever acknowledging it, they avoided each other. For two weeks, Taye and Charlie didn't fight, play, or swim together, which was longer than the time Charlie was sick with a sore throat.

Then one day, out of the blue, Taye took Charlie to their favorite spot, and they swam together. The moment they dove into the water, any awkwardness disappeared. They explored the sea like they'd done hundreds of times before, hand in hand. Then, at the end, unlike any time before, they kissed. At first, Charlie didn't know what Taye was doing when he drew her close, face to face with his arms around her waist. As he leaned in, she did too, and they banged their teeth. Blushing from the amateurishness of it all, they tried again. The second time was still sloppy, but better. By the sixth time, they'd greatly improved.

That day, the strange wall that had temporarily existed between them was kicked down. There was something new, something exciting that had been added. They were still the same Taye and Charlie. The kiss, and all the kisses that came after that, felt as right as the wrestling, fighting, and swimming they'd always done. But unlike the other physical stuff, this was theirs. Only to be shared by them; their lips, their hands, their bodies.

Now, as Charlie looked ahead, she saw bright patches of yellow and orange coral that lit up the dark water like a hundred burning candles. Taye tightened his grip around Charlie. She felt his heartbeat against her back. It was on these various ocean floors that they'd fallen in love.

A cold chill ran through her. These days, when she crept to the bottom of the sea, Taye wasn't with her anymore. The painful realization hit her like a hundred jellyfish stingers. She wasn't afraid to gill. She was afraid to feel how much she missed him.

Charlie started to kick her legs against Taye. Suddenly, she felt as though her chest had been ripped open. She broke free from his grasp and tugged hard on her rope.

"You were down there for over three minutes!" Liu exclaimed as Charlie's head broke through the surface a few long seconds later. "That's way longer than you've ever gone!"

Charlie ignored Liu as she gasped for air.

Taye popped up. "Hey, why'd you start freaking out?"

"Over three minutes!" Raquel cheered.

"Really?" Taye touched Charlie's shoulder. "That's a record for you!"

Charlie turned and wiped her tears. She didn't want to think about gilling, lirium, or Taye. More than that, she didn't want to feel this endless, aching longing inside. She lifted herself into the boat.

Taye joined her. "After Liu and Raquel take their turn, let's go for another round." He linked his fingers with Charlie's. "I knew you could gill!"

Charlie yanked her hand away. "Thanks for your help," she mumbled, afraid that if she spoke any louder, he'd hear her voice shaking. Charlie picked up a towel and started to dry herself off.

"Are we leaving already?" Raquel asked. "Charlie, are you okay?"

Charlie cringed. The last thing she wanted was for any of them to know. She cleared her throat. "Um, I just can't get into this. I really think we should all be with Ingela right now." Charlie knew it was low to use Ingela's condition, but she just couldn't bear a single second more.

"Of course, Ingela's more important than gilling. And we've already been here awhile," Liu muttered, as she picked up an oar and handed another one to Charlie.

Charlie breathed a sigh of relief. She tried her hardest to concentrate on the horizon, and not on Taye, as they rowed away.

***

Charlie, Liu, and Raquel jumped out of the rowboat and pulled it to shore. A few miles back, Taye had decided to swim back on his own and was somewhere in the Indian Ocean, which was just fine with Charlie.

"Ouch!" Charlie cried as she stepped onto the hot sand. She'd gone barefoot after gilling, but the scalding Marrakatran beach made it impossible to walk without shoes. Worries over Ingela, Zhang Tao, Rogers Barrish, and having no ship had kept her from enjoying any sightseeing excursions in the week they'd been in Marrakatra, but it was clear this tiny kingdom, tucked away between India and the Ottoman Empire, was breathtaking. Even now, with the blue ocean behind her and the white, sandy beach lined with bright pink and yellow flower bushes ahead, Marrakatra looked like a watercolor painting in one of those fancy European museums that Sadie had dragged her to. Charlie waded ankle-deep back into the water to cool her feet.

However, in all her travels, she'd never quite experienced heat like this. Marrakatra's scorching sun and boiling temperatures made her feel like she was trapped in a massive fire pit. "I think I'll go and change out of these wet clothes," Raquel announced.

"Me too!" said Liu, beginning to run after her. She'd been trying to patch things up with Raquel, but the girl could hold a grudge.

Up ahead, Sadie rushed toward them. Charlie froze.

Sadie never moved that fast unless it was an emergency. "Ingela's awake!" Sadie announced with tear-stained cheeks.

"¡Santo Cielos!" Raquel cried, her eyes instantly brimming with tears.

Raquel and Sadie fell into a hug.

Liu, who hadn't realized she'd been holding her breath, let it out. "Is she okay?" Her voice quivered.

Sadie nodded. "Amsha checked all her vitals and says she's going to make a full recovery, but she'll need about three more weeks of bedrest. That's going to be a nightmare for all of us!"

"Can we go see her?" Charlie asked.

"Yeah, she's stirring up trouble like usual. She already ate a whole chicken, and now she's having cake. And of course, she's cussing up a storm about her arm and boasting about how she saved us all from the gunfire." Sadie beamed. "Oh, and Princess Imera invited us to a party. Actually, it was Sultan Musef who invited us. That's what Amsha said, anyway." She fanned herself with her hand. "I was so excited that I ran all the way down here hoping to find you all. But boy, is it hot!"

"Any mention of a reward?" Liu asked. "I mean, does the sultan know we helped? Even if we didn't manage to actually save his fleet?"

"What am I going to wear?" Raquel asked at the same time.

"I think being invited to the sultan's palace is our reward. Amsha said she mentioned us in passing, but she didn't give any details." Sadie shrugged. "After all, we didn't save the treasure. And Raquel, the party isn't for another two weeks, so you have plenty of time to figure out what you're going to wear."

Raquel's eyebrows shot up. "All my good dresses were lost in the storm! I need something new. But what can I make in that short a time?" She looked at Liu, who usually sewed Raquel's designs, then turned away again. A dress was not worth calling a truce for.

Charlie's eyes glazed over with the talk of dresses. She'd been out here for just a few hours and could already feel the sunburn forming on her pale arms, legs, and back. "Hey, Sadie, I need some of that ointment stuff—I'm getting burned pretty bad out here."

Sadie raised an eyebrow. "Are you going to help me pick the aloe vera this time? You know how many times I got pricked by those pointy stems trying to make your ointment last time?"

Before Charlie could answer, Liu decided to speak up. "Guys! We need to talk about what happens after three weeks. I mean, what are we going to do when Ingela gets better and we need to leave Marrakatra?"

"This again? You really want to bring up our dismal futures twice in one day?" Charlie asked, but she knew they had to talk about it. "Well, at least let me cool off first." She was already wearing the cotton bottom of her swimsuit, and now she took off her oversized blouse to reveal her flimsy undershirt below.

"Charlie!" Raquel admonished.

"Oh, it's not a big deal, Raquel. Look around—there's no one on the beach, and the nearest boat is miles away. No one can see me." Charlie waded further into the ocean until she was deep enough to submerge her entire body. The cold water felt refreshing against her rapidly blistering skin. She was sure this was going to be a long talk, and immersed herself one more time before heading back to shore.

"What did I miss?" Charlie asked, as she joined the girls under the shade of a giant palm tree.

Sadie handed Charlie a palm frond. "Fan yourself with this." She turned to face the circle. "Like I was saying, we survived Len and Seth, we survived that wretched storm, and we survived the Blood and Bone Brothers! We should be proud of ourselves."

Liu sighed. "We are, Sadie. But the reality is that the storm wrecked our stolen junk ship. And just because we haven't heard from Zhang Tao in a while doesn't mean that he isn't going to find us again. In fact, he'll probably track us down pretty soon now that we're stuck in one spot.

That Marrakatran wall that tried to keep us out won't do the same for Zhang Tao. Remember, "Daddy Dearest" is a legitimate businessman and has the credentials to get in here if he needs to."

"We might have survived the BBB, but that whole botched mission cost us any chance of a reward," Charlie added. "So we're basically where we started—with nothing."

Raquel's shoulders slumped. She'd trade the invitation to the sultan's gala for a chance to be back on the sea in a heartbeat. Her hunger was even greater now that she'd seen the faceless soldier again. "What about our parents? Finding out about the DD? Have we just forgotten all of that?"

Charlie scoffed at the mere thought that they could somehow lose sight of what was most important to all of them. "Of course we haven't forgotten, Raquel!" She didn't want this conversation to end in an argument like before, so she took a few breaths and fanned herself. Once she was ready, she spoke again. "But how are we going to do anything without a ship?"

Sadie cleared her throat. She wasn't sure why she was even bringing this up, but she felt someone had to. "I don't love the idea, but we could always join the Castaways? At least until we make enough from gilling to get our own ship."

"No!" All three girls shouted in unison, which Sadie realized she was relieved to hear. The sea represented freedom, and as long as they were on someone else's ship, they'd never have it.

Liu sat up. "Wait! Maybe we could gill for a ship!" She looked at Charlie and held up her hand. "Hear me out before you object. We know it will take forever if we try to save up the money from gilling to get a ship, right? But what if we told Sultan Musef about lirium and used one of his ships to find it and bring it back to Marrakatra? I mean, this kingdom has everything but clean drinking water. Think of how happy he would be to offer that to his people."

"So you're saying that the sultan would commission us to find lirium. The way that royal courts give explorers money and ships to conquer new lands?" Sadie asked.

Liu nodded. "Something like that. Except that we wouldn't need to conquer anything."

Charlie moved back, readjusting herself against the tree. "Your plan is contingent on three things. First, we have to break our ancient secret about gilling, unless you think we can get a ship without telling the sultan the method for harvesting lirium. Second, we have to convince Sultan Musef that lirium is real. You know that to outsiders, clean drinking water is as farfetched as a pot of gold at the end of a rainbow. Which means that third, we probably have to find some lirium and show him how it works. Something we haven't been able to do yet."

"Correction. Something *you* haven't been able to do yet," Raquel countered. "As you pointed out, Liu and I just started today, and we're naturals. So if we go out every day for the next three weeks that we're in Marrakatra, we could easily find lirium."

"I'm pretty sure I didn't say you were naturals, and believe me, even if you go out every day, it's not that easy." Charlie was finding it hard to stay calm, between the combination of Raquel's over-positive attitude and this incessant heat. "We're really just going to spill our gilling secret for the world to know?"

"The Storm has shared lirium with villages, towns, and even cities all over the globe already, so that's not a major secret. No one else knows about gilling, but telling Sultan Musef isn't really blabbing it to the world. And we'd make sure to only explain the basic method, not the details." Sadie used her scarf to wipe off her sweaty face. "How do you plan for us to get to Sultan Musef, Liu?"

Liu cocked her head. "Through Amsha, of course. She's his personal physician, and obviously he listens to her if she managed to get us all invited to his gala."

Now it was Sadie's turn to become irritated. "Uh-uh." She crumpled her scarf between her hands. "We are not telling Amsha about the stolen junk ship and getting her involved in our mess." The past week that Sadie had spent with Amsha at her clinic was the best she'd had since DD, because, for the first time since losing her mother, she'd found someone to look up to. The initial animosity she'd felt toward Amsha had quickly melted into pure admiration. The last thing she wanted her new mentor to know was that they were just a bunch of ragtag thieves who didn't have a clue as to what they were doing. Without the Storm code, they were all hopelessly lost of any dignity or honor. It was only lately, and especially in this moment, that she was beginning to feel the true burden of that loss.

Raquel could feel Sadie's growing temper and quickly stepped in. "Sadie, we'd never ask you to embarrass yourself in front of Amsha. We know how much you look up to her. There's no need to go into the details of the stolen junk ship. All we need is for Amsha to help us get an audience with Sultan Musef."

"Besides saving Ingela's life and continuing to take care of her for free, Amsha has generously allowed us to stay here as her guests. I think we've already asked enough of her." Sadie used the scarf to tie her hair up off her neck.

Charlie toyed with her pearl necklace. She didn't even think Liu's plan would work, but she was annoyed by the way Sadie was intent on putting a damper on it. After they'd failed to save the sultan's treasure, she'd seen the faded faces of her girls, and she felt the same way. It was like their futures had been entirely erased once again, just like after the storm, and just like after the DD. Yet they'd managed to survive those horrible fates, and they would somehow survive this. She set aside her own misgivings and tried to find her captain's voice. "We'll find lirium, and we'll approach the sultan with Liu's idea at his party in two weeks." Charlie checked the group to gauge whether she'd sounded convincing enough. Liu and Raquel were beaming back at her, so apparently she had. A little part of her felt guilty for lying, but it didn't matter what she thought of Liu's plan. Right now, her crew needed something to believe in more than they needed honesty.

"Fine by me, as long as we keep Amsha out of it," Sadie muttered. "That also means that you two need to start talking to each other."

"You guys are still fighting?" Charlie ran her fingers through the sand, then looked up at Raquel and Liu. "Get over it."

Raquel and Liu didn't go so far as to speak, but they did make eye contact with each other, which was a good start.

"So now that we've resolved everything, can we finally go visit Squirt?" said Sadie, already standing up to leave.

As they walked off the beach, Charlie glanced at Liu and Raquel's excited faces. It was hard not to get caught up in their silly hope, even if she didn't feel it herself.

***

The Countess fingered her pearl ring. *Mind over body.* She couldn't get the words out of her head. If what Len had said was true, then all of this went much further than a botched raid on the sultan's fleet.

Barrish's incompetence had created quite a hassle for her on that front as well. She'd come to India under the guise of official court duties. Of course, she was really here to assess the damage after the failed attack. It seemed that Sultan Musef didn't suspect Sapphire East Trading of sabotage, but the company's stake in the region was too great to risk any possible retaliation from the powerful sovereign.

Barrish was still gathering information, but early reports mentioned something about girls fighting on the princess's ship against the pirates. The intel was vague, but the Countess felt it was safe to assume that these girls were none other than the Pirettes. If Barrish's reports could indeed be trusted, it also seemed that after saving the princess, the Pirettes had landed safely in Marrakatra. Having had her Plan B—which was to hold the sultan's daughter for a sizable ransom—ruined, the Countess now had to make sure those "do-gooders" kept their mouths shut. She couldn't afford to get her hands dirty with such business. That was what Barrish was for, if he could manage to get it right this time. She remembered the sound of breaking bone as the hammer crushed his right wrist. *Getting it right.* The Countess smiled at her pun.

No amount of torture that she doled out could surpass the atrocities she'd survived. She ran her hand along the rich, mahogany-stained railing. The greatest cruelty was being born a woman in a man's world. Especially one as intelligent, as strong, and as ambitious as her. Finally, after enduring one last depravity, she had learned her lesson and transformed from a duckling into a swan. Serene, beautiful, and poised on the surface, but ferociously kicking underneath.

The Countess looked down at her finger. Jewels dripped from her ears, neck, and wrists. But this simple pearl ring, a gift from a time when she actually believed there was a difference between good and evil, was the only jewelry to adorn her hands. *Mind over body.* Surely it wasn't possible.

Still, if there was even the slightest chance, then it went way above Barrish's pay grade. The Countess thought for another minute before deciding. She rang the bell.

A young servant boy hurried out. "Yes, Madam."

"Tell the captain there's been a change in plan. I need to get to Marrakatra."

The boy nodded and scurried away.

Marrakatra was only a six-day sail away. Seven if the winds were slow. Barrish would be less than pleased to see her. Their last visit had been terrifying—for him, at least.

Mind over body. The Countess twisted her ring. She needed to find out for herself. There were lives depending on it.

Chapter
FIFTEEN

I M BOORED. THATS WHY I M RITIN A SLOG WHEN WE R STILL STUK ON LAND.

WHAT'S WURS THEN SADIE??? SADIE AND AMSHA!!! ITS LIKE HAVIN 2 GRANMAS. I CANT FITE, FISH OR HUNT. JUST STUK IN BED. HELP!!!!!

 Ingela

The palace gates opened. The carriage drove down a long brick road that led to the charbagh, a rectangular Persian garden built to emulate Paradise. Raised pathways divided the land into four quadrants, each an avenue of flowers and trees. Sunken beds of chrysanthemums and cypress trees, brought all the way from Italy, surrounded a long reflective pool that covered the entire length of the garden.

Sadie gasped as the sultan's palace came into sight. An enormous structure made entirely out of black marble, it looked even more impressive against the orange-red sky of the setting sun. Charlie, Raquel, Liu, and Sadie hopped out of their carriage, mesmerized by the stunning beauty before them. Ingela had been moved out of the hospital to Amsha's guesthouse, but had been ordered to rest in bed and was therefore sulking at home.

In the small library at Amsha's guesthouse, Sadie had found a book explaining that what made Marrakatra such a wealthy independent kingdom were its vast diamond mines and its strong ties to India, Persia, and the Ottomans. These influences could be found in Marrakatran food, dress, literature, music, art, and especially the architecture. Sultan Musef's opulent residential palace, one of six built solely for his family, was often touted as the eighth wonder of the world by those who'd had the privilege of setting their eyes upon it. Sadie blinked. She couldn't believe she was actually standing right there in front of it.

"Are we really here?" Liu asked, voicing what the rest of them were thinking.

Two identical onion-shaped domes sat in the center of the building, each sitting on a cylindrical drum. These were surrounded on each side by three smaller domes. *Pishtaqs*, vaulted archways, framed the two huge *ishwans*, arch-shaped doorways that were decorated entirely in calligraphy.

Torches lit up the approaching night sky, and a band of musicians played on the balcony. Ladies with orchids in their hair welcomed the steady stream of guests with glasses of cool hibiscus tea.

Raquel tried to take it all in, but the beauty was blurred by the ugliness of her thoughts. She smoothed her fitted silk bodice. When Amsha had generously offered to have dresses made for each of the girls, only Raquel had actually taken her up on the offer. In fact, she'd spent hours poring over every button, fringe, and scallop until two days ago, when Axel had received some very unexpected intel from one of his underground sources. Now Raquel's focus was back to where it should never have strayed from—the faceless soldier. That's why she'd spent all of last night modifying the design of her one-of-a-kind dress to accommodate the hidden pockets she'd needed to conceal her daggers.

In the background, Raquel could hear Sadie's anxious lecture about onion domes and arches. They were all nervous, but for very different reasons. Raquel felt her own jitters growing with every minute they stalled outside the palace. She lifted her glass of tea and faced Liu, Charlie, and Sadie. Too bad this wasn't a costume ball, because it seemed none of them could mask the worry on their faces.

Raquel smirked. *They had no idea.* "To a night to remember," Raquel toasted.

***

Charlie's mind was many miles away, but even she couldn't resist the pure splendor of the sultan's palace. An official palace guide had taken them around a few of the palace's public areas, including the hall they were in now. Apparently, over 40,000 handmade ceramic tiles with sixty different floral patterns made up the entire interior of Sultan Musef's ballroom, which was nicknamed *jannah*, the Arabic word for garden. Brilliant designs of red poppies, yellow sunflowers, and blue irises lined the high vaulted ceiling, while more traditional roses and gerberas decorated the marble pillars. The floral motif extended to the floor with a gigantic mother-of-pearl mosaic depicting a bird of paradise, resplendent in its electric blue petals and vivid orange sepals. The sheer beauty was enhanced by two-hundred-and-fifty stained-glass windows that lined the walls, giving the gigantic hall an airy, spacious feel.

Long banquet tables were filled with gigantic platters of *mezes*, assortments of small plates of food, alongside piping hot ceramic baking dishes brimming with stews, grilled meats, and pilafs. Wafts of garlic, ginger, cumin, citrus, and cloves mingled in the air.

Charlie's stomach rumbled, but she wasn't going to be able to keep a single thing down until they finished what they'd come here to do tonight. She scanned the crowd, instantly spotting the Castaways, who were tucked away in the back of the room. Charlie pulled at her blouse. She hadn't allowed Amsha to make her a dress, but she'd conceded by wearing a pair of silk trousers. Much to her chagrin, the Castaways had turned up looking pretty impressive. Maybe not as regal as some of the royals and other fancy guests who were in attendance, but the boys cleaned up quite nicely when they wanted to. Especially Taye, who was wearing a dark navy silk waistcoat that seemed designed to accentuate his broad chest and shoulders.

"Do you see him?" Liu whispered.

Charlie's face clouded. She'd have a better view of the entire ballroom by moving toward the center, but she didn't want to bring any unnecessary attention to herself. Nor did she want Taye and Axel to see her yet. It was crucial they not get any hint of the girls' plan if this was going to work. To be specific, it was more like Liu and Charlie's plan, since neither Raquel nor Sadie really knew what was going on. "Not yet, but he's gotta be here!" Charlie said, checking around the corner.

Sadie leaned in. "Maybe Axel's info was wrong," she said, biting her lip. "Let's just join the guys and forget this whole thing!"

"No!" chimed Charlie, Liu, and, surprisingly, Raquel. Charlie looked at Raquel quizzically. She knew what she and Liu had at stake here, but what exactly was Raquel up to? Before Charlie could ask, her eyes landed on the target. She silently admonished herself for not noticing him before, since Rogers Barrish clearly wanted to be seen. He was dressed in a magnificent long red overcoat and black boots, despite the heat, and every hair on his head was perfectly in place. Barrish emanated authority and sophistication. As he basked in the glitzy glow of the bluebloods who surrounded him and seemed to hang on his every word, Barrish acted like he was the host of this gala instead of the sultan, who was yet to make an appearance. Charlie glowered. Barrish wore his two faces so well that it was difficult to know where one stopped and the other began.

Barrish looked like the same phony bastard as during the only time that Charlie had ever actually met him. There was one glaring difference, though—he was crippled. His right hand was now grotesquely deformed, the fingers crooked, mangled, and turning inward toward his palm as though he were holding an invisible cup. The injury looked excruciating, but Charlie had no mercy for the scoundrel who had raided the sultan's fleet and caused Ingela to be shot. "He's right there," Charlie pointed discreetly.

Sadie, Raquel, and Liu whipped around to finally get a long, hard look at the man who had been their nightmare for so long. No one said a word until Charlie finally broke the silence. "We've only got one chance, so make this count."

***

The servant presented the plate to the Countess. With all the flair befitting a stunning dish like kavun dolmasi, he dramatically lifted the cap of the hollowed melon to reveal a bubbling mixture of minced lamb and black currants inside. The intoxicating aroma of allspice and cinnamon wafted in the air. The Marrakatran imperial kitchen staff had worked solidly for a month perfecting the delicate balance of sweet, salty, and tartness necessary for this Ottoman specialty so as to be able to serve it at tonight's royal ball.

"Mmms" and "aaahs" carried across the table of dignitaries who used their silver spoons to scoop up the delicacy. The Countess feigned delight but didn't actually let a single morsel touch her lips. Eating had never produced the same level of pleasure for her as it did for many of her royal counterparts, not least her husband. With his stubby legs and flared nostrils, he'd always resembled swine, so it was only appropriate that he ended up looking like an overstuffed suckling pig, which was incidentally a favorite Sunday meal of his.

The Countess looked down the table at Barrish, who was busy holding court. Unbeknownst to him, he'd dined with her on several occasions. In fact, shortly after the "accident," they both received the same invitation to dine with King George III. She'd had to suppress a laugh as she watched Barrish struggle with his left hand to eat the tiny stuffed quails. The legs were so dainty that Barrish just didn't seem to have the dexterity as a leftie to manage. It looked like he was going to have to forgo the *kavun dolmasi* as well.

Barrish was sitting a mere three feet away from the woman who'd crippled him and he hadn't a clue. Of course, Barrish's ego prevented him from paying attention to anyone but himself, so it wasn't such a surprise he'd failed to recognize her. Again. But her successful "disguise" was based more on the fact that the Countess had mastered the art of hiding in plain sight.

Her public face was a world away from the woman who haunted Barrish's dreams. Here she was malleable, soft-spoken, and, dare she say, cheery. A benevolent widow who faded into the background. Being invisible gave her ultimate power. She could watch them all. Barrish. Sultan Musef. The Pirettes.

The best part of it all, the Countess thought, as she sipped her wine, was that they all laughed, drank, and ate merrily without the slightest inkling that their greatest fear was in their midst.

***

Charlie and Liu jumped up behind Rogers Barrish and pinned his arms back. Raquel followed, doing the same to the small man next to him after kicking away the leather briefcase he was holding. The girls had patiently waited for the last two hours to get Barrish alone, but after realizing his manservant was never more than a few steps away, they relented and struck both of them. Thankfully, the dimly lit balcony they were standing on was on the opposite side of the long hallway from the ballroom, and no guests or guards were present for the time being. Music and laughter from the increasingly merry crowd carried outside, but Charlie still knew how important it was to remain as quiet as possible so as not to draw any suspicion. "We don't have any weapons," Charlie whispered. This was a half-truth, since she had her trusted cutlass on her, for the reason that she never traveled without it. However, she'd promised the girls beforehand that she wasn't going to use it, since even she understood that physically assaulting one of the most important men in the world inside the sultan's palace was too dangerous for all of them. "We just want to talk."

"That is precisely why I allowed you to follow me out here," Barrish said, grimacing. "Now, I demand you remove your hands from my person."

Charlie raised her eyebrow. Rogers Barrish was such a good liar that it was difficult to determine whether he was bluffing or not about "allowing" them to follow him out here. But there were more important matters to get to. She and Liu let go of Barrish. Charlie stood directly in front of him, so close that she could smell Barrish's scotch-tainted breath.

"I have more important matters to attend to than you filthy sewer rats. So tell me, what is it you want?" Barrish eyed Charlie up and down. "A confession?"

Charlie was taken aback. She hadn't expected Barrish to acknowledge his deception so easily. Or was he just toying with them? "We know that Sapphire East Trading Company was behind the raid on the sultan's fleet," Charlie shouted. It was probably best to stay calm, but it was nearly impossible with slimy Rogers Barrish right in front of her.

Barrish grinned. Feisty gingers were always a treat. The sour taste of hate filled his mouth. Wisps of the Countess's red hair and echoes of her cold, menacing voice had been haunting his dreams since the night she'd permanently mutilated him. "Next time, get it right, Barrish," the Countess had laughed, before the hammer came crashing down on his wrist, shattering his bones and permanently severing all the nerves in his hand. The pain was excruciating—and continued to be—but that could be managed with enough scotch, opium, and other delights. Barrish had always attracted admiration, envy, and lust wherever he went. Now, with one strike of a hammer, the evil bitch had reduced him to a feeble cripple.

"And where exactly did you obtain this information from?" Barrish sneered at Charlie. He'd never have ended up in the Countess's dungeon had it not been for these miserable girls.

"Well, we first discovered your nasty little scheme with the map from your office. Then the two thugs that you sent after us told us your plans for raiding the sultan's fleet." Finally getting to throw all of Roger's misdeeds in his face was so satisfying. He'd tried to kill them, and had used his power to ransack innocent ships. Charlie looked down at his mangled fingers. She wished she'd been the one to do it.

Barrish straightened. Did she really think she had the upper hand? He was Governor Rogers Barrish, and she was nothing but a piece of pirate scum. Still, he hadn't had this much fun in a while, and he rather liked this game. "So, when you came here tonight, what were you believing would take place? Did you have a plan of any sort?"

"Our plan was to get you to confess," Raquel answered. The combination of the stilted air and Barrish's phoniness was nauseating.

"I see. A written confession, no doubt," he said, winking at the Spanish girl before turning his gaze back to Charlie. "And what did *you* want?"

Charlie looked at Liu. There hadn't been much time to plan, but she and Liu knew exactly what they had to do. It was the lowest she'd ever gone, far worse than mugging those drunks. Liu had been by her side during those times, and that's why Charlie could count on her now. Raquel and Sadie might talk about how they longed for their own ship, but only Charlie and Liu were willing to do what was necessary to make that happen.

They were going to blackmail Rogers Barrish into giving them a ship. Charlie gulped down the nausea she felt at the idea, and at herself for stooping to this. But it was their only way out. "We want a ship," Charlie fingered her necklace. "For our silence."

"What?" Raquel leaped forward. "That wasn't the plan—" The cold-eyed look Charlie shot her shut her up instantly.

"Please," Liu mouthed. Her stomach churned with a combination of fright, shame, and if she had to be honest, relief. Blackmailing anybody, even a crook like Rogers Barrish, was so far from the Storm code that Liu knew there was no going back after this. But there was no going forward if they *didn't* do this. They needed a ship, and they needed to escape Zhang Tao. If blackmail was their last chance at freedom, then Liu was ready to use it.

"I will assume you no longer have the map or my notes, since if you did, you would have surely brought them with you today. Therefore, without any written proof, it boils down to your word against mine," he sneered. "My word versus the word of pirate trash like the Pirettes, who are nothing but a bunch of rowdy kids, and two criminals." He decided it best not to mention that both Len and Seth were dead, lest it raise too many questions. "If I may share a few pieces of information I believe you all will find interesting." Barrish nodded to his manservant, who took out a blue folder from the attaché case he had managed to retrieve. He handed the folder to Charlie. "As you can see, there are tens of articles documenting all your exploits. Holding a group of robbers at gunpoint in the Carolinas, raiding a fleet of Portuguese merchant ships, inciting a mob in Shanghai, and ransacking a marketplace in Malé?" Barrish grimaced. It was actually fun to obliterate any sense of justice these idiots naively held onto. "Didn't you just come from the Maldives, where you heroically tried to save the sultan's ship?"

"Malé? But that's not supposed to be out yet," Charlie muttered to herself as she shuffled through the newspaper clippings. It was hard to see properly in the semi-darkness, but it looked like the article about the Pirettes in Malé had already been published in a French newspaper, despite Sadie having promised it wouldn't be out until they'd left the entire region in a month's time.

Charlie couldn't find words, but luckily Liu stepped in. "Are you hoping these stories will smear us in the eyes of the sultan?" she asked. Liu picked up an article. "So it becomes our word, a group of dangerous girl pirates, who also happened to save the princess, against the word of the mighty head of Sapphire East Trading Company, who also happens to be a lying snake?" She waved her hand in front of her nose. Liu was now also standing close enough to breathe in the strong scotch smell. "A snake with a drinking problem."

Barrish grimaced. Heroes nauseated him.

Liu crossed her arms triumphantly. "Exactly. We'll take our chances," she said, looking over at Charlie. If they were going to get Rogers Barrish, they had to do it now.

Charlie nodded. She took a deep breath and focused on Barrish's smarmy smile. "We don't really need the written proof, do we? I mean, just an accusation of this magnitude could have serious consequences for a public figure like you." Charlie tried to keep her heart from jumping out of her chest. She paused for a brief second before continuing. "Just think how detrimental it could be for you and Sapphire East Trading Company if Sultan Musef even suspected you of having anything to do with the raid on his ships." Barrish tried to put on his best worried face. "I see your point," he said. Ginger Junior was better at this game than he'd thought. A slow smile appeared on Barrish's face. But he'd invented it. Now it was time to school them all in the art of blackmail. "I could give you a ship to ensure your silence," said Barrish, signaling for another blue folder to be delivered, this time to Liu. "However, I believe that after you read the contents of that folder, you'll find that a ship is not necessary to keep you quiet."

Liu opened it and held it up to a lantern. Inside, there were stacks of documents with her father's name on them. Her stomach was doing too many flips for her to do anything but stare down at them. Sapphire East Trading Company insured his entire fleet of ships. How did Rogers Barrish know her identity? Shivers ran down her spine. "What are these?" she asked, putting on her best poker face.

Barrish smirked. "Sapphire East is the largest maritime insurance company in the entire world. And every one of the ships that we insure has a special serial number engraved on it. A number that Len was able to not only see, but to my surprise—and I'm sure yours—memorize." "We stole our ship. From a total stranger," Liu answered firmly. "Uh oh, our secret's out!" she cried mockingly, putting her hand over her mouth.

"Of course you stole your ship. That's the way most pirates get their ships," Barrish paused, savoring the moment before he threw the bomb. "From a Mr. Zhang Tao Shao, according to the stolen ship report he filed." Barrish let the words sink in before speaking again. "He listed it as an 'extremely valuable vessel.' No mention whom he thought had done it. I sent my team to investigate, as usual. We do that with all claims. And you know what they came back and told me? They told me that the rumor around town was that it was Zhang Tao's own daughter who'd stolen the ship. She'd fallen in love with some servant boy, and the two had run away together. Complete and utter scandal." Barrish was drunk with joy. They were all trying to stay composed, but he was sure he'd hit the mark.

A shiver ran down Liu's spine at the mention of Liang. Had he spread the lie that they had run away together as a cover for him, and maybe even Liu? "Make all the assumptions you want about filing claims, but like I told you, we stole the ship from a stranger." Liu didn't know why she was protecting "Daddy Dearest," but she couldn't throw him to Rogers Barrish—even if it was a fitting retribution. She tried to stop herself from shaking.

Barrish leaned forward. "Of course you'll keep on saying that, because you're a good little girl, aren't you? But you see, I heard this story of the runaway girl, and then I read the story of the Pirettes inciting a mob in Shanghai. In fact, the two events practically on the same day," said Barrish, lifting the newspaper article for show. He hadn't actually read the article himself, but an assistant had pointed it out to him.

"Good for you, Rog! You found us!" Liu quipped, while giving him her best "I don't care" look.

Barrish smirked. This girl's ashen face and shaky hands were a dead giveaway. She wasn't fooling anyone. Still, he liked to play. "But you don't know the lengths I had to go to just so I could find you all. First, I had to set up pirate attacks on two of Zhang Tao's ships, which cost him a lot of money and wasted much of my time. But he was getting much too close to catching you," Barrish mimicked a cut throat with his index finger.

"What?" Liu asked, trying to keep the concern out of her voice. She could feel the anxiety of the others, too.

"Funny you should worry about a stranger so much. He was coming after you all. In fact, he was pretty close, just a few hundred meters behind, when I thwarted him. Or, should I say, until my men blew his ship to pieces," Barrish beamed. Watching them all deflate like this was really too much fun.

Liu gulped. She thought back to Zhang Tao's ship chasing them, and how suddenly that third ship had appeared out of nowhere and shot it down. Her hand trembled. She'd thought it was a savior, some kind of mythical hero ship, but really it had just been sadistic Rogers Barrish and his endless games.

"Whether I'm right or wrong about him being your dear old dad, Sapphire East Trading Company is pulling all of the insurance from Mr. Zhang Tao Shao's entire fleet of ships. Which means he won't be able to import or export his goods, and his business will close. He'll lose that lovely house up on the hill—"

"What do you want?!" Charlie yelled. Their blackmailing plan had backfired. It was clear that Barrish had been pulling the strings all this time. The remorse she felt was accentuated by the contempt that boiled within her toward this loathsome creature in front of her.

Barrish's eyes burned with scorn. "Keep your mouths shut and stay out of all Sapphire East Trading Company business!" Venom dripped from every word he spoke. "Or Mr. Zhang Tao Shao loses *everything!*"

The color drained from Charlie's face, and Liu looked like she was going to be sick. Liu wished with every muscle in her body that she could look Barrish in the eye and tell him she didn't give a damn about what happened to Zhang Tao. Part of her really didn't. But a bigger part of her, the part that was scared to death of his threat, couldn't let her brothers—or even her doll-loving stepmother—suffer. Zhang Tao's financial ruin would result in utter devastation for them as well. Despite the fact that she felt like a stranger in Zhang Tao's family, Liu would not be responsible for its destruction. She nodded her head without saying a word.

"NO!" Raquel screamed. Before anyone knew what was happening, she drew a dagger from underneath her dress and held it to Barrish's throat.

"Raquel!" Liu shouted. "What are you doing?" "Stop!" Charlie yelled with wide-eyed terror. "The faceless soldier!" Raquel spit out.

Another girl who spoke in riddles. Barrish was growing tired of this entire crew of nitwits. "Perhaps this is as fine a time as any to inform you that my man here is a perfect shot. At my command, he'll draw any of the four pistols he's currently carrying on him."

Raquel pushed her blade against Barrish's skin. "The faceless soldiers, the black smoke, the fourth ship. The one that joined the ransacking on the sultan's fleet. We know you were behind all of it."

Liu slowly inched forward. "Raquel, please! Don't do this!"

Charlie wasn't going to wait this out and see what resulted. She drew her cutlass and swung directly at Raquel, knocking the dagger out of her hand. As Raquel reached for another knife, Charlie swung again, this time barely missing her arm. Raquel didn't have time to reach for her third blade before Charlie pinned her to the ground. This would no doubt mean she'd be getting a few weeks of the silent treatment herself, but Charlie could easily live with that instead of facing the consequences of a murdered Rogers Barrish.

Barrish looked down at Charlie. "I would have liked to properly acknowledge you for your chivalry, but it seems that the second part of my plan is commencing."

Two men dressed in white, with mustard-colored turbans, walked down the hallway toward the balcony doors carrying silver bayonets. Charlie instantly jumped up, helping Raquel to her feet.

"Sultan Musef has requested to see you," one of the men said as he approached the girls. He spoke English, but with a strange accent that Charlie couldn't quite place. "This matter is of urgent concern."

***

Charlie, Liu, and Raquel walked down the banquet hall, followed by the sultan's royal guards, with Barrish sauntering behind. When they reached the end of the walkway, they were stunned to see Sadie, Taye, Axel, Jimmy, and Javier surrounded by another set of stern-looking men.

"What's going on?" Charlie whispered to Sadie.

Sadie shrugged her shoulders. "You tell me! I was just keeping the boys distracted, like you ordered."

"To the right!" instructed one of the men.

The group entered through a scalloped archway onto a raised platform covered in lush Persian rugs. Everyone tried to hide their shot nerves, though they were all trembling for different reasons. Javier and Jimmy had never met royalty. On the other hand, the girls wondered if they'd end this evening behind bars—or worse.

On an elevated marble throne covered in a velvet canopy sat Sultan Musef, surrounded by his four wives, thirty-six children, and various other important-looking people. Among them was Amsha. This explained why Charlie hadn't seen her in the main dining room, but her presence here with Sultan Musef gave Charlie no comfort. The group went down on their knees and bowed. Somewhere in the crowd sat Princess Imera, but Charlie doubted she'd be pleased to see them. Likewise, to add to Charlie's growing discomfort, Rogers Barrish climbed up the canopy and joined the sultan.

Charlie studied the sultan from afar. This was apparently a man who appreciated fashion and was clearly not afraid of a little bling. Like most Marrakatran men, he wore a traditional Persian *jama*, a side-fastening floor-length coat with a nipped-in waist. Sultan Musef's jama showed his noble status with intricately embroidered gold braiding and a long, silk sash. As Marrakatran royals didn't wear crowns, the sultan wore a luxuriously ornamented turban instead, with decorative strands. At the center was a long curved feather, a symbol of power that went back to ancient times. To complete his regal swagger, since only royalty could wear precious stones in Marrakatra, the sultan was loaded down with thick gold chains covered in diamonds, sapphires, emeralds, and rubies.

What was more impressive than his appearance, though, was the air of gravitas and dignity he emanated, instantly commanding reverence and respect. According to Sadie's "fun facts," the sultan was somewhere around seventy-two years old. This meant that he had been ruling a long time, but one felt that even without all the opulence around him, the man would still seem royal.

The sultan said something in French, after which the crowd broke out in laughter. French was the preferred second language of the Marrakatran elite. However, since neither Charlie nor Liu spoke it, they looked on with blank expressions. Raquel, Sadie, and Taye were all fluent French speakers and would have laughed along if they had been in any sort of humorous mood.

Charlie tried to search Amsha's face for some indication as to what was happening, but Sadie's mentor was being unusually inscrutable. What had Barrish meant by "the second part of his plan"? At this point, Charlie hoped they'd be allowed to return to Amsha's guesthouse without an escort from the royal guard.

The grumpy-looking lady sitting in the throne next to the sultan growled in Marrakatran. Judging by her exalted status, she was probably Wife #1, and, given her similarly egg-shaped head, Princess Imera's mother.

Sultan Musef's expression grew weary. He made another joke in French that Wife #1 seemed to appreciate even less than the last joke. He clearly hadn't married this wife for her sense of humor.

"Please sit."

Sadie turned to Charlie and Liu and muttered the translation. Charlie and Liu followed Sadie, Raquel, and the Castaways to a set of divans. All of them were too nervous to get comfortable and sat on the edges of their seats.

Sultan Musef waved his family away. Then, to everyone's surprise, he switched to English. "I understand not all of you speak French, so I will use my English. I want to make sure you understand the grave matters that we must discuss now," said the sultan, before turning to Amsha. "Stay. You must hear this as well." Then he faced Rogers Barrish. "So should you, Mr. Barrish."

The girls took a collective gulp. Axel jittered, Taye cracked his knuckles, Raquel fanned herself profusely. Liu's gut did flips, Sadie bit her lip, and Charlie tried not to puke.

Sultan Musef snapped his fingers, and a boy appeared from the corner. The sultan barked out some orders in Marrakatran. Charlie could see where Princess Imera had gotten her imperious attitude. Then the sultan turned to the group and explained. "I am calling for the pastry chef. My sweet tooth is getting impatient."

Charlie cocked her head. Did emperors usually eat dessert before sending people to prison?

The sultan bit into a deep-fried semolina fritter covered in rose syrup. "Our kitchen makes the best *zienab*," he cheered in delight. "Better than in Persia, if you ask me. Do not tell the sultana that. The woman left her native land fifty years ago and still acts like she is in Marrakatra on a temporary exile!" He waved his hand. "Eat!"

Servants placed platters of sweets and pastries on the nesting tables. Charlie's sweet tooth could probably rival the sultan's, and because she felt it was important to humor him, she grabbed a mini pancake oozing with sweet cream and slathered in pistachios. The warm, soft gooey goodness melted in her mouth. If this was going to be her last supper, at least it was delicious. "Mmmmmm ..." she purred. Charlie was never strict about etiquette, but she was suddenly aware of her inappropriate loudness.

To Charlie's relief, the sultan chuckled.

"Aaah, you like it? Yes, *khataief asafiry* is my favorite, too." He motioned to a bearer. "Bring her more!" Sultan Musef grabbed the same pastry and shoved the entire piece into his mouth. A young boy holding a silk napkin immediately hurried over to wipe the pistachios that were hanging from his white beard.

Once the fussing was done, the sultan began to speak. "I understand we have some matters to discuss."

Everyone looked up from their dessert-filled plates. No one wanted to guess what possible matters were between them and the sultan. Charlie glanced up at Rogers Barrish. Judging by the smug smile on his face, whatever this was about, it most certainly involved Barrish.

"Mr. Rogers Barrish has passed on a bit of information," the sultan began.

Barrish nodded, his eyes flashing with satisfaction.

The girls all froze. Charlie put the pancake down, and Liu stopped eating her cinnamonand sugar-dusted dumpling. Raquel squeezed the arm of her chair so tightly that her knuckles turned white. She felt her head getting lighter and lighter. Liu reached out to steady Raquel.

The sultan cleared his throat. "Mr. Rogers Barrish alerted me to some most disturbing news a few days back." The sultan snapped his fingers. This time instead of confectionery, a familiar blue folder was brought out. The sultan grabbed it and held up a news article. "I read the stories of these girl pirates and was quite alarmed to hear that such girls of ill repute were in my kingdom."

The sight of the now all-too-familiar blue folder caused a wave of nausea in Charlie. Sadie looked up at Amsha, who sat in stony-faced silence. "I simply will not tolerate criminals!" the sultan roared.

Charlie hung her head. It sounded like their time in Marrakatra was coming to an end. She could see the victory glow practically emanating from Barrish.

"However, Amsha has assured me that you were all nothing but selfless and courageous when defending her and Imera. 'Heroes' is the word she used to describe you." The sultan motioned for Amsha, and she stepped next to him. "The written word is powerful." He held an article up.

"However, in this instance, the word of my favorite niece bares more weight."

Sadie gasped. All this time, she'd been working side by side with Amsha, and the humble woman had never once even hinted at her royal blood. Raquel started to breathe normally again. Amsha beamed down at all of them.

The sultan turned to Barrish. "I am humbled that you would show such deference for the well-being of Marrakatra, Mr. Barrish." The sultan snapped his fingers. "Please take our honored guest to a private suite. Make sure he is given all the food and drink he desires."

Barrish barely had time to wipe the furious expression from his face before a pair of guards escorted him off the podium. Charlie flashed Barrish a huge smile as he bristled past her. She knew the best thing would have been to stay neutral—this surely was not the last time they'd cross paths—but Charlie couldn't resist a chance to rub it in a little.

Sultan Musef turned his attention back to the group. "As appreciation for your valor, I would like to reward you all."

They looked at each other in astonishment.

"But your ship sank!" Raquel blurted, wiping the sweat from her throat with a lace handkerchief. "Your treasure was lost!"

Perhaps it was the heat that was getting to her, or maybe she needed to loosen her corset, but Liu really wished Raquel would shut up. If the sultan wanted to reward them, it was certainly not their place to stop him. Their stay in Amsha's luxurious guesthouse, where they could eat all the food they wanted, had been a much-needed respite from their desperate situation. The reality remained that they had nothing, and Zhang Tao was still on the loose. Even a pearl from the sultan's shoe would be helpful.

Charlie had the same thought as Liu, and gently but firmly placed her hand on Raquel's shoulder.

Sultan Musef smiled. "Those were very valuable things, and I am sorry to have lost them," he said, taking Amsha's hand. "But returning my niece and my daughter to me unharmed is a far greater treasure."

A medium-sized mahogany box was delivered to Taye. Charlie scowled. If this was a group effort, why was the box being handed to him directly?

"A token of my appreciation." The sultan motioned to the box. "Please, open it."

Shiny gold coins of all sizes filled the velvet interior of the box.

"Sultan Musef, thank you. This was unexpected and unnecessary," said Taye, as he stood up and bowed. "But most welcome. It has been an honor to be of service."

They all followed Taye and bowed. Liu couldn't help making a quick survey of the coins. Once the reward was divided evenly between them and the Castaways, it would be a little light. It was a decent contribution for the "new ship" piggy bank, but not enough to hold off Zhang Tao.

"Uncle? I believe you are forgetting somebody?" Amsha playfully chided the sultan. She grinned at the girls. "Or should I say, somebodies?"

"Yes, of course!" Sultan Musef patted his niece's hand. "Thank you for reminding me. My breakfast with Mr. Barrish two mornings ago greatly dissuaded me from following through with this." He held his finger up. "However, my lunch with Amsha later that afternoon convinced me to rethink my position." The sultan winked. "Goes to show that the early bird does not always catch the worm. Or perhaps my niece knows that I'm always more persuadable with a belly full of *shawarma*?" Sultan Musef smacked his lips. He had a sudden craving for something savory. "Bring me more of the roasted pigeon!"

"Uncle, please, may they open it?" Amsha pleaded. He nodded.

A scribe handed Charlie a dark envelope. Carefully, she tore the official royal seal. Then she pulled out the oversized piece of parchment paper, which contained the sultan's signature and personal stamp on the bottom. She was shaking too much to make out the words, and handed the document over to Sadie. She was, after all, the official "reader" in the gang.

Sadie also began trembling as she read the contents of the decree.

"What? What does it say?" All the girls wanted to knock Sadie over and read the paper for themselves, but they knew that would play right into Barrish's savage Pirettes argument.

Tears rolled down Sadie's cheeks. She held up the royal decree and took a deep breath so she could get the words out. "Sultan Musef is giving us a ship. Not on loan. It's ours. Forever." She turned to face Charlie, Raquel, and Liu. "We're free."

Chapter
SIXTEEN

SLOG
Date: January 15
Location: Marrakatra

We don't have a ship to write this from—yet. But we're picking it out ...TOMORROW. I don't know how to express our gratitude to Sultan Musef. Maybe I tried to save his fleet for the reward (though I think it was honestly more for the thrill), but never in my wildest dreams did I think we'd actually have our very own ship. This means Zhang Tao and Rogers Barrish can suck it. Speaking of Daddy Dearest, we've decided to go back to Shanghai and see if we can get some more answers from the shady Mr. Chang. We still gotta survive and we still gotta figure out DD but we're together. For good.

Happy New Year, World!

(Puke. I sound like Raquel with all my good cheer, who actually forgave me for not allowing her to kill RB.)

Charlie

"It's too prissy!" Ingela shouted.

Raquel's face fell. "But it's real cherry wood!"

"Ingela's right. All these ships are for a bunch of princesses." Charlie sat down on the edge of the pier.

Sadie took a seat next to Charlie. "Well, that's because they *are* for princesses. They're from the sultan's royal fleet." She tried to sound reasonable, but she felt the same way as Charlie and Ingela.

Sultan Musef owned 422 vessels, including some of the largest warships ever made. Of course, there was a limit to his generosity, but he'd allowed the girls to choose from an extraordinary selection of junks, brigs, and sloops. Each ship was magnificent, tricked out with the newest gadgets and made of the finest materials. But the girls had been desperately searching for over three hours and hadn't agreed upon a single one.

"They got no ..." Ingela searched for the right word. "Spirit?" Raquel asked, her shoulders falling. There was a lot of beauty here, but not a lot of heart.

"Maybe we should just come back tomorrow?" Charlie asked, trying to keep the disappointment out of her voice.

"We'll be clearer with fresh eyes." They all nodded reluctantly.

"Guys, I found it!" Liu yelped as she ran full speed down the pier. She panted heavily.

"Where?" Raquel asked.

Liu tried to catch her breath. "There." She pointed to an area a few hundred meters in front of them, away from the rest of the ships. "I'll show you."

They followed Liu down the pier.

"Is that a schooner?" Charlie asked in wide-eyed excitement as the ship slowly came into view. She ran ahead of them.

"Wait for me!" Ingela screamed.

"You can't get too excited! You're still recuperating." Sadie warned. "Ingela, slow down!"

Ingela ignored Sadie and took off behind Charlie.

Schooners were small, fast, and steady workhorses, with some of the best features desired in a ship. Their grace and speed were solely due to their firate construction. Charlie looked up at the masts. Schooners could have up to six masts, but this one only had two, the most popular design. The forward mast was smaller than the one at the rear, and had a gaff rig. Since the sails ran the length of the deck, the schooner could catch wind at a closer angle. This unique positioning not only made the schooner the fastest vessel on the sea, it also allowed it to make sharper, more precise turns.

"She's got a super shallow draft and a really narrow hull," Liu said to Charlie. They both smiled, knowing exactly what that meant. This ship was perfect for navigating shallow waters and hiding in coves.

A short man with a missing leg walked over to the girls. "I already told ya, friend. You don't want this ship." Curiously, the man spoke in a distinct Massachusetts accent. Given that she was part American, this interested Charlie. Storm One had spent an entire summer and fall sailing up the Eastern seaboard, and it was there that she'd become fascinated with the various American accents. Charlie wondered what this man was doing here all the way from Boston, but decided to forgo inquiries into his personal history to focus on questions about the ship. "Why? What's her history?"

"¡Y *dale*! Don't tell me it's haunted," Raquel fingered her crucifix necklace. "An angry ghost is impossible to get rid of!"

"Naw, nothin' like that." The man put a wad of chewing tobacco under his lip. "She's from the war in America. You know, the Revolution." He puckered his lips. "She's been a blockade runner."

Liu grinned. "So she's even faster than the regular schooners." Blockade runners were ships commissioned to bring supplies to blockaded cities during wartime. As they were often fired upon, they were specially rigged to be extremely lightweight and speedy, and have superior handling.

"She was the best, Miss. I can attest to that myself." The man lowered his head. "But she got pretty beat up in a skirmish with the British Navy, and, long story short, was traded to the sultan."

Sadie nodded. That explained the man's leg, and a bit of the story behind his travels to Marrakatra.

"This is our ship!" Ingela yelped as she ran above deck. "We're taking this one!"

The man nodded profusely. "No, that's just what I'm tryin' to tell yas. The old gal's been through a lot. She needs a lot of love."

"But she still runs fine?" Charlie asked.

"She runs great. Even better than before, if you ask me." He spit his wad of chew on the deck floor. "Just tested her myself with a small crew about a week ago."

"Then why can't we have her?" Raquel asked.

"Maybe it costs too much?" Sadie looked at the girls. The sultan's reward did have its price limits, and schooners were the top of the line, reserved for gentlemen of fortune.

Even the Castaways had yet to get their hands on a schooner. "Does the sultan want us to look at cheaper rigs? Like the sloops and the brigs?"

"No. He's got some brand-new schooners that are off-limits to you." The man dug his hands deep into his pockets. "But he doesn't even use this one."

"Then why can't we have her?" Raquel repeated, this time stomping her foot in frustration.

"Well, it's just that she ain't too pretty. I mean, I don't want the sultan comin' down on me 'cuz I gave you all an 'ugly duckling.'" He rested on his cane.

Liu, Charlie, Ingela, Sadie, and Raquel smiled at one another. They knew a thing or two about beat-up girls that just needed some tender loving care.

"A good cleaning and a little bit of wax and she'll shine like new," Sadie suggested.

"A few modifications so we can have our own souped-up ride," Liu added.

"We can trade the shells to buy our supplies," Raquel offered.

The great thing about growing up together was that sometimes you didn't need to speak to know exactly what the others were thinking. The girls had found their new home.

***

"I hate moving!" Raquel whined for the umpteenth time today. Though they were still staying at Amsha's guesthouse while they finished the renovations on their new ship, the girls had decided to move their stuff out of Holy Tide.

"Yeah, well, why don't you try it first?" Jimmy responded wryly. He didn't know how he'd gotten suckered so easily, but he found himself carrying yet another load of Raquel's stupid things. "I don't get it. I thought you guys lost most of your stuff in that storm. How do you have so much crap?"

Raquel fanned herself. They'd waited until just before sunset, when the air was cooler, to do all this manual labor, but the lingering humidity was suffocating. Maybe it was better for her to make some lemonade for everyone, she thought. "Jimmy, you take my things to the new ship. I'll catch up."

"No way, José," Jimmy smirked, using Raquel's favorite Spanglish saying on her. He threw the bag of ugly, frilly stuff at her. "Get to work, *muchacha*."

Charlie climbed on deck, balancing a load that was way too heavy for her. Taye ran up and tried to take some of the boxes from Charlie. "Here, let me have something."

Though she couldn't see him over her haul, Charlie held on even tighter.

"Charlie, seriously. It's gonna drop. Let me carry some of this stuff." Taye tried to grab the top box.

"No, I've got it," Charlie scolded.

"Give it to me!" Taye yelled back, now going for the bottom box.

"Let go!" Charlie warned, ignoring the fact that her arms were shaking under the weight.

Taye blocked Charlie. "Let me help you! You can't do it by yourself!"

"Yes, I can! Now get out of my way!" Charlie lunged forward. Taye fell back, while the boxes came crashing to the ground. "See what you did? Just leave me alone!" she shrieked.

Without a word, Taye stood up. Every muscle in his body tensed with sheer rage. Charlie took a step back, but it was too late. Taye hoisted her over his shoulder and began to walk.

"What the hell are you doing?" she shouted, pounding him on his back and kicking her legs as hard as she could. Flashbacks to the brute in the opium den flooded her mind. "Put me down! NOW!"

Taye ignored her. He walked over to the edge of the railing and threw Charlie overboard. Then he jumped over himself.

"Oye!" Raquel scurried over to the railing and put her bag down. "We gotta see this," she said to Jimmy, who'd already stopped to watch the show.

Charlie rose to the surface. "WHAT IS WRONG WITH YOU?" she shouted, before grabbing Taye's head and holding it underwater.

Axel put Sadie's things down. "Do I need to get into this, before she kills him?"

Sadie moved her box of books from the deck chair. "No, you're fine." As much as she loved gossip, she respected her big bro's privacy too much to stop and gawk. "Come on, Raquel. Get back to work." Sadie nudged her.

"Just a minute. Don't you want to see how this turns out?" "No!" Sadie gave Raquel a scary combination of the stink and evil eye.

Raquel jumped up. "Come on, Jimmy!" she ordered, and scurried away.

***

Taye extricated Charlie's hands off his head and came up for air. He took a giant breath. The ocean was cool and refreshing, with gentle waves, though swimming in his boots was kind of tough. "I threw you in here because the water is the only place we're normal anymore," Taye shouted.

Apparently Taye was intent on doing this right here, right now. Charlie looked up. It was back to business as usual on *Holy Tide*, but still she didn't want any of them to overhear. "Can we get out of here first?"

Taye nodded. It wasn't really necessary, but he obliged. They both swam forward until they were out of earshot. Taye jostled against a wave. They were a bit rougher here. "Don't yell at me for ruining your good clothes," he said as he treaded water, "because I know you don't own any."

Charlie laughed in spite of herself. Maybe the water *was* the only place she could be with him anymore. Which was why she hated him. At one time, he'd been one of the only people she could actually be herself with in the water and on land. "This isn't about what I've done, so don't put the blame on me!" Charlie splashed him in frustration.

Taye swallowed a mouthful of saltwater and coughed. "Sorry! I—" She reached out for him, then started to retreat.

Taye grabbed Charlie's arm and pulled her closer to him. She could feel his breath on her face. He wrapped his arms around her waist. Her body pressed against his. Everything dissolved in the sea. Here they were weightless.

He held her so tight, she almost couldn't breathe. Maybe she'd eventually stop breathing, except that every part of her tingled with anticipation, excitement, fear. His lips touched her forehead. The skin was slightly chapped. Rough and soft on her cheek, her chin. Down her neck. Slowly. Shivers running all the way to her fingertips. He lingered on a spot. His spot. She felt his tongue on her skin. It stirred the longing deep inside. Charlie knew what was next. Their lips grazed. Playing, biting. Charlie resisted. She turned her head, and he nuzzled her from her nape to her ear. Droplets of water glistened against the dark ebony of his smooth skin.

"Charlie," Taye whispered as he ran his fingers through her hair. Then he took his strong, beautiful hands and cupped her face. He opened his eyes. She did, too. "Charlie." She didn't resist anymore. They kissed. Softly at first, exploring with their fingers and tongues what used to be so familiar. The aching, which had been with Charlie for so long, floated away. Their mutual hunger grew, and their lips responded with a ferocity neither of them could help. "Charlie, Charlie, Charlie," he repeated. Each time more frenzied. Her long legs wrapped around him. She felt the steady weight of him underneath her. Their hands ran up and down each other. Her fingers traced his chest. First over his shirt, then under. His skin was cool and smooth. She lingered in the ridge between his pecs, then followed it down to his abs. Each defined muscle was so hard and firm to the touch. His sheer power made her feel safe and excited.

The waves rocked them gently from side to side, up and down. The hunger didn't subside, it only grew. She was lost in him. With him. Because of him. "Why did you leave?" she whispered, first only to herself. Her heart *hurt*.

"Why did you leave?" she asked, louder this time, so he could hear.

He stopped. It would always come down to this, and Taye would never be able to tell her the truth. "Not because of you. You have to trust me on that, Charlie."

His words were a current pulling her under. "Why did you leave? Tell me," she said, her gaze steady.

Taye stroked her cheek, but she turned away. "It's complicated. I've tried to tell you that."

She shook her head. "That's not an answer." "It's all I can give you."

Her heart exploded into a thousand little pieces. She broke away from his grasp. There would never be a "normal" between them ever again. There would always be this resentment, this pain, this rage. Enough to drown her, and him.

She started to swim away.

"Charlie! Don't leave it like this!" Taye reached out for her.

She shoved him, hard. He fell back slightly. "Everything's so black-and-white with you, Charlie!" He swam forward, the power of his stroke creating ripples all around them. "Stop pushing me away!" He grabbed her wrist and turned her toward him.

"Stop," he whispered.

Charlie wished with every muscle in her body, the same muscles that were fighting against her now, that she could just stop. She looked away. "No," she mumbled, either to him or maybe just to herself. One of them had to leave for good.

Charlie turned around and began to swim away. This time, it would be her.

***

Charlie vigorously scrubbed the main deck of their new ship, ignoring the hot tears rolling down her face. Cleaning was always a good remedy to clear her head, which was pretty mixed up right now.

They'd all agreed that the best plan was for the Castaways to follow Rogers Barrish back to England and try to find written evidence of his schemes to attack the ships insured by Sapphire East Trading Company. In the meantime, the girls would finish fixing up their ship before sailing to Shanghai. Then they'd all meet up again in Europe and see how they could finally take Rogers Barrish down—legally, this time. After barely escaping imprisonment for the attack on Barrish, Charlie wasn't even sure she wanted to test her luck any further and tangle with RB again. However, she supported the plan because it meant that she could say goodbye to the Castaways. At least temporarily.

Charlie twisted the sponge in the soapy water. She didn't know what pissed her off more, the fact that she'd never be rid of Taye, or the fact that she didn't want to be. She scoured the wooden floorboards.

Whatever it was, she sure as hell didn't want to pretend like everything was okay. Charlie's face burned. How could Taye think "It's complicated" was enough to explain why he'd left? They'd been each other's entire lives. Why couldn't he just tell her what she'd done to make him walk out on her?

The faint sound of singing carried across the water, which made Charlie seethe even more. The Castaways were throwing a "bon voyage" party on *Holy Tide*, which was anchored less than five hundred meters from their ship. She'd made an excuse about a headache and insisted Sadie, Liu, Raquel, and Ingela go without her. To Charlie's relief, the girls didn't pry any deeper and just left her alone.

It wasn't even sunset yet, but judging by the sounds of merriment, the party was already in full swing. Charlie had used the spyglass to peek in on the festivities a few times already, and was surprised at the number of people at the party. With all the mayhem surrounding Ingela's hospitalization and Rogers Barrish, when had the Castaways had the time to make all those friends in Marrakatra? Actually, Charlie couldn't care less who the Castaways were friends with. She bent over a grease spot in the wood, intent on rubbing it out.

A few minutes later, Charlie was forced out of her scrubbing therapy when she heard a hushed thud, followed by faint footsteps, behind her. What had Ingela forgotten now? Couldn't she just be left to clean and cry in peace? Charlie was mortified at the thought of anyone seeing her in this state, and wiped her snotty tears with the back of her sleeve. When she was better composed, Charlie threw the sponge in the bucket and turned around. "Squirt, what did you come back for—"

Charlie stopped mid-sentence. Standing no more than thirty steps ahead of her, against the pink splendor of the setting sun, was a masked woman holding a sword. Instinctively, Charlie reached down at her side for her cutlass, then remembered it wasn't there. She'd carelessly thrown her daggers, cutlass, and coat off of her when she began cleaning. Her sword lay on the ground, beside the masked woman.

Charlie hurriedly searched for anything around her that could be used as a weapon. "Not exactly a fair fight," she said, as she held up her empty hands.

The woman kicked Charlie's cutlass to her. Charlie was utterly confused by the gesture, but grabbed it and instantly jumped to her feet. Before she could do anything else, the woman saluted to Charlie before standing *en garde*. Charlie nodded in recognition. She was being challenged to a duel. On *Storm One*, Charlie had dominated her fencing classes and even held her own with Pop, who was her most frequent sparring partner. That, and the real-world experience she'd acquired in the last year, had solidified her confidence in sword fighting. In fact, these days, Charlie viewed her cutlass as an extension of her arm. She hadn't had a proper duel since the Storm days, but Charlie was more than certain she was ready.

"I accept," she called out, walking forward until she was standing opposite her opponent, sword-length apart.

Charlie pointed her front foot straight out, her back foot sideways, and bent her knees. She'd barely gotten into *en garde* position when the woman lunged at her, jumping forward with her sword held straight out. Charlie parried, barely blocking the opponent's sword from striking her. Their blades clashed, clanking loudly together. If the woman was going to play dirty, so was Charlie. She kicked her leg up high, landing her foot directly on her opponent's chin. Then she slashed from side to side, swishing by the woman's hip. The woman briskly retaliated and stuck her sword high in the air, yielding her blade from outside to inside in one fell swoop. Charlie smirked. Pop had also been left-handed. Charlie knew exactly how to win this.

Charlie charged with her sword. Her opponent swerved to the side. She and the woman circled each other like a pair of rabid dogs, blades locked.

"Scared to show your face?" Charlie taunted, motioning to the black mask her opponent wore. Before she could answer, Charlie rushed ahead.

The woman vaulted, then lunged after her. They thrust and parried over and over. The shrill ring of steel against steel pierced the air. The woman had no trouble keeping up with Charlie's speed and agility. They were a perfect match. Charlie saw the woman's shoulder muscles tense slightly before she sliced toward her head. She quickly jerked back, but not before the tip of her opponent's blade cut her chin. Droplets of blood trickled down her neck as Charlie raced to the other side of the deck. Just as she reached the rail, the woman grabbed Charlie's shirt. Charlie slammed the hilt of her sword into the woman's face. Using the railing for stability, Charlie whooshed around and slammed her cutlass into her opponent's left arm. The woman's sword fell to her side. Charlie dashed for it, but the woman grabbed it first.

With her right hand.

Charlie smiled. This was exactly what Pop had taught her. Now her opponent was forced to fight with her weak hand. The sounds of the party lingered behind her, but all Charlie could hear were the cheers of victory in her head. She was ready to finish this.

Charlie leapt forward, wielding her sword over her head while slashing with her backhand. The woman parried deftly. Charlie twisted around, but her opponent was quicker and countered. Charlie lifted her sword, but the woman blocked her.

Charlie tried to return with another backhand slice, but her opponent was too fast. She unleashed a fury of strikes, driving Charlie further and further back. Frantically, Charlie tried to dodge, sidestep, and parry, but her opponent was quicker, stronger, and better. The color drained from Charlie's face. *She'd been tricked.* The woman *was* right-handed.

Charlie stumbled over the mop bucket before losing her footing on the partially wet floor. She went crashing down, landing hard on her back. The blood rushed to her head. All it took was one savage slice with the flat side of the woman's blade and Charlie's cutlass went flying across the deck. Charlie tried to roll to the side, but the woman pinned her under her heavy, black boot. She pointed her blade at Charlie. The whoops and hollers of the partygoers mocked her now, reminding Charlie how nearby the girls were. She could try to yell for help, but it was pointless now. This was already over.

Charlie stared up at the woman. She had been so preoccupied with the fighting, Charlie only now noticed that her opponent was a redhead, too. Her mask was black, like everything else she wore, and covered her entire face. Charlie couldn't recognize the texture, but it fit her like a second skin, contouring to her bony cheeks and small forehead.

"At least let me see the face of my killer," Charlie spit out through gritted teeth.

She was frightened, but strangely, not for her life. Charlie knew she should be terrified, given that she was lying on the ground with her opponent's sword over her. However, something about it all—the ambush, the deception, even the mask—made Charlie feel like none of this was real. That this had all been a game. Charlie clutched at her necklace, wondering what the next move was going to be.

The woman's eyes flashed. She dropped her sword, then raced toward the gangplank.

Before Charlie could chase her, she was gone.

***

Charlie, we're so sorry!" Raquel cried. "We should have been here."

The girls had returned to the ship less than fifteen minutes after the attack. The assault in itself was surprising, but what baffled the other girls even more was how calm Charlie was when relaying the events, like she was telling them what she'd had for dinner last night.

"Let me take you to the clinic, just to make sure everything's fine." Sadie started to pull Charlie by the hand.

Charlie yanked her arm away. "I told you, I'm okay. Her blade barely touched my skin." She lifted the rag that was against her chin. "See, it's just a flesh wound."

The sky was dark now, with only a dim moon to light up the night.

"She must have been watching. She wanted me alone," Charlie thought aloud.

Liu reclined back, resting her head on Raquel's lap. "You're sure it was a woman?"

"Her clothes were form-fitting enough that I could definitely make out that she was a female. Although she did wear a strange kind of mask."

A light breeze blew strands of Charlie's long hair into her face. She brushed them back. It was humiliating to think that she'd spent the earlier part of the evening crying about Taye. Charlie ran her hand over the handle of her cutlass. Nothing like a sword fight to get the adrenaline pumping and her head in order. She had one job. To keep these guys safe. There was no time for broken hearts.

"So Rogers Barrish has lady goons, too?" Raquel asked. She shifted her weight to adjust for Liu's heavy head. "Or does she belong to Zhang Tao?"

Liu snorted. The last thing that Zhang Tao would employ was a female goon. "No way."

Charlie squinted, deep in thought. "I don't think this was a member of Barrish's hit squad."

"What?" Sadie sat up. "Why do you think that?" She'd spent weeks learning from Amsha not to jump to conclusions without evidence, and she was pretty sure Charlie was doing that now.

"She was good. Highly trained. Not like Len and Seth, who just used muscles or guns." Charlie bit her lip. "Mind over body."

Liu shrugged. "Okay, so you used mind over body. We all did the same thing when we fought Len and Seth."

"No, *she* used it. The attacker." Charlie replayed the fight in her head. "I can't explain it exactly, but I knew her moves. And she knew mine. It was like fighting …myself."

"How?" Sadie asked. She needed evidence to support Charlie's crazy theory, not just vague explanations.

Charlie sighed. She was embarrassed to admit how badly she'd been outfoxed, but she knew Sadie would drag it out of her eventually.

"She started out fighting left-handed." "Like Andrew used to do, right?" Raquel asked.

"Exactly. So I pulled the Storm's classic maneuver where I forced her to use her weaker hand, which should have been her right hand. Pop and I had practiced it hundreds of times, so I knew what I was doing. But it turns out she wasn't left-handed. She'd tricked me. Not only was she right-handed, once she'd switched, she was even faster and better." Charlie's brow furrowed. "That's what makes this whole thing feel like a set-up. It was like she faked being left-handed to see what I'd do."

"You're saying that she actually used a Storm tactic against you?" Sadie thought for a moment while she pieced this all together. "Then that means that she not only fought like you, Charlie, she *thought* like you, too." Sadie bit her lip. It just didn't make any sense. "How could she think and fight like you?"

Ingela picked up the attacker's sword. Let the rest of them spend useless time talking and talking while she actually did something. She ran her fingers over the handle, and then the blade. Ingela turned the cutlass in her hand slowly. Her shoulder was pretty much healed, but still got sore if she made sudden movements. She thumbed the engraved insignia. A shiver ran down her spine. Ingela carried the sword carefully back to the others. She laid it down in front of skeptical Sadie. "She fights like Charlie because she's Storm."

***

The Countess leaned against the cliff, shielded by the darkness and the dimly lit moon. The hot, heavy night air gave little relief from the day's stifling heat. She bent over to catch her breath, reaching between the rocks. She splashed water on her face, but its tepid temperature didn't refresh her.

Still, the Countess was invigorated. She felt her blood pumping fiercely through her veins. She'd cut a little flesh, drawn a little blood, but most importantly, she'd set the trap. She was satisfied. For now. She drew out her jewel-encrusted pocket watch, a departing gift from her husband, to check the time.

The dinner would start in less than an hour. That wasn't nearly enough time for her to attend to this cut on her left arm and still make herself presentable. Anyway, how many dinners, feasts, fetes, and celebrations did the Marrakatran royal court possibly need to throw? It seemed like Sultan Musef was quite the *bon vivant*. No wonder Rogers Barrish was always making excuses to travel down here. She'd feign a headache. Another advantage of merely blending in was that your absence was rarely noticed or missed. Benevolent widows like her were excused all their frailties and illnesses.

The Countess wrapped the cloth tighter around the wound. The girl was fast, agile, strong. Most of all, she was sharp. *Mind over body.*

She'd miss the sword. It was her first. But it was smarter to leave it with them. Now all she had to do was wait.

***

The girls raised their mugs. Tonight was their last night in Marrakatra. Tomorrow they would set sail for Shanghai.

Charlie inhaled. The scent of fresh lemons was everywhere. Since fruit trees grew all over Marrakatra, they'd easily collected bushels and bushels of lemons, limes, oranges, and grapefruit. Citrus was a great preventative against scurvy. Sadie had already brought out her recipes on bottling and preserving it, but the sheer citrus aroma made everything feel so fresh and clean.

Charlie looked around. Every corner of their ship sparkled like new. They had spent weeks scouring, scrubbing, painting, remodeling, and tricking her out. Just as they hoped, their new schooner was stronger, smarter, and faster than before. But the real test would begin in less than a day's time, when she hit the open waters.

They'd caught *Holy Tide* before it sailed and showed Taye and Axel the sword. Both guys verified what the girls already knew, that it was authentic Storm. Was Charlie's attacker really Storm? Did that mean there were more Storm out there? And most importantly, why the hell was she attacked? Charlie shook her head. Getting answers was more important than ever now, but they seemed to know less than when they started.

Despite not wanting to see Taye again, circumstances beyond her control had once again forced them to be together. This time it was the sword, but next time—and she knew there would be a next time—it would be something else. Just as she'd predicted, everything that had happened between them in the water had dried up instantly once they were back on land. Charlie hadn't even bothered to say goodbye before leaving. The worse part was seeing the relief on Taye's face as she walked away.

Charlie scanned the girls' faces. She'd always known her mission was to keep them safe, but she no longer worried about what that meant. These last few months had made her strong. With every strike of her sword, she grew surer and surer that she would do whatever it took. There was no going too far anymore.

No matter how much Raquel and Sadie wanted to convince themselves of it, the sword wasn't left accidentally. The only thing Charlie had to determine was if it was a clue or a trap.

"To fair winds," Liu began.

"No! No!" Raquel put her arm down. "Let's not say that. It's bad luck. That was what we toasted last time we sailed, and then we were hit by the storm and Ingela was shot." She looked at them. "We need to come up with something else. Something just for us."

Raquel was by far the most superstitious of the group, but the other girls had to admit that they were all feeling nervous about setting out to sea again. It wouldn't hurt to come up with something new.

They turned to Sadie, who was the resident wordsmith.

Sadie shrugged her shoulders. "Got nothing."

Raquel put her hand on her chin in an exaggerated pose of someone thinking, which meant that her mind was drawing a blank.

Liu spoke up. "What about something like, 'We don't know what we're doing or why we're doing it, but we've got the best intentions'?"

"It works," Ingela replied.

"I'm fine with it," Charlie said, raising her mug again.

Sadie kept her arm to her side. Best intentions meant deciding between right and wrong, good and bad. Like Raquel had mentioned, they'd been through so much. Sadie was still struggling to find answers to her endless questions about ethics and justice.

"How about skipping best and just going for good enough? Good enough intentions …good enough as we are. Plain old simple 'good enough.'"

The other girls smiled. Sadie had done it again. "*Good enough*," Raquel repeated.

They all raised their mugs.

Chapter
SEVENTEEN

SLOG
Date: Feb 27
Location: Somewhere around Ceylon (if you want specifics, ask Liu.)
Speed: Fast, fast, fast because our ship is awesome!
Weather: Curl frizz level is medium.

Dear Good Enough,

That's right. We finally have a ship with a name, because you are ours and nobody else's!!! Like Sadie said, if we're "good enough," then so are you. We're five days into our thirty-day journey, and you sail like a dream. Don't think we don't notice the twinkle in the merchant ships' eyes when you race by, sparkling from bow to stern. Dare I say, dear Good Enough, that you're the star of the sea?

Getting you was bittersweet (more sweet than bitter, though). Having our own ship means we're really on our own. So we're counting on you to take us where we need to go, which is still a long way from here. First, we gotta get to Shanghai in one piece. Believe me, easier said than done, but the upwinds are steady, and the Indian Ocean is behaving (for now, at least).

Between my shells and the coins that Amsha gave Sadie, we've been able to buy enough supplies to keep us going for a while. Sadie tried gilling, but she was really bad at it. Charlie's been conveniently avoiding it, so it's pretty much up to me and Liu. Technically, Ingela isn't supposed to gill until her shoulder is 100%, but we take her out anyway. It's not like we really have a choice, ,cuz she's an emotional blackmailer (Sadie's been reading a lot of medical ~~nonsense~~ books and labeling us all). We haven't found any lirium yet.

I sleep sometimes now. But most nights, I dance.

I know Charlie's going to yell at me for making this a diary, but I don't care. You're my ship, too, so I can do whatever I want.

Big, juicy, wet kisses (We love you, *Good Enough*!),

Raquel ♡

Liu tucked herself under the fluffy cotton blanket. Sadie had stuffed all their pillows with pouches of dried herbs. The scent of lavender flower and chamomile filled her nose. She'd spent most of her life sharing a room, either with her mother or Raquel. Yet after only two weeks having her own, she couldn't imagine life without her little oasis.

Good Enough had come with three spacious sleeping cabins that the girls (with some help from the Castaways) had renovated into five small but separate bedrooms. Each chamber was probably no bigger than a standard armoire for Princess Imera, but having such a space at all was a true luxury. Just like the girls who lived in them, their bedrooms couldn't be more different from one another.

Charlie's room was painted a cool, frosty blue, like the icy Antarctic sea, or the color of her eyes. It was incredibly neat (she dusted every day) and organized. She hung a display of swords, daggers, and other various weapons on the wall. Maybe as decoration, but it was clear that Charlie had used—or was planning to use—them all.

Like Sadie's colorful clothing, every wall in her room was a different color, with books stacked to the ceiling. Texts of all kind covered nearly every flat surface, despite the fact that they'd actually had enough space to fit a tiny library on the ship. If Sadie wasn't in her room, then she was usually either there or in the large galley kitchen, which was never a good sign.

Unsurprisingly, Raquel's chamber was fit for a queen. They'd let her use some of her shell fund to decorate it with luxurious silks, and she'd even managed to get Jimmy to construct a four-poster bed for her. Who knew Jimmy was a carpenter? Or a sucker for Raquel? Obviously, Raquel did. Ingela's room looked like a storm had ravaged it. There were piles of stuff that none of them wanted to go through, for fear that they'd find something dead or alive at the bottom. The mess didn't seem to bother her, though, as she still preferred sleeping on deck.

Finally, Liu had been true to her unique style when planning her room. After years of sleeping in a hammock, she decided she liked the gentle swinging motion, but it was time for an upgrade, so she designed her own "floating bed." Using heavy ropes, she suspended a large, round bamboo disc from the ceiling and then cushioned it with layers of cotton, coconut fiber, and horsehair. Soft linen sheets and lots of pillows added extra comfort—so much so that Liu found herself sleeping until pretty late every morning. A gigantic map of the world covered one entire wall.

In every room, there was a wooden chest from Amsha, their fairy godmother. She'd filled each one with a few pieces of clothing, some household stuff, and things that could help them smell better, but what was most touching was that she'd customized each chest with special gifts for each individual girl. Raquel's had a bottle of expensive perfume she cherished; Sadie's was filled with translated versions of classic Arabian literature; Charlie's contained the ancient weapons she then hung on her wall; Ingela's trunk had everything she needed to start her own gambling business; and Liu's contained the map.

Liu peered out the porthole. The calm night sea dazzled under the full moon. In such a short time, the girls had lost so much and gained so much in return. Maybe that was life. Calm waters and choppy seas following each other.

Most of all, they'd all changed. There was a new strength they all had that wasn't there before Rogers Barrish, Len, Seth, the Blood and Bone Brothers, and that stormy night. They'd *survived*. But like the butterfly fish that only swims in shallow waters, their newfound strength lived on the surface. Deeper down, in the blackness where lirium grew, was a fear that none of them could acknowledge. They'd survived Len, Seth, BBB, and the storm, but now they knew those kinds of horrors waited for them on every sea they crossed.

Liu blew out her lemon candle. To Sadie's annoyance, Raquel had confiscated over half their citrus supply to make scented candles. Though the candles were useless in protecting against scurvy, they did make the entire ship smell lemony fresh.

She flipped over onto her belly. Besides the trunks, their fairy godmother had given them another present. After finding out everything that Amsha had done for them on behalf of the sultan, the girls had shared their story with her. Not all of it, but enough so that she knew about Zhang Tao and the stolen junk. With yet another wave of what seemed like her magic wand, Amsha asked her father, the second largest shipping magnate in Marrakatra, for one of his junk ships as an early birthday gift. Then she'd insisted the girls use the junk to settle their debt with Zhang Tao.

Liu turned to her side. Tomorrow she would be in Shanghai. Liu had sent a letter before they'd left Marrakatra telling her father that she was ready to meet. Zhang Tao was expecting her.

Or should she say, he was expecting the obedient daughter who was running back "home" with her tail between her legs, so sorry to have brought shame on his good name and ready to do whatever it took to make him love her. What had Rogers Barrish called her? *A good little girl.*

She thought about Liang and the bamboo cane. The scared little boy who became a hateful young man. Hot tears spilled onto her pillow. Tomorrow, Zhang Tao would discover who his daughter really was.

***

Heavy drops of rain fell against the windows. It wasn't even lunchtime, yet the sky was dark, with gray clouds lurking low overhead. Liu shivered, both from the chill of her damp clothes and the natural chill she felt being in her father's home, anticipating what was to come. She scooted her maplewood hardback chair toward one of the two fires that crackled in the stone hearths on either side of the long, rectangular room. A warm cozy glow radiated against the cheery butter-colored walls. The whole snug atmosphere was, of course, the opposite of Zhang Tao, and seemed oddly out of place in his austere house, possibly because this was his European room, which was used only when he entertained Western visitors.

She stroked the bamboo cane that lay across her lap. Once she'd made her decision, she'd only had a few days to construct it, scrambling to find the wood and tools she needed to carve it. Her finger caught a nick in the wood. The finish wasn't as smooth as she'd wanted, but it would have to do for now.

The other girls had wanted to come with her, but Liu wanted to end this with just her and Daddy Dearest. She checked her pocket watch. Zhang Tao was a stickler for punctuality; it wouldn't be long now.

Thirty seconds later, he breezed through the door wearing a Western-style suit, confirming he had Europeans in town, which always made him anxious and irritable. Zhang Tao despised everything Western, except for the piles of money that hungry European consumers brought in. So he obliged to them when necessary and adapted to the clothing and customs. However, now that he was safely out of the view of his visiting guests, he hastily untucked his ruffled shirt and threw off his waistcoat, while eying his only daughter with an expression of suspicion and hostility that was usually reserved for foreigners.

Liu tried to stop her shivering and rubbed her hands quickly over the fire before turning her full attention toward her father. A servant followed him inside and set up a tea service between Liu and Zhang Tao. She was certainly not going to have another cup of tea in this house, and politely declined. The windows rattled loudly in protest at the heavy rain, which was now pelting against them.

"Are you here to apologize?" he asked, sipping his tea.

Zhang Tao didn't have much patience for small talk.

Liu saw the blue vein rise on the left side of her father's neck. As a little girl, she would run and hide when she saw the "blue snake" appear, knowing there was only fury to follow. Liu stopped her voice from shaking before she spoke.

"You first."

He balked. "The only thing I feel sorry for is having you as my daughter. A liar, a thief, and if rumors are to be believed," Zhang Tao paused, "a whore." His upper lip furled in disgust. Yet he didn't look away, which confirmed her suspicions. If he'd actually thought the rumor had a merit of truth, Zhang Tao would not have even let her back into his house.

Liu crossed her arms. "I felt sorry that I stole your junk. That I ran away. That your name and your house were shamed. That your ship was attacked by pirates while you tried to chase me."

"If you are ready to atone," he put down his teacup, "I am ready with your punishment." Except for his pulsing vein, nothing in Zhang Tao's cool demeanor changed.

Chills ran up and down Liu's spine. She regained her composure and tried her best to ignore his threat. "I just don't feel sorry anymore." She took a breath to calm herself.

Liu couldn't believe that she was able to be so strong. A loud clap of thunder shook the room.

Zhang Tao pulled out his shiny gold pocket watch. "I don't have time for this nonsense. If you haven't come to ask for my forgiveness, then what are you here for?"

"You know who changed my mind? I mean, about feeling sorry?" Liu tapped her foot. "Rogers Barrish."

Zhang Tao flinched slightly. "Oh, yes? And how so?" "He told me about this rumor that had surfaced about Liang and me running away together."

This time Zhang Tao did look away. "That boy was nothing but a piece of servant trash."

Liu clenched her jaw. As much as he'd like her to erupt, she wasn't going to give in. Her father was no longer the puppet master pulling the strings.

She sat back against the rigid chair. The fire next to her was now blazing, and tiny sweat beads were beginning to form on her hairline. "I knew that I hadn't left with Liang. So naturally, I thought Liang had made up the rumor. To explain why he was missing."

Zhang Tao nodded. "That would certainly be plausible." "Yes, indeed it would," said Liu, keeping his steady gaze.

"But you know what else Rogers Barrish mentioned?" "Oh, please, do tell me." Zhang Tao put down his empty teacup.

Despite his sarcastic tone, what mattered to Liu was that Zhang Tao was talking. In fact, he was being more candid with Liu than he would have been with any male in this situation—even his own sons—which was exactly what Liu was counting on.

"Barrish told me that your ship had come very close to finding me." Liu used the back of her sleeve to wipe the sweat off her forehead. "Is this true? Were you really that close?"

"Until the pirate attack," replied Zhang Tao, waving his hand as though the question and the questioner were nuisances. "Yes, I believe my ship was extremely close to catching the junk. Only about a half a day behind ..." Zhang Tao stopped, realizing his mistake.

All her life, her father had always underestimated her because she was a girl. That's why, even in this moment, he hadn't bothered to put up his guard. Liu smirked. His own prejudice had led him straight into her hands.

Zhang Tao bristled. He'd been caught, and he knew it. He looked across at Liu and noticed the bamboo cane. "So you're going to beat me with that cane? Is your mother telling you stories from her grave?" He fingered the scar on his right temple.

"I will hurt you, yes. And I have my own stories to tell. I'd like to finish this one, please. We're almost at the end."

The wind howled outside, while the branches from the rare golden larch scraped against the windowpanes.

"Hurry up then," he scowled.

"Like I said, I felt sorry for stealing your ship and causing you harm. But at the same time, I wasn't going to agree to an arranged marriage and live here for the rest of my life. So I went back and forth between feeling sorry and hating you."

Liu paused the way Raquel would have done. She wanted to make sure Zhang Tao caught every word she said, for there was no doubt he would play this conversation in his mind for years to come. "Then, about a week ago, I realized I just hated you. It took me months, but I finally put it together."

Zhang Tao sat back. "This is riveting, Liu. Please do tell me what you put together. What horrible deed do you think I've done that merits a beating with the sacred bamboo cane?"

"You murdered Liang!"

Though he maintained the same steely expression, the color drained from his face.

"How did you know to go south? And so quickly? Because you found Liang and you beat it out of him. Or whatever you do these days. Then you made up the rumor that we'd run off together. To cover up the real reason he was missing. Which was because you'd killed him."

Zhang Tao grimaced. "Interesting theory. Do you have any proof?"

Liu shook her head. "Nope. Except for my gut instinct and the guilt written all over your ghost-white face."

"Well, that isn't going to get you very far with the lawmen, now is it?"

Lighting flashed outside the window, followed by another boom of thunder.

"I'm not looking for justice."

Zhang Tao smiled knowingly. He reached for his wallet. "How much?"

"I don't want your money." Liu stood up and held the bamboo cane by its brass handle. She pointed directly at Zhang Tao. "I want revenge." Before he could move, she fired. "For Liang."

The bullet directly pierced Zhang Tao's median nerve, just like Liu had planned. She'd hollowed out the bamboo cane to fit a long rifle, which was much easier to shoot accurately than a flintlock. Rifles of this quality were difficult to track down, but Liu had found one in the Shanghai black market. Blood gushed from his left arm. He howled in agony, but Liu ignored his pain.

"This will hurt. For a long time. And it will never quite heal. You'll have full use of your arm, but whenever you try to lift it and come down with force, like if you try to give anyone a beating with a cane, you will feel a sharp, paralyzing pain radiating throughout your body." Liu reached into her long navy coat.

Zhang Tao cowered, just like Liang had done from him all those years ago. She ignored his fear, just as he'd done to Liang. "This is the deed to your new junk ship." Liu picked up the bamboo cane. "I always pay back."

She hid the cane inside the long, narrow inner pocket she'd sewn into the lining of her coat. Then, without so much as a look back, Liu walked out the door.

***

The girls walked along the bridged pathway holding torches. Liu begrudgingly followed Charlie, who was leading the way. She looked up. The black sky was moonless and starless. They should have picked another night to do this, or at least come up with a better plan that didn't have to rely completely on Liu's ability to pass as a local.

The Old City was no place for foreigners. Had she known about Charlie and Raquel's trip there last time, she would never have let them go. Though technically Liu was from Shanghai and spoke Shanghainese, she wasn't exactly embraced as a local, for lots of reasons her brothers loved to tease her about. For one thing, she moved clumsily for a Chinese girl, with big strides and swinging arms. There was no way she'd get past the guards at the gate.

"Guys, this plan sucks." Liu stopped. She blew into her hands to keep them warm in the frosty air. Ever since her confrontation with Zhang Tao a few days back, Liu had felt like an enormous weight had lifted. Now she was free to re-focus on what was important, which was finding out everything they could about the DD. When she broached this with the rest of the girls, they all expressed agreement, since the issue of having a ship of their own was finally resolved. So when Charlie had mentioned going back to the opium den this morning, it seemed like a good idea. Except now Liu found herself on the way to Mr. Chang with no actual plan, and a snowball's chance in hell that she was going to get them past the Old City.

Raquel shivered. The temperatures were lower than she'd thought. She should have worn another layer of stockings. "I'm so glad you said that, because I don't think this is going to work either."

"Can we at least go a little further?" Ingela asked. They hadn't had any fun since the chase with the Blood and Bone Brothers, and she'd been unconscious for that.

"No. Liu knows best here, and if she says we can't do this, then we shouldn't." Sadie was tired of letting Ingela and Charlie's mistaken ideas of excitement put them in constant harm's way.

"Well, I've actually done this, Sadie. Let's at least get to where the rowboats are." Charlie was frustrated with everyone in this pathetic group of scaredy-cats, except Ingela. Plus, Charlie trusted Ingela to have her back much more than Sadie, who despite her uselessness, had insisted on coming.

"If it looks like it's not safe a bit further on, then we can go back to the ship," she halfheartedly added in order to shut Sadie up.

Liu stomped her foot. "You know damn well that it will be too late to turn back then."

"And I also know that we can't get to the opium den unless we cross through the Old City." If there was any chance of her passing as a local, Charlie would have used it. But unfortunately, she had to rely on Liu, who was really letting her down.

"Come on Liu, all you have to do is make it past the guards and then let us in through the hidden door before you reach the big *paifang*."

"Oh, is that all she has to do, then?" Raquel spat. When Charlie got an idea in her head, it was impossible to talk her out of it—even if it meant Liu ending up in a Chinese prison. "I was with you last time, remember? We barely made it out of the Old City, and we were with that Chinese woman."

"But Liu is a Chinese woman!" Ingela shouted.

Charlie's patience was wearing thin. "Seriously, if you guys were so against this, why did you agree to do it in the first place?"

Raquel crossed her arms and jutted out her hip. "We all want to do this, Charlie. But only after we come up with some sort of sensible plan. Instead, you just took off running like a headless chicken. So now, we're just basically here to stop you and this *niñata* from getting yourselves killed!"

"Well, adios then, 'cuz we don't need you fatheads!" Ingela shouted way too loudly. She stormed off toward the stone tunnel.

"I second that." Charlie had become much more comfortable with her cutlass since the last visit to the opium den, and she felt confident that this time around, she could compel Mr. Chang to be more talkative. It would have been nice to have the other girls (except Sadie) for backup, but it wasn't necessary. Especially since they were acting like brats.

"See ya!" she said, waving mockingly.

Charlie entered the dark tunnel only minutes after Ingela. She momentarily got a glimpse of a figure standing over the little girl before her torch was stolen. Charlie instantly reached for her cutlass, but someone pinned her arms behind her back, while another person placed a gloved hand over her mouth.

Charlie heard the approaching footsteps of Liu, Raquel, and Sadie. She thrashed around, but the attackers were already tying her hands and feet together with intricate sailing knots. They gagged her before she could scream a warning to the other girls.

"Fine, we'll go with you to the rowboats and then—" Suddenly, three more attackers stepped out of the darkness and grabbed Liu, Raquel, and Sadie in a matter of seconds. Even with three lit torches, the images were hard to make out, but to Charlie's wide-eyed astonishment, one or possibly more of the assailants appeared to be women. Charlie recalled the sword fight in Marrakatra. Were they linked? She felt someone standing behind her, tying a blindfold around her eyes. Charlie took the opportunity to throw her head back as hard as she could, knocking the forehead of the person behind her. An explosion of profanities in a language Charlie recognized as German erupted from a distinctly female voice.

"Yeah, well this mangy mutt bit me!" Charlie heard someone growl a few feet down from her. She couldn't make out if it was a male or female, but she was pretty sure she heard an Irish lilt, and it was speaking about Ingela.

"Help here!" called out another woman, this one clearly not a native English speaker. "Her tall man-boots stab my toes."

"Yeah, they're all a bunch of fighters. We're never gonna get them back to her like this."

"Think we better use the heavy stuff."

"She's gonna be pissed. She specifically forbade us." "Well, we gotta improvise."

A pungent, sulfuric odor filled the air. Charlie's heart raced as she frantically tried to free herself. Charlie heard Sadie mumble something, but it was impossible to understand her with the gag over her mouth. Suddenly, Charlie was forced down on her knees. Sharp stones jabbed into her legs, and then her mouth was covered with a rag. Now she knew what Sadie had been trying to say. *Ether.* A rotten egg smell filled Charlie's nostrils and mouth. It only took seconds for her body to go limp before falling forward with a loud thud against the grainy pathway.

"She's waiting for us at headquarters," the Irish woman said in an authoritative voice as she surveyed the five bodies clumsily sprawled out in front of them. "We'd better get moving."

That was the last thing Charlie heard before she lost consciousness.

***

Charlie had been the last one to go down, which meant that she'd inhaled the most ether and was therefore the last to wake up. Slowly, she opened one eye and then the other. Her head felt groggy, her muscles ached, and her throat was burning from the drug. Her blindfold and gag had been removed, but her hands and feet remained bound. She turned slowly to see each of the girls tied to a chair like she was. On one side of her sat Liu, while Sadie was to the left of her.

"I think we're on a ship," Ingela whispered to Liu, who'd only woken up a few seconds before Charlie and was still adjusting her eyes.

Liu blinked. The room was dimly lit with a few candles, but still brighter than the blackness of the tunnel. "It's anchored. It looks like we're in some kind of control center." They'd been placed in the corner of a huge, dank room that made Liu feel like they were submerged deep in the ocean. All around them, the area buzzed with activity as people consulted maps, studied sail charts, and used strange-looking devices that Liu had never seen before.

"Do you notice there aren't any boys here?" Raquel said in a hushed voice. "I mean, like no men in sight."

Sadie turned her head from side to side. Raquel was right. The whole room was filled entirely with women, which was strange enough, but these women looked like pirates. They didn't have uniforms, but they were all dressed in some variation of breeches, doublets, waistcoats, and tri-cornered hats. "They really are all women." A flurry of conversation whirled through the room. Sadie strained to hear. She picked up bits and pieces of a few languages, but it sounded like there were at least a half-dozen different tongues being spoken in the room. "Seems like they're women from all over the world, too."

The effects of the ether were slowly wearing off, and Charlie was already thinking of how to escape. She tried to contort her body so that she could free her hands, but the ropes had been tied with the same deft sailor knots as before. "It was a bunch of women who attacked us. I think I heard German and picked out an Irish accent as well."

"Was one of them the woman who left the Storm sword?" Liu asked quietly.

Charlie shrugged. "I really don't know. But we can figure that out after we get out of here."

Sadie shook her head. "None of this makes sense. I mean, where are we anyway?"

"Shhh!" Raquel admonished. "We don't want them to hear us!"

"You're on my ship, Sadie," a gravelly voice replied.

Sadie looked up to see a petite woman with stick-straight black hair stride toward them. The air in the room seemed to shift immediately as all activity ceased. The other women saluted as this woman walked by.

She turned to face them. "At ease." Upon her instruction, the women went back to work.

"How—how do you know my name?" Sadie asked in complete bewilderment. She squinted hard to see if she recognized the woman, but from her chair, she only had a partial view of her.

"I know all of you. Ingela, Liu, Raquel, Sadie." She paused and turned to face them all head-on, revealing the leather eye patch that covered her right eye. "And Charlie."

Everyone sat in stunned silence except for Charlie, who was mumbling something incoherent.

"Charlie?" Sadie asked quietly. "Do you know her?" Charlie's skin was sallow and her voice barely audible. "Yes." She began trembling uncontrollably. "She's my mother."

***

After promising they wouldn't fight back, the girls were untied. This might have been a gesture of goodwill, but it was clear that neither side trusted the other. In each corner, a different woman had been positioned, each of whom was heavily armed.

However, Liu wasn't as concerned with them as she was with Charlie, who'd been fingering her cutlass for the last ten minutes. The tall woman with cropped blond hair standing to the right of Charlie was carrying at least two flintlock pistols, while eying Charlie suspiciously.

They'd all voluntarily moved to another room, this one with a long table and several chairs. The lighting was much better here, with dozens of lanterns illuminating every crevice, but there was a draft that sent a chill through the air.

Sadie studied Eliza. She couldn't say it was like seeing a ghost, because she barely remembered Charlie's mother. But it did feel like she'd been brought back from the dead. Maybe that's why Eliza had an eerie, almost creepy vibe to her, which was only enhanced by the stark blackness of her hair against her translucent skin. Charlie was also pretty pale, but not in the same way. Sadie looked at Charlie. In fact, Charlie and Eliza didn't share a strong physical resemblance.

"I understand that the methods of getting you here were extreme," Eliza said with a faint Southern drawl. She was small, but her presence filled the room. "Particularly the ether, which I had given strict orders against."

Sadie smiled to herself. Eliza spoke with such a coolness that it wasn't clear if she was trying to apologize or was simply stating facts. They may not have shared that many physical attributes, but Charlie was certainly domineering and imposing like her mom. For the sake of science, Sadie did have to acknowledge that Andrew Drake had been quite overbearing himself, so it would only make sense that Charlie's hyperimperious nature was a result of both her mother and father.

"We needed to kidnap you now," Eliza tapped the wooden table. Behind her, there was a massive symbol of a human eye that covered the wall. It matched the eye watermarked in the letter that Charlie had received, and the small tattoo on Eliza's inner left wrist. "Before you went to the Old City, which was just too risky. There was no way you were going to make it." She paused. "Liu, you weren't ready—"

"No worries. I knew I couldn't get us through," Liu smiled despite herself. Charlie's mom wasn't exactly the milk-and-cookies type, but she also didn't seem like the kind of monster that would abandon her only child.

Eliza flinched. "Yes, the Old City is very risky. That's why I sent Jun last time to help you."

Both Charlie and Raquel turned to see the woman who had led them to the opium den. Raquel waved, while Charlie glared at Eliza.

"You were the one who sent that letter?" Charlie blurted, practically spitting out every word.

Eliza met Charlie's angry stare. "Yes. I knew you weren't ready to see me, but I had to lead you to the source somehow." She leaned against the table. "However, I did follow you back from Mr. Chang's."

Raquel beamed. "See? I told you I had a feeling someone was tailing us."

Eliza kept her eyes on Charlie. "I had to ensure you didn't take Mr. Chang's information to the authorities."

Charlie smirked. "We're not snitches."

Ingela watched, wondering to herself which one of these two lady tigers would win in a fistfight, as it certainly seemed that hotheaded Charlie was ready to come to blows. She sat back in her chair. Charlie was definitely tough, but Eliza looked like she had some fierce tricks up her sleeve as well.

"So, you know about the Day of Destruction?"

"I've been trying to find out what happened. Why it happened. Who was behind it," said Eliza, keeping her eyes down on the papers in front of her. "We've got an extensive network of sources, and I'm piecing things together."

Charlie kicked the table leg. "Who's 'we'? Why do you want to help us? And why should we trust you?"

"Charlie!" Sadie admonished.

"I have some information you need to know." Eliza's jaw tensed. Underneath the table, she flexed her fist open and closed.

"You have nothing I need." Charlie knocked her chair over as she stood up. She started walking toward the door. Eliza jumped up and swiftly grabbed Charlie by the arm.

Her daughter stood nearly a head taller than her, but that didn't stop Eliza from shoving Charlie back down in her chair. "I said I have information for you." Eliza dug her weight into Charlie's shoulders to keep her in place.

One by one, she eyed each of the girls. Only when she knew she had their full attention did Eliza resume speaking.

"Your parents are alive."

Acknowledgements

I think it's only fitting that a story about girl pirates involves three of the most kickass women I have ever had the pleasure to work with. To my fellow geeky book girls with big glasses, thank you. Ilona—you put me on this journey, and for that, I will always be grateful. Laura N.: Oh Captain, My Captain. And Laura A.: Your pushing, prodding, and invaluable wisdom got us here—thank you for your trust. The support at Rovio has been overwhelming, and I can't begin to name all the people who have dedicated their time and energy in helping Storm Sisters come alive. To mention a few: Terhi, Chris, Laura K., Rollo, Blanca, and Sanna L.

Many thanks to Elina and her power pink posse for their tireless efforts and dedication.

To my soul sisters: Lamb, Tanja, Suzy, Bron, Venla, Rena, Jen, Shad and Liis—thank you for a lifetime of unconditional love, unconditional encouragement, and unconditional wine. To my soul bros, Oliver and Markus—cheers. To my soul kids—Vens, who will always set her own course, and Lo, you inspired every scowl, growl, glare, and grimace. Much love and appreciation to the global Das-Koivisto family, with its satellite offices around the world. To the wacky, wonderful Indian crew—you've given me enough material for a hundred more books. To the Finnish branch: Thank you Piini and Tarmo for the encouragement, enthusiasm, and best joulu kinkku ever. To the American headquarters: Sne, thank you for teaching me how to be strong *and* kind. Dad: Your Shakespearean bedtime tales were my first lessons in storytelling; your fearlessness was my most important lesson in life. All my love to Dada, Sarah, and Lowy. To Mommy, Ita, Dede, and Koko; you are the stars in the night sky that guide me.

Finally, every girl pirate needs a home. Thank you, Kalle, for being mine. With your synthesizer beats, 80s grooves, and Roxy music, your sheer brilliance inspires me every day.